WAIT FOR YOU

Jennifer L Armentrout, also known as J Lynn, is the *USA Today* bestselling author of the Lux and Gamble Brothers series. She is also the author of the award-winning Covenant series. She writes young adult fiction and adult fiction. When she's not busy writing, which is almost next to never, she can be found procrastinating on Twitter or messing with her dog Loki. She lives with her husband in West Virginia and is addicted to 5-Hour Energy Drinks.

J LYNN

Wait for You

HARPER

Harper
An imprint of HarperCollins*Publishers*
77–85 Fulham Palace Road,
Hammersmith, London W6 8JB

www.harpercollins.co.uk

A Paperback Original 2013
2

A catalogue record for this book
is available from the British Library

ISBN: 978-0-00-753098-4

Set i...

Dedicated to those who are reading this book right now. Without you, none of this would be possible. You guys rock my fuzzy socks.

Chapter 1

There were two things in life that scared the ever-loving crap out of me. Waking up in the middle of the night and discovering a ghost with its transparent face shoved in mine was one of them. Not likely to occur, but still pretty damn freaky to think about. The second thing was walking into a crowded classroom late.

I absolutely loathed being late.

I hated for people to turn and stare, which they always did when you entered a classroom a minute after class started.

That was why I had obsessively plotted the distance between my apartment in University Heights and the designated parking lot for commuter students over the weekend on Google. And I actually drove it twice on Sunday to make sure Google wasn't leading me astray.

One point two miles to be exact.

Five minutes in the car.

I even left my apartment fifteen minutes early so I would arrive ten minutes before my 9:10 class began.

What I didn't plan for was the mile-long traffic backup at the stop sign, because God forbid there be an actual light in the historical town, or the fact there was absolutely no parking left on campus. I had to park at the train station adjacent to the campus, wasting precious time digging up quarters for the meter.

'If you insist on moving halfway across the country, at least stay in one of the dorms. They do have dorms there, don't they?' My mom's voice filtered through my thoughts as I stopped in front of the Robert Byrd Science Building, out of breath from racing up the steepest, most inconvenient hill in history.

Of course I hadn't chosen to stay in a dorm, because I knew at some point, my parents would randomly show up and they would start *judging* and start *talking*, and I'd rather punt-kick myself in the face than subject an innocent bystander to that. Instead, I tapped into my well-earned blood money and leased a two-bedroom apartment next to campus.

Mr. and Mrs. Morgansten had hated that.

And that had made me extremely happy.

But now I was sort of regretting my little act of rebellion, because as I hurried out of the humid heat of a late August morning and into the air-conditioned brick building, it was already eleven minutes past nine and my astronomy class was on the second floor. And why in the hell did I choose astronomy?

Maybe because the idea of sitting through another biology class made me want to hurl? Yep. That was it.

Racing up the wide staircase, I barreled through the double doors and smacked right into a brick wall.

Stumbling backward, I flailed my arms like a cracked-out crossing guard. My overpacked messenger bag slipped, pulling me to one side. My hair flew in front of my face, a sheet of auburn that obscured everything as I teetered dangerously.

Oh dear God, I was going down. There was no stopping it. Visions of broken necks danced in my head. This was going to suck so—

Something strong and hard went around my waist, stopping my free fall. My bag hit the floor, spilling overpriced books and pens across the shiny floor. My pens! My glorious pens rolled everywhere. A second later I was pressed against the wall.

The wall was strangely warm.

The wall chuckled.

'Whoa,' a deep voice said. 'You okay, sweetheart?'

The wall was *so* not a wall. It was a guy. My heart stopped, and for a frightening second, pressure clamped down on my chest and I couldn't move or think. I was thrown back five years. Stuck. Couldn't move. Air punched from my lungs in a painful rush as tingles spread up the back of my neck. Every muscle locked up.

'Hey …' The voice softened, edged with concern. 'Are you okay?'

I forced myself to take a deep breath—to just breathe. I needed to breathe. Air in. Air out. I had practiced this over and over for five years. I wasn't fourteen anymore. I wasn't there. I was *here*, halfway across the country.

Two fingers pressed under my chin, forcing my head up. Startling, brilliant blue eyes framed with thick black lashes fixed on mine. A blue so vibrant and electric, and such a stark contrast against the black pupils, I wondered if the color was real.

And then it hit me.

A guy was holding me. A guy had never held me. I didn't count that one time, because that time didn't count for shit, and I was pressed against him, thigh to thigh, my chest to his. Like we were dancing. My senses fried as I inhaled the light scent of cologne. Wow. It smelled good and expensive, like *his* …

Anger suddenly rushed through me, a sweet and familiar thing, pushing away the old panic and confusion. I latched on to it desperately and found my voice. 'Let. Go. Of. Me.'

3

Blue Eyes immediately dropped his arm. Unprepared for the sudden loss of support, I swayed to the side, catching myself before I tripped over my bag. Breathing like I'd just run a mile, I pushed the thick strands of hair out of my face and finally got a good look at Blue Eyes.

Sweet baby Jesus, Blue Eyes was …

He was gorgeous in all the ways that made girls do stupid things. He was tall, a good head or two taller than me, and broad at the shoulders, but tapered at the waist. An athlete's body—like a swimmer's. Wavy black hair toppled over his forehead, brushing matching eyebrows. Broad cheekbones and wide, expressive lips completed the package created for girls to drool over. And with those sapphire-colored eyes, holy moly …

Who thought a place named Shepherdstown would be hiding someone who looked like this?

And I ran into him. Literally. Nice. 'I'm sorry. I was in a hurry to get to class. I'm late and …'

His lips curved up at the corners as he knelt. He started gathering up my stuff, and for a brief moment I felt like crying. I could feel tears building in my throat. I was really late now; no way could I walk into that class late, especially on the first day. Fail.

Dipping down, I let my hair fall forward and shield my face as I started grabbing up my pens. 'You don't have to help me.'

'It's no problem.' He picked up a slip of paper and then glanced up. 'Astronomy 101? I'm heading that way, too.'

Great. For the whole semester I'd have to see the guy I nearly killed in the hallway. 'You're late,' I said lamely. 'I really am sorry.'

With all my books and pens back in my bag, he stood as he handed it back to me. 'It's okay.' That crooked grin spread, revealing a dimple in his left cheek, but nothing on the right side. 'I'm used to having girls throw themselves at me.'

I blinked, thinking I hadn't heard the blue-eyed babe right, because surely he hadn't said something as lame as that.

He had, and he wasn't done. 'Trying to jump on my back is new, though. Kind of liked it.'

Feeling my cheeks burn, I snapped out of it. 'I wasn't trying to jump on your back or throw myself at you.'

'You weren't?' The lopsided grin remained. 'Well, that's a shame. If so, it would have made this the best first day of class in history.'

I didn't know what to say as I clutched the heavy bag to my chest. Guys hadn't flirted with me back at home. Most of them hadn't dared to look in my direction in high school and the very few that did, well, they hadn't been flirting.

Blue Eyes's gaze dropped to the slip of paper in his hand. 'Avery Morgansten?'

My heart jumped. 'How do you know my name?'

He cocked his head to the side as the smile inched wider. 'It's on your schedule.'

'Oh.' I pushed the wavy strands of hair back from my hot face. He handed my schedule back, and I took it, slipping it into my bag. A whole lot of awkward descended as I fumbled with my strap.

'My name is Cameron Hamilton,' Blue Eyes said. 'But everyone calls me Cam.'

Cam. I rolled the name around, liking it. 'Thank you again, Cam.'

He bent over and picked up a black backpack I hadn't noticed. Several locks of dark hair fell over his forehead and as he straightened, he brushed them away. 'Well, let's make our grand entrance.'

My feet were rooted to the spot where I stood as he turned and strolled the couple of feet to the closed door to room 205. He reached for the handle, looking over his shoulder, waiting.

I couldn't do it. It didn't have anything to do with the fact that I had plowed into what was possibly the sexiest guy on campus. I couldn't walk into the class and have everybody turn and stare. I'd had enough of being the center of attention everywhere I went for the last five years. Sweat broke out and dotted my forehead. My stomach tightened as I took a step back, away from the classroom and Cam.

He turned, brows knitted as a curious expression settled on his striking face. 'You're going in the wrong direction, sweetheart.'

I'd been going in the wrong direction half my life, it seemed. 'I can't.'

'Can't what?' He took a step toward me.

And I bolted. I actually spun around and ran like I was in a race for the last cup of coffee in the world. As I made it to those damn double doors, I heard him call out my name, but I kept going.

My face was flaming as I hurried down the stairs. I was out of breath as I burst out of the science building. My legs kept moving until I sat down on a bench outside of the adjacent library. The early-morning sun seemed too bright as I lifted my head and squeezed my eyes shut.

Geez.

What a way to make a first impression in a new city, new school … new life. I moved more than a thousand miles to start over and I had already mucked it up in a matter of minutes.

Chapter 2

I had two options at this point: let go and move on from my disastrous attempt to attend my first class of my college career or go home, climb into bed, and pull the covers over my head. I so wanted to indulge in the second option.

If running and hiding wasn't my MO, I would've never survived high school.

Reaching down, I checked the wide, silver bracelet on my left wrist, making sure it was in place. I almost *didn't* survive high school.

Mom and Dad had pitched a fit when I'd informed them of my plans to attend a university clear across the country. If it had been Harvard, Yale, or Sweet Briar, they would have been all about it. But a non-Ivy-League university? For shame. They just didn't understand. They never did. There was no way in holy hell I was going to attend the college they had gone to or enroll where half the country club back home forced their kids to attend.

I wanted to go where I wouldn't see a familiar sneer or hear the whispers that *still* dripped from people's lips like acid. Where people hadn't heard the story or whatever version of the truth had been repeated over and over again, until sometimes even I questioned what had really happened Halloween night five years ago.

None of them mattered here, though. No one knew me. No one suspected anything. And no one knew what the bracelet hid on summer days when a long-sleeve shirt wouldn't work.

Coming here had been my decision and it had been the right thing to do.

My parents had threatened to cut off my trust fund, which I'd found hilarious. I had my own money—money they had no control over once I turned eighteen. Money I had *earned*. To them, I had let them down yet again, but if I stayed in Texas or around any of those people, I would be dead.

Glancing at the time on my cell phone, I pushed to my feet and slung my bag over my shoulder. At least I wouldn't be late to my history class.

History was in the social sciences building, at the bottom of the hill I had just raced up. I cut through the parking lot behind the Byrd building and crossed the congested street. All around me students walked in groups of two or more; many obviously knew each other. Instead of feeling left out, I felt a precious sense of freedom in walking to class without being recognized.

Pushing my epic fail of a morning out of the way, I entered Whitehall and took the first set of steps to the right. The hallway upstairs was crowded with students waiting for the rooms to empty. I threaded through the laughing groups, dodging some who still looked half-asleep. Finding an empty spot across from my classroom, I sat down against the wall and crossed my legs. I ran my hands over my jeans, excited to be starting history. Most people would be bored to tears in History 101, but it was my first class in my major.

And if I got lucky, five years from now, I'd be working in a silent and cool museum or library, cataloging ancient texts or artifacts. Not the most glamorous of professions, but it would be perfect for me.

Better than what I used to want to be, which was a professional dancer in New York.

Yet another thing Mom had to be disappointed over. All that money thrown at ballet lessons since I was old enough to walk was wasted after I turned fourteen.

I did miss it though, the calming effect dancing had brought on. I just couldn't bring myself to do it ever again.

'Girl, what are you doing sitting on the floor?'

My head jerked up and a grin broke out across my face when I saw the wide, bright smile stretching across the caramel tone of Jacob Massey's boyishly handsome face. We'd buddied up during freshman orientation last week and he was in my next class, plus art on Tuesdays and Thursdays. I'd immediately warmed to his outgoing personality.

I glanced at the expensive-looking jeans he wore, recognizing the tailored cut. 'It's comfortable down here. You should join me.'

'Hell, no. I don't want my fine ass to be tainted by sitting on that floor.' He propped a hip against the wall beside me and grinned. 'Wait. What are you doing here already? I thought you had a class at nine.'

'You remember that?' We'd exchanged schedules for, like, a half a second last week.

He winked. 'I have a frightening memory for things that are virtually useless to me.'

I laughed. 'Good to know.'

'So did you skip already? You bad, bad girl.'

Wincing, I shook my head. 'Yes, but I was running late, and I hate going into a classroom after class starts, so I guess my first day will be Wednesday if I don't drop it before then.'

'Drop it? Girl, don't be stupid. Astronomy is a cake class. I would've taken it if it hadn't filled up in two seconds flat when all the damn upperclassmen took the class.'

'Well, you didn't nearly kill a guy in a hallway racing to class—a guy who happens to also be in said cake class.'

'What?' His dark eyes widened with interest and he started to kneel down. Someone caught his attention. 'Hold on a sec, Avery.' Then he started waving his arm and jumping. 'Yo! Brittany. Get your ass over here!'

A short blond girl jerked to a stop in the middle of the hall and turned toward us, her cheeks flushing, but she smiled as she saw Jacob hopping around. She cut her way over, stopping in front of us.

'Brittany, this is Avery.' Jacob beamed. 'Avery, this is Brittany. Say hi.'

'Hi,' Brittany said, giving me a little wave.

I waved back. 'Hey.'

'Avery is about to tell us how she almost killed a guy in a hallway. Thought you'd like to hear the story too.'

I winced, but the spark of interest in Brittany's brown eyes was kind of funny as she looked at me. 'Do tell,' she said, smiling.

'Well, I really didn't almost kill someone,' I said, sighing. 'But it was close and it was so, so embarrassing.'

'Embarrassing stories are the best,' Jacob threw out, kneeling down.

Brittany laughed. 'That is true.'

'Spill it, sister.'

I tucked my hair back and lowered my voice so the whole hall didn't revel in my humiliation. 'I was running late to astronomy and I sort of ran through the double doors on the second floor. I wasn't watching where I was going and I plowed into this poor guy in the hallway.'

'Yikes.' A sympathetic look crossed Brittany's face.

'Yeah, and I mean, I almost knocked him over. I dropped my stuff. Books and pens flew everywhere. It was pretty epic.'

Jacob's eyes gleamed with humor. 'Was he hot?'

'What?'

'Was he hot?' he repeated as he smoothed a hand through his cropped hair. ''Cuz if he was hot, you should've used it to your benefit. That could've become the best icebreaker in history. Like, you two could fall madly in love and you get to tell everyone how you plowed him before he actually *plowed* you.'

'Oh, my God.' I felt a familiar heat cross my cheeks. 'Yeah, he was really good-looking.'

'Oh no,' said Brittany, who seemed to be the only other person to recognize how a hot guy made the situation all the more embarrassing. I guess you needed a vagina to understand that, because Jacob looked even more thrilled by the news.

'So tell me what this good-looking man candy looked like? This is a need-to-know kind of detail.'

Part of me didn't want to say, because thinking about Cam made me about a thousand different levels of uncomfortable. 'Uh … well, he was really tall and nicely built, I guess.'

'How do you know he was nicely built? Did you feel him up, too?'

I laughed as Brittany shook her head. 'I seriously ran *into* him, Jacob. And he caught me. I wasn't feeling him up on purpose, but he seemed like he had a good body.' I shrugged. 'Anyway, he had dark, wavy hair. Longer than yours, kind of messy but in a—'

'Damn, girl, if you say messy in a I-don't-care-I'm-a-sexy-beast kind of way, I want to run into this guy.'

Brittany giggled. 'Love hair like that.'

I wondered if my face looked as hot as it felt. 'Yeah, it was like that. He was really gorgeous and his eyes were so blue they looked—'

'Wait,' Brittany gasped, her own eyes widening. 'Were his eyes, like, so blue they almost looked fake? And did he smell, like, really good? I know that sounds creepy and weird, but just answer the question.'

That was kind of creepy and weird and really funny. 'Yes to both.'

'Holy shit on a shoe.' Brittany let out a loud laugh. 'Did you get his name?'

I was starting to get worried, because Jacob also had this dawning expression on his face. 'Yeah, why?'

Brittany elbowed Jacob, and then she lowered her voice. 'Was it Cameron Hamilton?'

My jaw hit my lap.

'It was!' Brittany's shoulders shook. 'You ran into *Cameron Hamilton*?'

Jacob wasn't smiling. He was just staring at me in … awe? 'I am so incredibly envious of you right now. I would give my left testicle to run into Cameron Hamilton.'

I half laughed, half choked. 'Wow. That's pretty serious.'

'Cameron Hamilton is serious, Avery. You wouldn't know. You're not from around here,' Jacob said.

'You're a freshman, too. How do you know about him?' I asked, because Cam looked too old to be a freshman. He had to at least be a junior or senior.

'Everyone on campus knows him,' he replied.

'You've been on campus for less than a week!'

Jacob grinned. 'I get around.'

I laughed, shaking my head. 'I don't get it. Yeah, he's … hot, but so what?'

'I went to school with Cameron,' Brittany explained, glancing over her shoulder. 'I mean, he was two years older than me, but he was, like, the shit in high school. Everyone wanted to be around him or with him. It's pretty much the same here.'

Curiosity rose in spite of how what Brittany said reminded me of someone else. 'So you guys are from around here?'

'No. We're from outside of the Morgantown–Fort Hill area. I don't know why he chose this school instead of WVU, but I did because I wanted to get out of town versus being stuck with the same old people.'

I could understand that.

'Anyway, Cameron is known around campus.' Jacob smacked his hands together. 'He lives off campus and supposedly throws the best parties ever and—'

'He had a reputation in high school,' Brittany cut in. 'A reputation that was well earned. Don't get me wrong. Cameron has always been a really cool guy. Very nice and funny, but he put the "or" in man-whore back then. Seems to have settled down a bit, but a leopard and their spots …'

'Okay.' I fiddled with my bracelet. 'Good to know, but it doesn't really matter. I mean, I ran into him in a hallway. That's the extent of my knowledge of Cam.'

'*Cam?*' Brittany blinked.

'Yeah?' I shoved to my feet and grabbed my bag. Doors would open soon.

Brittany's brows knitted. 'People who he doesn't know call him Cameron. Only his friends call him Cam.'

'Oh.' I frowned. 'He told me people called him Cam, so I assumed that's what people called him.'

Brittany didn't say anything, and I honestly didn't see what the big deal was. Cam/Cameron/Whatever was just being polite after I ran him over. The fact that he was a reformed party playboy meant nothing to me other than that I should stay far, far away from him.

Doors swung open and students spilled into the hallway.

Our little group waited until it cleared before we headed inside, picking three seats in the back, with Jacob in between Brittany and me. As I pulled out my massive, could-knock-someone-out-if-hit-with-it, five-subject notebook, Jacob grabbed my arm.

Mischief and total mayhem filled his gaze. 'You cannot drop astronomy. To get through this semester, I must live vicariously through you and hear about *Cam* at least three days a week.'

I laughed softly. 'I'm not going to drop the class'—even though I sort of wanted to—'but I doubt I'm going to have anything to tell you. It's not like we're even going to talk again.'

Jacob let go of my arm and sat back, eyeing me. 'Famous last words, Avery.'

The rest of the day wasn't nearly as eventful as my morning had been, much to my pleasure. No more innocent hot boys almost knocked over or other humiliating incidents. Although I had to relive the experience all over again at lunch for Jacob's entertainment, I was happy that he and Brittany had a break around the same time I did. I'd really been planning on spending most of my day being a loner, so it was nice to actually talk to people … my own age.

Being social was like riding a bike, I guess.

And besides Jacob's unneeded advice, which entailed me purposely running into Cam the next time I saw him, there hadn't been any awkward moments. By the end of the day, I honestly had pretty much forgotten about Cam.

Before I left campus, I headed down to the financial building to pick up an application for work-study. I didn't need the money, but I needed the time suckage to keep my mind occupied. I had a full load—eighteen credit hours—but I would have a crap ton of free time. A job on campus seemed like the right thing to go for, but there were no spots open. My name went on an extended waiting list.

The campus was really beautiful in a quaint, peaceful sort of way. It was nothing like the sprawling campuses of huge universities. Nestled between the Potomac River and the tiny, historical town of Shepherdstown, it was like something you'd see on a postcard. Large buildings with steeples mixed in among more modern structures. Trees everywhere. Fresh, clean air and everything you needed within walking distance. I could actually walk on nicer days or at least park on West Campus to avoid paying the meter.

After giving my information for the waiting list, I hoofed it back toward my car, enjoying the warm breeze. Unlike this morning when I'd been running late, I got a chance to check out the houses on the way to the train station. Three houses, side by side, had porches full of college-aged guys. Most likely this school's version of fraternity row.

One guy looked up, beer in hand. He smiled, but then turned as a football flew out from the open door, smacking him in the back. Curses exploded.

Definitely fraternity row.

My spine stiffened as I picked up my pace, hurrying past the houses. I hit an intersection, stepped out, and nearly got slammed by a silver truck—one of those big ones, maybe a Tundra—as it sped onto the narrow road I needed to cross. My heart jumped as the truck slammed its brakes, blocking my path.

I took a step back onto the curb, confused. Was the driver going to yell at me?

The tinted passenger window rolled down, and I about fell flat on my face.

Cameron Hamilton grinned at me from behind the wheel, baseball cap on, turned backward. Wisps of dark hair curled up under the band. And he was shirtless—totally shirtless.

And from what I could see of him, just his chest, it was a mighty fine chest. Pecs—the guy had pecs. And a tattoo. On the right side of his chest, a sunburst, flames trailing back over his shoulders in vibrant hues of red and orange.

'Avery Morgansten, we meet again.'

He was the last person I wanted to see. I had the shittiest luck known to man. 'Cameron Hamilton … hi.'

He leaned over, dropping an arm over the steering wheel. Correction. He also had some really nice biceps. 'We have to stop meeting like this.'

And that was the truest thing ever spoken. I needed to stop staring at his biceps … and chest … and tattoo. Never thought the sun could be so … sexy. Wow. This was awkward.

'You running into me, me almost running over you?' Cam elaborated. 'It's like we're a catastrophe waiting to happen.'

I had no idea what to say to that. My mouth was dry, thoughts scattered.

'Where are you heading?'

'My car,' I forced out. 'I'm about to run out of time.' Not necessarily true, because I had been generous with the quarters so I wouldn't end up with a parking ticket, but he didn't need to know that. 'So …'

'Well, hop in, sweetheart. I can give you a ride.'

Blood drained from my face and rushed to other parts of my body in a really odd and confusing way. 'No. It's okay. I'm right up the hill. No need at all.'

The grin spread up on the side, revealing that one dimple. 'It's no problem. It's the least I can do after almost running you over.'

'Thank you, but—'

'Yo! Cam!' Beer Guy jumped off the porch and jogged down the sidewalk, passing me a quick look. 'What you up to, man?'

Saved by the frat boy.

Cam's gaze didn't veer from me, but his grin started to slip. 'Nothing, Kevin, just trying to have a conversation.'

Giving Cam a quick wave, I hurried around Kevin and the front of the truck. I didn't look back, but I could feel him watching. Over the years, knowing when someone was staring at you when you weren't looking had become a talent of mine.

I forced myself not to run to the train station, because running away in front of the same guy twice in one day was beyond the acceptable level of weirdness. Even for me.

I didn't realize I'd been holding my breath until I was behind the wheel of my car and had the engine humming.

Jesus.

I dropped my head against the steering wheel and groaned. A catastrophe waiting to happen? Yeah, sounded about right.

Chapter 3

Sitting through a three-hour-long sociology class Tuesday night hadn't been as bad as I thought it would be, but by the time class let out, I was starving. Before I headed back to my apartment, I stopped by Sheetz—a convenience store/ gas station we didn't have in Texas—and got an MTO. A made-to-order salad, heavy on the fried chicken strips and ranch dressing.

Mmm. Healthy.

My apartment building parking lot was packed with cars, some even in the nearby field that butted up to West Campus. It hadn't been like this when I'd left for my evening class and I wondered what was going on. I managed to find a parking spot all the way near the main road and as I turned off the ignition, my cell rattled in the cup holder.

I grinned when I saw it was a text from Jacob. We'd exchanged numbers earlier in class since he lived in one of the dorms.

Art sucks was all his text said.

Laughing, I sent him a quick text back about our home-work, which was to identify what painting belonged to what era. Thank God for Google, because that was how I was completing the assignment.

Gathering up my bag and food, I climbed out of my car. The air was sticky and I lifted my hair off my neck, wishing I had pulled it up into a ponytail. The scent of autumn was in the air, though, and I was eager to see cooler weather. Maybe even snow in the winter. I headed across the brightly lit parking lot, toward the center cluster of apartments. I was on the top floor—the fifth. It seemed like a lot of students lived here and most hadn't really started to arrive until today, but as soon as I stepped up on the sidewalk, I knew where all the cars were coming from.

Music thumped from somewhere inside my apartment building. A lot of lights were on, and I could pick up pieces of conversation as I headed up the stairs. On the fifth floor, I found the culprit. The apartment across the hall, two doors down, was throwing a party. The door was cracked open, and light and music spilled into the open hallway.

A little bit of jealousy wiggled inside my chest as I unlocked my door. All the laughter, the noise, and the music sounded fun. It all seemed so normal, like something I *should* be doing, but parties …

Parties didn't end well for me.

Closing my door behind me, I kicked off my shoes and dropped my bag on the couch. Furnishing this apartment had put a dent in my account, but I'd be here for four years and I figured I could sell everything when I left or take it with me.

And it was all *my* stuff. That meant a lot to me.

The party raged on across the hall, long after I finished my not-so-healthy salad, changed into sleep shorts and a long-sleeve shirt, and finished my art homework. It was just after midnight when I gave up on reading my English assignment and started back toward my bedroom.

But I stopped in the hallway, my toes curling into the carpet.

A burst of muffled laughter rang out and I knew the door of the party apartment must've been open, because it sounded louder than before. I was frozen, worrying my lower lip. What if I opened the door and recognized someone from class? It was obviously a college kid throwing the party. Maybe I would know the person? So what if I did? Wasn't like I was going to join in when I was braless, wearing my jammies, and rocking the messiest ponytail known to man.

I turned and flipped on the bathroom light, staring at my reflection. Scrubbed of all makeup, the freckles on the bridge of my nose stood way out and my face seemed more flushed than normal. I leaned against the sink my mom would've laughed at and pressed my face closer to the mirror.

With the exception of my reddish-brown hair, which came from my father, I was the spitting image of my mom—straight nose, rounded chin, and high cheekbones; with all the cosmetic help she'd had over the years to stay looking *fresh*, we looked more like sisters than mother and daughter.

Footsteps echoed out in the hall. More laughter.

I made a face at my reflection and pushed away from the mirror. Back in the hall, I told myself to go to sleep, but I found myself walking toward my front door. I had no idea what I was doing or why I was being so nosy, but everything sounded … warm and fun out there and everything in here was cold and boring.

Warm and fun?

I rolled my eyes. God, I sounded lame. It was cold in here because I had the central air cranked like a mother.

But I was at the door and there was nothing stopping me. Yanking it open, I peered out into the stairwell, seeing two heads disappear down the steps. The door to the party was still open, and I stood there, torn. This wasn't home. No one was going to send me a scathing look or yell obscenities at me. If anything, they'd probably think I was some kind of freak just standing there, half out my door, all bug-eyed, and letting all the cold air out.

'Bring Raphael back!' exclaimed a familiar voice and a deep laugh that had my stomach dropping in stunned disbelief. 'You fucktard!'

I recognized that voice! Oh my God …

It couldn't be. I hadn't seen the big-ass silver truck outside, but then again, there were so many cars and it wasn't like I was searching for his truck.

The door swung all the way open, and I froze as a guy stumbled out, laughing as he set a tortoise—*what the fuck?*—on the floor. The thing stuck its head out, looked around, and then disappeared into its shell.

A second later, the guy who'd put the tortoise outside was pulled back into the apartment and Cam appeared in the doorway in all his shirtless glory. He reached down and scooped up the little green guy. 'Sorry, Raphael. My friends are complete, fucking …' He looked up.

I tried to jerk back inside, but it was too late.

Cam saw me.

'Assholes …' He did a double take. 'What the … ?'

Would dive-bombing into my apartment seem weird? Yes—yes it would. So I went with a very lame, 'Hey …'

Cam blinked several times, as if he sought to clear his vision. 'Avery Morgansten? This is becoming a habit.'

'Yeah.' I forced myself to swallow. 'It is.'

'Do you live here or are you visiting?'

I cleared my throat as the tortoise's legs started moving like it was trying to wiggle away. 'I … I live here.'

'No shit?' Those baby blues widened and he swaggered around the railing. I couldn't help but notice how his gym shorts hung way low on his narrow hips. Or his stomach.

22

It was ripped, taking six-pack into eight-pack territory. 'You really live here?'

I forced my gaze up and got stuck on the sun tattoo. 'Yes. I really live here.'

'This is … I don't even know.' He laughed again, and I met his stare. 'Really crazy.'

'Why?' Besides the fact he was standing in my apartment hallway, shirtless and barefoot, holding a tortoise named Raphael?

'*I* live here.'

I gaped at him. The whole half-naked thing sort of made sense now and I guess so did the tortoise, but it couldn't be true. Way too many coincidences. 'You're joking, right?'

'No. I've been living here for a while—like a couple of years with my roommate. You know, the fucktard who put poor Raphael outside.'

'Hey!' the guy yelled from inside their apartment. 'I have a name. It's *Señor* Fucktard!'

Cam laughed. 'Anyway, did you move in over the weekend?'

I found myself nodding.

'Makes sense. I was back home, visiting the fam.' He shifted Raphael to his other hand, cradling the squirming thing to his chest. 'Well, hell …'

I was gripping the door so hard my knuckles ached. 'That's … um, your tortoise?'

'Yeah.' A half grin appeared as he lifted the little guy. 'Raphael, meet Avery.'

I gave the tortoise a little wave, feeling stupid afterward for doing so. It just stuck its head back in its green-and-brown shell. 'That's a very interesting pet.'

'And those are very interesting shorts.' His gaze dropped. 'What are they?' He leaned forward, his eyes narrowing, and I stiffened. 'Pizza slices?'

Heat swamped my cheeks. 'They're ice cream cones.'

'Huh. I like them.' Straightening, his gaze drifted up me slowly, leaving an unfamiliar wake of heat behind. 'A lot.'

I immediately let go of the door and crossed my arms over my chest. One corner of his lips tipped up. My eyes narrowed. 'Thanks. That means a lot to me.'

'It should. They have my seal of approval.' He bit down on his lower lip as his lashes lifted. Those eyes pierced mine. 'I need to get Raphael back in his little habitat before he pees on my hand, which he's bound to do, and that sucks.'

My lips twitched into a small grin. 'I can imagine.'

'So, you should come over. The guys are about to leave, but I'm sure they'll be around for a little longer. You can meet them.' He inched closer and lowered his voice. 'They're no way as interesting as I am, but they're not bad.'

I glanced over his shoulder, part of me wanting one thing and the other part wanting nothing to do with any of this. That part won out. 'Thanks, but I was heading to bed.'

'This early?'

'It has to be after midnight.'

His grin was spreading. 'That's still early.'

'Maybe to you.'

'Are you sure?' he asked. 'I have cookies.'

'Cookies?' My brows rose.

'Yeah, and I made them. I'm quite the baker.'

For some reason, I couldn't picture that. 'You baked cookies?'

'I bake a lot of things, and I'm sure you're dying to know all about those things. But tonight, it was chocolate and walnut cookies. They are the shit, if I do say so myself.'

'As great as that sounds, I'm going to have to pass.'

'Maybe later then?'

'Maybe.' Not likely. I stepped back, reaching for the door. 'Well, it's good seeing you again, Cameron.'

24

'Cam,' he corrected. 'And hey, we didn't almost run each other over. Look at us, changing up the pattern.'

'That's a good thing.' I was back in my apartment and he was still in front of my door. 'You should get back before Raphael pees on your hand.'

'Would be worth it,' he replied.

My brows knitted. 'Why?'

He didn't answer that, but he did start backing up. 'If you change your mind, I'll be up for a while.'

'I'm not going to. Good night, Cam.'

His eyes widened only a fraction of inch, but his grin slipped into a full smile, and my stomach sort of flopped, because his smile was wow. 'See you tomorrow.'

'Tomorrow?'

'Astronomy class? Or are you skipping again?'

My cheeks heated all over again. God, I had *almost* forgotten about running away in front of him like a total idiot. 'No.' I sighed. 'I'll be there.'

'Great.' He started backing up again. 'Good night, Avery.'

Ducking behind the door, I closed it and then locked it. I swore I heard him chuckle, but I had to be crazy.

I stood there a few moments and then I whipped around and raced back to my bedroom. Diving under the covers, I rolled onto my stomach and shoved my face into a pillow.

Sleep. Just go to sleep.

Cam lived across the hall?

You need to get up early. Go to sleep.

How in the world was that possible? He was everywhere I went.

Go to sleep.

And why did he have a pet tortoise? And did he seriously name it after the Teenage Mutant Ninja Turtles? Because that was kind of funny.

Morning's going to come soon.

Does he only wear a shirt during class? Oh my God, he seriously lived across the hall. Jacob was going to flip … and probably move in. That would be fun. I really liked Jacob, but I had a feeling he'd borrow my clothes.

Go the fuck to sleep.

I couldn't believe the hot dude I ran into and then ran away from lived across the hall. I don't even know why I cared. It didn't matter. I wasn't interested in guys, or girls, but he was extraordinarily hot … and kind of funny … and kind of charming.

No. No. No. Stop thinking about him, because it's pointless and hopeless, so go to sleep.

Did I eat all that salad? Man, those cookies sound good right about now.

'Ugh!' I groaned into the pillow.

This crap went on for about an hour before I gave up and threw myself out of bed. Out in the living room, I didn't hear any music or noise coming from Cam's apartment. He was probably sleeping soundly while I was up obsessing over cookies and chicken tenders and ripped stomachs.

Stomping into the extra bedroom that had become more of a library/office, I powered on my laptop and brought up my e-mail. There was one unread e-mail in my in-box, from my cousin. I deleted that without even opening it. On the left toolbar, I saw I had a few unread e-mails in my junk folder. Bored out of my mind, I clicked on the link and scanned the prescription drug offers, the 'I have money in a foreign account' e-mails, and the notice that Bath & Body Works was having a sale. My eyes narrowed on the subject line of the one e-mail, which had come in at around eleven the previous night.

It read AVERY MORGANSTEN and was from an e-mail address I didn't recognize.

Well, that was strange, because my e-mail wasn't set up under my real name, so it would be unlikely that it was a phishing scam. Only my parents and cousin had my e-mail address because, even though they had my telephone number, I'd rather have them contact me that way instead of calling. No one else had it.

My finger hovered over the mouse pad. Unease rose as knots formed in my stomach. Tucking my legs against my chest, I told myself not to open it, to just delete it—but I clicked because I had to. It was like looking at a bad car accident alongside the road. You knew you shouldn't, but you did.

I immediately wished I hadn't. The knots in my stomach tightened and a lump formed in the back of my throat. Nauseous, I pushed away from the desk and slammed the laptop shut. Standing in the middle of the room, I sucked in a deep breath and curled my hands into fists.

It was just two lines.

That was all.

Two lines erased thousands of miles.

Two lines ruined my entire night.

Two lines found me all the way in a little college town in West Virginia.

You're nothing but a liar, Avery Morgansten. You'll get yours in the end.

Chapter 4

I dragged myself into astronomy class ten minutes early and picked what I believed to be an inconspicuous seat in the middle of the amphitheater-style classroom. A few other students were already there, sitting up front. Yawning, I scooted down in my seat and rubbed my eyes. The gallon of coffee I drank this morning hadn't done a thing for me, given that I only got an hour of sleep.

Two little sentences.

Squeezing my eyes shut, I rested my head on my forearm. I didn't want to think about the e-mail or the fact that I had reopened my laptop and gone into my trash folder to see what my cousin had said. His e-mail had just been one giant bitch fest on how I was letting my parents down and how his were worried sick and afraid I was going to put Mom and Dad through another episode. *You need to come home*, he had written. *It is the right thing to do*. It was the right thing for them, and while my cousin sided with my parents and, oh, about ninety-nine percent of the town, I doubted he had been behind the other e-mail.

The e-mail address was unrecognizable to me, and while there were a lot of people that it could've come from, I really didn't know who it was. It couldn't be *him* because even he wasn't stupid enough to try to contact me.

Or was he?

A shudder rolled down my spine. What if it had been Blaine? What if he found out where I'd moved to? My family wouldn't have told him. Then again, they could've told his parents because they were, after all, country club pals. I was going to murder them if they had. Seriously. Catch the next flight to Texas and murder them, because the whole point of coming here was to get away from—

'Morning, sweetheart,' came a deep voice.

I jerked my head up and twisted around. Surprised into speechlessness, I watched Cam slide into the empty seat next to me. I must have been a little slow on the uptake, because I knew I should've said the seat was taken or tell him to move, but all I could do was stare.

He settled back, looking at me sideways. 'You look a little rough this morning.'

And he looked remarkably refreshed for someone who had been partying last night. Hair damp and all over the place, eyes bright. 'Thanks.'

'You're welcome. Glad to see you made it to class this time.' He paused, tilting his head back and kicking his feet up on the seat in front of us, his eyes on me. 'Though I kind of missed the whole running-into-each-other thing. Provided a lot of excitement.'

'I don't miss that,' I admitted, bending over and rummaging through my bag for my notebook. 'That was really embarrassing.'

'It shouldn't have been.'

'Easy for you to say. You're the one who got plowed. I was doing the plowing.'

Cam's mouth opened. Oh my God, had I really just said that? I had. Flushing to the roots of my hair, I flipped open my notebook.

'Raphael is doing great, by the way.'

A relieved grin snuck out. 'That's good to hear. Did he pee on your hand?'

'No, but it was a close call. Brought you something.'

'Turtle pee?'

Cam laughed and shook his head as he reached into his backpack. 'Sorry to let you down, but no.' He pulled out papers stapled together. 'It's a syllabus. I know. Thrilling shit right here, but figured since you didn't come to class on Monday, you'd need one, so I got it from the professor.'

'Thank you.' I took the papers from him, somewhat shocked by the act. 'That was really thoughtful.'

'Well, prepare yourself. I am all kinds of thoughtful this week. I brought you something else.'

As he rooted around in his backpack, I bit down on the edge of my pen and took the moment to openly gawk at him without him knowing. It really had been a long time since I had held a conversation with a member of the opposite sex who wasn't related to me, but from all the people-watching I'd done over the years, I thought I was handling this well. Besides the plowing comment, I was sort of proud of myself.

Cam pulled out a napkin and unfolded it with long fingers. 'Cookie for you. Cookie for me.'

Removing the pen from my mouth, I shook my head. 'You didn't have to do that.'

'It's just a cookie, sweetheart.'

I shook my head again, because it just didn't make sense to me. Cam didn't make sense to me. Hell, most people didn't make sense to me.

He looked up through those impossibly long lashes and

31

sighed. Tearing the napkin in half, he folded up one of the cookies and then dropped it in my lap. 'I know they say you shouldn't take candy from strangers, but it's a cookie and not candy and technically, I'm not a stranger.'

I swallowed.

Cam took a bite of his cookie and closed his eyes. A deep sound emanated from his throat—a growl of pleasure. My heart jumped and my cheeks heated even more as I stared at him. He made the sound again, and my mouth dropped open. A row down, a girl turned in her seat, her eyes clouded over.

'Is it really that good?' I asked, glancing down at the cookie in my lap.

'Oh, yeah, this is the shit. I told you that last night. Be better if I had some milk.' He took another bite. 'Mmm, milk.'

I dared another peek at him and he looked like he was on the verge of having an orgasm or something.

One eye opened. 'It's the combination of walnut and chocolate. You mix that together and it's like an explosion of sex in your mouth, but not as messy. The only thing better would be those teeny tiny Reese's Cups. When the dough is warm, you plop those suckers in … Anyway, you just need to try it. Take a small bite.'

Oh, what the hell? It was just a cookie, not a crack pipe. I was being stupid. I unfolded the napkin and took a bite. The cookie practically melted in my mouth.

'Good?' Cam said. 'Right?'

I took another bite and nodded.

'Well, I have a whole ton of them at home.' He stretched as he rolled up his napkin. 'Just saying.'

Finishing off the cookie, I had to admit that it was a pretty damn good cookie. Wiping off my fingers, I started to roll up the napkin, but Cam reached over and took it from me. He twisted a bit in his seat, causing his knee to brush my leg.

'Crumb,' he said.

'What?'

A slight grin appeared on his face and then he reached out, without the napkin, and before I knew what he was doing, he smoothed his thumb over my bottom lip. Every single muscle in my body locked up and became painfully tense. My eyes widened and the air caught in my throat. The touch was slight, barely anything, but I felt it in several parts of my body.

'Got it.' His grin spread.

My lip still tingled. That was all I could think about. I didn't move, not until the door at the front of the classroom opened and the strangest man I'd ever seen rolled in. Dressed head to toe in olive-green polyester, the man had thick, curly hair that went in every which direction, peppered black and gray. His glasses were huge, resting on the tip of his nose. As he crossed the main stage, I noticed he was wearing a pair of checkered Vans … that matched his bow tie.

Cam chuckled softly. 'Professor Drage is a very … unique man.'

'I can see,' I murmured.

Professor Drage had an accent I couldn't quite place, but based on his olive skin tone, I was going with Mediterranean or Middle Eastern. He launched right into the topic—no roll call or warning. I scrambled to catch up to his introduction to the field of astronomy and units of measurement while Cam scooted even farther down in his seat and opened his notebook. His pen was making quick, short strokes over the paper, but he wasn't taking notes.

He was drawing.

Cocking my head to the side, I tried to focus on what the hell an astronomical unit meant, which was some crazy number I couldn't even begin to remember. Turned out to be the average distance at which the Earth orbits the sun. That was important because astronomical units were used to determine most distances in our solar system, but I found myself glancing at Cam's notebook.

What the hell was he drawing?

'Now, most of you kiddos don't care about astronomical units or have never really heard of them,' Professor Drage went on, passing the length of the stage. 'What you are familiar with is the term "light-year." Although, I doubt any of you really, truly understands what a light-year is.'

I was pretty sure Cam was drawing Bigfoot.

The lecture went on until Professor Drage suddenly changed gears at the end, catching me and everyone else besides Cam off guard, and started passing out star maps. 'I know today is only Wednesday, but here is your first assignment for the weekend. Skies are supposed to be clear as a baby's bottom on Saturday.'

'Clear as a baby's bottom?' I muttered.

Cam chuckled.

'I want you to find the Corona Borealis in the sky—the actual real, honest to goodness, night sky,' Professor Drage explained, smiling as if he said something funny, but we all stared at him. 'You won't need a telescope. Use your eyes or glasses or contacts or whatever. You can view it either Friday or Saturday night, but the weather is looking sketchy on Friday, so choose wisely.'

'Wait,' someone from up front said. 'How do you use this map?'

Cam handed me a map that had been passed down our row, along with several grid sheets.

Professor Drage stopped in front of the class. 'You look at it.'

I bit back a laugh.

The student huffed. 'I get that, but do we hold it up to the sky or something?'

'Sure. You could do that. Or you could just look at each of the constellations, see what they look like and then use your own eyes and brains to find it in the sky.' The professor paused. 'Or use Google. I want all of you to start to get familiar with stargazing. You're going to be doing a lot of that this semester and you'll appreciate doing it now when it's warm. So get with your partner and pick out a time. The grid will be turned back in to me on Monday. That's all for the day. Good luck and may the force of the universe be with you today.'

Several students laughed, but my stomach dropped out of my butt.

'Partner?' I said, voice low as I frantically looked around the classroom. Almost everyone was turned in their seats, talking to another person. 'When did we pick partners?'

'On Monday,' Cam replied, closing his notebook and shoving it into his backpack. 'You weren't here.'

My heart thumped in my chest as I scooted to the edge of the seat. *Shit*. Professor Drage had already bounced from the room. Half the students were already out the door.

'Avery?'

How in the hell was I supposed to get a partner now? I really shouldn't have run like a little baby on Monday. This was all my fault.

'Avery.'

Where was the professor's office? I was going to have to find the dude and explain I didn't have a partner. I bet his office smelled weird, too, like mothballs.

'*Avery.*'

'What?' I snapped, turning to Cam. Why was he still sitting here staring at me?

His brows rose. 'We're partners.'

'Huh?'

'We. Are. Partners,' he repeated, and then sighed. 'Apparently, Drage had the class pick their partners right at

35

the beginning of class on Monday. I walked in afterward and at the end he told me to partner with anyone who joined the class on Wednesday or I'd be partnerless. And since I don't like the idea of being partnerless, you and I are partners.'

I stared at him. 'We have a choice to do this on our own?'

'Yeah, but who wants to go out staring at the sky at night by themselves?' He stood and slung his backpack over his shoulder as he started down the row. 'Anyway, I know a perfect place we can do our assignment. Has to be Saturday, because I have plans Friday.'

'Wait.' I stood, rushing after him. 'I do.'

'You have plans on Saturday?' He frowned. 'Well, I might—'

'No. I don't have plans on Saturday, but we don't have to be partners,' I explained. 'I can do this by myself.'

He stopped so suddenly in front of the doors that I nearly had a repeat of Monday. 'Why would you want to do all the assignments—and if you look at his class outline, there are a lot—all by yourself?'

'Well, I don't really want to.' I shifted my weight from one foot to the next. 'But you don't have to be my partner. I mean, you don't owe me or anything.'

'I don't get what you're saying.' Cam tilted his head to the side.

'What I'm saying is that ...' I trailed off. What the hell was I saying? The problem was I just didn't get him—any of him. He didn't know me. I didn't know him and yet he was so ... so *friendly*. The next words just came out of my mouth. 'Why are you being so nice to me?'

A brow rose. 'Is that a serious question?'

'Yes.'

He stared at me a moment. 'All right, I guess I'm just a nice guy. And you're obviously new—a freshman. You seemed to be a little out of it on Monday and then you ran off, wouldn't even come into class, and I—'

'I don't want your pity.' I was horrified. He was being nice to me because he thought I was a freshman freak. Oh God, that was …

Cam frowned, and I mean really frowned. 'You don't have my pity, Avery. I'm just saying you seemed out of it on Monday and I figured we'd just be partners.' He stopped and his eyes narrowed. 'I can see that you don't believe me. Maybe it was the cookie? Well, you refused to taste my cookies last night and, honestly, I was going to eat the other cookie, but you looked so tired and sad sitting there, I figured you needed the cookie more than I did.'

I couldn't tell if he was joking or not, but there was a distinct gleam of amusement in his eyes.

'And you're pretty,' he added.

I blinked. 'What?'

That frown had faded as he opened the door, ushering me out of the class and into the hall. 'Do not tell me you don't know you're pretty. If so, I'm about to lose all faith in mankind. You don't want to be responsible for that.'

'I know I'm pretty—I mean, that's not what I meant.' God, I sounded vain. I shook my head. 'I don't think I'm ugly. That's what—'

'Good. Now we've cleared that up.' Tugging on my bag, he steered me toward the stairwell. 'Watch the door. It can be tricky.'

I ignored that. 'What does the whole pretty comment have to do with anything?'

'You asked why I'm so nice to you. It's mutually beneficial.'

It sank in, and I stopped on the stair above him. 'You're nice to me because you think I'm pretty?'

'And because you have brown eyes. I'm a sucker for big old brown eyes.' He laughed. 'I'm a shallow, shallow boy. Hey, it helps that you're pretty. It brings out the nice guy in me. Makes me want to share my cookies with you.'

I stared at him. 'So if I was ugly, you wouldn't be nice to me?'

Cam pivoted around, facing me. Even a whole step below, he was taller than me. 'I'd still be nice to you if you were ugly.'

'Okay.'

A wicked grin slipped over his full lips. He bent his head down and whispered, 'I just wouldn't offer you any cookies.'

I folded my arms and tried to ignore the close proximity of our faces. 'I'm beginning to think cookies is a code word for something else.'

'Maybe it is.' He tugged on my bag again as he took a confident step back, forcing me down another step. 'And just think about it. If cookies is a code word, whatever it symbolizes, it's been in your mouth, sweetheart.'

Part of me was slightly disturbed by that, and the other part? A laugh bubbled up my throat and came out, sounding a bit hoarse. 'You are really …'

'Amazing? Awesome?' He paused, brows raised. 'Astonishing?'

'I was going to go with bizarre.'

'Well, hell, if I had feelings that might actually hurt.'

I grinned, falling into the easy banter with him. 'I guess it's a good thing that you don't have feelings then, huh?'

'Guess so.' He went down a couple more steps and stopped on the landing. 'You better hurry or you're going to be late to your next class.'

Holy shit! He was right.

Cam laughed at my wide eyes and stepped out of my way as I charged down the steps. 'Damn, if only you moved that fast for my cookies, I'd be a happy guy.'

'Shut up!' I tossed over my shoulder as I hit the next set of steps.

'Hey!' he yelled after me. 'Don't you want to know what cookies is a code word for?'

'No! Good God, no!'

His laughter followed me into the hall and all the way to my next class.

Chapter 5

'Your apartment is nice,' Brittany said from my couch. A history text lay open but unread in her lap. 'I would love not to have to live in a dorm. My roommate snores like a banshee.'

I hovered between the coffee table and the TV, really unsure how Brittany and Jacob had ended up in my apartment after class. At lunch, we'd talked about getting together and exchanging notes from history, and somehow my place was offered up. I thought it was Jacob's idea, and since both of them were here we were getting absolutely no studying done.

Anxious energy buzzed through me like a hummingbird. It had been so long since I had people in my space. Back home, no one but family came around, and only the maid entered my bedroom. Not only had I been a virtual pariah in my town and at school, it had been the same way inside my house. But before that Halloween party, *everyone* hung out at my house, especially the girls from the studio. Everyone had still talked to me then, and I'd still danced. Before that party, things had been normal.

I fiddled with my bracelet, nervous. I liked having them here because it was normal and reminded me of the *before*.

It was what people in college did, but it was so ... different to me.

Jacob resurfaced from my kitchen, a bag of chips in hand. 'Forget about the apartment. Don't get me wrong. It is a nice apartment, but I want to hear more about Cam's *cookies*.'

I took a chip from the bag. 'I should've never told you about that conversation.'

'Whatever,' he replied, mouth full.

Brittany giggled. 'I am so dying to know what cookies are slang for.'

'Probably his cock.' Jacob plopped down on the arm of the couch.

'Oh my God,' I said, taking a handful of chips. I needed the calorie fortitude for where this conversation was heading.

Brittany nodded. 'Makes sense then. I mean, with the whole not sharing cookies with ugly girls.'

'I don't think he really meant that,' I said, popping a chip in my mouth. 'So, back to our history notes ...'

'Fuck history. Back to Cam's cock,' Jacob said. 'Do you know, if cookies are a code word for cock, then that means his cock was in your mouth.'

I choked on the chip and grabbed my can of soda, inhaling the liquid as my face burned.

'Figuratively speaking, that is,' Jacob added, grinning like a total shithead. He hopped up. 'I don't know how you do it, Avery. If I lived across the hall from him, I'd be plastered to his front door noon to midnight. And I'd be all over his *cookies*. Yum.'

Waving a hand in front of my face, I shook my head. 'You can have his cookies.'

'Oh, honey, if he swung batter-batter for my team, I'd be all over that in a heartbeat.'

Brittany's eyes rolled. 'Big surprise there.'

'What I don't understand is how come you aren't all over his *cookies*.'

I opened my mouth, but Brittany shook her head and said, 'I don't think cookies mean cock. I think it might mean his balls, being that it's plural and all.'

Jacob burst into loud laughter. 'Then that means his balls were in your mouth, figuratively speaking! Damn, that's some dirty baking.'

I gaped at the two. Was this typical conversation? 'Oh my God, can we please stop talking about his cock and balls or I'll never be able to eat cookies again. Like, ever.'

'No. Seriously. How come you aren't all up on that?' Jacob climbed onto the back of the couch like an overgrown cat. 'He's obviously flirting with you.'

'So?' I replied, believing it might be safe to eat another chip without dying.

Jacob's jaw dropped. 'So?'

Brittany closed the history book and dropped it on the floor with a loud thump. Guess there went studying completely. 'Jacob is like a sex-starved woman in her mid-thirties, so he can't possibly understand why you wouldn't want to take a ride on the town bike.'

I glanced at Jacob, and he just shrugged and said, 'Very true.'

'Even I have a hard time understanding that. Cameron is really good-looking,' Brittany continued. 'And I've never heard any girl talking crap about him, so he must treat them good.'

Having no idea what to say, I dropped into the black moon chair near the TV. Explaining to them the why behind it all was a big fat no go. 'I don't know. I'm just not interested.'

'Do you have ovaries?' Jacob asked.

I shot him a look. 'Yes.'

He slid down the back of the couch and sat beside Brittany. 'Then how are you not interested?'

Shoving the rest of the chips in my mouth, I struggled to respond without coming across like a frigid prude. But I was a total frigid prude, wasn't I? Or afflicted, depending on who you asked. Either way, while the idea of cocks and balls interested me, the thought of actually getting up close and personal with them made me break out in a cold sweat.

And I was sweating now. The chips were already souring in my stomach. I'd be breaking out the Tums later. My mind immediately went straight to the e-mail from last night.

Liar.

Wiping my hands over my jeans, I shook my head. 'I'm just not interested in a relationship.'

Jacob laughed. 'We're not saying that Cam is either, you know? You don't have to want to be in a relationship for a little bow-chicka-bow-wow.'

Brittany looked at him slowly. 'Did you really just say that?'

'I did. And I owned it. Gonna make me a shirt that says that.' Jacob flashed a grin. 'Anyway, all I'm saying is he's an opportunity you might not want to pass up.'

I didn't even give that a thought. 'Why are we even talking about this? We have one class together and he lives across the hall—'

'And you're partners for the rest of the semester,' Brittany added. 'Kind of romantic, going out at night and gazing up at stars.'

My stomach tightened. 'It's not romantic. Nothing is romantic.'

Her brows rose as she ran her hand through the short locks of blond hair. 'Well, hello, Debbie Downer.'

I rolled my eyes. 'All I'm saying is that I don't know him. He doesn't know me. And he's just a flirt. You've even said he's the town bike. This is just probably how he is. He's a nice and friendly guy. That's all. So can we just forget about it?'

'Yeah, you bitches be boring me to tears,' Jacob said, and Brittany stuck her pierced tongue out at him. Light glinted off the bolt, and I winced, thinking that had to have hurt. 'And I need some salsa to go with these chips.'

'In the bottom cupboard,' I shouted, but he was already halfway in the kitchen, doors opening and slamming.

Much to my relief, the topic veered away from me and the nonexistent whatever with Cam. Hours passed and I became more comfortable with having them there, and we even cracked open our history books for a few short seconds. When it got close to nine, they packed up their stuff and headed toward the door.

Brittany stopped and sprang forward. Before I could prepare myself, she gave me a quick hug and peck on the cheek. I stood there, sort of shell-shocked. She smiled. 'There's a big party at one of the frats Friday night. You should come with.'

I remembered Cam saying he was busy Friday and since he obviously liked to party, that was probably why. I shook my head. 'I don't know.'

'Don't be antisocial,' Jacob said, opening the door. 'We're cool people to hang with.'

I laughed. 'I know. I'll think about it.'

'Okay.' Brittany wiggled her fingers. 'See you tomorrow.'

Out in the hall, Jacob started pointing at Cam's door as he thrust his hips and wiggled his ass. I bit down on my lip to stop laughing. It went on until Brittany caught the collar of his polo and yanked him down the stairs.

Smiling, I shut the door and locked it. It didn't take much time for me to clean up and get ready for bed. The whole bed thing was pointless because I wasn't sleepy, and since I was avoiding the laptop and therefore my e-mail, I ended up watching reruns of *Ghost Hunters* until I was convinced there was a poltergeist in my bathroom. Turning off the TV, I stood and ended up doing something I hated.

Pacing my apartment like I used to do in my bedroom back home. With the TV off and my apartment quiet, I could hear little minute noises from the other apartments. I focused on those noises instead of letting my mind do the wander thing because tonight had been good and I didn't want to ruin it. The last couple of days had been great, with the exception of the whole plowing-into-Cam thing. Things were good.

I stopped behind my couch, only realizing then what I was doing.

Looking down, I saw the sleeve of my shirt pushed up and my fingers wrapped around my left wrist. Slowly, meticulously, I lifted up my fingers, one by one. There were faint pink indents from the bracelet pressing into my skin. For the last five years, I only took the bracelet off at night and when I showered. Those indents would probably be permanent.

Just like the jagged scar the bracelet hid.

I removed my hand completely. The two-inch stretch of a deeper pink slashed down the very center of my wrist, over the vein. It had been a deep cut made with broken glass from the picture frame I'd thrown after the first picture had circulated the high school.

When I'd made that cut, it had been the lowest point of my life and I hadn't been joking around. There would've been a matching violent slash on my right wrist if it hadn't been for the maid hearing the glass break.

The picture had been of me and my best friend, the very same best friend who had been one of the first to turn her back and whisper words like *whore* and *liar*.

46

I had wanted to end it then. Just check out, because at that point in my life, nothing could've been worse than what had happened to me, what my parents had agreed to, and the subsequent fallout. In a matter of months, my life had utterly separated into two ragged chunks: before and after. And I hadn't been able to see a possible *after* when the entire school got behind Blaine.

Now? The after seemed endless, but shame burned like a low fire in my belly as I stared at the scar. Suicide was never the answer and if anything, *checking out* was letting all of them win. I'd learned the lesson all by myself, since therapy had never been an option. My parents would've rather cut off their legs than suffer through the embarrassment of having a daughter who had tried to commit suicide and needed therapy. More money had exchanged hands to keep my afternoon hospital run quiet.

Apparently my parents were okay with having a daughter labeled a lying whore.

But I hated seeing the physical embodiment of my weakness, would be beyond humiliated if anyone ever saw it.

Sudden deep laughter from the hallway drew my attention—Cam's laughter. My head swiveled toward the kitchen. On the stove, the clock read near one in the morning.

I tugged my sleeve down.

'Can't you skip it Friday night?' a feminine voice asked, slightly muffled through the wall.

There was a pause and then I heard Cam say, 'You know I can't, sweetheart. Maybe next time.'

Sweetheart? Oh! I heard their footsteps round the railing outside the apartment, hitting the stairwell.

Rushing around the couch, I made my way over to the window. Since my apartment was at the end and overlooking the parking lot, all I had to do was wait. And then there they were, a shirtless Cam and a girl.

A really tall, leggy brunette wearing a cute denim skirt. That was all I could make out from the window as they crossed the parking lot. The girl stumbled but caught herself before Cam had to intervene. They stopped behind a dark-colored sedan. I felt like a total peeper watching them, but I was riveted.

Cam said something and laughed when the girl playfully shoved his shoulder. A second later, they hugged and then he stepped back, giving her a little wave before turning back to the apartment building. Halfway back, he glanced up toward our floor, and I jumped back like a total idiot. He couldn't see me. There was no way without any lights on in my apartment.

I laughed at myself and then quieted when I heard a door shut down the hall.

Relief poured into me, easing the muscles that had been tightening on and off. Seeing him with another girl was ... good. Totally reaffirmed the fact that Cam was a very charming, harmless flirt who liked to hand out cookies to pretty girls and had a pet tortoise named Raphael. That was good. That was doable. I could handle that. Otherwise, what Brittany and Jacob were suggesting made me itchy and antsy.

Maybe Cam and I would become friends. I was okay with that, because it was nice to have more friends like *before*.

But as I climbed into bed and lay awake, staring at the ceiling, for a moment, a really brief moment, I wondered what it would be like if Cam were interested in me like *that*. To have something like that to look forward to. To be giddy and excited whenever he looked at me or when our hands accidentally touched. I wondered what it would be like to be interested in him like that, or in any guy for that matter. To look forward to dates, to first kisses, and all the things that came after that. I bet it would be nice. It would be like *before*.

Before Blaine Fitzgerald had taken all of that away.

Storm clouds were rolling in Thursday morning and it looked like it would be a rainy, cruddy day on campus. Luckily I only had two classes to sloth through, so before I headed out, I grabbed a hoodie and slipped it over my shirt. I thought about changing out of my shorts and flip-flops, but decided I was feeling way too lazy to go to that much trouble.

Texting Jacob to see if he wanted me to pick up any coffee before I hit art class, I slipped out of my apartment and made it to the stairwell before Cam's apartment door flew open and a guy came out, pulling a shirt down over his head. His shaggy, shoulder-length blond hair poked through, and I recognized him as the guy with Cam's tortoise—the roommate.

The moment our eyes met, a big smile broke out across his tan face, exposing a row of ultrawhite teeth. 'Hey! I've seen you before.'

My gaze flicked behind him. He'd left the door wide open. 'Hey, you are … tortoise guy.'

Confusion flickered across his face as his sandals smacked off the cement. 'Tortoise guy? Oh, yeah.' He laughed, the skin crinkling around his brown eyes. 'You saw me with Raphael, right?'

I nodded. 'And I think you called yourself Señor Fucktard.'

Letting out another loud laugh, he joined me on the stairs. 'That's my drinking name. Most days people know me as Ollie.'

'That sounds much better than Señor Fucktard.' I smiled as we rounded the fourth-floor landing. 'I'm—'

'Avery.' When my eyes widened, he gave a toothy grin. 'Cam told me your name.'

'Oh. So … um, you're heading to—'

'Yo douche bag, you left the door open!' Cam's voice boomed down the stairwell, and a second later, he appeared at the top of the stairs, the black baseball cap on. A lopsided grin appeared as he spotted us and bounded down the steps. 'Hey, what are you doing with my girl?'

My girl? What? I almost tripped over my feet.

'I was explaining to her how I go by two names.'

'Oh yeah?' Cam dropped an arm over my shoulders, and one of my flip-flops snagged in the back of my other one. His arm tightened, pulling me to his side. 'Whoa, sweetheart, almost lost you there.'

'Look at you.' Ollie hopped down the steps. 'Got the girl tripping all over her feet.'

Cam chuckled as he reached up with his free hand and slid the cap around backward. 'I can't help it. It's my magnetic charm.'

'Or it could be your smell,' Ollie retorted. 'I'm not sure I heard a shower this morning.'

Cam gasped in mocked outrage. 'Do I smell bad, Avery?'

'You smell great,' I murmured, feeling my face heat. It was the truth, though. He smelled wonderful—a mixture of fresh linen, faint cologne, and something else that was probably all him. 'I mean, you don't smell bad.'

Cam watched me for almost a moment too long. 'Heading to class?'

We were walking down the steps, but his arm was still around my shoulders and the entire side of my body seemed to tingle like it had fallen asleep. He was so … casual about it. Like it was nothing to him and it probably wasn't. I remembered how he and the girl had hugged last night, but to me, it was …

There were no words.

'Avery?' Cam's voice lowered.

I wiggled free, and I saw the way Ollie's grin spread. I headed down the stairs, needing distance. 'Yeah, I'm heading to art. What about you guys?'

Cam easily caught up with me on the third floor. 'We're going out to breakfast. You should skip and join us.'

'I think I've done enough skipping this week.'

'I'm skipping,' Ollie announced, 'but Cam doesn't have a class until this afternoon, so he's a good boy.'

'And you're a bad boy?' I asked.

Ollie's grin was contagious. 'Oh, I'm a bad, bad boy.'

Cam shot his friend a look. 'Yeah, as in bad at spelling, math, English, cleaning up after yourself, talking to people, and I could go on.'

'But I'm good at the things that count.'

'And what are those things?' Cam asked as we exited the building. Outside the air carried the faint scent of dampness, and the clouds looked plump with water.

Ollie jogged out in front of us and turned so that he was facing us as he walked backward, completely ignoring the red truck trying to back up. He held up a tanned hand and started ticking off his fingers. 'Drinking, *socializing*, snowboarding, and soccer—remember that sport, Cam? Soccer?'

The easy grin slipped off Cam's face. 'Yeah, I remember it, asshole.'

Ollie just laughed and turned, heading toward where the silver truck was parked. I glanced up at Cam, curious. He stared straight ahead, jaw set and eyes like chips of ice. Without looking down at me, he shoved his hands into his jeans and said, 'See you around, Avery.'

With that, he joined Ollie over at his truck, and I'd swear the temperature dropped to match the sudden coolness in Cam's attitude. Didn't take a genius or an overly intuitive person to figure out that Ollie had touched on a sore spot and Cam hadn't been in the mood to elaborate.

51

Shivering, I hurried to my car and jumped in. Not a second too soon as a big, fat raindrop splatted against the windshield. As I backed out, I glanced over, my eyes finding them. Both guys were standing by the bed of the truck, Ollie smiling and Cam with the same distant, rigid set to his expression as he spoke. Whatever he was telling his friend, he wasn't happy about it.

Chapter 6

I had no idea how I let Cam talk me into riding with him and not taking two cars, but Saturday night—the night of our assignment—just before dusk, I found myself climbing into the massive silver truck. My stomach had been in knots since Friday night, when Jacob started hounding me about the party he and Brittany were going to. It had been good-natured and I wanted to go, but I couldn't bring myself to really do it. Besides, I had no idea where the house was, it had been late when he'd started texting, and it had been storming again.

And now I was as nervous as a mouse in a room full of hungry cats. As lame as this was, I'd never been in a car with a guy before. Man, even admitting that to myself sounded incredibly pathetic. Like take-that-little-secret-to-my-grave level of pathetic.

Cam shoved the keys into the ignition as he glanced over at me. The baseball cap was on again, twisted backward. Behind the thick lashes, his eyes glimmered a bright azure. 'Ready steady?'

Tugging my lightweight cardigan around me, I nodded. When I saw him in astronomy yesterday morning, he was his usual self—joking, flirting, and offering cookies. I hoped that meant whatever had gone down between him and Ollie had been worked out. 'Are you sure we can't just do this around here?'

'This place will be perfect. I will never lead you wrong, sweetheart.'

'Okay,' I murmured, clasping my hands together tightly. I turned to the side window, watching as we blew past the campus and crossed the bridge into Maryland.

Fifteen minutes later, Cam turned onto the road leading to the visitors' center in Antietam National Battlefield. The history nerd in me started doing cartwheels, but I was way too nervous about being out here at night with Cam. Not that he seemed like the type to try anything, but if I knew anything, there was no 'type' when it came to that sort of thing. My nerves felt stretched thin and frayed at the edges.

'Are you sure we're allowed to be out here at night?' I asked, glancing around.

'Nope.' He pulled into a parking spot. There were only a handful of cars.

I stared at him. 'What?'

He laughed as he killed the engine. 'I'm kidding. All we have to do is tell one of the rangers that we're from the university. They'll be cool about it.'

I hoped so. The idea of being chased off the battlefield by a park ranger wasn't on my list of things to accomplish before I died.

However, from a quick look at Cam, it looked like something he'd be down for.

'You ready?'

Grabbing my bag off the floor, I opened the truck door. 'Yeah, let's get this over with.'

Cam grabbed a flashlight out of the glove box as he chuckled. 'Don't sound too excited.'

I sent him a quick grin. 'I'm not.'

'Don't lie.' He walked around the hood and joined me, pointing over to where a cement tower with a red top rose into the sky. 'That's where we want to go.'

'The tower on Bloody Lane?'

He shot me a quick look. 'You've been here before?'

'No.'

'Then how did you know that's Bloody Lane?'

I smiled slightly as I picked up a strand of my hair, twisting it between my fingers. 'I'm a history major, so places like this appeal to me. Read up on it before. Bloodiest day of the whole war took place on that little stretch of dirt road.'

'Yeah, that's what they say. Hold on a sec.' He turned to where a ranger was cutting across the field. 'Be right back.'

I watched him jog over to where the ranger waited. Words seemed to be exchanged and then Cam showed him his notebook. The ranger laughed and they shook hands. Tipping my head back, I could already see tiny stars appearing in the deep blue sky. Nightfall would be on us in minutes.

I took a deep breath and let it out slowly.

Cam swaggered back to my side. 'We're good to go. And we're not the only ones. There are a few students down by the other side of the tower.'

'Cool.' I fell in step with him, keeping a healthy distance between us. 'Why do so many people come here to do this? I'm sure there are places closer to campus.'

'Not like this. Look around.' He shoved the flashlight in his back pocket. 'Besides the houses across the street, there are no city lights or towers everywhere. It's just the sky.'

'And cornfields,' I pointed out.

He nodded. 'Lots of cornfields.'

We hit the paved portion of the lane and started toward the tower. 'How long do you think this will take?' I asked.

'Why? You got a hot date tonight?'

I barked out a short laugh. 'Uh, no.'

One single dark brow arched up. 'You sound like that's an insane idea. That no one would go out on a Saturday night for a date.'

Dropping the piece of hair I was playing with, I forced a casual shrug. 'I'm not dating anyone.'

'So why the rush?'

Admitting that I was seriously uncomfortable being out here would be embarrassing and rude, so I said nothing.

'Are you worried that I've brought you out here for my own nefarious plans?'

I came to a complete stop. Knots formed in my stomach. 'What?'

Cam stopped and turned toward me. His grin slipped a notch. 'Hey, Avery, I'm just joking. Seriously.'

Heat swamped my cheeks and the knots unraveled, replaced by a strong feeling of total lameness. 'I know. I'm just …'

'Jumpy?' he supplied.

'Yeah, that.'

He studied me a moment longer and then started walking again. 'Come on. It'll be dark soon.'

Trailing behind him, I pictured myself running straight into the old wooden fences and impaling myself on one of the pointy ends. God, I needed to get a grip. Not every guy was like Blaine. I knew that. Totally understood that. I wasn't completely damaged by my *affliction*.

On the other side of the tower, near the plaques, two students from our astronomy class sat on the bench, notebooks in their laps. They waved at us and as we waved back, Cam headed a little farther down the wide parking lot and then veered off toward the grassy hill overlooking the dirt path of Bloody Lane.

Cam picked a spot and pulled out the flashlight before he sat down. I hovered a few steps back, listening to the low hum of the crickets. The ground had dried out from yesterday's weather, but even if it were wet, it wouldn't have stopped me from sitting down. I was just too keyed up.

'Join me?' Patting the spot beside him, he inclined his head. 'Pretty please? I'm lonely all by myself over here.'

Biting down on my lip, I sat a few feet away from him and then busied myself with finding my astronomy notebook. As I pulled it out, I glanced over at him and our eyes locked. I couldn't look away. *Intense.* That was the first word that came to mind. His stare was intense, like he was seeing right through me.

Clearing my throat, I fixed my attention on the notebook. Finally, Cam spoke. 'What constellation are we supposed to be mapping?'

He held the flashlight while I skimmed through my notes. 'Um, the Corona Borealis, I think.'

'Ah, the northern crown.'

I glanced at him, brows raised. 'You knew that off the top of your head?'

He laughed. 'I might not take notes, but I do pay attention.'

I was pretty sure he slept through the vast majority of the class yesterday. I slid out the grid Professor Drage made for us and then the star map and found the Corona Borealis on it. 'I really don't understand how anyone sees shapes in the stars.'

'Really?' He scooted over and peered over my shoulder. 'The shapes are pretty obvious.'

'Not to me. I mean, it's just a bunch of stars in the sky. You can probably see whatever you want to see.'

'Look at the Borealis.' He tapped his finger off the map. 'It's obviously a crown.'

I laughed. 'It does not look like a crown. It looks like an irregular half circle.'

He shook his head. 'Look. You can see it now easily. That's a crown. Come on, see the seven stars.'

I craned my head back as I grabbed a pen from my bag. 'I see the seven stars, but I also see about a hundred others peeking out. I also see the cookie monster.'

Cam burst into laughter. It was a nice sound, deep and rich. 'You're ridiculous.'

My lips pulled into a smile as I hovered my pen over the grid. I had no idea what latitude line to start at. I glanced up toward the Borealis and managed to draw a line where I thought I should, connecting two dots.

'You know where the name comes from?' When I shook my head, he reached over and took the pen from my hand. His fingers brushed mine, and I pulled my hand back, planting it in the lush grass. 'It represents the crown given by the god Dionysus to Ariadne. When she married Bacchus, he placed her crown in the heavens in honor of their marriage.'

I stared at him. 'Professor Drage didn't teach that in class.'

'I know.'

Leaning back, I studied him. 'Then why do you know that?'

'Why don't you know that?'

I cocked my head to the side, brows raised.

'Okay. Maybe most people wouldn't know that off the top of their head.' He twirled my pen between his fingers. 'I actually took part of this class as a freshman, but had to drop it.'

'Really?'

He nodded, but didn't elaborate.

'You're, what, a junior?'

'Yep. I ended up having to take a year off, which put me behind.'

I wanted to ask why but decided it was none of my business. 'Why did you retake astronomy?' I decided that was a safe topic. 'Is it a part of your major?'

'No. I just like the class and Professor Drage.' He paused, flipping off the flashlight. 'I'm studying recreation and sport. Would like to get into sport rehabilitation.'

'Oh. Did you …' I trailed off as the girl behind us broke out into a fit of giggles. Glancing over my shoulder, my eyes widened.

The two students from our class were definitely a couple or well on the way to becoming one. Their notebooks were forgotten on the bench. She was in his lap, their faces inches apart, and his hand was slipped under the hem of her skirt.

'Now that is an interesting form of stargazing,' Cam commented.

I was grateful for the darkening sky, because my face started to heat. I knew I should turn away, because watching them made me a total creeper, but I couldn't. Not even when the girl's hand threaded through the boy's hair, pulling his head to hers, and they started really kissing and his hand was all the way up her skirt, to his forearm.

Wow.

Cam poked me in the arm with my pen, drawing my attention. He looked … curious. 'What?' I said.

'Nothing. It's just that …' He seemed to choose his next words wisely. 'You're watching them like … you've never seen a couple do that before.'

'I am?'

He nodded. 'So unless you were raised in a convent, I imagine you've been in a lap a time or two, right?'

'No, I haven't!' I winced, because I practically yelled that. 'I mean, I haven't been in a guy's lap.'

'What about a girl's lap?'

'What? No!'

59

A slow grin spread across his face. 'I was joking, Avery.'

I gritted my teeth. 'I know, it's just that …'

'What?' He poked me again. 'You what?'

My mouth opened and the worse kind of verbal vomit happened. 'I've never been in a relationship.' The moment those words came out of my mouth I wanted to kick myself in the boob. Who admitted that to a virtual stranger? Clenching the edges of my notebook, I peeked up at Cam. He was staring at me like I'd just claimed to be the Virgin Mary. My cheeks burned. 'What? It's not a big deal.'

He blinked and gave his head a little shake as he turned back to the sky. 'You've never been in a relationship?'

'No.' I shifted, uncomfortable to the max, like I'd laid my soul bare.

'Nothing?'

'That's what no means.'

Cam's mouth opened and then closed. 'How old are you?'

I rolled my eyes as I wiggled. 'I'm nineteen.'

'And you haven't been in a single relationship?' he asked again.

'No.' The paper was starting to crumple under my fingers. 'My parents … they were strict.' Such a lie, but it sounded believable. 'I mean, *really* strict.'

'I can tell.' Cam tapped my pen off his notepad. 'So have you gone on a date or anything?'

Sighing, I cast my eyes to my paper. 'I thought we were supposed to be mapping stars?'

'We are.'

'No, we're not. All I have is a scribbly line and you have nothing.'

'That *scribbly* line is between the Delta and Gamma.' He leaned over, connecting two of the dots. 'Here is the Theta and this is the Alpha—brightest star. See, we are halfway done.'

I frowned as I glanced up, tracing the pattern of the stars in the sky. Hell, he was getting it right. Then he leaned in again, his shoulder pressing into mine as he drew a perfect line to another dot on the map. I bit down on my lip as he continued to finish the map without looking up once or at the star map. I was acutely aware of how warm his arm felt even through the two layers of clothing. The warmth from the contact spread up my shoulder and across my chest, kicking my pulse up.

He turned his head toward me. 'Now we're done mapping stars.'

I sucked in a sharp breath. Our faces were inches apart, and he was way too close. My gaze fell to his lips. They were curved up on one side and that dimple started to appear in his left cheek. His lips started moving, but I didn't hear a word he was saying. I wanted to move away, but I ... I didn't want to. Confusion swept through my body as I struggled not to shy away ... and not to move closer. It was like being caught between two opposing magnets.

Maybe I should stop staring at his lips.

Sounded like a good plan, because staring at a guy's lips was kind of creepy, so I forced my gaze up. Oh boy, wrong move, because now I was staring into those panty-dropping eyes, as Jacob had referred to them earlier when he texted. And Jacob had been right. I bet there was a legion of discarded panties in the wake of wherever Cam went. It should be illegal for a boy to have lashes as thick as his. Even in the darkness, his eyes were the shade of denim. The somewhat tolerable warmth turned into near unbearable heat as it sped through my veins.

I squirmed again, unable to remember feeling like this in a long time. At least not since the Halloween party. Maybe before. Definitely before. There was just something about Cam that sort of made me forget everything except what was happening that very moment. Sounded normal. I liked it, for the most part.

'Are you listening to me?'

I blinked slowly. 'Huh? Yes! Yes. Totally.'

His grin turned knowing, and I wanted to crawl under a prickly bush. 'Yeah … so, you haven't been on a date?'

'What?'

Cam chuckled softly. 'You really haven't been listening to me at all. You've been too busy staring at me.'

'I have not!' My entire face burned with that little fib, and I hastily focused on where the couple had been. They were gone now.

He nudged my shoulder. 'Yes, you have.'

I screwed up my face. 'You are so beyond the acceptable level of arrogance.'

'Arrogant? I'm just stating the truth.' Cam tossed his notebook on the ground and leaned back on his elbows, eyeing me through his lowered lashes. That damn, insufferable lopsided grin was on his face. 'There's nothing wrong with staring at me. I like it.'

My mouth dropped open. How in the world was I supposed to respond to that? 'I wasn't staring at you. Not really. I sort of … dazed out. That's how *thrilling* talking to you is.'

'Everything about me is thrilling,' he replied.

'About as thrilling as watching your tortoise cross a road.'

'Uh-huh. Keep telling yourself that, sweetheart.'

'Keep calling me sweetheart and you're going to be limping.'

Cam's eyes widened. 'Oh, listen to you.'

'Whatever.'

'We should do it.'

My mind went straight to where it shouldn't have gone, and my skin started to prickle. 'Do what? Go home? I'm all about going home, like, right now.'

'Go on a date.'

Obviously I had missed an important part in this conversation. I closed my notebook and reached around, grabbing my bag. 'I'm not sure I'm following this conversation.'

'It's really not that complicated.' He laughed when I shot him a look. 'We should go out on a date.'

My stomach dropped as I looked back at him. He looked so content, half sprawled on the ground. Was he joking? Was he high? I shoved my notebook into my bag, along with my pen. 'I don't understand.'

Cam lay back and stretched his arms above his head, causing his shirt to ride up and expose a slice of tan skin and two indents on either side of his hips … dear God. I looked away and took a huge gulp of air.

'Typically going on a date is when two people go out for the evening, or sometimes during the day. Really, it can be any time of the day or night. It usually involves dinner. Sometimes a movie or a walk in the park. Though I don't do walks in the park. Maybe on a beach, but since there aren't any—'

'I know what a date is,' I snapped, shoving to my feet.

He remained on the ground, and he didn't look like he was moving anytime soon. I should've taken my own car. 'You said you didn't understand,' he pointed out gamely. 'So I'm explaining what a date means.'

Frustrated … and reluctantly amused, I crossed my arms. 'That's not the part I don't understand and you know that.'

'I was just making sure we were on the same page.'

'We're not.'

Cam lowered his arms, but there was still a gap between his shirt and jeans. Was he wearing underwear? All I saw was a leather belt and jeans. Okay. I didn't need to start thinking about that. 'So now that we both know what a date entails, we should go out on one,' he said.

'Uh …'

Cam laughed as he sat up in one fluid moment. 'That's not really a response, Avery.'

'I …' A date? A date with Cameron Hamilton? Two things rose at once: unease and interest. I took a step back, putting distance between me and him and everything else. 'Don't you have a girlfriend?'

His brows shot up in surprise and he laughed. 'A girlfriend? No.'

'Then who was that brunette stumbling out of your apartment Wednesday night?' I asked.

Cam's grin spread into a wide smile. 'Have you been watching me, Avery?'

'No. No! What? I wasn't watching you. I do have a life.'

He arched a brow. 'Then how do you know about Stephanie?'

'That's her name?'

'Yes, and no, she's not my girlfriend.' He cocked his head to the side as he stared up at me. 'And she wasn't stumbling. Maybe shuffling.'

I rolled my eyes.

'So how did you see her if you weren't watching me?' he asked as he crossed his ankles. 'And I don't mind the idea of you watching me. Remember, I like that.'

I forced myself to take a deep, slow breath before I walked up and kicked him in the leg. 'I wasn't watching you. I couldn't sleep and I was staring out my living room window. I just *happened* to see you walking her out to her car.'

'Well, that makes sense. Not nearly as entertaining as you standing by your window hoping to catch a glimpse of me.'

All I could do was stare at him.

He winked, and damn, if he didn't look good doing it. 'Steph's not my girlfriend by the way. We aren't like that.'

Which meant they were most likely hooking up, and there was nothing wrong with that. And maybe that was what he wanted from me with this whole date thing. Jacob would be thrilled to hear that. Mental note to self: so not telling him about this. 'I'm not like that.'

'Like what?' he asked.

So he was going to make me spell it out. Of course. Why not? 'I'm not like her.'

'Do you know her?'

My eyes narrowed. 'I don't just hook up with guys for fun, okay? I don't see anything wrong with it. Totally not judging here, but that's not me. So I'm not interested. Sorry.'

'Wait a sec. I'm confused. You're not judging her, but you've made the assumption that she's into random hookups? That she's my fuck buddy? Isn't that kind of making a rush judgment based on assumptions?'

Damn it, he had a point. 'You're right. I don't know if that's what you guys are about. Maybe you're just childhood buddies or something.'

'We're not.' That mischievous grin was back. 'We hook up every once in a while.'

I gaped at him. 'I was right! Then why did you accuse me of being judgmental?'

'I was just pointing it out,' he replied, eyes twinkling like those damn stars in the sky. 'And for the record, we didn't hook up Wednesday night. Not for the lack of trying on her part, but I wasn't feeling it.'

I remembered how the girl had looked, and I wondered what red-blooded male wouldn't have been feeling that. 'Whatever. This is a stupid conversation.'

'I like this conversation.'

Shaking my head, I bent and reached for my bag, but Cam shot to his feet and grabbed it before I could get my fingers around the strap. I sighed as I held out my hand. 'Give it to me.'

'I'm trying to.'

I shot him a disgusted look.

Chuckling, he stepped forward and laid the strap over my shoulder. His fingers brushed my neck, and I couldn't stop my body from jumping at the slight touch. He stepped back and picked up the flashlight. 'See? I was just being a gentleman.'

'I don't think you're a gentleman,' I grumbled as my fingers tightened around the strap. 'But thank you.'

He swiped his notebook off the ground and we headed back to where his truck was parked, passing the now empty bench. He shone the flashlight when we hit the field, lighting our path. I guess to prove me wrong, he opened the door for me when we stopped in front of his truck. 'M'lady.'

'Thank you,' I said, a little more appreciative sounding than before.

Instead of closing the door, Cam leaned against the frame and placed a hand on the edge of the open door. 'So, what about it?'

'What about what?'

He eyed me with the same intense interest he had earlier. 'Go out on a date with me.'

I stiffened. 'Why?'

'Why not?'

'That's not an answer.' Yanking the strap on the seat belt, I busied myself with securing it. My hands were shaking, so I kept missing the latch.

'What kind of question was that? How am I—hey, it's just a seat belt. Not that hard.' He leaned over, taking control. His hands brushed over mine, and I jerked back against the seat. He paused and looked at me; those lips usually tilted up started to tip down at the corners. Something flared in his eyes. I don't know what it was, but it was gone as he snapped the seat belt in place. He didn't move back, though. 'Why shouldn't we go out on a date?'

I strained back against the seat, my hands curling into fists in my lap. It wasn't that I was that uncomfortable with him being so close. It was that I was uncomfortable with the way I noticed every slight touch of skin or look. 'Because … because we don't know each other.'

His lips tipped up again. I decided I liked them like that better than the frowny face. 'That's what a date is all about. Getting to know each other.' Cam's eyes dropped to my mouth. 'Go out on a date with me.'

'There's nothing to know about me.' The words came out in a heady whisper as my chest rose sharply.

He tilted his head to the side. 'I'm sure there is tons to know about you.'

'There's not.'

'Then we can spend the time with me talking.'

'That sounds like fun.'

'Oh, it will be more thrilling than watching Raphael cross a road.'

'Ha.'

He grinned. 'Thought you'd like that.'

I felt the side pocket of my bag vibrate against my leg once. A text message? Probably from Jacob. I wanted to reach for it, but I would end up smacking my head into Cam's. Not something I wanted to repeat. 'Can we go yet?'

'Can we go on a date?'

'Good God, you don't give up.'

'Nope.'

I laughed, couldn't help it, and his smile spread in response to the sound. 'I'm sure there are plenty of girls who want to go out on a date with you.'

'There are.'

'Wow. Modest, aren't you?'

'Why should I be?' he shot back. 'And I want to go out on a date with you. Not them.'

'I don't understand why.'

His dark brows rose. 'I can think of a few reasons. You're not like most girls. That interests me. You're awkward in this really ... adorable way. You're smart. Want me to list more?'

'No. Not at all,' I told him quickly. I needed to nip this in the bud. Reputation aside, he was a hell of a lot more than I could ever hope to handle. He would expect things I couldn't give him. Holding a conversation with him was difficult enough sometimes. 'I don't want to go out on a date with you.'

Cam didn't look surprised by my response, or the least bit daunted. 'I figured you'd say that.'

'Then why did you ask?'

He finally—*thank God*—backed away and gripped the side of the door. 'Because I wanted to.'

'Oh. Well. Okay. Glad you got it out of your system.'

His brows knitted. 'I haven't gotten it out of my system.'

Oh no. 'You haven't?'

'Nope.' He flashed a charming grin. 'There's always tomorrow.'

'What about tomorrow?'

'I'll ask you again.'

I shook my head. 'The answer will be the same.'

'Maybe. Maybe not.' He reached out and tapped the tip of my nose. 'And maybe you'll say yes. I'm a patient guy, and hey, like you said, I don't give up easily.'

'Great,' I muttered, but ... oh, oh man, there was an unfamiliar stirring in my chest.

'Knew you'd see it that way.' Cam tweaked the tip of my nose, and I swatted his hand away. 'Don't worry. I know the truth.'

'The truth about what?'

Cam stepped back. 'You want to say yes, but you're just not ready.'

My jaw dropped.

'It's okay.' His grin turned cocky. 'I'm a lot to handle, but I can assure you, you'll have fun handling me.'

Then before I could muster up a response worthy of that statement, he tapped my nose once more and then shut the door in my face.

Back in my apartment, I dropped my bag on the couch and collapsed next to it. Go out on a date with Cameron? Was he insane? He had to be joking or just flirting. On the ride home, he hadn't mentioned it again; instead he spent the time drilling me about my schedule. Question by question, he dragged out every detail about the classes I was taking. By the time we got back to the building, I was exhausted.

Leaning my head back against the cushion, I closed my eyes. My heart was beating pretty fast for just sitting down. Was he being serious about not hooking up with Stephanie on Wednesday? Seemed odd to me that he hadn't if she really had been all over him.

Honestly, it didn't matter.

I couldn't do a relationship of any sort. Maybe one day. Hopefully one day, because I didn't want to be like this for the rest of my life. Eventually I wanted to be the girl who got excited about being asked out on a date instead of the girl who came home and did this.

Opening my eyes, I groaned. 'I'm Señor Fucktard. Or Señorita Fucktard.'

I pushed to my feet and started halfway to the bedroom before I remembered my vibrating bag. 'Shit.'

Hurrying back to the couch, I reached into the side pocket and pulled out my cell. I tapped the screen, fully expecting to see a text from Jacob or Brittany pop up. Instead I saw a missed call and a voice-mail message.

'What the hell?'

I ran my fingers along the side and figured out I'd knocked the damn thing to silent. Sliding my figure along the screen, I unlocked it and saw that the call was from an UNKNOWN CALLER.

My heart skipped a beat.

No big deal. Probably a wrong call or a telemarketer. I went to the voice-mail screen, and my finger hovered over the delete button. The past raised its ugly, bitter head. How many times had I gotten prank calls from people blocking their numbers? Too many to count, but that couldn't be it. My number was new, like my e-mail …

I cursed again.

Taking a deep breath, I hit the message icon and raised the phone to my ear. There was a pause and then a gravelly, indistinguishable voice crackled through the phone. 'You know what happens to liars and skanks? They get a big, fat—'

Crying out, I hit the delete button before I could hear anything more. I dropped the phone on the couch instead of tossing it against the wall and backed up like it was some kind of venomous creature perched on the cushions.

Any method of communication could become poisonous. Didn't I already know that firsthand? A strangled laugh escaped me. Really, did they have nothing better to do? It had been five years. Five years! They couldn't let go of the past.

Just like, deep down, I couldn't.

Chapter 7

I jerked straight up in bed, confused and disoriented. It was damn near close to four A.M. when I'd finally fallen asleep and I had no idea what woke me. I twisted in bed, groaning when I saw that it was only eight in the morning.

On a Sunday.

Flopping onto my back, I stared up at the ceiling. Once I was awake, there was no hope of ever—

Thump. Thump. Thump.

I sat up again, frowning. Someone was banging on a door—*my door*. What the hell? Throwing off the covers, I swung my legs off the bed. My toe caught on the sheet and I nearly ate the carpet.

'Holy crap.'

Cursing, I raced through the apartment before the entire building was woken up. I stretched up, peering through the peephole. All I could see was a mass of wavy dark hair. Cam?

Something had to be wrong. Maybe the building was on fire, because I couldn't think of any other reason why he'd be banging on my door on a Sunday morning.

'Is everything okay?' I winced at the sound of my voice as I opened the door.

Cam spun around. A crooked smile appeared, taking his already extraordinary face and making it boyishly sexy. 'No, but it will be in about fifteen minutes.'

'W-w-what?' I stepped—or was forced—aside as he entered my apartment, carrying something wrapped in tinfoil: a carton of eggs—*huh?*—and a tiny frying pan. 'Cam, what are you doing? It's eight in the morning.'

'Thanks for the update on the time.' He headed straight for my kitchen. 'It's one thing I've never been able to master: the telling of time.'

I frowned as I padded after him. 'Why are you here?'

'Making breakfast.'

'You can't do that in your own kitchen?' I ask, scrubbing at my eyes. After the astronomy assignment and the phone call, he was the last person I wanted to see at a buttcrack time in the morning.

'My kitchen isn't as exciting as yours.' He put his stuff on the counter and faced me. His hair was damp and curlier than normal. How was it possible for him to look so good when it was obvious he'd just rolled out of bed and showered? There wasn't even a dusting of morning scruff on his smooth cheeks. And he made sweats and a plain old T-shirt look damn good. 'And Ollie is passed out on the living room floor.'

'On the floor?'

'Yep. Facedown, snoring and drooling a little. It's not an appetizing atmosphere.'

'Well, neither is my apartment.' He needed to go. He had no business being here.

Cam leaned against my counter, folding his arms. 'Oh, I don't know about that …' His gaze moved from the top of my disheveled head and all the way down to the tips of my curled toes. It was like a physical touch, causing my breath to catch. 'Your kitchen, right this second, is very appetizing.'

72

A flush crawled across my cheeks. 'I'm not going out with you, Cam.'

'I didn't ask you at this moment, now did I?' One side of his lips curved up. 'But you will eventually.'

My eyes narrowed. 'You're delusional.'

'I'm determined.'

'More like annoying.'

'Most would say amazing.'

I rolled my eyes. 'Only in your head.'

'In many heads is what you meant,' he replied, turning back to my stove. 'I also brought banana nut bread baked in my very own oven.'

Shaking my head, I glared at his back. 'I'm allergic to bananas.'

Cam spun around, brows raised in disbelief. 'Are you shitting me?'

'No. I'm not. I'm allergic to bananas.'

'Man, that's a damn shame. You have no idea what you're missing out on. Bananas make the world a better place.'

'I wouldn't know.'

He cocked his head to the side. 'Anything else you're allergic to?'

'Besides penicillin and guys who bust into my apartment? No.'

'Hardy-har-har,' he replied, bending down as he started opening cabinets. 'How many weaker, less assured guys have you slayed with that tongue of yours?'

'Apparently not enough,' I muttered. I went to adjust my bracelet and realized I wasn't wearing it. My heart dropped. 'I'll be right back.'

Humming to himself, Cam nodded. I darted back to my bedroom and grabbed the bracelet off the nightstand and slipped it on. A shudder of relief went through me. Halfway out of the bedroom, I glanced down and cursed again.

No bra.

The thin material of my shirt stretched taut across my chest and my nipples were poking out, saying hello. 'Oh, Jesus.'

Tossing the shirt off, I grabbed a sports bra out of my dresser.

'Hey! Are you hiding back there?' yelled Cam. 'Because I will come back there and drag you out.'

Sports bra stuck around my head and breasts bouncing everywhere, I blanched. I yanked it down, smushing my right boob. Ow! 'Don't you dare come in here!'

'Then hurry up. My eggs wait for no one.'

'Oh my God,' I muttered, pulling my shirt back on. I made it to the hallway before I then realized I also hadn't brushed my teeth. Cam and his eggs were going to have to wait.

When I returned to the kitchen, he had several eggs boiling in water, and a perfect sunny-side-up egg in the little frying pan he'd brought. He'd found the bag of shredded cheese in my fridge and was sprinkling it across the eggs.

Seeing him in my kitchen, at my stove, unnerved me. Knots formed low in my belly as he easily found the plates and silverware. I crossed my arms, shuffling from side to side. 'Cam, why are you over here?'

'I already told you.' He slid the eggs onto a plate and then walked them over to the bistro set butted up to the wall. 'Do you want toast? Wait. Do you have bread? If not, I can—'

'No. I don't need toast.' He'd taken complete control of my kitchen! 'Don't you have anyone else to bother?'

'There are a shit ton of people that I could *reward* with my presence, but I chose you.'

This had to be the most bizarre morning ever. I watched him a moment longer. Giving up on getting him out of my apartment, I sat in the high-rise chair, tucking my legs against my chest. I picked up a fork. 'Thanks.'

'I choose to believe that you mean that.'

'I do!'

He flashed a quick grin. 'I doubt that for some reason.'

Now I felt like a total bitch. 'I do appreciate the eggs. I'm just surprised to see you here … at eight in the morning.'

'Well, to be honest, I was planning to woo you with my banana nut bread, but that shit ain't happening now. So all I have left is my delicious eggs.'

I took a bite of the cheesy goodness. 'It is really good, but you're not wooing me.'

'Oh, I'm wooing.' He opened up the fridge and grabbed a bottle of OJ. Pouring two glasses, he sat one in front of me. 'It's just all about the stealth. You don't realize it yet.'

Dropping that no-win conversation, I moved on. 'Aren't you eating?'

'I am. I like boiled eggs.' Cam gestured to the stove as he sat in the chair opposite of mine. He propped his chin on his fist, and I focused on my plate. The bastard looked too adorable and cute. 'So, Avery Morgansten, I'm all yours.'

I almost choked on the piece of egg. 'I don't want you.'

'Too bad,' he replied, grinning. 'Tell me about yourself.'

Oh hell to the no, the bonding shit wasn't happening. 'Do you do this often? Just walk into random girls' apartments and make eggs?'

'Well, you're not random, so technically no.' He got up and checked the eggs boiling. 'And I might be known to surprise lucky ladies every now and then.'

'Seriously? I mean, you do this normally?'

Cam glanced over his shoulder at me. 'With friends, yes, and we're friends, aren't we, Avery?'

My mouth opened. Were we friends? I guessed so, but still. Was this normal? Or was Cam just that confident? He did things like this because he knew he could, knew that no one would really make him leave. Most people probably wouldn't want him to leave. And I could've made him get the hell out if I'd really wanted to, and that was the truth. Cam was the kind of guy who was probably used to getting what he wanted.

Just like Blaine.

That thought turned the eggs in my stomach, and I placed my fork down. 'Yeah, we're friends.'

'Finally!' he shouted, making me jump a little. 'You've finally admitted that we are friends. It's only taken a week.'

'We've only known each other for a week.'

'Still took a week,' he replied, poking at the eggs in the water.

I pushed the last remaining chunk of eggs around my plate. 'What? Does it normally take you just an hour to have someone declaring best friends forever?'

'No.' He pulled out the eggs, dropping them in a bowl. Coming to the table, he sat again. His eyes met mine, and it was hard to maintain that stare. Those eyes really were a beautiful shade of azure, sharp and clear. The kind of eyes you could easily get lost staring into. 'It usually takes me about five minutes before we've moved on to best friend status.'

A smile snuck out as I shook my head. 'Then I guess I'm just the odd one.'

'Maybe.' His lashes lowered as he started peeling his boiled egg.

I took a drink. 'I guess it's different for you.'

'Hmm?'

'I bet you have girls hanging all over you. Dozens would probably kill to be in my spot and here I am, allergic to your bread.'

He looked up. 'Why? Because of my near godlike perfection?'

A laugh burst from me. 'I wouldn't go that far.'

Cam chuckled and then shrugged. 'I don't know. Don't really think about it.'

'You don't think about it at all?'

'Nope.' He popped a whole freaking egg into his mouth. Besides that, he had impeccable table manners. Chewing with his mouth closed, wiping his hands on the napkin he'd pulled from the holder, and not talking with his mouth full. 'I only think about it when it matters.'

Our gazes collided, and my cheeks flushed. I ran my finger along the rim of my glass. 'So you're a reformed player?'

He paused, egg halfway to his mouth. 'What makes you think that?'

'I heard you were quite the player in high school.'

'Really? Who did you hear that from?'

'None of your business.'

A brow arched. 'With that mouth of yours, you don't have a lot of friends, do you?'

I flinched, because that was a spot-on observation. 'No,' I heard myself saying. 'I wasn't really popular in high school.'

Cam dropped his egg on the plate and sat back. 'Shit. I'm sorry. That was an asshole thing for me to say.'

I waved it off, but it stung.

He watched me through thick lashes. 'Hard to believe, though, that you weren't. You can be funny and nice when you're not insulting me, and you're a pretty girl. Actually, you're really hot.'

'Uh … thanks.' I squirmed, holding my glass close.

'I'm serious. You said your parents were strict. They didn't let you hang out in high school?' When I nodded, he finished off the egg he'd dropped. 'I still can't imagine you not being popular in high school. You rock the trifecta—smart, funny, and hot.'

'I wasn't. Okay?' I set my glass down and moved on to tugging at a loose string on the hem of my shorts. 'I was, like, the very opposite of popular.'

Cam started peeling another egg. I wondered how many he'd eat. 'I am sorry, Avery. That … that sucks. High school is a big deal.'

'Yeah, it is.' I wetted my lips nervously. 'You had a lot of friends?'

He nodded.

'Still talk to them?'

'Some of them. Ollie and I went to high school together, but he spent his first two years at WVU and transferred down here, and I see a few around campus and back home.'

Wrapping my arms around my legs to keep from fidgeting, I rested my chin on my knees. 'Have any brothers or sisters?'

'A sister,' he replied, picking up the last egg—the fourth one. A genuine smile appeared. 'She's younger than me. Just turned eighteen. She graduates this year.'

'You guys close?' I couldn't imagine having a brother like Cam.

'Yeah, we're close.' A dark look crossed his face and vanished quickly, but it left me wondering if they really were that close. 'She means a lot to me. How about you? A big brother I have to worry about visiting and kicking my ass for being here?'

'No. I'm an only child. Have a cousin who's older, but I doubt he'd do that.'

'Ah, good.' Devouring that egg, he sat back and patted his stomach. 'Where you from?'

I pressed my lips together, trying to decide if I should lie or not.

'Okay.' He dropped his arm off the back of the metal chair. 'You obviously know where I'm from if you've heard of my extracurricular activities in high school, but I'll just confirm it. I'm from the Fort Hill area. Never heard of that? Well, most people haven't. It's near Morgantown. Why didn't I go to WVU? Everyone wants to know that.' He shrugged. 'Just wanted to get away, but be somewhat close to my family. And, yes, I was … very busy in high school.'

'You're not anymore?' I asked, not really expecting him to answer, because it wasn't my business, but, hey, if I could keep him talking, I didn't have to say anything.

And I was … interested in learning more, because Cam, he was fascinating in a way. He was like every überpopular, sexy guy in high school, but he wasn't a dick. That alone made him worthy of a scientific study. Also, it was better than sitting around alone and thinking about harassing phone calls and e-mails.

'Depends on who you ask.' He laughed then. 'Yeah, I don't know. When I was a freshman—those first couple of months, being around all the older girls? I probably put more effort into them than I did my classes.'

I grinned, easily able to picture that. 'But not now?'

He shook his head. 'So where are you from?'

Okay. Obviously what changed his ex-player status was something he didn't want to talk about. Visions of pregnancy scares danced in my head. 'I'm from Texas.'

'Texas?' He leaned forward. 'Really? You don't have an accent.'

'I wasn't born in Texas. My family was originally from Ohio. We moved to Texas when I was eleven and I never picked up any accent.'

'Texas to West Virginia? That's a hell of a difference.'

Unfolding my legs, I stood and picked up my plate and

his bowl. 'Well, I lived in the strip mall hell part of Texas, but besides that, it's kind of the same here.'

'I should clean up.' He started to stand. 'I made the mess.'

'No.' I backed away with his bowl. 'You cooked. I clean.'

He relented, opening the foiled bread. It did smell wonderful. 'What made you choose here?'

I washed the dishes and his little frying pan before answering that doozy. 'I just wanted to get away, like you.'

'Got to be hard, though.'

'No.' I picked up the pot he used to boil the eggs. 'It was incredibly easy to make the decision.'

He seemed to consider that as he broke the bread in half. 'You are an enigma, Avery Morgansten.'

I leaned against the counter, my eyes widening as he proceeded to eat *half* the loaf. 'Not really. More like you are.'

'How so?'

I gestured at him. 'You just ate four hard-boiled eggs, you're eating half a loaf of bread, and you have abs that look like they belong on a Bowflex ad.'

Cam looked absolutely thrilled to hear that. 'You've been checking me out, haven't you? In between your flaming insults? I feel like man candy.'

I laughed. 'Shut up.'

'I'm a growing boy.'

My brows rose, and Cam laughed. As he finished off the loaf, he talked a little about his parents. I made my way back to the table and sat, genuinely interested. His father ran his own law firm, and his mother was a doctor. That meant Cam came from money, not the kind that my parents rolled around in, but enough that it most likely paid his rent. He was obviously close with them too, and I envied that. Growing up, all I wanted was for my parents to want to be around me, but with the benefits, the jet setting, and all the dinners, they'd never been home. And after everything that had happened, the few instances they were there, neither of them could even look at me.

'So you flying back to Texas for fall break or Thanksgiving?' he asked.

I snorted. 'Probably not.'

He cocked his head to the side. 'Got other plans?'

I shrugged.

Cam dropped the subject, and it was close to noon by the time he left. Stopping at my front door, he turned to me, flipping the tiny skillet in one hand, banana nut bread in the other. 'So, Avery …'

I popped my hip against the back of the couch. 'So, Cam …'

'Whatcha doing Tuesday night?'

'I don't know.' My brows lowered. 'Why?'

'How about you go out with me?'

'Cam.' I sighed.

He leaned against the jam. 'That's not a no.'

'No.'

'Well, that's a no.'

'Yes, it is.' I pushed off the couch and grabbed the door. 'Thanks for the eggs.'

Cam backed up, lopsided grin in place. 'How about Wednesday night?'

'Good-bye, Cam.' I closed the door, grinning. He was completely insufferable, but like the night before, being around him did something sort of miraculous. Maybe it was the verbal dueling, but whatever it was, I tended to act … normal. Like I used to.

Heh.

After showering, I puttered around the apartment and debated texting Jacob or Brittany to see what they were up to. Eventually, I tossed my cell on the couch and dragged my laptop out. I couldn't avoid my e-mail forever.

In my junk folder, there were a few suspicious-looking e-mails. Two with my name as the subject. After receiving the last e-mail, I had learned my lesson, and I clicked delete with a certain amount of glee.

The e-mails, though—it was strange to get them now. While I'd been in high school, it had been one thing. I'd been surrounded by the kids, but now, after we'd all left for college? Something just wasn't right about that. Like, did they seriously have nothing better to do? I doubted it could be Blaine, because as twisted as he was, he stayed far away from me. And the phone call? I refused to change my number. Back during the worst of it, when I'd get three to four phone calls a day, I'd gone through a series of telephone changes and they always found out the new ones anyway.

Shaking my head, I clicked on my in-box and found another e-mail from my cousin. Seriously? I was half tempted to not click on it, but I opened the stupid thing.

Avery,
I really need to talk to you ASAP. Call me whenever. It's very important. <u>Call me</u>.
David

My finger hovered on the mouse pad.
Delete.

Chapter 8

Over the next couple of weeks and as summer finally loosened its grip, a sort of odd routine started to occur. Monday through Friday, I got up and went to class. With each passing day, I started to look forward to astronomy. Not so much because I never knew what Professor Drage was going to say or what he would wear. A few days ago, he'd been rocking a pair of acid-wash jeans and a tie-dyed shirt. I think I focused on that more than anything else. But crazy-pants professor aside, it was a certain class partner who made the fifty minutes pretty damn entertaining.

Between Cam's side comments during Drage's lecture and his surprisingly accurate knowledge of solar systems, running away from astronomy on the first day had really ended up paying off in the long run. With Cam as my partner and seatmate, there was no way I would fail the class.

I spent lunch three days a week with Jacob and Brittany and even went to one of the football games with them. Parties were still a no go, something that neither could really understand, but they didn't abandon me. Twice a week, they hung out at my place. Not a lot of studying got done, but I wasn't complaining. I liked it when they came over. Okay, 'like' wasn't a strong enough word. They were great, and it had been way too long since I had friends like them who didn't seem to care when I acted like a spaz, which was quite a bit.

At least twice a week, I turned Cam down.

Twice. A. Week.

It got to the point where I sort of looked forward to how he was going to slide it into conversation. The boy was relentless, but it was more of a running joke between us than anything else. At least in my opinion.

I also started to look forward to Sundays.

Each Sunday morning since the very first, Cam showed up at my door at some ungodly hour with eggs and something he'd baked. The second Sunday, it was blueberry muffins. The third Sunday it was pumpkin bread—from a box, he'd admitted. The four and the fifth Sunday, it was strawberry cake and then brownies.

Brownies in the morning were the shit.

Things were really … good with the exception of e-mail and phone. At least once a week, I'd get a call from an UNKNOWN CALLER. I deleted the messages and the e-mails without opening them. There were at least fifteen unread e-mails from my cousin. One of these days I was going to read them, but I couldn't bring myself to do that or call my parents.

They hadn't called me, so I didn't see the point.

By the beginning of October, I was happier than I'd been in so long. The scent of autumn, something I'd missed while living in Texas, was in the air; I could wear long sleeves without looking like a freak; and cramming for midterms during lunch included M&Ms and Skittles.

'Can someone please tell me where Croatia is on this map?' Jacob groaned. 'Like, is there a song I can come up with that will somehow remind me of this?'

'Hungary, Slovenia, Bosnia,' I said, pointing at the blank map of Europe. 'And then there is Serbia.'

Jacob glared at me. 'Fucking overachieving bitch.'

I popped a red Skittle in my mouth. 'Sorry.'

'Can you imagine a song with those names?' Brit dipped her fries in mayo.

'That is so gross,' Jacob muttered.

She shrugged. 'It's yummy.'

'Actually, I'm going to nerd out on you, so prepare.' I picked up an M&M and held it in front of Jacob. His eyes widened, like he was a puppy about to get a treat. 'With the exception of Hungary, all the countries next to Croatia end with an *a*. They all sound alike. Think of it that way.'

His eyes narrowed. 'That didn't help.'

I sighed. 'You want a song?'

'Yes.' He stood up at our table, in the middle of the Ram's Den, and shouted. 'Yes! I want a song!'

'Wow.'

He raised his hands as several students turned in their seats. 'What? What?' He turned back to me. 'Was that a little too much?'

'Yes,' I said. 'Most def.'

Brit put her forehead on her textbook. 'Seriously,' she groaned. 'I can't believe he's making us map Europe on our midterm. I thought I'd left that shit behind in high school.'

'Give me a song, nerd,' Jacob demanded.

'Oh, my God, you're ridiculous.' Shaking my head, I placed my hands on the table. 'Okay. Here you go. Hungary to the upper left, upper left, Serbia to the lower left, lower left. Bosnia on the bottom, on the bottom. Slovenia to the top, to the top. And where's Croatia?'

'Where? Where?' Jacob sang.

'It's next to the Adriatic Sea, across from Italy!'

Jacob popped up straight. 'Again! Again!'

I went through the song twice more while Brit gaped at the both of us. By the time Jacob whipped out his pen and started scribbling countries across the map, my face was the shade of a tomato, but I was giggling like a hyena.

And he got the map right, with the exception of putting France where the United Kingdom was supposed to be, but I think he was just testing me on that one, because seriously.

I tossed an M&M at his mouth. It bounced off his lower lip. On the replay, I got the M&M in his mouth. He swallowed and shot forward, lowering his face next to mine. 'Guess what?'

'What?' I leaned back.

He blinked two times. 'Here comes your boyfriend.'

Looking over my shoulder, I spotted Cam entering the Den with not one girl but a girl on either side of him, both gazing up at him like he was the last eligible hot guy on campus. I rolled my eyes at Jacob. 'He's not my boyfriend.'

'Gurl, you got competition.' Jacob folded his arms on the table. 'That's Sally and Susan—beta, delta, boogie-sigma-chi-latte VPs.'

Brit's brows lowered. 'That's not even close to a sorority name.'

'Whatever.'

'It's not a competition, because it's not like that between us.' Slowly, surely, I looked over my shoulder. The trio had stopped by the couches. Cam was paying attention to whatever the two girls were saying to him. One of the girls, the blonde, had her hand on his chest and was moving it in tiny circles. My eyes narrowed. Was she giving him a breast exam? I turned back to Jacob.

He raised his brows.

'They can have him,' I said, throwing three Skittles in my mouth.

'I don't get you two,' Brit said, closing her book. Study time was over. 'You guys see each other practically every day, right?'

I nodded.

'He comes over every Sunday and makes you breakfast, right?' she added.

Jacob flipped me off. 'I hate you for that.'

'Yeah, he does, but it's not like that.' Thank God I'd never told them about him asking me out because I'd never hear the end of it then. 'Look, we're friends. That's all.'

'Are you gay?' Jacob demanded.

'What?'

'Look, I'm the last person to judge your sexual preference. I mean, come on.' He jerked his thumbs back at himself. 'So are you gay?'

'No,' I said. 'I'm not gay.'

'I'm not either, but I'd go gay for you.' Brit smiled.

'Thanks.' I giggled. 'I'd go gay for you too.'

'How cute,' Jacob said. 'Not the point. That fine mother-fucking specimen of a man is all up in you—oh my God, he's ditched the ra-ras and is coming over.'

My stomach knotted and I prayed to God, Shiva, and Zeus that Jacob didn't say anything that would make me want to kill him later.

'Damn,' Jacob said, shaking his head. 'He makes jeans look like they were molded to fit his—hey, Cameron! How's it going?'

I closed my eyes.

'Hey, Jacob. Brittany.' Cam dropped into the seat beside me and nudged my arm. 'Avery.'

'Hey,' I murmured, acutely aware of Jacob and Brittany staring at us. I closed my text and shoved it in my bag. 'What are you up to?'

'Oh, you know, mischief and mayhem,' he replied.

'That so reminds me of Harry Potter,' Brit said, sighing. 'I need a reread.'

We all turned to her.

Two bright spots appeared in her cheeks as she tossed her blond hair back. 'What? I'm not ashamed to admit that random things remind me of Harry Potter.'

'That guy over there reminds me of Snape,' Cam said, jerking his chin to the table behind us. 'So I understand.'

The guy with the jet-black hair did kind of look like Snape.

'Anyway, what are you guys doing?' Cam shifted and his leg rested against mine. I swallowed. 'Playing with M&Ms and Skittles?'

'Yes, that, and we're studying for our history midterm next week. We have to map out Europe,' Jacob explained.

'Ouch.' Cam knocked me with his leg.

I knocked his leg back.

'But Avery, wonderful Avery …' Jacob glanced at me, his grin spreading, and my eyes were narrowing. 'She's been helping us study.'

'That she has,' Brit said.

Cam sent me a sidelong glance, and I scooted away from him.

Popping his chin on his hand, Jacob smiled at Cam. 'Before we started studying, I was telling Avery that she should wear the color green more often. It makes her sexy with that hair of hers.'

My mouth dropped open. He had so not even said that about the stupid cardigan I was wearing.

'Do you like the color green on her, Cam?' Brit asked.

Oh my God.

Cam turned to me, his blue eyes as deep as the waters off the coast of Texas. 'The color looks great on her, but she looks beautiful every day.'

Heat crept across my cheeks as I let out a low breath.

'Beautiful?' Brit repeated.

'Beautiful,' Cam repeated, reclaiming what little distance I'd managed to put between us. He nudged my knee again. 'So did you guys learn anything from studying?'

I let out the breath. 'I think we got it.'

'Because of you.' Jacob glanced at Brit, and my stomach dropped. 'Avery came up with this song to help me remember where the countries were.'

Oh no.

'Sing him your song.' Brit elbowed me so hard that I bounced off Cam and ricocheted back.

Interest sparked in Cam's eyes. 'What song?'

'I am not singing that song again.'

Jacob beamed up at Cam. 'It's the Croatia song.'

I shot him a death glare.

Cam laughed. 'The Croatia song? What?'

'No,' I said again. 'I am not singing again. That is so not my talent.'

'What kinds of talents do you have?' Cam asked, and when I looked at him, I kind of got hung up on the cut line of his jaw, on the way his hair brushed his temples. What the hell? Cam was staring back at me, brows raised. 'Avery?'

'Do tell,' Jacob coaxed.

Brit nodded. 'Talents are fun.'

'They can be.' Cam's gaze dropped, and I sucked in a soft breath. He leaned over and there wasn't more than an inch or two separating our mouths. I heard Jacob's audible gasp. 'Tell me what your talents are, sweetheart.'

'Sweetheart,' Jacob murmured with a soft sigh.

'Dancing,' I blurted out. 'I danced. I *used* to dance.'

Curiosity filled Cam's face. 'What kind of dancing?'

'I don't know.' I grabbed the bag of Skittles and dumped the rest of them into my palm. 'Ballet, jazz, tap, contemporary—that kind of stuff.'

'No shit?' Jacob exclaimed. 'I did tap when I was like six, for about a month, and then decided I wanted to be a fireman or something like that. That shit was hard.'

Brit smirked. 'I tried dance and discovered I had no coordination or grace beyond shaking my ass. Were you any good at it?'

I shrugged, uncomfortable. 'I took classes for about ten years, did some competitions and a lot of recitals.'

'Then you were good!' Brit said. 'I bet you did all those crazy turns and tricks.'

I used to be able to do a ton of them and was at one point crazy flexible, but the thing I was really good at had been the turns—the *fouetté tour*—arguably the hardest series of spins in ballet.

Cam had been quiet for a few moments, a very odd thing indeed. 'My sister did dance since she was around five. Still does. I think she'd cut someone if they made her stop.'

Shoving the rest of the Skittles in my mouth, I nodded. 'Dancing can be addictive if you like it.'

'Or are good at it,' Brit interjected.

Cam bumped me with his shoulder. 'Why'd you stop?'

I'd loved to dance—loved every part of it. The training, the rehearsing, and especially the anticipation leading up to the moment you stepped out onto the stage. Nothing felt like that moment when you waited in the wings for your name to be called; the first breath you took as you stepped onto center stage and stood under the bright lights. The quiet moment when you closed your eyes while you waited for your music to begin, knowing that everyone was focused on you.

Shrugging my shoulders, I reached for what was left of the M&Ms. 'I guess I got tired of it,' I said finally. The lie was a big one. I didn't grow tired of dancing. I missed it more than anything, but I couldn't stand for people to stare. 'Does your sister do competitions?'

He nodded. 'She's traveled all over and spent the summer at the Joffrey School of Ballet on a scholarship.'

'Holy shit,' I gasped, my eyes widening. 'She must be damn good.'

Cam smiled proudly. 'She is.'

Envy grew like a cancer, deep and invasive. That could've been me dancing at one of the most well-known training centers in the world. It should've been me, but it wasn't and I needed to just deal with that.

Conversation sort of just fell apart after that, at least for me. Cam chatted with Brit and Jacob while I was lost in my own thoughts until it was time to go to class. I made plans for another study session and then said my good-byes.

Cam followed me out in the bright sunlight and the steady, cool breeze that warned that colder weather was well on its way. He didn't say anything as we walked over to Knutti Hall. Sometimes he did that, and I never knew or could begin to speculate on what he could be thinking during those quiet moments.

It was in that moment, as we crossed the congested street and he waved at a group standing in front of the Byrd Science Building, that I realized how different he was from when I saw him with the two girls earlier. It bothered me and I didn't know why I even cared.

'Are you okay?' he asked when we stopped by the benches in front of Knutti Hall.

I squinted up at him. 'Yeah, I'm fine. Are you?'

He gave me a tight-lipped smile and nodded. 'We still on for tomorrow night?'

'Tomorrow night? Oh! The astronomy assignment.' As part of our midterm grade, Drage was making us partner up to use the Observation Center. We'd have to turn in our images the following Wednesday. 'Yeah, it works for me.'

'Good.' Cam backed away. 'See you then.'

I started to turn, but stopped as something occurred to me. 'Cam?'

'Yeah?'

'What were you doing in the Den? Don't you normally have class, like, right now?'

His lips curved up at the corner and that damn dimple appeared. When he smiled like that, it felt like a balloon had suddenly inflated in my chest. 'Yeah, I normally have class right now,' he said, eyes a startling azure in the sun. 'But I wanted to see you.'

Words left me as I watched him pivot around and hit the road, heading in the opposite direction of my building. I stood there for a moment and then turned. There was no stopping the smile that split my lips and remained.

Chapter 9

'Are you sure you know how to use this thing?' I asked, staring at the telescope.

Cam shot me a look over his shoulder. 'What? You don't?'

'Nope.'

'Weren't you paying attention in class when Drage went over this and the imaging cameras?'

I crossed my arms. 'You were drawing the cast of *Duck Dynasty* when he was going over that.'

He laughed as he turned back to the telescope and started adjusting the knobs and buttons and other things I couldn't remember. 'I was listening.'

'Uh-huh.' I inched closer, using his body as a shield against the cool wind whipping across the roof of the Observation Center. 'You're actually a pretty good artist.'

'I know.'

I rolled my eyes, but he really was. The sketches were disturbingly lifelike, right down to the beards.

He bent over, moving a lever. 'I've used a telescope a time or two in my life.'

'That's random.'

'Okay. I used it when I had the class previously,' he corrected, sending me a quick grin as he straightened. Tipping his head back, he checked out the dark sky. 'Man, I don't know if we're going to be able to get anything before those clouds roll in.'

Following his gaze, I winced. Intense, tumultuous clouds were obscuring most of the night sky. There was a wet feel to the air, a smell of rain. 'Well, you better hurry then.'

'Bossy,' he murmured.

I grinned.

'Come over here and I'll show you how to use this.' He stepped back, and with a sigh, I took his place. 'Are you going to pay attention?'

'Not really,' I admitted.

'At least you're honest.' Cam leaned around me, putting his fingers on the telescope. His arm brushed mine, and I didn't mind. He was really blocking the wind now. 'This is a Philips ToUcam Pro II.' He pointed at a silver thing that reminded me of a webcam. 'It hooks to the telescope. At these settings, you should be able to get a clear image of Saturn. Press this and it will capture an image.'

'Okay.' I brushed my hair back. 'I don't think we're supposed to be getting an image of Saturn.'

'Huh.' He paused. 'Hey.'

'Hey, what?'

'Go out with me.'

'Shut up.' Grinning, I leaned forward, pressing my eye to the telescope. And all I saw was pitch black. Astronomy hated me. 'I don't see anything.'

'That's because I haven't taken the lens off.' Cam laughed.

I jerked my elbow back. It connected with his stomach, which was equivalent to hitting a wall. 'Asshole.'

Still laughing, he reached for the lens. Cam could've

moved, because I was so in the way, but he didn't. His entire front pushed against my back, and I stilled, closing my eyes.

'What?' he asked.

'It would've been easier for you to just go to the side and do that,' I pointed out.

'True.' He lowered his head so his lips were beside my ear. 'But what fun would that be.'

A shiver raced across my shoulders in spite of myself. 'Go have fun by yourself.'

'Well, that's really no fun,' he said. 'Try it again.'

Taking a deep breath, I pressed my eye in again and holy crap, I saw it. The planet was a little blurry, but the faint brownish hue was visible, as were the rings. 'Wow.'

'You see it?'

I pulled back. 'Yeah, that's pretty cool. I've never really seen a planet in real life. I mean, like, taken the time to do so. It's awesome.'

'I think so, too.' He looked away as he caught a few strands of my hair, pulling them off my face. 'What are we supposed to be looking at?'

'Sagittarius and then the Teapot asterism and its steam, whatever—'

A big, fat, cold raindrop splattered off my forehead. I jumped back, smacking off Cam. 'Oh, crap.'

Another fat glob of rain hit my nose and I squeaked. My eyes met Cam's. He swore and then grabbed my hand. We started running across the roof, our shoes slipping on the wet surface. We'd almost made it to the door when the sky ripped open and chilly rain poured down, soaking us within seconds.

He let out a loud laugh as I shrieked. 'Oh my God,' I yelled. 'It's so freaking cold.'

Stopping abruptly, he turned and pulled me against him.

My eyes widened as I was suddenly and most unexpectedly flush against his hard chest. My head jerked up and our gazes locked. Rain streamed down on us, but in that second, I didn't feel a thing.

He smiled.

That was his only warning.

Wrapping an arm around my waist, he dipped and lifted me off my feet, laying me over his shoulder. I shrieked again, but it was lost in his laugh.

'You were running too slow,' he yelled over the rain.

I gripped the back of his hoodie. 'Put me down, you son of a—'

'Hold on!' Laughing, he took off for the door, his arm clamped across my hips, holding me in place.

A couple of times he slipped in the puddles forming, and my heart dropped. I could easily see my skull cracking wide open. Each step jolted through me, causing little grunts to escape in between my continuous threats to do him bodily harm.

He ignored them or just laughed.

Cam skidded to a stop and threw open the door. Ducking down, he entered the dry, slightly warmer landing above the stairwell. Still laughing his head off, he gripped my hips. I was prepared to lay into him the moment he let go, but as he lowered me to my feet, my body slid down his, inch by inch. It must've been our wet clothing, because the friction that occurred caused the air to punch from my lungs.

His hands were still on my hips, the touch searing through my jeans. And he stared down at me, the hue of his eyes darkening into a deep, intense blue that was as consuming as it was shattering. Those perfectly formed lips of his parted, and his warm breath was slightly minty.

My entire front was pressed against his. Sensation exploded in various parts of my body; deep in my stomach, my muscles coiled, the tips of my breasts tightened, and my thighs tingled. My hands were pressed to his chest, and I wasn't sure how that happened. I didn't remember putting them there, but they were, and his heart pounded under my palm, a steady thump that matched my own.

One hand slid up my side, leaving behind an unfamiliar, heady rush of shivers. I gasped as his fingers trailed across my cheek, brushing the wet strands of hair back behind my ear.

'You're soaked,' he said, his voice deeper than normal.

Mouth dry, I swallowed. 'So are you.'

His hand lingered, fingers splayed so that his thumb was against my cheek. He made tiny, idle circles on my skin. 'I guess we're going to have to try this another night.'

'Yeah,' I whispered, fighting the urge to close my eyes and lean into his touch.

'Maybe we should've checked the weather first,' Cam said, and I had to smile at that.

Then he shifted just a fraction of an inch. A slight movement that somehow brought us even closer together, hip to hip. A shudder rocked its way down my spine. The awareness of my body and *his*—all of it was overwhelming. I was responding to him in an instinctual way, in a manner I was wholly unaccustomed to.

My body knew what to do, what it *wanted*, even though my brain was firing off so many warnings I felt like Homeland Security during a Code Red.

I jerked back, breaking contact. My breath was coming in and out in short bursts as I kept backing up, hitting the wall behind me. Soaked, cold clothing and I was too hot. Burning up. My voice sounded unfamiliar when I spoke. 'I think we … we should call it a night.'

Cam leaned back, resting his head against the opposite

wall, legs spread slightly apart. Everything about him looked tensed and strained. 'Yeah, we should.'

Neither of us moved for a full minute, and then we did, quiet as we made our way back down and out to his truck. Whatever had passed between us lingered in tense silence and by the time we arrived back at our apartment building, anxiety had built in the pit of my stomach, erasing the few moments back in the stairwell when I'd been nothing but sensation instead of thinking.

Muscles tense, I climbed out of his truck and raced under the awning of our building. Cam was beside me, shaking the rain out of his hair. I hovered at the bottom of the stairs, fingers twisting around my keys. I needed to say something. I needed to somehow make all of this go away, because I didn't want our friendship to be strained or for it change.

It struck me then, and a horrible twisty motion occurred in my stomach.

I didn't want to lose Cam.

Over the last month and weeks, he'd become such an intricate part of my life, weaving himself into my every day, that if things were to change …

But I didn't know what to say, because I didn't know what had happened back in the stairwell. My heart pounded at a sickening rate as he took one step and then stopped, turning to me.

'Go out with me?' he asked, running a hand through his wet hair, pushing it back from his face.

'No,' I whispered.

And then the dimple appeared in his cheek, and I let out the breath I was holding. He started up the steps. 'There's always tomorrow.'

I followed him. 'Tomorrow's not going to change anything.'

'We'll see.'

'There's nothing to see. You're wasting your time.'

'When it concerns you, it's never a waste of my time,' he replied.

Since his back was to me, he didn't see my smile. I relaxed. I warmed up. Things were normal again and with Cam, everything would be okay.

Chapter 10

Twenty-five e-mails from my cousin, ranging from the end of August straight up till October fourteenth.

That was absolutely ridiculous.

I'd waited until after midterms before subjecting myself to the unnecessary what-the-fuckery that was sure to occur from opening any of these. Part of me just wanted to delete them. What was the point in reading the e-mails? Same shit, different day.

But I leaned back in my desk chair, exhaling loudly and obnoxiously.

I told myself I'd read them Monday. Didn't do it. Told myself I'd read them Tuesday. Nope, didn't happen. Now it was Wednesday, six in the godforsaken morning, and I'd been staring at my in-box for thirty minutes.

David was Blaine's age, three years older than me. He'd been seventeen at the time everything had gone down. He'd been friends with Blaine, but he hadn't been at the party. After everything had happened—the truth, the deal between the parents, and the subsequent lies and nonstop shit storm that had become my life—David knew about the settlement, but he had believed what everyone else had.

That I had a mad case of buyer's remorse.

But David had stopped being friends with Blaine, because to my cousin, whether or not I'd been telling the truth in the beginning, it hadn't mattered. The whole thing had just been *nasty* to David. Hadn't made him one bit sympathetic to me for the past five years.

Scrolling down to the first unread e-mail dated back at the end of August, I shook my head and clicked it open. Same as the one I had read before. I needed to call him or my parents. Immediately. I rolled my eyes. Couldn't have been that important, because you'd think one of them would've picked up the phone and called me if it had been.

That was my family, though. Every one of them felt as if they should not have to pick up the phone. They were too busy for that, too important. Even my cousin, who apparently had a shit ton of time to send e-mails.

I deleted that one.

On to the next one.

Same stuff, but there were a couple more sentences. Something to do with a girl from high school. Molly Simmons. She'd been a year younger than me and of course I hadn't been friends with the chick. I couldn't even remember what she looked like. David needed to talk to me about her. Was he, like, dating her and getting married? If so, I was surprised that he'd even let me know.

That's one wedding I probably would not be attending.

I deleted that e-mail and was about to move on to the next one when my cell chirped. Dropping my feet onto the floor, I picked it up. It was a text from Brittany, wanting to know if I'd meet her for coffee before my astronomy class. I sent a quick text back, saying yes.

Closing my laptop, I jumped up, deciding that a coffee date with Brit was a million times better than going through the slush pile of my e-mail.

*

At lunch, Jacob was acting like a cracked-out jackrabbit because we didn't have classes Thursday or Friday due to fall break. He and Brit were excited about going home. I was happy for them, but also a little disappointed. Four-day weekends were what life was made of for college students, but for me, it meant four days of doing absolutely nothing but bouncing off walls and nerding out by reading ahead in my classes.

But their mood was contagious and I found myself laughing as Jacob tried to convince a guy at another table that if a zombie bit a vampire, then it would become a zombie vampire, while the other guy was convinced that it would become a vampire zombie.

Brit looked like she was hoping a zombie would crash through the Den and bite them all. 'So what are you doing for break?' she asked.

'Just staying here,' I said, and then added my ready-made excuse. 'It's just too far to travel for four days.'

'Understandable.' She picked up a rolled-up napkin and tossed it at Jacob's back, but he was in way too deep with his zombie/vampire fetish. 'I'm leaving after my last class today.' She rested her head on my shoulder. 'I'm going to miss you.'

'Me too.'

'You'll be bereft without me.'

'I know.'

She sat up, eyes glimmering with excitement. 'You know, you could always come home with me.'

'Oh, Brit …' I wanted to hug the girl or cry. The offer seriously meant a lot to me. 'Thank you, but that's your time with your family and stuff.'

'Well, think about it. If you change your mind between now and three, text me and I'll zip you away.' She took a drink of her soda. 'What's Cam doing? Is he going home?'

Good question. Before I could respond, Jacob whipped around like someone had yelled his name. 'What about my fantasy husband?'

Brit laughed. 'I was asking Avery if he was going home for break.'

'Is he?' he asked.

Tucking my hair back, I shrugged. 'I don't know.'

Jacob's brows lowered. 'What do you mean you don't know?'

'Um, I just don't know. He hasn't brought it up.'

The two of them exchanged a look and Brit said, 'I'm kind of surprised he hasn't said anything to you about it.'

Confusion rose. 'Why are you surprised?'

Jacob shot me a duh look. 'You guys are, like, attached at the hip—'

'No, we're not.' I frowned. Were we? 'No.'

'Okay, do I need to list how often you guys are together?' Jacob raised his brows. 'I think it would be safe to assume that you knew about his plans *and* the size of his cock by now.'

'Oh my God.' I dropped my face into my hands.

Brit giggled. 'You're making Avery blush.'

He was.

Jacob snickered. 'I think you're having a closet relationship with him.'

'What?' Lifting my head, I stared at him. 'I am not having a closet relationship with him. Trust me, he's asked me—' I cut myself off. 'We're not.'

'Whoa. Whoa. *Whoa*.' Jacob practically fell over. 'He's asked you what?'

'Nothing.' I sat back, crossing my arms. 'He hasn't asked me anything.'

Jacob looked at Brit. 'Is it just me or is she just not that smooth to pull off a lie?'

'Not that smooth,' Brit commented, twisting toward me. 'What has he asked you?'

'Nothing!'

'Bull poop!' She punched me in the arm. 'You're lying!'

'Ouch! I—'

Jacob shook his head, looking like he was seconds from falling on the floor. 'We are your friends. It is the law of friendship that you tell us things you don't want to tell us.'

My mouth dropped open. 'What? That makes no sense.'

'It is the law.' Brittany nodded solemnly.

'What has he asked you?' Jacob persisted. 'Did he ask you to eat more of his *cookies*? Did he ask you to be his baby mama? How about marry him? Or to just warm his bed every morning, afternoon, and evening? Did he—?'

'Oh my God!' There was no way out of this. I knew Jacob. He'd just keep going until the whole Den thought I was getting married and having a baby. 'Okay. I'll tell you if you promise not to freak out and scream.'

Jacob made a face. 'Uh, I don't know.'

'He promises!' Brit shot him a glare. 'Or I will physically maim him.'

He nodded. 'I promise.'

I exhaled harshly. 'Okay. It's not a big deal. Let's get that established first. Everyone understand? Good. All right, so Cam has kind of been asking me out—'

'What?' Jacob screeched, and several heads turned.

My shoulders slumped. 'You promised.'

'Sorry.' He crossed his heart. 'I just … wow. Got excited.'

'I can tell,' I said wryly.

Brit's hands were clasped in front of her chest. 'He's been asking you out, like in the plural sense?'

I nodded. 'Yeah, but I've said no each and every time.'

'You've said no?' Jacob shouted, and I shot up and

smacked his arm. He gave me a bright smile. 'Sorry. Sorry. Don't hit. Bitches be scary when they hit.'

Sitting back down, I eyed him. 'Yes. I've said no.'

'Why?' he demanded.

'And he keeps asking?' asked Brit at the same time.

'Yes, he keeps asking, but it's like a … running joke between us. He's not serious.'

Brit tugged at her hair like I was stressing her out or something. 'How do you know he's not being serious?'

'Come on.' I raised my hands. 'He's not serious.'

'Why?' Jacob was stunned, apparently. 'You're a smart and funny girl. You don't like to party, but you're hot, and that kind of makes up for that.'

'Gee, thanks.'

'What I'm trying to say is how do you know he hasn't been serious?'

I shook my head. 'He's not.'

'Get back to the important question,' Brit said. 'Why would you tell him no?'

'Why would I say yes?' Could a hole open up and swallow me? Please? 'We barely know each other.'

'Oh, what the fuck? You guys are like soul twins right now. And what do you think the purpose of going out on a date with someone is?' Jacob rolled his eyes. 'It's about getting to know someone. And you do know him, so that's a lame excuse.'

It was a lame excuse, but it was the best I had. 'How do you really ever truly know someone?'

Brit smacked her hands to her cheeks and shook her head. 'He's not a serial killer.'

'Speaking of serial killers, everyone thought Ted Bundy was a really charming, handsome man. And look how he turned out. Psycho.'

Jacob stared at me, jaw slightly unhinged. 'He's not Ted Bundy.'

'I don't understand,' Brit whispered. 'It's like someone saying that Earth is flat. Cam is like one of the most eligible bachelors on this campus, probably in this county and state.'

I said nothing.

'I'm pretty sure I've been stunned speechless.' Brit shook her head slowly. 'I'm absolutely speechless. Someone capture this with a picture.'

'Ha.' Jacob's grin made my anxiety rise. 'Here comes Cam. What a coinkydink.'

I face-planted on the table and groaned as Brit started giggling. Under the table, Jacob kicked my leg, and two seconds later, I *felt* Cam before he even spoke a word. I also caught his fresh scent. Was it weird that I knew him by his smell? That did sound weird. It was weird.

'Uh, what are you doing, Avery?'

In my head, I strung together as many fuck bombs as I could come up with, because I knew—oh, I knew—that Jacob would not keep quiet. 'Napping.'

'Napping?'

'Yeah.'

Cam tugged on the back of my cardigan. 'Why do I think that's not what you're doing?'

I gave an awkward shrug.

He sat beside me, his hand on my lower back, and my clothes must've gotten thinner, because I could really feel his hand. 'Are you sick?'

'Aw, he's so concerned!' Jacob exclaimed. 'Avery, you're such a bitch.'

Cam stiffened, and his tone was low and something I'd never heard from him before. 'Excuse me?'

I lifted my head, eyes narrowed at Jacob. 'I'm not sick.'

'Okay.' Cam glanced around, and Brit broke out into a fit of giggles. 'What's going on?'

Before they answered, I jumped in. 'Aren't you supposed to be in class?'

He frowned. 'Class was let out early. Don't change the subject.'

I opened my mouth, but freaking Jacob swept in. 'Avery has just informed us that you've been asking her out and she's been saying no, and we've been explaining to her that she's insane.'

'Well, then.' The hard look slipped off his face, and I wanted to slide under the table. 'I like this conversation.'

Ugh.

'So it's true?' Jacob asked, plopping his elbows on the table. 'You've been asking her out?'

Cam cast me a sideways glance. 'I have been, almost every day since the end of August.'

On the other side of me, Brit squealed like she was a plush toy that had been squeezed. 'Since August?'

He nodded.

Brit turned wide eyes on me. 'And you haven't said a word?'

'I'm sort of offended,' Cam commented.

I elbowed him in the side. 'No, you're not. And it's not like it's everyone's business.'

'But we're your friends.' Jacob sounded so pitiful that I started to feel bad. He turned to Cam. 'We totally support her going out with you.'

Okay. I didn't feel bad for him.

'I like your friends, Avery.' Cam grinned at my arched eyebrows.

'Oh, we think she should,' Jacob said. 'Like, she should do it right now.'

'We also told her you weren't a serial killer,' Brit interjected.

Cam nodded. 'That's a glowing recommendation. Hey, at

108

least he's not a serial killer. I'm going to put that on my Facebook profile.'

I smirked.

Jacob was positively beaming. 'And she compared you to Ted Bundy.'

'I hate you,' I muttered, pushing my hair back from my face. 'I didn't compare you to Ted Bundy. I just said that you never really know a person. Everyone thought Ted Bundy was a pretty cool guy.'

Cam stared at me, amusement twinkling in his eyes. 'Wow. This just keeps getting better.'

'Sorry?' I said, fighting a grin.

He sighed, turning back to my friends. 'She keeps turning me down. Breaks my little heart.'

I sighed. 'He's not being serious.'

'He looks serious,' Brit said, all doe-eyed as she stared at Cam. He'd roped her in, dammit.

Cam made the most pitiful sound known to man, and I rolled my eyes. 'And now she thinks I'm the next Ted Bundy.'

'I don't think you're the next Ted Bundy.'

'Besides, she has the wrong hair color for Ted Bundy,' Brit said. We all looked at her. 'What? Ted Bundy liked girls with brown hair parted down the middle. Avery's hair is pretty red.'

'Am I the only person who finds it disturbing that you know that?' Jacob asked.

Brit's lips pursed. 'I'm a psych major. I know these kinds of things.'

'Uh-huh,' I murmured.

'Anyway, this is not about me and my vast knowledge of serial killers. I can wow you later about that. This is about you, Avery.' She grinned as I glared at her. 'This fine young gentleman, who is not a serial killer, is asking you out. You're single. You're young. You should say yes.'

109

'Oh my God.' I scrubbed my hands over my hot face. 'Is it time for all of you to go home yet?'

Cam's deep chuckle crawled under my skin. 'Go out with me, Avery.'

Stunned, I turned to him. I couldn't believe he'd actually ask me out in front of them after all of this. 'No.'

'See?' Cam grinned at my friends. 'Keeps turning me down.'

Jacob shook his head. 'You're an idiot, Avery.'

'Whatever,' I grumbled, grabbing my bag. 'I'm going to class.'

'We love you,' Jacob said, smiling.

'Uh-huh.'

Brit giggled. 'We do. We just question your decisions.'

Shaking my head, I stood. 'Be careful when you guys drive home.'

'We're always careful,' she said, jumping up and giving me a quick hug. 'Remember what I said about coming home with me. If you change your mind, text me before three.'

'Okay.' I hugged her back and gave a little wave at Jacob. Of course, Cam was already on his feet, waiting for me. I shot him a look. 'Following me?'

'Like a true serial killer,' he replied.

I cringed as we crossed the Den and headed outside. 'You know we weren't being serious, right? And I'm sorry about saying something to them about it. They just started pestering me about you and the next thing I know—'

'It's okay.' He cut me off, dropping his arm over my shoulders as we stopped by the cluster of trees between the two buildings. 'I don't care.'

Looking up at him, I squinted. 'You don't care?'

He shook his head, and I was sort of floored. What person would want anyone to know that they'd been asking someone out and that person had been repeatedly turning

110

them down? I wouldn't want that known. And why was Cam still asking me out? It wasn't like I was the only option for him. With the unruly dark waves, the luminous true blue eyes, the face and body to covet, Cam was hands-down gorgeous. I doubted there was a single girl on campus who didn't think that. But he was more than a swoon-worthy hot guy. Cam was charming, nice, sweet, and funny. He was the kind of guy you wanted to bring home and show off—the kind of guy who was never single for too long and the one you fell head over heels in love with.

Cam had a lot of options, so why not explore them? Maybe he did. Contrary to what Jacob and Brit thought, I wasn't around him twenty-four seven. He hung out with the chick named Steph a lot and I always saw him with other girls around campus. The asking me out bit had to be something he didn't take seriously.

It couldn't be, not after almost two months of it.

An uncomfortable knot formed in my stomach. What if he was dating other girls? Hooking up with them? I mean, totally his right, and I didn't care. Totally didn't care.

'Uh-oh,' he said.

'What?'

He dropped his arm but caught a strand of my hair that was blowing across my face and tucked it back. 'You're thinking.'

I tried to ignore how my cheek tingled when his fingers grazed it. Maybe I was coming down with a nerve disorder. 'I am.'

'About?' he asked.

'Nothing important.' I smiled as I pushed away thoughts of him with other girls. So was not going there. 'You going home this weekend?'

'I am.' He stepped closer, blocking the glare of the sun. As he spoke, he reached out and gathered up my hair, separating it into two long pigtails on either side of my face. 'I'm leaving tomorrow morning, bright and early. I'm not coming back until Sunday night. So no eggs for you this week.'

'Boo.' I squelched the very real, rising disappointment. Eggs on Sunday had become a weekend staple.

'Don't cry too much about it.' A slight grin appeared as he tickled my face with the edges of my hair. 'Are you going to take Brit up on her offer and go home with her?'

I shook my head. 'I'm just going to hang out here and get some reading done.'

'Nerd.'

'Jerk.'

The grin spread as he dropped my hair across my shoulders. 'You know what?'

'What?'

Cam stepped back, shoving his hands into the pockets of his jeans. 'You should go out with me tonight, since I'll be gone all weekend.'

I laughed. 'I'm not going out with you.'

'Then hang out with me.'

My smile started to slip. 'How's that any different from going out with you?'

'How is me asking you to hang out with me tonight any different than us hanging out on Sunday?'

Ah, he had a good point. My heart rate kicked up as I watched him. 'What do you want to do?'

He shrugged. 'Order some food in and watch a movie.'

I shifted from side to side, suddenly very wary. 'That sounds like a date.'

'That's not a date with me, sweetheart.' He laughed. 'I'd take you out, like out in public. This is just two friends hanging out, watching a movie and eating food.'

Pressing my lips together, I looked away. Somehow I knew that wasn't what this was about, but then again, what the

112

hell did I know about guys and having guy friends? I didn't think twice when Brit or Jacob came over. Why should I treat Cam any differently?

Because he was very different to me.

None of that mattered, because I did want to hang out with him. Cam was fun. So I sighed and said, 'Yeah, sure. Come over.'

Cam made a face. 'Wow. Calm down before you get too excited.'

'I am excited.' I shoved him in the shoulder. 'When are you coming over?'

'How's seven?'

In the pit of my stomach, a nest of butterflies were born and began drinking energy drinks. 'Works for me. See you then.'

I made it onto the sidewalk before he stopped me.

'Avery?'

I turned. 'Yeah?'

His lips formed a crooked smile. 'See you tonight.'

My stomach flopped. This was going to be a *long* afternoon.

Chapter 11

The nest of butterflies had moved on from drinking energy drinks to smoking crack. I alternated between feeling like I was going to hurl and wanting to run around my apartment like a lunatic.

I was totally overreacting.

According to Cam, this wasn't a date. Just two friends hanging out. Not a big deal, nothing to get overworked about. It wasn't like it would be the first time we'd hung out. It would just be the first time he'd *asked* before coming over.

I took a shower—second of the day.

I cleaned up the apartment and then changed my outfit three times, which was really stupid, because I ended up settling on a pair of yoga pants and a long-sleeve shirt. Then I spent an ungodly amount of time coaxing my hair into manageable waves that fell down to the middle of my back. I put some makeup on, scrubbed it off entirely, and then reapplied.

By the time there was a knock on my door, I wanted to slam my head through a wall.

Cam looked like he always did as he stepped into my apartment—absolutely, disgustingly divine. Dressed in worn jeans and a shirt with some long-forgotten band name on it, he had the baseball cap on, pulled low. In one hand was a stack of DVDs and in the other was a bag that smelled like Chinese.

My stomach grumbled. 'Oh! What you got in there?'

'The stuff dreams are made of.'

Making grabby fingers, I grinned. 'Shrimp stir-fry?'

'Yep.' He handed the bag off, and I rushed into the kitchen like a starving kid. 'I brought a couple of movies over. Had no idea what you're in the mood to watch.'

Pulling out dishes from the cabinet, I glanced over my shoulder. Cam took his cap off and ran a hand through his hair. The dark waves were an adorable mess. He caught me looking and his lips formed a half grin. I looked away, flushing. 'So, um, what did you bring?'

'Let's see … We've got a good selection here. In the horror movie genre, I've got the last two *Resident Evil* movies.'

'Two movies?' I placed the plates on the counter.

He chuckled. 'You're not getting rid of me easily.'

'Damn it. What else do you have?'

'In the comedy department, I have the latest Vince Vaughn and Will Ferrell movies. For action, I have a James Bond flick and another where a bunch of shit blows up. And I have *The Notebook*.'

I whipped around, almost dropping the silverware. '*The Notebook*? You own *The Notebook*?'

Cam stared at me blankly. 'What's wrong with that?'

'Oh, nothing is wrong with that. It's just such a … uh, chick flick.'

'I'm confident enough in my masculinity and sexuality that I can say that Ryan Gosling is just *dreamy* in this movie.'

My jaw hit the floor.

The blank expression slipped away and he started laughing.

116

'I'm joking. I don't own *The Notebook*. Never watched it. Didn't bring any romance movies.'

I rolled my eyes. 'You douche.'

Cam laughed again.

'I've never watched *The Notebook* either. Not big on romance flicks,' I admitted, opening the huge cartons.

'Really? I thought every girl has seen that movie and can quote it at a drop of a hat.'

'Nope.'

'Interesting.'

'Not really.' I grabbed a spoon. 'How much do you want?'

'Get what you want, and I'll make do with whatever is left over.' He walked up behind me, and I stiffened. Tiny hairs rose on the back of my neck. I shifted so I was standing sideways. He tilted his head to the side. 'You are so jumpy.'

'I did not jump.'

'It's a figure of speech.'

I slopped a heaping of fried rice and shrimp on my plate. 'It's a stupid figure of speech.'

Cam looked like he wished to say something else but changed his mind. 'What movie do you want to watch?'

'Let's go with *Resident Evil*.'

'A girl after my own heart.' He picked up two DVDs and headed into the living room. My gaze followed him. 'Zombies for the win.'

Sighing, I shook my head. I dumped most of the stir-fry on his plate and then carried our dishes out to the living room, putting them on the coffee table. Cam was over by the TV, messing with the DVD player. I turned the lamp on, giving him light in the shadowy room. 'What do you want to drink?'

'Do you have milk?'

'You want that with Chinese food?'

He nodded. 'Need my calcium.'

My stomach turned, but I got him a glass of milk and me a can of Pepsi. 'That's kind of gross, you know?' I sat on the couch and tucked my legs under me. 'Weird combination.'

He sat beside me with the remote in hand. 'Have you ever tried it?'

'No.'

'Then how do you know it's gross?'

I shrugged and picked up my plate. 'I'll go with my assumption that it is.'

He cast me a sidelong glance. 'Before the end of the year, I will have you trying milk and Chinese.'

Not bothering to respond to that, I sat back and dug into my food. Cam got the movie started and settled on the couch, his thigh pressed to my knee. We were about ten minutes in when he said, 'Question?'

'Answer.'

'So, it's the zombie apocalypse, right? Zombies are coming out of the ass, running amok through buildings and streets. You've already almost died three times by this point and have been mutated by the T virus *twice*, which appears to be painful. Would you take time in your obviously hectic daily routine to do your hair and put makeup on?'

A laugh burst from me at his absurd question. 'No, not at all. I'm not even sure I'd take the time to brush my hair. And another thing. Have you noticed how everyone has a blinding white smile? Society collapsed, like, six years ago. No one is going to the dentist. Yellow their teeth.'

Cam finished off his stir-fry. 'Or how the one chick's hair changes color from one movie to the next.'

'Yes, because in a zombie apocalypse, there's a lot of downtime to get your hair done.'

He chuckled. 'Still love these movies.'

'Me too,' I admitted. 'It's pretty much the same stuff every movie, but I don't know. There's something addictive about watching Alice kick zombie ass. And I hope that when there is a zombie outbreak, I look half as good as she does spin-kicking zombies in the face.'

Laughing, he gathered up the now empty plates and took them into the kitchen. He returned with a fresh cup of milk and another can of soda for me.

'Thank you,' I said.

He sat back down and the couch dipped a little, moving me closer. 'I live to service you.'

I grinned.

Through most of the first movie, we continued to pick apart all the what-the-fuck moments, laughing at our overly critical stupid comments. Right when Alice was about to break out some bad-assery on Rain, my phone rang. Thinking it was Brittany or Jacob already bored back home, I leaned forward. Unease raced down my spine as I saw UNKNOWN CALLER on the screen. I quickly sent the call to voice mail.

'Not going to answer?' Cam asked, brows raised.

I shook my head as I covertly turned my phone off and then placed it back on the coffee table, screen down. 'I think it's rude to answer the phone when you have company.'

'I don't mind.'

Sitting back, I nibbled on my thumbnail as I focused on the TV. I wasn't really seeing what was going on, realizing the film had ended only when Cam got up to put the newest one in. I told myself not to think about the phone call or the message I knew was waiting. After the first phone call, I'd deleted all the messages without listening to them. Once more I considered going to the phone store and changing my number, but to me, that seemed like letting the asshole win. I still had no idea who it could be. Couldn't be Blaine, but what did I know? Whoever it was, I treated them like an Internet troll. Do not engage.

Cam's fingers were suddenly wrapped around my wrist, causing my head to snap up. He was watching me instead of the movie. 'What?' I asked, my gaze dropping to his hand. It completely circled my wrist.

'You've been biting your nail for the last ten minutes.'

That long? Well, that was kind of gross.

He lowered my arm to the top of my thigh but didn't let go. 'What's up?'

'Nothing,' I replied. 'I'm watching the movie.'

'I don't think you're really seeing the movie.' Our eyes locked, and my heart skipped a beat. 'What's going on?'

I tugged my arm back and he let go. 'Nothing is going on. Watch the movie.'

'Uh-huh,' he murmured, but he dropped the subject.

The comments were fewer this time around and my eyelids started to fall. Each time I blinked, it seemed to take longer to reopen them. Cam shifted beside me, and I sank farther into the couch, closer to him. My side rested against his, and I thought I should scoot away, but he was warm, and I was comfortable, feeling way too lazy to put the effort into it. Besides, he didn't seem to mind. If so, wouldn't he have moved away or pushed me off?

I must've drifted off during the second movie, because when I opened my eyes, it seemed like the TV had changed positions. I was slow to realize that I had, and—*oh, sweet baby Jesus*—how did I end up here?

Curled up on my side, with a blanket from the back of the couch spread across me and my head in Cam's lap.

On his thigh, to be exact.

My breath caught in my throat as my heart stuttered and my eyes widened. There was a slight weight on my hip, the feel and the shape of a hand—Cam's hand. Was he asleep? Oh good God, I had no idea how this happened. Had I done it in my sleep and now poor Cam was stuck here because I was sleeping on him?

Okay. I had two options at this point. I could roll off the couch and make a mad dash for my bedroom or I could actually act like an adult and see if he was awake.

Surprisingly, I sided with the whole acting-like-an-adult part and slowly rolled onto my back. And that was a horrifically bad move, because the hand on my hip moved when I did and was now resting against my lower stomach.

Oh sweet Lord …

His hand rested below my belly button, spanning southward, and his fingers reached the waistband on my yoga pants. It was close, really close to somewhat uncharted territories. A ball of ice formed in my chest, but lower, much lower, something else entirely was happening. Sharp tingles shot from my belly and spread below in a warm wave of shivers. How was it possible to feel so cold and hot at the same time?

His thumb moved, and I bit down on my lip. It had to be an accident or some idle movement in his sleep. Then his thumb moved again, but this time in a slow, lazy circle under my belly button. Oh shit. My pulse kicked up and that warmth increased. His thumb kept moving, at least for a half a minute, until I couldn't take it any longer. Parts of my body were aching in a way that was entirely unfair and unfamiliar, and that shouldn't be happening.

But oh it was.

I drew in a deep breath, but it did nothing to relax my muscles or to ease the tension building deep inside me. And I knew that if I looked down, my nipples would be straining against the thin shirt I wore. With each breath I took, I could feel them rubbing against my bra. I desperately

121

wanted to be that girl who knew how to handle this, the kind of girl that I knew Cam probably really wanted and was used to.

But I wasn't her.

I tipped my head back and looked up at Cam.

His head was turned to the side, away from mine, and back against the cushion. A faint shadow appeared on the strong line of his jaw. There was a slight smile on his face. Son of a bitch.

'Cam.'

One eye opened. 'Avery?'

'You're not asleep.'

'You were.' He lifted his head, turning it side to side, working out a kink. 'And I was asleep.'

And his hand was still on my lower stomach, incredibly heavy. Part of me wanted to tell him to get his paws off me, but that's not what came out of my mouth. 'I'm sorry I fell asleep on you.'

'I'm not.'

Wetting my lips nervously, I had no idea what to say to that, so I went with a, 'What time is it?'

His gaze had dropped to my mouth, and my entire body tensed in a way that wasn't unpleasant at all. 'After midnight,' he responded.

My heart was pounding. 'You didn't even look at the clock.'

'I just know these kinds of things.'

'Really?'

His eyes were hooded. 'Yes.'

'That's a remarkable talent.' My hand curled into a fist beside my thigh. 'What time are you leaving in the morning?'

'Are you going to miss me?'

I screwed up my face. 'That's not why I was asking. I was just curious.'

122

'I told my parents I'd be home by lunch.' With his other hand, he scooped a few strands off my face and that hand lingered too, in my hair. 'So I probably have to leave between eight and nine.'

'That's early.'

'It is.' His hand smoothed over my head, and my eyes drifted shut again, relaxing in spite of myself. 'But the drive is easy.'

'And you're not coming back until Sunday night?'

'Correct,' he murmured, and I felt his chest move with a deep breath. 'Are you sure you're not going to miss me?'

My lips cracked a small grin. 'It'll be like a vacation for me.'

He chuckled. 'That was entirely mean.'

'Wasn't it?'

'But I know you're lying.'

'You do?'

'Yep.' His hand moved, and I felt the tips of his fingers graze my cheek. My eyes flew open. He was smiling down at me. Not a big smile that showed off his dimple, though. 'You're going to miss me, but you're not going to admit it.'

I didn't say anything, because I was trying not to think about the next four days. And then his fingers moved, trailing the curve of my cheekbone, and I wasn't really thinking about anything. They drifted to my jaw and one finger carved a path to my chin. Air leaked slowly out of my lungs as the finger hovered near my bottom lip.

He tilted his head to the side. 'I'll miss you.'

My lips parted. 'Really?'

'Yeah.'

I closed my eyes against the sudden burn of tears. I had no idea why those three words affected me so, but they did, and for a teeny, tiny moment, I admitted to myself that I didn't want him to leave. That made the burn worse.

Several minutes passed and the only sound was the low hum of the TV. He traced the outline of my lower lip, never quite touching it but coming close with each pass. I wondered if he would ever touch my lip, and if I wanted him to.

I think I sort of did.

'You talk in your sleep,' he said.

My eyes popped open. Screw the touching of the lip. 'I do?'

He nodded.

Oh God. My stomach dropped. 'Are you messing with me? Because I swear to God, if you're messing with me, I'm going to hurt you.'

'I'm not messing with you, sweetheart.'

I sat up, and both his hands dropped away. I twisted on the couch, facing him. My pulse was pounding for a whole different reason. 'What did I say?'

'Nothing, really.'

'For real?'

Leaning forward, he scrubbed his hands down his face. 'You were just murmuring stuff. I couldn't really make out what you were saying.' He lifted his head. 'It was kind of cute.'

My heart started to slow down as the fear loosened its grip on my chest. God only knows what I could've been saying when I slept. Glancing at the clock, I saw it was past three in the morning. 'Holy crap, you suck at your special ability at knowing the time.'

Cam shrugged as he slid forward. 'I guess I should be going home.'

I opened my mouth and then closed it. What was I about to do? Ask him to stay? Like have a slumber party on my couch? Real smooth. I doubted he was interested in PG-13 couch parties. 'Be careful when you drive,' I finally said.

He stood, and I stared at the spot he'd occupied. 'I will.' And then he swooped down, moving faster than I could figure out what he was up to. He placed his lips to my forehead. 'Good night, Avery.'

I closed my eyes and my hands balled into fists. 'Good night, Cam.' He made it to the door before I sprang up, clutching the back of the couch. 'Cam?'

He stopped. 'Yeah?'

Taking a deep breath, I forced the words out. 'I had a really good time tonight.'

Cam stared at me a moment and then he smiled. The dimple appeared in his left cheek, and my own lips responded in kind. 'I know.'

Chapter 12

Tossing my history text onto the edge of my bed, I flopped onto my back and smacked my hands over my eyes. It was only Thursday afternoon and I already felt like I was about to crawl out of my skin.

I guess I could clean something.

Yawn.

My cell chirped from the nightstand, and I rolled over, grabbing it. Half afraid to look at the screen, I did so with one eye closed. Like that somehow made things less shitty if it was the friendly neighborhood asshole.

It wasn't.

Sitting up, I opened the text from Cam. Two words and I was grinning like a fool. *Miss me?*

I responded back with: *No.*

The response was almost immediate. *If u were Pinocchio, ur nose wld span the state.*

Crossing my legs, I leaned against my headboard. *Pinocchio? Sounds like your reading level.*

Ha. U wound me. Deeply.

Thought you didn't have feelings?

I lied. I have so many feels for u. Before I could respond, another text came through. *When I lie something else grows on me.*

I laughed out loud. *Thanks for sharing.*

Ur welcome. Just keeping u updated.

You can keep that to yourself. Biting down on my lip, I texted back: *Did you make it home?*

A few minutes passed while I stared at my phone. *Yeah. Fam showering me with affection. U cld learn frm them.*

I think you get enough attention.

I'm needy.

Boy, don't I know that.

There was another span of minutes. *What r u doing?*

Lying on my back, I crossed my ankles. *Reading.*

Nerd.

Jerk.

Bet u miss me.

My grin had reached embarrassingly epic proportions. *Bet you have better things to do right now.*

Nope. A few seconds later, *Who is this???* I frowned as I sat up. And then, *Sorry, my sister just stole my phone.*

I relaxed. *Sounds like a pretty cool sister.*

She is. Sometimes. She's needier than I am. Gotta run.

I texted back: *TTYL.*

The rest of the afternoon dragged, and by nine o'clock, I was briefly considering taking some NyQuil just to go to sleep. From the living room I heard my cell chirp again. Throwing my toothbrush into the sink, I made a mad four-foot dash to my living room and then slowed as I approached my phone.

Go out with me.

Laughing, I forgot I had toothpaste in my mouth and ended up spewing white, foamy gunk all over my chin and shirt. 'Jesus, I'm a dork.'

I cleaned myself up and then responded to Cam. *Asking me over text is no different from in person.*

Thought I'd give it a try. What r u doing now? I'm beating my dad at poker.

Picturing him with his family, I smiled. *Getting ready for bed.*

Wish I was there.

My eyes widened. What the what?

Wait r u naked?

No!!! I sent back. *Perv.*

Damn. At least I have my imagination.

That's all you will ever have.

We'll c.

No you won't.

I choose to ignore that. Ok. Gotta go. Dad is kicking my ass.

Night Cam.

Good night, Avery.

I held on to the phone for an indecent amount of time after that and then took it into my bedroom. Lately, I'd taken to the habit of turning my ringer off at night, because I never knew when I'd get the UNKNOWN CALLER messages. But tonight, I left it on.

Just in case.

Sunday morning didn't feel right without Cam: his obsession with hard-boiled eggs, that damn little skillet, and all those yummy baked goods. I woke up early, as if some internal clock was expecting him to knock on my door. Of course, it didn't happen, and he hadn't texted all day Saturday. I imagined that he was hanging out with his family and friends who were still living up there.

I tried not to miss Cam, because he was just a friend, and while I wished Brit and Jacob were around, it wasn't like I *missed them,* missed them. It wasn't the same. Or maybe it was.

Pulling out a box of cereal, I made a yuck face. I really could go for some blueberry muffins. I ate my cereal, feeling all kinds of grumpy. I'd just finished washing the bowl when my phone rang.

I hurried into the living room and drew up short when I saw the name on my caller ID.

Mom.

Ooooh fuck.

The phone kept ringing while I debated picking it up and tossing it out the window. I had to answer, though. Mom and Dad *never* called. So it had to be important. Answering the phone, I winced. 'Hello.'

'Avery.'

Ah, there was the voice—the cultured, clipped, highly impersonal, and cold voice of Mrs. Morgansten. I bit back a string of curses that would burn her perfect ears. 'Hi, Mom.'

There was a huge gap of silence. My brows rose as I wondered if she had misdialed me or something. Finally she spoke. 'How is West Virginia?'

She said 'West Virginia' like it was some kind of venereal disease. I rolled my eyes. Sometimes my parents forgot where they came from. 'It's really good. You're up early.'

'It's Sunday. Theo has insisted on doing an early brunch with your father at the club. Otherwise I would not be up at this time.'

Theo? I plopped down on the couch, my mouth hanging open. For the love of little babies everywhere, Theo was *Blaine's* father. My parents, they were such … fuckers.

'Avery, are you there?' Impatience filled her tone.

'Yes. I'm here.' I grabbed a pillow and shoved it in my lap. 'You're going to have brunch with Mr. Fitzgerald?'

'Yes.'

And that was all she said to that. Yes. Like it was no big deal. The Fitzgeralds paid off the Morganstens and I was labeled a lying whore, but it was all good in the hood, because they all could still have brunch at the club.

130

'How is school?' she asked, but she sounded bored. She was probably surfing the Internet for her next cosmetic procedure. 'Avery?'

Oh, for fuck's sake. 'School is perfect. West Virginia is perfect. Everything is perfect.'

'Don't you take that tone with me, young lady. After everything you put us through—'

'Everything I put *you* through?' I was living in an alternate universe.

'And are still putting us through,' she continued as if I hadn't spoken a word. 'You're clear across the country, going to some little university in *West Virginia* instead of—'

'There's nothing wrong with this school, Mom, or West Virginia. You were born in Ohio. Not that different—'

'That is something I try not to remember.' Her huff was pretty epic. 'Which brings me to the point of this call.'

Thank God, baby Jesus, and the Holy Ghost.

'You need to come home.'

'What?' I clenched the pillow to my chest.

She sighed. 'You need to stop playing around and come home, Avery. You've made your point quite clear by up and doing something as childish as this.'

'Childish? Mom, I hated being there—'

'And who do you have to blame for that, Avery?' Some of the coolness slipped from her voice.

My mouth dropped open. This wasn't the first time she'd said something like that. Not by a long shot, but it was like a punch in the chest. I stared at the window, shaking my head slowly.

'We only want the best for you,' she began again, regaining the cool aloofness with a line of pure bullshit. 'That's all we've wanted, and the best thing for you to do is to come home.'

I started to laugh, but it got stuck in my throat. Coming

131

home was in my best interest? The woman was crazy. Just talking to her made it feel like I got the crazy on me.

'Some things have happened here,' she added, and then cleared her throat. 'You should come home.'

How many times had I done what they wanted? Too many, but this was one time I couldn't back down. Going home was equivalent to sticking my head in a meat grinder and then asking why it hurt. I took a deep breath and opened my eyes. 'No.'

'Excuse me?' My mother's voice turned shrill.

'I said, no. I'm not coming back home.'

'Avery Samantha Morgan—'

'I've got to go. It was nice talking to you, Mom. Good-bye.' And then I hung up the phone before she could say anything else. I placed the cell on the coffee table and waited.

One minute went by, two minutes, and then five minutes. Letting out a sigh of relief, I collapsed against the couch. I shook my head, literally blown away by the conversation. My mother was insane. I closed my eyes and rubbed my temples. What a way to start a Sunday morning.

A sudden knock on the door startled me.

Hopping to my feet, I hurried around the couch, wondering who it could be. It was too early for any of my friends to have come home. Hell, it wasn't even nine yet, which meant it was probably also too early for a serial killer to pay a visit.

I stretched up and peered through the peephole. 'No way.' My heart did a series of backflips as I yanked open the door. 'Cam?'

He turned around, lips forming a crooked grin. In his hand was a grocery bag. 'So, I woke up around four this morning and thought, I could really eat some eggs. And eggs with you is so much better than eggs with my sister or my dad. Plus my mom made pumpkin bread. I know how you like pumpkin bread.'

132

Struck silent, I stepped aside and watched him carry his bag into the kitchen. The back of my throat burned; my lower lip was doing this really weird tremble thing. A knot somewhere deep inside my chest unraveled. My brain clicked off. I didn't even shut the front door or feel the cool air washing over my bare ankles. I shot forward, crossing the distance between the door and the kitchen. Cam turned just as I launched myself at him.

He caught me and stumbled back a step with his arms around my waist. I buried my head against his chest, eyes closed and heart thumping. 'I missed you.'

Chapter 13

Hunkered down in my hoodie, I shivered as the cold wind whipped between Whitehall and Knutti, rattling the brown and yellow leaves above us. Several were tossed into the air and they spiraled down to the ground, joining the thick carpet of leaves.

Brit drew in a deep drag of her cigarette and let it out slowly. 'So the next time I answer a late-night booty call from Jimmie and I actually go over to his place, what will you do?'

I hobbled from side to side. 'Punch you in the vagina?'

'Exactly!' She took one last draw and then put the cigarette out. 'God, why are we girls so stupid?'

I fell in step beside her, keeping my arms wrapped around me. 'Good question.'

'I mean, I totally know he doesn't want to be in a relationship, that all he wants is sex, and he's usually a little drunk and yet I still go over there. Seriously?'

'Do you want to be in a relationship?'

Her lips pursed as she pulled her knit cap down over her ears. 'You know, I don't think so.'

I frowned. 'Then why are you so upset that he doesn't want to be?'

'Because he should want to be in a relationship with me! I'm friggin' awesome.'

Fighting a grin, I glanced at her. 'You are awesome.'

Brit smiled. I'd met Jimmie a couple of times around campus with Brit. He seemed like a pretty okay guy, but I really believed she could do better than some guy who only called her when he was drunk. So I told her that.

'And that's why we're friends,' she responded, wiggling her arm through mine. 'Man, where did fall go? It's like winter came out of nowhere and bitch-smacked us.'

'I know.' I shuddered as we stopped at the intersection. 'I feel sorry for the kids who are about to go trick or treating tomorrow night. They're going to freeze.'

'Fuck the kids,' she said, causing me to giggle. 'I'm dressing as an angel—a slutty angel.'

'Of course.'

'And that means I'm basically wearing lingerie. My nipples will probably freeze and fall off. Speaking of which, don't think I haven't noticed how you've been avoiding the whole party topic.'

I had no idea how she went from frozen nipples to that.

Outside of the registrar's office, she pinned me with a look. 'You have to go with us. Everyone is going to be there.'

Looking away, I watched campus police doing a car unlock for an unlucky person. 'I don't know. Not big on Halloween parties.'

'You're not big on any parties. Come on, you've got to come. I need you there. Jimmie will be there and I'll need you to punch me in the vagina.'

I laughed. 'I'm sure Jacob will gladly do that for you.'

'It's not the same! He doesn't understand, and he gives the worst advice. He'd probably tell me to go hook up with him,' she protested, and I had to imagine that was true. 'You have to come. Please. Pretty please.'

My resolve to not even consider this party started to crack. Jacob had been talking about it all week. Last night, as Cam and I had been finishing up our assignment and in between him asking me out, he'd even brought up the party his friend Jase was throwing. Jase was a year younger than Cam and pretty high up in one of the frats, which one I couldn't remember. I'd seen Cam with him a couple of times, but we'd never spoken. Not that any of that mattered, because even considering going to this party had the beginnings of an ulcer forming in my stomach.

'I've got to head in here and take care of the stupid scheduling for next semester.'

She'd been having a hell of a time getting classes. I'd been lucky and got into all the ones I'd wanted. 'Are you going to cut a bitch?'

'Maybe.' Brit gave me a quick hug. 'Thank you for walking me here.'

'No problem.' I was done for the day, so I didn't have much else to do.

She started up the wide steps but turned around. 'Think about the party. Please? You need to go, not just for me; it will be fun. You'll get to let loose a little. Okay?'

I took a deep breath. 'I'll think about it.'

'Like, really think about?' When I nodded, she said, 'Promise?'

'Promise.'

Brit headed into the building, and I was probably going to be heading to the store to get some Tums. I was going to need them.

There were times in my life when I knew that what I was thinking was wrong. Knowing that didn't make things any easier. Going to a Halloween party shouldn't have me sitting in my moon chair with a bottle of Tums beside me and a carton of Ben & Jerry's in my hands.

A *half-empty* carton of Ben & Jerry's ice cream.

I felt like I was well on my way to becoming the neighborhood cat lady. All I needed were the cats.

Shortly after leaving campus, I had gotten a text from Cam about the party. He wanted me to go. Brit wanted me to go. Jacob wanted me to go. I wanted to go, but …

Groaning, I put the lid on the ice cream and shoved to my feet. I was nineteen years old. Living on my own. I had told my mother to suck it and I'd actually hugged Cam and told him that I missed him. Going to this party shouldn't be that big of a deal. It was about time that I did something like this. If I didn't do it now, would I ever do it?

Probably not.

I put the ice cream away and then moved on to the spray bottle stashed under the sink. Spraying the surface of everything in my kitchen, I started cleaning with a wicked vengeance.

I could do it.

My heart flopped in my chest, and it felt like my stomach had dropped to my feet.

No, I couldn't.

As I was scrubbing the counter by the stove, the light reflected off my silver bracelet, catching my attention. I stopped, unable to look away from something that had become a staple in my everyday life. Putting the bottle down and dropping the cloth, I reached out and slid the bracelet off. Turning my arm over, I forced myself to look at the scar. I was ashamed of it, did everything in my power to hide it, but for what? Staying in my apartment, being antisocial and a general loser? Certain things were probably always going be a no go for me, or insanely awkward, but going to a fucking party? Was I really so crippled by what happened that five years later I couldn't go to one?

I put the bracelet back on as I leaned against the counter.

I had to do this. I needed to do this. At least try to do this. My heart started its panicked thumping as I pushed off the counter and headed into the living room. I dug my phone out of my bag and before I thought about what I was doing, I opened a text Cam had sent earlier and sent *Okay*.

A few seconds passed and then there was a text back. *Incoming*.

'Incoming?' What in the—?

There was a knock on my door.

Rolling my eyes, I tossed my phone on the couch and went to open the door. 'You didn't have to come over.'

Cam strolled right in, twisting his cap on backward.

'Well, help yourself.'

He stopped near the kitchen and frowned. 'Why does your apartment smell like Clorox?'

'I was cleaning.'

A brow went up.

'The whole kitchen,' I said sheepishly. 'You know, you could've saved yourself the trip and just responded to the text.'

Casting me a long look, he sat on the couch. 'I needed the exercise.'

Yeah, he did not need the exercise.

He patted the spot beside me. 'Come sit with me.'

I stared.

'Come on.'

Muttering under my breath, I stepped over his legs and sat. 'All right, I'm sitting.'

His lashes lowered, and I felt his gaze on my mouth. Warmth spread across my cheeks, and his grin went up a notch. 'So you texted me with the word "okay." I've asked

139

you two things today. So I'm curious to which one you're finally agreeing to.'

I pulled my legs up to my chest and wrapped my arms around my knees. 'You asked me about the Halloween party tomorrow night.'

'Yes, I did.' He reached over and tugged on my arm until I let go of my knees. 'But I asked you something else.'

My eyes narrowed.

Then he got a hand on the hem of my jeans and pulled my legs away from my chest. 'I also asked you out.'

'You know the answer to that.'

He narrowed his eyes.

My lips twitched. 'I was saying okay, I'll go to the party.'

'Smart choice. It'll be fun and you'll have a good time.' Once I was apparently sitting to his approval, he sat back. 'When do you want me to pick you up?'

I shook my head. 'I'm going to drive myself.'

'Why would you do that? We live in the same building and are heading to the same place.'

'Thanks, but I'll drive.'

He studied me a moment. 'If you don't want to go with me, then at least get a ride with Brittany.'

I said something along the lines of agreeing to that, but I wasn't planning on it. Taking my own car meant I could leave whenever I wanted to. I needed that lifeline.

'Hey,' Cam said.

Turning my head toward him, I raised my brows. 'Hi.'

'Go out with me.'

I smiled. 'Shut up, Cam.'

I was so nervous that my phone felt slippery in my hand and my seat belt felt like it was pressed too tightly against my chest. I was sitting in the parking lot, thirty minutes past the time I should've left for the Halloween party at Jase's house. I'd like to say that I was just being fashionably late, but that was so not the truth.

I was, like, two steps from a panic attack.

'So you didn't get a costume?' Brit said, and over her voice, I could hear music and muffled laughter. 'It's not a big deal. There are lots of people here that aren't dressed up.'

Well, there went that excuse. After talking to Cam last night, I'd briefly considered the idea of making a last-minute run to the store to find a costume, but dressing up would probably be too much.

'Are you almost here?' Brit asked. 'Because I'm lonely—hey!'

A second later, Jacob's voice came through the phone. 'Hey, girl, hey, where you at?'

I closed my eyes. 'I'm getting ready to leave.'

'You better, because Brit is getting on my nerves asking for you. So get your ass here.'

'I'm coming. I'll be there in a little bit.'

Hanging up, I tossed the phone onto the seat next to me and gripped the steering wheel. *I can do this.* That's what I kept telling myself as I glanced back up at my apartment. I'd left a light on and it was like a damn beacon right now, enticing me back to the safety that was pure boredom.

I was being stupid, totally understood that, but it didn't change the fact that my heart was thundering in my chest or that I was nauseated. What I was experiencing wasn't normal to anyone else, and that was the key. I didn't want *this* to be normal for me.

'Fuck.'

I needed to be brave.

I knocked the car into reverse and backed out. My arms were trembling by the time I made it to the end of the road and turned onto Route 45. Jase's house wasn't that far from

University Heights. Only a few miles, back in a nearby subdivision where several larger frats had taken up residency.

On the drive to his house, I focused on listing as many constellations as I could. Andromeda, Antlia, Apus, Aquarius, Aquila, Ara, Aries, Auriga—who came up with these names? Seriously. I'd made it to the D's when I spotted the line of cars pouring out of a large three-story home's driveway. Cars were everywhere, parking along the road, in the yard, and down the street. I ended up having to turn around so I could park on the other side of the street, about a block down.

The night air was chilly and the streets were void of children. Trick or treat had ended about an hour before, and there were pieces of dropped candy every few feet.

Bright light spilled out from the windows, casting a luminous glow along the porch. There were a few people outside, leaning against the railing. Shoving my hands into the pockets of my hoodie, I avoided the garage, where a mean game of beer pong was going down, and walked through the open front door.

Holy crap …

The house was packed. People were everywhere, crowding a TV, in groups by the couch, on the floor, and in the hallway. Music thumped along with my heart as I scanned the crowd, searching for a sexy angel. There were a lot of angels— naughty angels in red, sexy angels in white, and, I guess, very bad angels in black.

Hmm.

I squeezed past a girl dressed like Dorothy from *The Wizard of Oz*, if Dorothy had been a stripper. She smiled at me and I smiled back. It felt wobbly and weird. Sliding past a group at a card table, I saw Cam's roommate, Ollie, at the table. He was too immersed in the game to notice me. I stretched up on the tips of my toes. The inside of the house had a slightly suffocating feel to it with all the people.

There was a nearby high-pitched squeal and I turned, having only seconds to prepare myself before I was attacked by an angel in white.

'You're here!' Brit shrieked, squeezing me. 'Holy shit! I didn't think you'd actually come. I thought you were going to bail.'

'I'm here.'

She squeezed me again and then grabbed my hand. 'Come. Jacob is out in the garage. So is Cam.'

My overworked heart did some more cardio as she pulled me around the card table. A few guys looked up, dismissing me and my jeans outright and then settling on the tiny white dress Brit had on. Interest sparked in their eyes. One guy leaned back in his chair, brows knitting as he took her in. I couldn't blame him. She looked hot.

'Coming through!' Brit announced, free hand in the air. 'Beep. Beep.'

The air was easier to breathe in the garage, the light not so bright, and while there were more people out here, the muscles in the back of my neck relaxed. Brit led me toward a guy who had on an old-school black bowler hat and a purple blazer.

'Jakey-Jake, look who I found!' Brit yelled.

Purple blazer turned, and a genuine smile broke out across my face as I saw the big black-rimmed glasses. 'Bruno Mars?' I asked.

'Yes! See, Brit, some people get my costume!' Jacob shot her a dirty look before turning back to me. He frowned. 'What are you dressed as?'

I shrugged. 'A lazy college student?'

Jacob laughed as Brit bounced over to the keg. 'What do you have on under this godawful sweatshirt?'

'What's wrong with my hoodie?' I demanded.

He gave me a bland look. 'Nothing's wrong with it if you

143

just rolled out of bed and were going to class, but you're at a party.' He went for the zipper on my hoodie and pulled it down. 'Take it off or I'm taking it off.'

'He's being serious.' Brit returned with two red plastic cups in her hand. 'He once took my shirt off because he wanted to try it on and there I was, standing in a room full of girls, in just my bra.'

I slipped my keys into my jeans and took my hoodie off, dropping it on the back of a nearby camping chair. 'Happy?'

Jacob took in my fitted black turtleneck, lips pursed. 'Hmm …' He tugged the hem of my sweater up so that it exposed a slice of my lower stomach. Then roughed his hands through my hair, causing the waves to go every which way. 'Better. You have a tight little body. Fucking own it, girl. Now you're dressed as a sexy, lazy college student.'

I took the drink Brit shoved in my hand. 'Are you done dressing me like I'm your own personal Barbie?'

'Bitch, if you were my Barbie, you'd be half naked.'

I laughed. 'Good thing I'm not.'

He dropped an arm over my shoulder. 'I'm glad you're here. For real.'

'Me too.' And once I said that, I *was* glad. I was here. I made it. This was huge. I even took a sip of my beer. Look at me. Party animal extraordinaire.

Telling myself I wasn't looking for anyone in particular, I glanced around the garage. It didn't take long to find Cam. Being that he was a good head taller than most of the guys around, he was easy to pick out. Seeing that he wasn't dressed any differently than he normally was brought a smile to my face.

Cam was standing near the beer pong table, arms folded across his chest. His biceps stretched the short-sleeve shirt he wore. I didn't know what it was with guys dressing like it was warm outside when it was obviously not.

144

Beside him was Jase, who was as tall as Cam, and just as nice to openly gawk at with his slightly longer brown hair. He too was dressed like it was sweltering, and a dark tattoo peeked out from underneath his sleeve.

Brit followed my stare and sighed. 'I don't know which one is hotter.'

Cam, to me, won hands down. 'Me neither.'

'I'd take them both,' Jacob commented.

'At the same time?' Curiosity filled Brit's tone.

Jacob grinned. 'Hell yeah.'

'A Cam and Jase sandwich.' Brit shivered. 'I wish that was on the Dollar Menu.'

I laughed. 'I think they'd cost more than a dollar.'

'True,' she murmured and then sighed out, 'I need to get laid.'

Jase elbowed Cam and said something. A moment later, Cam looked in our direction. A wide smile broke out across his striking face. He put his cup down on the edge of the Ping-Pong table.

'And here comes one of them,' Jacob said, looking at me slyly. 'It's about to become a Cam and Avery sandwich.'

'Shut up,' I said, flushing.

People got out of the way for Cam. He was like a hot Moses, parting a sea of drunk college students. I took a step back, suddenly nervous.

Cam didn't hesitate. There was a confident ease in everything he did. His arms were around my waist in under a second, lifting me off my feet in a bear hug. Brit wisely grabbed the cup from my hand before Cam spun around. I clutched his shoulders as the walls of the garage whirled.

'Holy shit, I can't believe you're actually here.'

It seemed that no one really thought I'd show. It made me warm and fuzzy to know that I had. 'I told you I was coming.'

He set me on my feet but didn't let go. 'When did you get here?'

I shrugged. 'I don't know. Not that long ago.'

'Why didn't you come say hi?' The dimple was there, and I found myself staring at it.

'You were busy and I didn't want to bother you,' I admitted, noticing that quite a few people were staring at us.

Cam lowered his head and his lips brushed my ear as he spoke, sending a burst of shivers along my spine. 'You are *never* a bother to me.'

My heart skipped in my chest like I was poised atop a roller-coaster ride. I turned my head slightly, and our eyes locked. Thoughts scattered, and when Cam's hands tightened on my arms, I was flying down that roller coaster. For a moment, the sounds of the party were drowned out. The pupils of his eyes were so large, a startling contrast against the bright blue.

'Yo, Cam!' Jase yelled. 'You're up.'

The moment was shattered, and I let out the breath I hadn't realized I was holding. He grinned. 'Don't go too far.'

I nodded. 'Okay.'

Cam returned to Jase's side and picked up a Ping-Pong ball.

'Whoa,' Brit breathed, handing my drink back to me. 'That was …'

'Really hot,' Jacob finished. 'I thought you two were going to rip off each other's clothes and start making babies right here on the dirty, beer-covered floor. Like I was going to have to start charging admission for what was about to go down.'

I shot him look. 'I think that's a tad bit on the overexaggeration side.'

'Not from where we were standing,' Brit said, fanning herself. 'How long are you going to string that boy along?'

A frown pulled at my lips. 'I'm not stringing him along.'

Her brows rose, but she didn't say anything. Luckily the conversation moved away from me when Jimmie appeared and started messing with Brit's wings. Our threesome turned into a foursome and before I knew it, we had our own little party off to the side. I was totally out of my element, but I kept up with the conversation. I knew as I sipped my beer that I was being labeled as the quiet chick at the party, but that was better than the last party label I ended up with.

The group had grown outside, the music was slightly louder, and clusters of people started to dance. Somehow, among all the noise, a deep, husky laugh drew my attention, and I turned halfway.

Coming through the garage entrance were two girls who looked like they belonged on a Victoria's Secret runway. One was dressed as a devil, which was really just a red teddy, a pointy tail, and horns. Boobs were everywhere. The other was a very sexy version of Little Red Riding Hood. Several things immediately happened as they prowled in on mile-high heels.

A lot of guys literally stopped what they were doing and looked, like, midconversation. Jimmie's mouth hit the floor. Even Jacob was staring like he was about to change sexual preferences. My stomach sort of twisted as I eyed the Riding Hood costume and I tried not to even think about the fact that I had worn a costume just like that to the Halloween party years before. Besides, right now, that didn't seem like the biggest deal to contend with, which spoke volumes for a lot of things.

Little Red Riding Hood was also known as Stephanie Keith, a.k.a. Steph.

The girl was gorgeous in a way that made any girl feel underdressed and on the wrong side of ugly. The hem of her sparkly red dress ended just below the ass, and her legs were stunning. Her outfit was complete with red lips, smoky eyes, and two pigtails.

She was hot.

And she was going straight for Cam.

Steph threw her arms around him, which caused her dress to hike up, revealing ruffled black panties that read SPANK ME across her ass cheeks. Cam didn't run from her, but turned, giving her that damn lopsided smile of his. She took the ball from him, backing up and giggling as her friend was all up on Jase.

Something ugly unfurled in the pit of my stomach like a noxious weed. Why wasn't Cam running away from her instead of following her around the table?

That was a stupid question.

What guy would be running from Steph?

Someone bumped into me from the side, an apology was muttered, but I was focused on Steph. She was holding the ball close to her breasts, grinning wickedly as Cam stalked her.

Brit took the cup from me and grabbed my hand. 'Let's dance.'

I dug my feet in, blinking at her. 'I don't dance.'

'No. We are going to dance.' She cast a look over her shoulder. Cam had somehow gotten the ball from Steph. 'Because if we don't, you're just going to stand there and glare at them like a pissed-off girlfriend.'

Shit. She had a point. I let her drag me toward a group of girls who were dancing, which was conveniently close to the Ping-Pong table. Brit held on to my hand as she shimmied around me, singing along to the song. It took a couple of moments to work up the nerve to do another thing I hadn't done in years and I sort of wished I'd finished off the beer.

Closing my eyes, I let myself feel the music and catch the beat. Once that happened, my hips were swaying and I was smiling. Eyes open now, I still held on to Brit's hand as we danced together. The group around us grew larger and over Brit's shoulder, I saw Cam.

He wasn't paying attention to Steph.

He was watching us—watching *me*.

Brit was a freaking genius.

She looked behind her and then turned back to me, biting her lip. 'Fuck 'em.'

I threw my head back and laughed. 'Fuck 'em.'

'That's my girl.'

Jimmie joined us, coming up behind Brit, dropping his hands on her waist. I raised my brows, and she shrugged, which was code for holding off on the punching in the vagina. My hair was damp along my temples and my sweater had ridden up. The three of us were joined by Jacob, who pretty much flailed around. I was so caught up in laughing at him that when hands landed on my hips, I jumped a good five inches off the floor.

Brit's eyes widened.

I looked over my shoulder and saw a relatively unfamiliar face. The guy's cheeks were red, eyes slightly glazed over as he ground his hips.

'Hey,' he slurred, smiling.

'Hi.' I turned back around, making a face at Brit as I stepped forward. I made it about an inch before Drunk Guy's grip tightened.

'Where you going?' he said. 'We're dancing.'

I twisted to the side, and the guy followed, staying at my back. My stomach dropped, and a strange, shivery sensation crawled up the back of my neck, raising the tiny hairs there.

Thrown back several years, I froze for a second. Brit, Jacob, the party—everything—disappeared. I felt him pull me back against him, his hands on the bare skin of my stomach. Without any warning, reality seemed to shift.

I wasn't here.

I was back *there*, with *his* hands under my skirt, and I couldn't breathe or see, the fabric of the couch rough against my cheek.

'Baby,' the guy crooned in my ear. 'Dance with me.'

'Baby,' Blaine had said, his breath heavy in my ear. 'You can't tell me you don't want this.'

The garage shifted to a basement and back again. I tried to pull away, my heart beating so fast I was going to be sick. 'Let me go.'

'Come on, it's just a dance.' His hand was on my stomach, under my sweater. 'You—'

'Let me go.' My breath caught in my throat as I struggled. 'Let me go!'

There was a surprised shout and a squeal. Suddenly I was torn out of the drunk guy's grip. I stumbled back, bumping into someone. Heart racing, I pushed my hair out of my face and lifted my head.

Oh my God.

Cam had the guy against the wall.

Chapter 14

A small crowd had already circled Cam and the guy. Some watched with interest; others jeered and urged on the fight.

Cam had pinned the guy with one hand shoved into his chest. He was right up in his face, his free hand curled into a fist at his side. 'What the fuck, man? Do you have a fucking hearing problem?'

'I'm sorry,' the guy blubbered, hands raised at his sides. 'We were just dancing. Didn't mean any shit by it.'

'Cam.' My voice came out strangled, hoarse as I started forward.

Brit was beside me, capturing my arm. 'Do not get involved, Avery.'

How could I not get involved? My stomach roiled, and what little beer I had consumed rose in my throat.

Cam shoved the guy back into the wall again and then Jase was suddenly there, getting an arm around Cam's waist, pulling him back. The guy slumped against the wall, eyes closed.

'You need to chill the fuck out,' Jase said.

Cam sidestepped his friend, eyes narrowed on the other guy. 'Let me the fuck go, Jase.'

'Fuck no.' Jase got in between them, putting his hands on Cam's chest. 'You don't need this, remember? Getting into a fight is the last thing you fucking need right now. So back down.'

Something in what Jase said seemed to reach Cam. He cast one last promising look at the guy against the wall and then shrugged off Jase's hands. Cam turned, thrusting his hand through his hair. Through the people standing between us, his gaze landed on me and Brit. He started forward, but Jase said something that made him stop. Out of nowhere, Ollie appeared, shoving a bottle of beer in Cam's hands. Between the two of them, they ushered him back into the house. I started after them, but Brit hauled me into a corner, her wings bouncing as she turned to me. 'What the hell happened?'

'I don't know.' My chest rose and fell sharply. 'The guy wouldn't let me go and Cam just came out of nowhere. I need to—'

'No.' She stopped me, blocking my path. 'You need to let him cool down. He's with his boys, let him be.'

Smoothing my hands over my hips, I was slow to process what Brit was saying. There was a good chance I was going to hurl. I looked around, willing my heart to slow down. Some people were staring at us. Others had lost interest the moment it was obvious there wouldn't be a fight. Steph was at the Ping-Pong table, lips thinning as our gazes collided. Music picked back up, thumping in tune with my heart. Sweat dotted my brow.

'Hey, Avery, you okay?' Brit asked.

I forced a nod, but I wasn't okay. The garage was shifting again—all the costumes and the sounds amplified. Pressure clamped down on my chest. The smell of beer, perfume, and sweat clouded the air. I took a breath, but it didn't seem like enough.

152

'I need fresh air,' I told Brit, pulling free.

'I'll go with you.'

'No. No, I'm fine. Stay here.' I didn't want to ruin her night. 'I'm okay. Really. I just need some fresh air.'

Brit relented with a little more coaxing, and I hurried out of the garage, feeling like a hundred eyes were on my back even though I knew probably no one was looking.

Cool air lifted the damp hair off my neck, but I didn't really feel it. I didn't stop. I kept walking, my hands opening and closing at my sides. I was by my car before I realized it. Digging my keys out of my pocket, I got behind the wheel.

Hands shaking, I pressed them against my face. Oh God, I could still feel his hands—not the drunk guy's but Blaine's. I could hear him whispering in my ear, feel him behind me and the pressure ... Throwing my head back against the headrest, I squeezed my eyes shut. 'No. I'm not doing this.'

The words seemed to echo in the car and were thrown back in my face, because I was doing this. I was doing exactly what I shouldn't do.

I couldn't go back in there, not for my friends or for my hoodie.

Shoving the keys into the ignition, I eased out from between two cars.

I don't even know how I got home. I didn't remember anything from the ride, just that I was standing in the middle of my apartment, trying to catch my breath.

I made it to the hallway before I slid down the wall, bringing my knees against my chest. I curled up, thrusting my hands into my hair. I squeezed my eyes shut, but the tears snuck free, spilling down my cheeks.

There was no doubt in my mind that I had screwed up—I'd overreacted. The guy at the party had been obnoxiously grabby, but I had overreacted. I'd let the past distort what had been really happening. I'd panicked and Cam almost got into a fight over it.

I pressed my forehead against my knees, pulling my hair back. I couldn't do it. I'd tried and I had turned a good time into an epic fail. What was wrong with me?

There were several valid answers to that—a lot was wrong. Not breaking news there but this … I had wanted so badly for tonight to be good, for tonight to be that extra push in the right direction, whatever direction that was. A sob rose and I clamped my jaw shut until my molars ached. Instead, I was here, back to where I started.

The throbbing in my head had increased until it felt like the entire apartment was pounding right along with it. Wincing, I opened my eyes and realized I was where I'd sat down, in the hall, and my entire body ached. I'd fallen asleep, maybe for an hour or two.

And the thumping wasn't just in my head—it was on my door.

I pushed off the floor, hurrying to the door in a haze. I was so out of it I didn't even check to see who it was.

Cam barreled through the door, and I was against his chest before I processed what was happening. Strong arms swept around me and his hand came up, cradling the back of my head. I inhaled deeply, drawing in the faint scent of cologne and alcohol.

'Jesus Christ,' he said, his hand fisting in my hair. 'Why haven't you answered your damn phone?'

'I left my phone in the car, I think.' My voice was muffled against his chest.

He swore again as he pulled back. His hands went to my cheeks, holding me in place in a way that didn't trigger dark memories. 'I've been blowing up your phone—so have Jacob and Brittany.'

154

'I'm sorry.' I blinked slowly. 'I didn't—'

'You've been crying.' His eyes narrowed until only a thin strip of blue showed in both. 'You've been fucking crying.'

'No, I haven't.' The lie sounded lame.

'Have you looked in the mirror?' he demanded. When I shook my head, he dropped his hands and closed the door behind him. He then took my hand. A muscle ticced along his jaw, and when he spoke, his voice was hard. 'Come on.'

I let him pull me into the hallway bathroom. When he flipped on the overhead light, I winced and then I saw myself in the mirror. 'Oh God …'

My eyes were puffy and red, but it was the streaks of black mascara that truly cemented the fact that my first attempt at attending a party in five years had not ended well. My gaze met Cam's in the mirror and embarrassment swamped me. I dropped my head in my hands and muttered, 'Perfect—just perfect.'

'It's not that bad, sweetheart.' His voice softened as his hands settled on my upper arms. He gently pulled my hands. 'Sit down.'

I sat on the closed toilet seat. Staring at my fingers, I forced my sluggish brain to catch up. 'What are you doing here?'

'What am I doing here?' He ran a washcloth under the tap and knelt down in front of me. 'Is that a serious question?'

'Guess not.'

'Look at me.' When I didn't, he repeated it. 'Dammit, Avery, look at me.'

Whoa. Anger rose like smoke through me. My chin lifted. 'Happy?'

The muscle was back, ticking away. 'Why would I come here? You left a party without saying a word to anyone.'

'I told—'

'You told Brittany you were getting some fresh air. That was three hours ago, Avery. They thought you were with me, but when they saw me later they knew you weren't. After what happened with that asshole, you scared them.'

My anger seeped out of me, replaced by guilt. 'I didn't mean to. I just left my phone in the car.'

He didn't say anything as he smoothed the washcloth under my eyes, wiping away the mascara. 'You didn't need to leave.'

'I overreacted.' My lashes lowered and I let out a breath. 'The guy … he really hadn't done anything wrong. He just surprised me and I overreacted. I ruined the party.'

'You didn't ruin the party. And that son of a bitch shouldn't have been grabbing you. Fuck. I heard you say "let me go" and I know damn well he did too. Maybe I shouldn't have reacted as … strongly as I had, but fuck it. He was grabbing you and I didn't like it.'

Yeah, I had told the guy to let me go, but he'd been drunk and stupid. All he had wanted to do was dance with me. I knew when a guy became a threat. He hadn't hit that stage. Who knew if he would have, but it had been the memories that had sent me over the edge.

'You didn't need to come here,' I said finally, suddenly very tired. 'You should be at the party having fun.'

Cam was quiet so long that I had to look at him. The expression on his face was a cross between wanting to strangle me and something far, far different. There was a dipping motion in my stomach, very much like it had been at the party before everything went to hell.

'We're friends, right?' he said in a quiet, low voice.

'Yes.'

'This is what friends do. They check on each other. Brittany and Jacob would've been here, but I made them stay there.'

156

Maybe I totally misread that moment we were having. 'I need to get my phone and call—'

'I'll text Brittany. I got her number.' He rocked back on his heels, watching me. 'The fact that you wouldn't expect anyone to check up on you is … I don't even know what it is.'

I didn't say anything and started to look away, but his hand came up, resting against my cheek. His thumb moved, smoothing across my skin. Our eyes met, and I wished I had something witty to say, something that would erase this night. Well, everything except the way he'd looked at me at the party. I sort of liked that.

Okay. I had really liked that, but whatever.

'Why were you crying?' he asked. 'Wait. Did that fucker hurt you, because I will—'

'No! Not at all,' I said quickly. I had a feeling he'd track that guy down and beat the crap out of him if he thought he'd hurt me.

'Then why?' His thumb moved again, and I moved out of some long-forgotten instinct. I turned my head into his palm. 'Talk to me?'

Talking was so easy for most people, but most people had things they actually wanted to talk about. 'I don't know. I guess I was just being a girl.'

His brows rose. 'You sure that's all?'

'Yes,' I whispered.

He didn't say anything again for another long moment. Instead, his eyes moved over my face in a slow perusal. 'You okay?'

I nodded.

His hand moved down and his thumb brushed the edge of my lip. I sucked in a sharp breath, becoming hyperaware of how close we were. Strange, I realized. I had wanted something to say to make the night disappear, but it wasn't necessarily words I needed.

A touch, a single look was just as powerful.

I wasn't thinking of anything but him in that moment. There was a freedom in that I hadn't experienced before.

His gaze was centered on my lips and as soon as I realized that, my heart kicked up, sending my blood rushing. There wasn't a lot of space separating us. All he'd have to do was move two or three inches and that would be it.

Then his gaze flicked up.

Cam closed the little distance between us before I had a chance to move away. My heart leaped in my chest at the thought that he might kiss me, that I was literally seconds away from my first kiss, and I had no idea what to do. My mouth felt funny after all the crying and I was sitting on a toilet, which probably wasn't the most romantic of all settings.

But he didn't kiss me. He pressed his forehead against mine and let out a ragged breath that smelled of mint. 'You drive me fucking insane sometimes.'

I drove myself fucking insane. 'Sorry.'

Cam pulled back a little, his eyes searching my face. 'Don't run off like that again, okay? I was worried shitless when I couldn't find you and no one knew where you were.'

I almost apologized again, but apologies were really like wishes. There was an abundance of both in my life, and neither really made a difference. So I did something I don't think I'd ever done, not even *before*.

Scooting forward, I pressed my lips to his smooth cheek. His eyes widened, and I inched back. Under his intense stare, I wondered if that had been the wrong thing to do.

Cam started to move forward and then stopped. His eyes were so large, and they were truly beautiful, unique in the way the hue seemed to deepen and darken. 'Avery?'

I swallowed. 'Cam?'

He didn't give me his lopsided grin or show off his one dimple. 'Go out on a date with me.'

There was a tugging in my chest and I was reminded of that moment when he'd come back to campus early after fall break and had come straight to my apartment. Something had cracked inside me then and it did so now, like a wall of … reservation. The party hadn't worked out, but Cam … he was different. He'd always been different.

And he was here. That had to mean something. It sure felt like it did.

My brain was telling me this was a bad idea and I told my brain to shut the fuck up, because it rarely told me anything helpful. I took a breath. 'Yes.'

Jacob sat across from Brittany and me in the small coffee shop in town, rocking a pair of dark shades and the bowler hat from his Halloween costume. The three of us had skipped history. It had been his idea, and honestly, I was way too wired to be sitting in class. Besides, the only class I'd missed all semester had been the first day of astronomy. Skipping one more time, even if it was my major, couldn't be that big of a crime.

He groaned as he sipped his latte. 'Whoever let me drink as much as I did last night should be smacked in the face.'

I glanced at Brit as I picked at my chocolate chip scone. She shot him a sheepish look. 'Well, you let me spend "quality time" with Jimmie, so whatever.'

'And how did that go?' he asked, sliding his glasses down and pinning her with bloodshot eyes. 'You looked like you were walking a little funny to the car.'

Brit snorted. 'Yeah, you're giving Jimmie way too much credit. I left with you and when Jimmie did text me later, because hello, why wouldn't he? I didn't answer. I was a good girl.'

'Good, because if the guy isn't making you walk funny after sex, then he probably isn't anything to write home to Mom about.' Jacob shifted his gaze to me. 'But you, missy, I'm still ticked at you.'

'So am I,' Brit joined in, smacking my arm as I reached for my hot chocolate. 'You scared the shit out of me last night. I thought you had been kidnapped.'

'I really am sorry for that. I went home and left my phone in the car.' When I thought she wouldn't whack me again, I wrapped my fingers around my cup. 'I do feel terrible. I didn't want either of you to worry.'

'Well, we did …' He grinned. 'When we realized you were missing. That took about an hour or so.'

Brit made a face as she nodded. 'That's true. So if you *had been* kidnapped, well, that would've sucked.'

I laughed, almost choking on my drink. 'Wow. I don't know if I should feel less guilty now.'

'Yeah, we're shitty friends.' Jacob sat back, tipping his hat up. 'Except we totally redeemed ourselves by involving Cam.'

My heart did that cartwheel again.

'We really thought you were with him,' Brit said, sneaking a piece of my scone. 'That's why it took us so long, but then we saw him coming out of one of the rooms with Jase and Ollie.'

'He was really worried when we asked if he'd seen you.' Jacob rubbed the skin above his brows. 'He went right out of there with Ollie and started looking for your car.'

Brit nodded as she eyed my scone. 'It was kind of romantic, especially since you weren't lying dead anywhere.'

I laughed as I slid the scone toward her.

'And then he rushed off, like a knight in shining armor, leaving the party and one very unhappy Little Skanky Red Riding Hood behind.' Brit dug into the scone happily. 'Seriously, Avery, I know you're saying you're not taking

160

hard to get to a whole new level, but you need to go out with him.'

'I am,' I said quietly, holding on to my hot chocolate.

'Because he's not going to keep asking,' she continued blithely. 'He's going to move on and you're going to be sitting in your apartment, crying your little heart out and—'

'Brit, shut it for a second.' Jacob leaned forward and slid his sunglasses down. 'Wait. Did you just say you were going out with him?'

'Yeah.' Now my heart did a backflip. Just talking about it filled me with an absurd amount of nervousness. 'He asked me again and I said yes.'

Brit lowered my scone from her mouth, her eyes wide. 'What? When did this happen?'

'Last night,' I answered.

'When he left to check on you?' Jacob asked.

I nodded.

'Holy shit,' Brit whispered. 'You're going out with Cam.'

'On a date,' I added. 'It's really not that big of a deal.'

Of course, it was a big deal to me. This would be my first date—this was huge. No way was I sharing that little tidbit with them. It was bad enough that Cam already knew that embarrassing secret.

'I would be clapping like a seal right now if I weren't so fucking hungover, just so you know. Inside, I am doing happy jumping jacks for you with glittery pom-poms.' Jacob laughed at the face I made. 'It's about time. He's only been asking you out for …?'

I shrugged. 'Not that long.'

Brit gaped at me and a piece of scone hit the table, causing me to giggle. 'He's been asking you out since the end of August. It is the first day of November, Avery, just in case you can't tell time. Most guys don't even remember a girl's name for that length of time.'

My brows rose.

'It's true,' Jacob commented. 'I forget your name about once a week.'

I laughed.

'So when are you guys going out?' she asked, tugging her ponytail down and then redoing it. 'What are you doing?'

I was pretty sure that my heart was now doing the jumping jacks that Jacob claimed were going on inside him. 'We're not going out until next weekend. He's got a paper he's got to write this weekend and he's already got plans with Ollie—something about one of those mixed martial arts fights on pay-per-view.' Cam had invited me to come over then, but it seemed like it was a guy night. 'I think we're going to some restaurant in Hagerstown next Saturday.'

Brit's eyes lit up. 'Oh, my God, girl, we so have tons of time to get ready.'

'I need a week to get ready?'

Her head bobbed vigorously. 'You've got to get your hair done, your nails done, and then you should get waxed, you know, down—'

'All right, when you guys start talking about waxing unmentionable places, that's my cue to get the hell out of here.' Jacob grabbed his bag and stood. Stopping by me, he kissed my cheek. 'Seriously, it's about time.'

My cheeks warmed and I murmured 'Thanks' but didn't really know why because it seemed like a weird time to say thank you.

After Jacob stumbled out the door, Brit picked up her cup. 'Serious moment?'

'Okay.' I figured I was about to get a detailed lesson on Brazilian waxes and prepared myself.

Brit twisted toward me and when she spoke, her voice

was uncharacteristically low. 'Last night at the party, when that guy tried to dance with you …'

Uh-oh. My stomach shot straight to my toes. 'Yeah?'

'What happened between you two?' She wetted her lips. 'I saw him grabbing you.'

I looked away, swallowing against the sudden nauseous feeling. 'That's all he did. He just surprised me and I over-reacted. I feel like a total idiot.'

Brit sucked her lip between her teeth as she watched me. 'Not that some guy grabbing you is cool—because it's not, and although it freaking happens at parties all the time, it's really annoying—' She paused. 'Why did you overreact?'

Shifting in my chair, I slid my hands over my thighs. 'Like I said, I was just surprised. He caught me off guard.'

'He caught you off guard …' she repeated and then took a deep breath. 'Okay. I'm going to be real with you. That's what friends do, right?'

Unease rose swiftly, snaking its way through me. 'Right.'

There was a pause. 'I saw your face, Avery. You were scared out of your mind. It wasn't just being caught off guard or because you don't go to parties. And I'm not trying to be ignorant by saying this, so please God don't take it that way, but that's not a normal reaction.'

Not a normal reaction. Didn't I know that? I glanced at her, and all of a sudden I wanted to tell her the truth—tell her everything. The need was inexplicable and rode me hard. It came up, making it to the tip of my tongue. Years' worth of silence hung in the air between us. Brit waited with an open look etched upon her face, and already, before I even opened my mouth, I could see it in her eyes and in the taut pull around her lips. She wasn't stupid. She suspected some-thing, maybe even the worst. Sympathy, maybe even pity, shone in her eyes.

163

'Did … did something happen to you, Avery?' she asked quietly.

The need to tell her, to tell *someone*, deflated like a balloon with a tiny pinprick in it. My gaze shifted to the window and beyond, to the congested street outside. I shook my head. 'No, nothing has happened to me.'

Chapter 15

Brit didn't bring the conversation up again after that morning in the coffee shop, and as Jacob had promised, the following day he'd been excessively excited—jumping, clapping, doing a little dance—over the upcoming date with Cam. One would think Jacob was actually going out with him.

I tried not to obsess over the date, as impossible as that was. Even harder to not think about it every time I was around Cam. Nothing had changed between us, but in a way, everything had. When he sat beside me in class, I became absurdly aware of him. Each time he moved and his leg or arm brushed mine, a prickling sensation would wash over my entire body and would last the rest of the hour. I wasn't sure if he noticed and I really hoped he didn't.

Over the next week, an early deep freeze had settled over the Panhandle. The trees were bare and the wind off the Potomac rattled them like hollow, dry bones, and it had been a long time since I'd been in this kind of weather. No matter how much I bundled up, I felt like I was in Alaska every time I walked to class.

The Friday before the 'big night' Cam was in an odd mood, actually taking notes in class.

'Look at you,' I murmured as Professor Drage flipped through pictures of the Milky Way on the projector. 'You're paying attention.'

Cam sent me a sidelong glance. 'I always pay attention.'

'Uh-huh.'

He twirled his pen between his fingers, keeping his eyes glued to Drage. 'You'd fail if it weren't for me.'

My lips curved up. 'I'd be able to concentrate more if it weren't for you.'

'Is that so?' He leaned in so that his shoulder pressed into mine. Watching the front of the class for a moment, he then turned. When he spoke, his lips brushed my temple, causing heat to rise to my skin. 'Why do you find me so distracting, sweetheart?'

'Not the reason you think,' I said, which was a lie.

'Keep telling yourself that.'

'One day your ego is going to make your head implode.'

'I doubt that day will ever come,' he replied, and then he trailed the edge of his pen across the back of my right hand, right up to the edge of my sweater. 'Is that distracting?'

At a total loss for words, my fingers stilled around my pen.

'Is it?' The pen moved back down my hand, over my knuckles. 'Did you pick up how many stars make up Orion's belt? No?' The pen was on the move again, and who knew a pen could be so … so sensual. 'There are three stars that make up the belt, sweetheart.'

I bit down on my lip.

A soft, low rumble emanated from his chest. 'That's fucking distracting,' he murmured, 'whenever you do that.'

My eyes widened as the air pushed from my lungs.

He chuckled deeply, and a delicate shiver coursed down my spine. 'You know what?'

'What?' I whispered.

Cam shifted closer, acting like he was stretching. I tensed, having no idea what he was up to. His arm came behind me and then his lips were warm and firm against my skin, below my ear. A pulse shot through me, unnerving and something else—something exciting.

His lips curved against me, and I shuddered. 'I cannot wait for tomorrow night.'

Sucking in a deep breath, I closed my eyes. Cam chuckled again and settled back in his seat, eyes on the front of the class, pen scribbling across his notebook. I was so done with class. Nothing was getting through the fog that was my brain now, and I was so, so incredibly in over my head with him.

Brit and I spent Saturday afternoon getting our nails done. It had been so long since I'd had a manicure and a pedicure that I forgot how incredibly bored I got during the procedures and how once there was wet nail polish gleaming on my nails, I wanted to touch everything I laid eyes on.

'Are you nervous?' Brit asked as she wiggled her hot pink toenails.

Resisting the urge to pull my hands out from the lamps and through my hair, I nodded vigorously. 'Yes, I'm nervous. Does that make me lame? Because if so, I am the queen of lame right now.'

She giggled. 'I don't think so. Being nervous means you're excited. Hell, I'm excited! I'm so living vicariously through you. You have to call me immediately afterward tonight.' A sly look crossed her face. 'Unless tonight turns into tomorrow …'

My mouth dropped open.

Another fit of giggles took her as she pressed back in her chair. 'Okay. I doubt that's going to happen, but you need to call me right away. I have to know if he's a good kisser.'

'How do you know if we're going to kiss?'

'Seriously?' she said, gaping at me. 'He's so going to kiss you.'

My stomach did the dipping thing. 'Maybe not.'

'Oh, no, he's going to kiss you. He's probably going to want to do lots, lots more, but he'll kiss you. I just know it.' Brit let out a squeal that brought a nervous grin to my face. 'I bet he's an awesome kisser.'

If I had to base his kissing skills off what I already knew of him, I'd have to say he was probably a great kisser, especially if he could have me damn near squirming in my seat just by running a pen along my hand. It was like foreplay … with a pen.

I giggled.

After the mani and pedi, Brit made me promise once more that I'd call her as soon as I could after my date, and then I headed back to my apartment. Careful with my shiny purple nails, I took the longest shower of my life and then went through my entire closet. Every time I looked at the time and saw it getting closer and closer to seven, I felt my heart throw itself against my ribs like it was just about to climb out of my chest.

I had my whole freaking closet on my bed and half on my floor. Seemed kind of stupid to be this indecisive about what to wear, but I honestly had no idea. Finally, after almost breaking down and calling Brit for advice, I settled on a pair of skinny jeans tucked into black boots and a deep green cap-sleeve blouse that was a little dressy and flirty.

I spent the same amount of time on my makeup and hair, just as bad as it had been when he'd come over to watch movies. It struck me funny as I applied mascara that I'd be this concerned with my appearance when he always saw me looking like a ragamuffin on Sundays when he came over to cook eggs.

Oh my God, tomorrow was Sunday, which was a big duh, because that day always came after Saturday, but tomorrow would be a different Sunday. It would be the first one after our date. Would we still be doing eggs? What if the date did end up turning into a tomorrow morning thing? I wasn't naive. Cam could easily expect that this date was going to lead somewhere.

In my reflection, my eyes were unnaturally wide in the mirror, and the mascara wand was dangerously close to my eyeball.

The date was so not leading to my bedroom, because it looked like Old Navy had thrown up in there.

Okay. I was being stupid. Tomorrow would be no different from today. Tonight was not going to become a sex-fueled all-nighter for several reasons. And there was no reason for me to act like I had no idea that Sunday was the day after Saturday.

Finishing my little come-to-Jesus pep talk, I forced myself out of the bathroom. The nervous excitement humming through my veins wasn't a bad feeling. It was quite ... different, like a good kind of anxiousness. I was literally two seconds away from doing a little ass-shaking jig in the middle of my living room when Cam showed up.

He stepped into my apartment, his gaze starting at the top of my head and making it all the way down to the pointy tips of my black boots. Amazing how a look could feel like a touch, and I felt it in a way that put my earlier edginess to shame.

Cam cleared his throat. 'You look ... really, really great.'

I flushed. 'Thank you. So do you.'

And that was the freaking truth. Cam was just in dark jeans and a black V-neck sweater that stretched across his broad shoulders; with his dark hair tumbling over his fore-head and the slight half grin on his face, he was absolutely stunning. So much so, I sort of wondered what I was doing here, about to go out on a date with him.

'You ready? Got a jacket?'

Snapping out of it, I nodded and raced back to my bedroom, nearly eating the floor when my heel snagged in a sweater. I grabbed my coat and slid it on as I joined him. Amusement glimmered in his eyes as he picked my purse up off the back of the couch. Feeling about nine kinds of awkward, I thanked him.

'Ready,' I said, breathless.

'Not quite yet.' Cam reached out and started pushing the large buttons on my coat through the holes. 'It's freezing outside.'

I just stood there, absolutely still and enthralled by the simple act. He'd started at the bottom and as he worked his way up, my pulse thudded. I held my breath as he neared my chest. The sides of his hands brushed across the front of my coat and I stiffened. Layers of clothing vanished as an unexpected jolt of heat shot to the tips of my breasts.

'Perfect,' he murmured. Through his lashes, his eyes were a heated, startling blue. 'Now we're ready.'

All I could do was stare at him for a moment, and then I had to force my legs, which felt wobbly, forward. The moment we stepped out into the hall, Cam's apartment door flung open.

Ollie appeared, a cell phone in one hand and Raphael wiggling in the other. 'Smile!' he shouted as he snapped a picture on his phone. 'It's like my two kids are going to prom.'

Both Cam and I were dumbstruck.

Ollie beamed. 'Putting this in my scrapbook. Have fun!' He popped back into their apartment, closing the door behind him.

'Um ...'

170

Cam laughed loudly. 'Oh God, that was different.'

'He doesn't normally do that?'

'No.' He laughed again, putting his hand on my lower back. 'Let's get out of here before he tries to go along with us.'

I grinned. 'With Raphael?'

'Raphael would be welcomed. Ollie, however, would not be.' He grinned as we hit the steps. 'The last thing I'd want is for you to be distracted on this date.'

Distracted? I already was.

Chapter 16

By the time the bread arrived with our drinks and was placed on the glossy square table between us, I'd gotten better control of my breathing. The nervousness had returned in the truck ride to the restaurant, though Cam didn't seem to notice and was completely at ease.

I spent way too much time poring over the menu as I resisted the urge to start chewing on my pretty nails.

Cam nudged me under the table with his foot and I looked up. 'What?'

He nodded to my left, and I saw the waiter standing there with a smile. 'Oh, um, can I get the ...' I picked the first thing my eyes centered on. 'Stuffed chicken marsala?'

The waiter scribbled that down and then Cam ordered a steak, medium rare with a side salad and baked potato. When the waiter left, Cam went for the bread. 'Want a piece?'

'Sure.' I hoped I didn't choke on it. I watched him slice a piece in half and then butter it up. 'Thank you.'

He arched a brow but said nothing as I nibbled the bread, a tiny piece at a time. I racked my brain for something, anything to say. It didn't even have to be interesting. I just needed to speak. For some reason, the conversation he'd had with Ollie resurfaced and I latched on to it. 'Do you play any sports?'

Cam blinked as if caught off guard.

I flushed. 'Sorry. That's really random.'

'It's okay.' He chewed the bread slowly. 'I used to play.'

Thankful that he was playing along, I relaxed a little. 'What sport?'

He cut off another slice of bread. 'I played soccer.'

'Really?' Why were all soccer players hot? Was it some kind of universal law of soccer? 'What position?'

Even though I knew Cam probably suspected I didn't know squat about soccer, he went along with it. 'I was a striker, which is a middle player position.'

'Oh!' I nodded like I had a clue what any of that meant.

Cam flashed that dimple. 'That means I did a lot of scoring.'

'So you were good?'

'I was decent. Had to be fast, so a lot of running.'

That's pretty much all I knew about soccer—a lot of running. 'Did you play in high school?'

'High school, rec league, and my first year of college.'

I dared another bite of bread. So far so good. 'Why'd you stop?'

Cam opened his mouth, but then closed it. Staring over my shoulder, several moments passed before he shrugged. 'Just not something I wanted to do anymore.'

I was the queen of giving evasive answers, so I knew one when I heard one. And I so wanted to dig deeper and find out more, but I had given the same lame answer when he'd asked me about dancing. I wasn't really in the position to push.

His ultrabright gaze settled on me and in the dim lighting,

I felt my face turn a deeper shade of pink. Jesus, I needed to stop blushing.

He chuckled, and I wanted to throw my bread in his face. 'Avery ...'

'Cam?'

He leaned over onto the table and the small candle in the center sent dancing shadows across his face. 'You don't have to be so nervous.'

'I'm not.'

His brows rose.

I sighed. 'Okay. I am. Sorry.'

'Why are you apologizing? You don't need to. This is your first date.'

'Thanks for reminding me,' I muttered.

His lips twitched as if he wished to smile. 'It's not a bad thing. You're going to be nervous.'

'You're not.'

'That's because I'm awesome.'

I rolled my eyes.

He laughed, and the sound was deep and rich. 'You just don't have to be. I want to be here with you, Avery. You don't have to worry about impressing me or wowing me. You've already done that.'

'That's ...' I shook my head, ignoring the lump in my throat. I stared at him. 'You're just so ... I don't know. You just know what to say to ...'

'To?'

I tucked my hair back and then dropped my hand in my lap. It was shaking. 'You just say the right stuff.'

'It's because I'm—'

'Awesome,' I supplied. 'I know that.'

Cam leaned back. 'I wasn't going to say that, but I'm glad you're starting to realize my awesomeness.'

'Then what were you going to say?'

'That I said that because it's true and I want to.'

'Why me?' I blurted out, and then closed my eyes briefly. 'Okay. Don't answer that.'

The food arrived just then—thank God—and the conversation was deterred … for about two minutes. 'I'm going to answer that question,' Cam said, peering at me through his lashes.

I wanted to face-plant in my stuffed chicken. 'You don't have to.'

'No, I think I do.'

Clenching my silverware, I drew in a deep breath. 'I know it's a stupid question to ask, but you're gorgeous, Cam. You're nice and you're funny. You're smart. I've been turning you down for two months. You could go out with anyone, but you're here with me.'

'Yes, I am.'

'With the girl who's never been out on a date before,' I added, looking at him dead-on. 'It just doesn't seem real.'

'Okay.' He cut off a piece of steak. 'I'm here with you because I want to be—because I like you. Ah—let me finish. I've already told you. You're different—in a good way, so get that look off your face.'

My eyes narrowed.

He grinned. 'And I'll admit, some of the times I asked you out, I knew you weren't going to say yes. And maybe while I wasn't always being serious when I did, I was always serious about wanting to take you out. You get that?'

Um, not really, but I nodded.

'And I like hanging out with you.' He popped a piece of steak into his mouth. 'And hey, I think I'm a pretty damn good catch for your first date.'

'Oh my God.' I laughed. 'I can't believe you just said you were a good catch.'

176

He shrugged one shoulder. 'I am. Now eat your chicken before I do.'

Smiling, I started to pick it apart, going for the stuffed part first. With the exception of asking a stupid question, my first date was going well. Cam started steering the questions and I wasn't a mute just sitting here. Though, every so often, our gazes would lock and I'd forget what I was doing or completely lose track of what he was saying. But I was having a good time—I was enjoying myself and Cam. And the best part? I wasn't thinking beyond right now. I was just … *here*, and it was a nice place to be.

Toward the end of dinner, Cam asked, 'So what are you doing for Thanksgiving? Going back home to Texas?'

I snorted. 'No.'

His brows knitted. 'You're not going home?'

Finishing off my chicken, I shook my head. 'I'm staying here. Are you going home?'

'I'm going home, not sure exactly when.' He picked up his glass. 'You're seriously not going home at all? It's more than a week—nine days. You have time.'

'My parents … are traveling, so I'm staying here.' That wasn't a huge lie. Around this time of year, between Thanksgiving and Christmas, my parents took cruises or went on ski trips. 'Do your parents do the big Thanksgiving dinner?'

'Yeah,' he murmured, his gaze falling to his empty plate.

Conversation lulled a little at that point, and as the check arrived, Cam didn't seem like he wanted to linger. Outside, the night air was beyond chilly and our breaths formed puffy, misty white clouds. A fierce wind kicked up, picking up my hair and throwing it around my face. I shivered and hunkered down in my jacket.

'Cold?'

'It's not Texas,' I admitted.

177

Cam chuckled and stepped closer, dropping his arm over my shoulders. His body warmth immediately slipped over mine, and I worked hard at not tensing and falling flat on my ass. 'Better?' he asked.

All I could do was nod.

Once in the truck and out of the brutal wind, I buckled myself in. Cam climbed in, started the engine, and then smacked his hands together, rubbing them. He glanced over at me. 'Did you have a good dinner?'

'Yes. And thank you for the food. I mean, dinner. Thank you,' I stumbled over my words, closing my eyes. 'Thank you.'

'You're welcome.' Amusement colored his tone. 'Thank you for finally agreeing to let me take you out.'

He turned the radio on after that, not loud enough that we couldn't talk, but I was too busy focusing on important stuff. Somewhere between Hagerstown and University Heights, I had made an extremely important decision.

If Cam kissed me, I would not freak.

Nope. Nope. Nope.

I would act like a fucking nineteen-year-old girl with an iota of experience and not freak. Then again, he might not kiss me. He might've realized at some point during our date that I wasn't kiss-worthy and hightail his ass back to his apartment to hang out with Ollie and Raphael. And if so, that would be okay. I *would* be okay with that.

But when we got back to our apartment building and as we reached the fifth floor, I realized I didn't want the night to be over yet. We stopped in front of my door, and I turned to face him, twisting my fingers along the strap of my purse.

His lips quirked up on one side. 'So …'

'Would you like to come in? For something to drink? I have coffee or hot chocolate.' Hot chocolate? Seriously? Was

I twelve? Fuck me. 'I don't have any beer or anything more—'

'Hot chocolate would be good,' he cut in. 'Only if you have the kind with those tiny marshmallows.'

My lips spread into a smile and I didn't care how big or goofy it looked. 'I do.'

'Then lead the way, sweetheart.'

Heart pumping, I let us into my apartment and turned on the lamp beside the couch. Shedding my jacket, I headed into the kitchen. Cam sat on the couch while I whipped us up some hot chocolate. While the water heated up, I yanked off my shoes. I brought two steaming cups back.

'Thank you.' He took one. 'Got a question for you.'

'Okay.' I sat facing him, tucking my legs under me.

He took a sip. 'So based on your first date experience, would you go out on a second?'

A pleasant feeling hummed in my chest. 'Like a second in general?'

'In general.'

I shrugged and then tried some of my hot chocolate. 'Well, this was a very good first date. If second dates were like this, then I guess I would.'

'Hmm. With just anyone or …?'

My lashes lowered. 'Not with just anyone.'

'So it would have to be someone in particular?'

The pleasant feeling spread into my limbs. 'I think it would have to be.'

'Interesting,' he murmured, taking another drink. When he looked at me, his eyes positively twinkled. Christ. I was screwed. Eyes were twinkling at me. 'Is this someone in particular going to have to wait another two months if he asks you out?'

I couldn't fight the smile, so I took a drink. 'Depends.'

'On?'

179

'My mood.'

Cam chuckled. 'Get ready.'

'Okay.'

'I'm going to ask you out again—not dinner, because I like to change things up. It's to the movies.'

I pretended to think about it, but I already knew I'd say yes. Might be a dumb move or pointless, but I wanted to go out on another date with him. 'Movies?'

He nodded. 'But it's a drive-in movie, one of the last ones around.'

'Outside?'

'Yep.' His grin spread. 'Don't worry. I'd keep you warm.'

I didn't know if I should giggle or tell him that last statement was kind of adorably corny. 'Okay.'

His brows rose. 'Okay to the movies?'

Biting down on my lip, I nodded.

'Seriously, it isn't going to take me another two months?'

I shook my head.

Cam looked away, laughing under his breath. 'Okay. How about Wednesday?'

'This Wednesday?'

'Nope.'

I sat my hot chocolate down on the coffee table. 'The following Wednesday?'

'Yep.'

Counting the days down, I ended up frowning. 'Wait. That's the Wednesday before Thanksgiving.'

'It is.'

I stared at him. 'Cam, aren't you going home?'

'I am.'

'When? After the movies, in the middle of the night, or Thanksgiving morning?'

He shook his head. 'See, the drive-in movie theater is just outside of my hometown. About ten miles out.'

I leaned back against the couch, confused. 'I don't understand.'

Cam finished off the hot chocolate and twisted toward me. He scooted over so only a handful of inches separated us. 'If you go on this date with me, you're going to have to go home with me.'

'What?' I shrieked, sitting up straight. 'Go home with you?'

He pressed his lips together and nodded his head.

'Are you serious?'

'Serious as my pierced eardrum,' he said. 'Come home with me. We'll have fun.'

'Go home with you—to your parents' house? Basically for Thanksgiving?' When he nodded again, I smacked him on the arm. 'Don't be stupid, Cam.'

'I'm not being stupid. I'm being serious. My parents won't mind.' He paused, nose wrinkling. 'Actually, they'd probably be happy to see someone other than me. And my mom likes to cook way too much food. The more mouths, the better.'

There were no words.

'We can leave whenever you want, but obviously before Wednesday afternoon. You finishing the rest of your hot chocolate?' When I shook my head, he grabbed my cup. 'And we can come back whenever.'

I watched him drink the rest of my hot chocolate. 'I can't go with you.'

He raised his brows. 'Why not?'

'Because of a hundred obvious reasons, Cam. Your parents are going to think—'

'They're not going to think anything.'

I shot him a look.

He sighed. 'Okay. Look at it this way. It's better than you sitting home, by yourself, all week. What are you going to do? Sit around and read? And miss me, because you're going to miss me. And then I'm going to have spend most of my time texting you and feeling bad that you're sitting home, all alone, and can't even eat McDonald's because they're closed on Thanksgiving.'

'I don't want you to feel sorry for me. It's not a big deal. I have no problem staying here.'

'I don't want you sitting here alone, and you're making this into a big deal. I'm a *friend* asking a *friend* to come hang out with me over Thanksgiving break.'

'You're a *friend* who just took a *friend* out on a date!'

'Ah,' he said, sitting my cup down. 'That's a good point.'

Shaking my head, I picked up a pillow, holding it to my chest. 'I can't do that. Visiting family over the holidays? That's way too—'

'Fast?' he supplied.

'Yes. Way too fast.'

'Well, then, I guess it's a good thing that we're not seeing each other, because, yes, it would be too fast if that was the case.'

'What the what?'

Cam pulled the pillow away and tossed it behind him. 'You and I are two friends who went out on one date. Maybe two if you come with me. We're not dating each other. We're just friends who had one date. So we will be going back to my house as friends.'

My head was spinning. 'You make no sense.'

'I make perfect sense. We haven't even kissed, Avery. We're just friends.'

I gaped at him.

He shrugged one shoulder. 'Come home with me, Avery. I promise you it won't be uncomfortable. My parents would be happy to have you. You will have a good time and it will be better than what you'd end up doing here. And nothing, absolutely nothing is expected from you. Okay?'

182

The word no formed on my tongue, but for some reason it didn't come out of my mouth. My thoughts raced from vaguely entertaining the idea to flat out telling him he was insane. Go home with him? That was … way better than spending Thanksgiving here alone. It had been bad enough when I did live at home and my parents skipped out of town without me, but at least the maid made me a turkey dinner. Mrs. Gibson. She'd baked me a turkey for the last three years. And was McDonald's really closed? Man, that sucked. But going home with Cam was insane. His reasoning made no sense whatsoever. It was like backward logic or something. It was reckless and just so unlike anything I'd ever do.

Unlike anything I'd ever do.

I looked up, meeting his steady gaze. His eyes … were such an astonishing shade of blue. Was I really considering this? My heart started thumping in my chest. I swallowed. 'Your parents really would be okay with this?'

Something glinted in his eyes. 'I've brought friends home before.'

'Girls?'

He shook his head.

Well, that … that was interesting. 'And your parents are really going to think we're just friends?'

'Why would I have a reason to tell them we weren't dating if we were? If I say we're friends, that's what they'll think.'

Every logical part of me was screaming no. 'Okay. I'll go home with you.' Once the words were out, I couldn't take them back. 'This is an insane idea.'

'It's a perfect idea.' A slow smile spread across his lips. 'Let's hug on it.'

'What?'

'Hug on it.' That glint in his eyes went up a notch. 'Once you hug on it, you can't go back on it.'

'Oh my God, are you serious?'

'Very serious.'

Rolling my eyes, I grumbled as I rose onto my knees and stretched my arms out. 'All right, let's hug to seal our deal before I change—' My words ended in a squeak as Cam's arms went around my waist and he tugged me over to him. I ended up sitting right next to him, practically on him, with my left leg tangled between his knees.

Cam hugged me. It wasn't a tight one, not like it would've been if we were standing, but the fact we were so close this way had such a powerful effect on me. 'Deal is sealed, sweetheart. Thanksgiving is at the Hamiltons'.'

I said something to the affirmative and as I pulled back a little, our faces were perfectly lined up. And I suddenly understood that glint in his eyes. 'You …'

He chuckled, and low in my stomach, muscles tightened. 'Smooth move, huh? Got you all the way over here. I would've taken you on your word.'

I was fighting a grin. 'You're so wrong.'

'I'm wrong in all the right ways. I have to admit something.' He regained that tiny distance I'd put between us. His lips brushed my cheek, and I found it hard to concentrate. 'I lied earlier.'

'About what?'

His hands slid to my lower back. 'When I said you looked great? I wasn't being completely honest.'

That was not what I expected. I turned my head the slightest and then bit back a gasp. Our mouths were *centimeters* apart and I thought about Brit's certainty that he would kiss me tonight. I forced my tongue to work. 'You don't think I look great?'

'No,' he said, his expression serious as one hand followed the line of my spine, resting below the edges of my hair. He lowered his head so that his temple pressed against mine. 'You look beautiful tonight.'

My breath caught. 'Thank you.'

He didn't say anything as he shifted his head. His lips brushed the curve of my cheek, and I stiffened in his arms. My heart was thundering with excitement and a different kind of emotion. Fear? Was that what I tasted in the back of my throat? It had come out of nowhere, raw and powerful. The mixture of the two, the need to stay where I was and to pull away, was consuming.

Cam's lips swept over the hollow of my cheek, and then his nose brushed mine. His breath was warm against my lips and smelled of sweet chocolate. Would it taste that way? The curiosity rose and I reached up, putting my hands on his biceps.

'Avery?'

My eyes drifted shut. 'What?'

'You've never been kissed before, right?'

My pulse exploded. 'No.'

'Just so we're clear,' he said. 'This isn't a kiss.'

I opened my mouth, and then his lips were on mine. A sweet sweeping of his lips across mine, breathtakingly tender and soft, and way too quick.

'You kissed me,' I gasped, my fingers digging into his sweater.

'That wasn't a kiss.' His lips brushed mine as he spoke. Shivers raced up and down my spine. 'Remember? If we've kissed, then that means you going home with me could potentially mean something more serious.'

'Oh. Okay.'

'This is also not a kiss.'

The press of his lips the second time consumed me, awakened me. His mouth was all I could think about, all I wanted to think about. A wonderful warmth slipped down my neck, spreading across my chest, and then lower, between my thighs. He kissed me gently, tracing the pattern of my lips

185

with his own. Something deep inside me was rising, opening, and aching. I clung to him as he shifted, and I was suddenly on my back.

Cam hovered over me, the powerful muscles of his arms flexing under my hands. His mouth was still on mine. No other part of our bodies touched and I wasn't sure if I should be relieved or disappointed by that. But his lips … oh, God, his lips moved against mine. I started to kiss him back, slower and clumsy where he had been sure, practiced. I was worried I was doing it wrong, but then a deep sound came from him, almost a growl, and instinctively I knew it was a sound of approval. A shudder rocked its way down my body. The ache was spreading, intensifying, and it was terrifying in its own way.

His kiss deepened, coaxing my lips to open to his. My senses spun as his tongue slipped in, licking over mine. I gasped at the sensation, and his tongue delved deeply. I fell into the kiss, my fingers clenching and my neck arching. He tasted of chocolate and man, and I was coming out of my skin as lust stirred in the pit of my stomach, followed by a burst of fluttery panic. That was smoothed away as his tongue flicked along the roof of my mouth. When he lifted his head again, he caught my lower lip between his teeth and a pleased whimper escaped me. Both of us were breathing heavily.

'Still not a kiss?' I asked.

Cam sat back, pulling me up into a sitting position. His eyes were that intense blue, hot and searing. I felt flushed all over. My chest rose and fell rapidly. My hands were still attached to his arms. He reached up, tracing the line of my lower lip, and then he leaned in again.

'No, that wasn't a kiss.' His lips brushed mine in the most tantalizing, promising way. 'That was a good night.'

Chapter 17

Long after Cam had left, I lay awake in bed. This sleepless night was different from all others. Blew them right out of the water. My body felt foreign to me, achy and way too hot. I pushed the comforter off me, and the thin sheet still abraded my skin. I rolled onto my side, biting down on my lips as my thighs squeezed together.

I hated Cam.

Not really.

But I hated him for his 'good night,' and for leaving, and for me being strung so tight that every time I shifted, my ultrasensitive skin demanded more.

More.

I didn't hate Cam.

Flopping onto my back, I shoved the sheet down. Cool air washed over my bare arms and across my chest. Underneath my cotton tank top, the tips of my breasts hardened and tingled, to the point that it went beyond annoying and straight into almost painful territory.

I brought my knees up, and a moan escaped my parted lips as the pressure pulsed from between my thighs to my breasts. Straightening my legs, I clenched the fitted sheet under me and tried to empty my thoughts, but all I could think about was Cam's kiss, the way his lips felt against mine, how his tongue had been wet and warm inside my mouth. I could still taste the chocolate, and I could still feel his muscles flexing under my hands. My breath caught at the phantom touch the memory of the backs of his hands brushing my breasts provoked.

What I was feeling was entirely new to me. It was like Cam's kiss had thrown a switch in my body, but I wasn't stupid. I wasn't naive or so inexperienced to not realize that I was turned on. My body had been woken up, like Sleeping Beauty coming out of her deep slumber, and my body demanded more.

My hand fluttered to my stomach and I jumped. Along my throat, my pulse kicked up, my heart stuttered. Between my thighs, the ache intensified. My eyes flew open and fixed on the dark ceiling. I held my breath as I slid my hand down. It was like an out-of-body experience, like I really didn't have control of what I was doing.

I closed my eyes as I slipped my hand under the loose band of my sleep shorts. The muscles in my belly tightened, my breath quickened. The edges of my fingers reached the bundle of nerves down there and a shot of pure electricity lit through my veins. I bit down on my lip to stop the cry building in my throat. Heart now pounding, my fingers slid through the wetness that had gathered there.

Part of me couldn't believe I was doing this.

I couldn't believe that it took *this* long to do this.

But I was beyond the point of stopping. In my mind, the image of Cam appeared. His blue eyes on fire with heat and his mouth against mine, coaxing me open, heavenly patient and yet determined. My fingers fumbled, because I really had no idea what I was doing, but it seemed to be working. I stroked myself and it felt good, but all it seemed to do was flame the fire, making it burn hotter. I felt swollen and I was sure I was going to scream my head off if the aching grew any more.

I caught my lower lip between my teeth. My finger flicked back and forth before I drew in a deep breath and pushed in. A gasp escaped me as tension coiled. Okay. That was good. I pushed a little deeper and the pressure of my palm against the apex sent another jolt through me. My hips jerked and the burning in my core spread. Instinct seemed to have taken over. My hips rocked in a tiny circle, and the tension built deeper and deeper. The noise that came out of my throat would've embarrassed me if anyone had ever heard it, but right now, in the darkness of my room, it made me hotter.

My hips ground against my hand, and it felt like a cord was being pulled into a tight knot deep inside me. I could feel it and I knew that it was coming, seconds away. In an instant, I pictured Cam doing this—*his* hand, *his* fingers, and that was it. A moan erupted from deep inside my body as the cord unraveled, whipping through my body and scattering all my thoughts.

As my heart rate returned to normal and the trembles subsided, I collapsed back against the pillows, arms and legs shaking. Holy crap, so that was what that felt like? I rolled onto my side, my lips spreading into a weak grin. The pillow muffled my throaty laugh.

Somehow though, even as the pleasant, languid peace invaded my body, carrying me off to sleep, I knew that whatever I had just felt was lacking. That with a guy I wanted to be with—*with Cam*—all of that would've been amplified, and I wanted that.

I wanted to feel that with Cam.

Brit and Jacob were just as surprised as I was that I'd agreed to go home with Cam over Thanksgiving break. I'd been afraid they'd lecture me on how absolutely insane this was, but they hadn't. Both had acted like it was no big deal.

Maybe the crazy was contagious? Besides, they'd been more interested in the other details of the date.

'So is he a good kisser?' Jacob asked.

I glanced around the class, praying that no one was paying attention. The professor hadn't arrived yet, and most looked half asleep.

Brit giggled. 'Tell him what you told me yesterday.'

My cheeks warmed as I thought about what I'd told her on the phone when she'd asked me the same question.

'So he did kiss you?' Jacob's dark eyes widened, but thankfully he kept his voice low.

Clenching my notebook to my chest, I ignored the way Brit bounced in her seat. 'Yes.'

'Tell him,' she whispered.

Jacob nodded. 'Tell me.'

I closed my eyes. 'He's a good kisser—a great kisser.'

'That is not what you said.'

A frown pulled at Jacob's lips. 'Tell me or I'm going to start shouting you kissed—'

'Okay,' I hissed, my entire body heating. The first kiss had been tender and soft. Even the second one had been a controlled exploration, but when I had lain back and he'd hovered over me? The ache was back just thinking about it, and, well, that was awkward being that I was in history class. 'He kissed me like he wanted to … eat me up.'

Brit giggled around her Twizzler.

Jacob's mouth worked for several seconds and then, 'I bet he did.' His brows were raised as he jerked his chin down. 'Like he really wanted to eat—'

'I get what you're saying. Thanks. Back to the important stuff,' I said, placing my notebook on my desk. 'You don't think going home with him is insane?'

Brit shook her head. 'People go home with other people all the time. You know Rachel Adkins, right? She's in your art class. She's going home with Jared instead of flying back out to California.'

'Aren't those two dating?' Jacob asked.

My shoulders slumped.

'Not anymore,' Brit said, pulling another Twizzler from her pack. She pointed the ropey red candy at me. 'They broke up, but she still goes home with him.'

Still didn't make me feel that much better about this. Throughout class, while I nibbled on the Twizzler I'd swiped from Brit's bag, I alternated between paying attention to the lesson on the Middle Ages and wondering if I was really going to go through with this next week.

The truth was that going home with Cam wasn't really even the issue. Yeah, it was about twenty-one flavors of crazy, but a huge part of me was even looking forward to it. I wanted to know more about Cam—to see his family and how he interacted with them. I wanted to know why he quit playing soccer and what he did every Friday night.

And I wanted … I wanted Cam.

In the way I hadn't wanted a guy before, hadn't even thought I'd truly be capable of wanting one. What I felt when he had kissed me was what I was supposed to feel. A tiny bit of panic had been there, was still there, but the curiosity overwhelmed that fear. So did the baffling warmth I felt whenever Cam was near.

There was no doubt in my mind that I wanted to kiss Cam again. I wanted to experience with him what I had after he'd left. Kissing him wasn't the problem. Going home wasn't the problem.

I just didn't know how much of this I was capable of. How far this—whatever it was—would actually go before old fears overshadowed the warmth.

*

191

Over the next week, I talked myself into and out of going with Cam about a million times. Right up to the moment I packed a weekender bag, I wavered back and forth. It wasn't until I was sitting beside him in his truck Wednesday morning that I realized I was really doing this.

'Are you sure your parents are okay with this?'

Cam nodded. I'd only asked the question around a hundred times.

I started nibbling on my thumb. 'And you did actually call them and ask, right?'

He slid me a sideway look. 'No.'

My jaw hit my lap. 'Cam!'

Tipping his head back, he laughed deeply. 'I'm kidding. Chill out, Avery. I told them the day after you said you'd go. They know you're coming, and they're excited to meet you.'

Glaring at him, I went back to chewing on my nail. 'That wasn't funny.'

He laughed again. 'Yes, it was.'

'Jerk.'

'Nerd.'

I stared out the passenger window. 'Bitch-ass.'

'Oh.' Cam whistled. 'Them be fighting words. Keep it up and I'll turn this truck around.'

I grinned as we hit I-70. 'Sounds like a good idea.'

'You'd be distraught and in tears.' There was a pause. He reached over, pulling my hand away from my mouth. 'Stop doing that.'

'Sorry.' I glanced at him. 'It's a bad habit.'

'It is.' He threaded his fingers through mine, and my heart skipped a beat. Our joined hands rested on my thigh, and I wasn't sure what to think about that. 'My sister won't be home until early tomorrow morning. She's doing a show in Pittsburgh tonight.'

'What kind of show?' My gaze flicked from our hands to the window and back again.

'I think it's a ballet recital.'

My attention was focused partly on the weight of his hand in mine. 'Is ballet her favorite?'

'A mix between that and contemporary.'

Contemporary used a lot of ballet and it would make sense that she'd like a mixture of those. Cam eventually let go of my hand, which was a good thing because I was sure my palm was starting to sweat and that was just gross. The two-hour drive went by way too fast. It seemed like only minutes had passed when he got off the interstate and entered a small, hilly town that seemed to have been built into the side of the mountain.

And, boy, were we smack-dab in the middle of Mountaineer Country. Every storefront displayed a WVU flag, as did the porches of the small homes. We continued through the town and out onto country roads that looked like they'd just been paved recently.

I couldn't remember the last time I'd been this nervous. My stomach roiled as Cam slowed and hooked a right onto what looked like a private road crowded with tall oak trees. My mouth was completely dry as he rounded a bend and a large, stately manor came into view.

It wasn't so much that it was a huge house—the thing was big, colonial style, white pillars in the front, and three stories—but that it reminded me of my parents' home. Cold and perfect on the outside and most likely the same on the inside.

Cam followed the driveway behind the house, and I got a closer view of the manicured lawn and beautiful, rustic landscaping. I swallowed, but my throat wasn't really working. He pulled in next to a detached garage that was probably the size of a small ranch-style home. Beyond the garage, I could see a covered in-ground pool.

He turned the engine off and faced me, a slight smile on his face. 'You ready?'

I wanted to scream no and then take off, running straight for the nearby woods, but that seemed like a bit of an overreaction. So I nodded and opened the door, stepping out into temps that were at least ten degrees cooler than back at the apartment. I reached for my bag, but Cam tugged it out along with his much smaller one.

'I can carry it,' I said.

Cam grinned as he glanced at the bag he'd slung over his shoulder. 'I'll carry it. Besides, I think the pink-and-blue flower print looks amazing on me.'

In spite of my nerves, I laughed. 'It's very flattering on you.'

'Thought so.' He waited for me to join him on the other side, and then we started up a slate pathway that led up to a covered patio at the back of the house. He stopped just outside the glass door, beside a wicker chaise longue. 'You look like you're about to have a heart attack.'

I winced. 'That bad?'

'Close.' He stepped closer to me and his hand moved so fast. Tucking my hair back behind my ear, he lowered his head slightly. A look crossed his face, deepening the hue of his eyes until they were the darkest shade of blue. My stomach fluttered in response. 'You have no reason to be nervous, okay? I promise.'

My cheek tingled where his fingers grazed, and as close as we were I thought about our kiss that wasn't a kiss. He hadn't done anything like that since the night of our first date, but right now, I think he wanted to. 'Okay,' I whispered.

He stared at me a moment longer and then shook his head. Dropping his hand, he turned to the door and opened it. A wave of warm air that smelled of apple and spice spilled out, an alluring, welcoming scent. I followed him inside, eyes wide as I took in the room on the lower floor.

It was a game room of sorts. A large pool table sat in the middle, with a stocked bar to the right, and in the back, near the stairs, was a large TV with several comfy-looking chairs in front of it. My parents had something like this, but the pool table had never been used, Mom only drank from the bar when she thought no one was paying attention, and the TV in our basement had never been turned on.

But everything looked … lived in down here.

The balls weren't racked up in the middle, but spread across the table like someone had stopped in the middle of a game. A bottle of scotch sat on the bar top beside a glass, and the chairs were worn, obviously older furniture that had been moved down from upstairs. Unlike my parents who had to have new stuff in every room in the house.

'This is the man cave,' Cam said as he headed for the stairs. 'Dad spends a lot of time down here. There's the poker table he kicked my ass on.'

I looked over to the left, and there was just an average card table sitting there. A small smile pulled at my lips. 'I like it down here.'

'So do I,' he replied. 'Mom and Dad are probably upstairs …'

Nodding, I pulled myself away from the center of the room and trailed behind him. We ended up in a living room that, like the basement, had a well-lived-in feel. A huge sectional couch took up most of the room, placed directly in front of another large TV. Magazines were scattered across the coffee table, and potted plants, rather than weird statues and paintings, filled almost every corner.

'Living room,' Cam commented, going through an archway. 'And this is the second living room or some room that no one sits in. Maybe it's a sitting room? Who knows?

And this is the formal dining room that we never use but have—'

'We do too use the dining room!' came a woman's voice. 'Maybe once or twice a year, when we have company.'

'And break the "good dishes" out,' Cam commented drily.

My legs stopped working at the sound of Cam's mother's voice. I hovered at the end of the table, heart in my throat, as his mother came through the door.

Cam's mom was as tall and striking as he was, with raven-colored hair pulled back in a loose ponytail. Her eyes were brown and free of makeup. Tiny crow's-feet appeared at the corners as a wide smile broke out across her face when she spotted her son. She wore a pair of jeans and a baggy sweater.

She rushed across the room, enveloping him in a hug. 'I don't even know where the "good dishes" are, Cameron.'

He laughed. 'Wherever they are, they're probably hiding from the paper plates.'

Laughing softly, she pulled back. 'Good to have you home. Your father is starting to get on my nerves with all his going-hunting talk.' Her gaze shifted over his shoulders and she smiled welcomingly. 'And this must be Avery?'

'Oh, God, no,' Cam said. 'This is Candy, Mom.'

His mother's eyes widened, and a bit of color infused her cheeks. 'Uh, I'm …'

'I'm Avery,' I said, shooting Cam a look. 'You had it right.'

She spun around, smacking Cam across the arm. Hard, too. 'Cameron! Oh my God, I thought …' She smacked him again and he laughed. 'You're terrible.' Shaking her head, she turned back to me. 'You must be a patient young lady to have survived a trip here with this idiot.'

Thinking I hadn't heard her right, I blinked and then a laugh burst from me as Cam scowled. 'It wasn't that bad.'

'Oh.' His mom glanced over her shoulder at Cam. 'And she's well mannered. It's okay. I know my son is a … handful. By the way, you can call me Dani. Everyone does.'

Then she hugged me.

And it was a real hug—a warm, affectionate hug. I couldn't even remember the last time my mom hugged me. Emotion crawled up my throat and I squelched it before I made a fool out of myself.

'Thank you for letting me come up,' I said, happy that my voice didn't crack.

'It's no problem. We love having the company. Come on, let's go meet the guy who thinks he's my better half.' His mom dropped an arm around my shoulders and squeezed. 'And dear God, I apologize ahead of time if he starts talking to you about how many eight-point bucks he's planning to hunt this weekend.'

As she led me toward the foyer, I glanced over to where Cam waited. Our gazes locked, and that flipping motion occurred in my chest. A smile spread across his face, revealing the dimple in his left cheek.

Cam winked.

And my smile widened.

Chapter 18

Cam got those blue eyes from his father, as well as his sense of humor … and the ability to string together the most confusing rationales on this earth, which was what probably made Richard Hamilton such a successful lawyer. Within a few short hours, he nearly had me agreeing to try deer jerky for the first time.

Nearly.

If it weren't for Cam continuously whispering 'Bambi' in my ear every couple of minutes, I would've caved. But I couldn't eat Bambi, no matter how succulent Mr. Hamilton made it sound.

We stayed in the spacious kitchen, at the scuffed oak table that was just the right size to seat four or five people, drinking the coffee Cam's mother had made. My sides were actually aching from laughing so hard at Cam and his father. The two of them were identical. Wavy, uncontrollable hair, bright blue eyes that sparkled with pure mischief, and the rare talent for turning every word around.

'Look, Dad, seriously, you're embarrassing yourself here.'

His father glanced at me, brows raised in a fashion that was so like Cam. 'Do I look embarrassed, Avery?'

Pressing my lips together, I shook my head.

Cam shot me a look that said I wasn't helping. 'You're sitting here trying to convince me, Mom, Avery, and baby Jesus that Bigfoot must exist because apes exist?'

'Yes!' the older Hamilton shouted. 'It's called evolution, son. Are they teaching you anything at college?'

Cam rolled his eyes. 'Well, Dad, they aren't teaching me about Bigfoot at college.'

'Actually,' I said, clearing my throat. 'There is the whole missing link theory when it comes to primates.'

'I like this girl.' Mr. Hamilton winked at me.

'You're not helping,' Cam grumbled.

'All I'm saying is once you've been out in the woods and heard the things I've heard,' his father continued, 'you'd believe in Bigfoot and the chupacabra.'

'Chupacabra?' Cam's jaw hit the table. 'Aw, come on, Dad.'

Mrs. Hamilton shook her head fondly. 'These are my boys. I'm so proud.'

I grinned as I took a sip of the rich coffee. 'They really are quite something else together.'

'Something else?' She huffed as she pushed from the table, grabbing her husband's empty coffee cup. 'That's the nice way of saying they're bat-shit crazy.'

'Hey!' Mr. Hamilton's head whipped around, eyes dancing. 'You listen here, woman.'

'You can listen to my foot up your ass if you call me woman again.' Mrs. Hamilton refilled the cup and reached for the sugar. 'And you can take that to court.'

Cam sighed and lowered his head.

I smothered my giggle with my hand.

His family was … wonderful. They were friendly and warm. Nothing like my own. I doubted my mom knew how to use the coffeemaker or would lower herself to serving someone, even my dad.

Mrs. Hamilton put the cup down in front of her husband. 'Aren't you two going to the drive-in tonight?'

'Yep,' Cam said, standing. He picked up our bags. 'We need to get going so we get a good spot.'

'Make sure you grab some thick blankets,' she said, sitting back down at the table. 'It's been getting really cold at night.'

I was kind of reluctant to leave his family, even if the conversation was pretty bizarre. I stood, thanking his mother for the coffee.

'No problem, honey.' Mrs. Hamilton turned to her son. 'I have the yellow room ready for her, Cameron. Be a gentleman and show her where it is.'

A strange look crossed Cam's face, but it was gone by the time we stepped out into the foyer. I followed Cam up the stairs. 'I like your parents. They're very nice.'

'They're pretty cool.' He trailed his hand along the wooden banister. 'Is your dad convinced that Bigfoot exists?'

I laughed. 'No.'

'How about the chupacabra?'

Laughing again, I shook my head. 'Definitely no.'

He headed down the hall on the second floor. 'My parents have a room upstairs, and my sister has one at the start of the hall.' He stopped outside of a door and nudged it open with his hip. 'This is the yellow room, because it's yellow.'

The room was yellow, but a pretty buttercup shade, not school bus. Cam put my bag on the bed as I made my way over to the window overlooking a side garden below. I turned, catching a fresh scent of vanilla. 'It's really pretty. I hope your mom didn't go through any trouble.'

'She didn't.' He stretched his arms above his head, cracking his back. 'You think you'll be ready in about thirty minutes?'

I sat on the edge of the bed. 'Yep.'

Cam backed toward the door, arms still raised. He tapped the top of the door's frame. 'Guess what?'

201

'What?'

A slight grin appeared. 'My bedroom is right across the hall.'

My tummy tumbled. 'Okay.'

The grin spread, turning wicked. 'Just thought you'd be happy to hear that.'

'Thrilled,' I murmured.

He chuckled as he left the room, closing the door behind him. I sat there for a second and then threw myself onto my back. Cam was right across the hall, which was no different from at the apartment building, right? Wrong. Tonight and tomorrow night he'd be closer than he ever had before.

About an hour and a half later, I stood beside his truck as he put two long pillows up against the back of the truck's bed. He'd backed the vehicle into the spot so we could sit out and have a lot more space. We weren't the only ones daring the cold temps at night. Several big trucks were parked alongside us, doing the same with pillows and blankets. One even had an air mattress.

Cam came over to the tailgate and offered his hands. 'Ready?'

I placed my hands in his and he lifted me up. The sudden shift in weight caused him to stumble back a step and his hands dropped to my hips to steady himself. An immediate rush of heat pooled in my stomach as I looked up.

Cam's thick lashes hid his eyes as his hands seemed to flex. His lips parted, and my body tensed with anticipation. Under the starry night, it seemed like the perfect atmosphere for a kiss. I could practically feel his lips against mine.

He dropped his hands and turned to the two bags near the stack of blankets and pillows. Disappointment rose as he knelt down. Why hadn't he kissed me?

Hell, why hadn't he kissed me since our date?

'Here,' he said, rising. 'Brought you something to help keep you warm.'

He held one of his skullcaps and as he raised his hands, I caught the scent of his shampoo. I stood still as he pulled it down over my head, taking the time to tuck my hair back behind my ears before he was done.

'Thank you,' I told him.

Cam smiled as he grabbed the other bag and moved back against the pillows. I carefully made my way over to him and sat beside him. He pulled out the bucket of fried chicken and drinks we'd picked up on the way.

The movie started to play—an old one that seemed to be some kind of yearly custom, because there were several shouts and cheers as the first scene rolled across the massive screen.

'*Home Alone*?' I asked, looking at Cam.

He snickered. 'It's like a Thanksgiving tradition around these parts.'

I grinned. 'I haven't seen this movie in forever.'

As Kevin McCallister appeared on screen, pouting and glaring at his family, we dug into the chicken, leaving a path of crumpled napkins in our wake. By the time Kevin's mom yelled his name on the plane, my tummy was full, and I was sure that Cam had eaten an entire chicken.

The blanket around my shoulders kept the bulk of the cold air away, but every so often, I shivered, especially when the wind picked up.

'Why don't you come over here?' Cam said, and I turned to him, brows raised. 'You look cold.'

I shifted closer, but that apparently wasn't close enough. He tugged the blanket off me and then leaned back. Lifting me up, he placed me between his widespread legs.

My eyes practically popped out of my head.

Cam spread the blanket over me, tucking the edges around my neck. I sat with my spine straight for several moments, staring at the screen, but not really seeing it. Then his arms snaked under the blanket and around my waist. He tugged me back so I was fitted against his front.

Muscles tense, I forced myself to take several slow, deep breaths. Just as I had my breathing somewhat normal, his hands slid to my stomach.

'Is this warmer?' he asked, his breath stirring the hair around my ear.

Throat closed off, I nodded.

One hand moved up, settling under my breasts, and the other shifted to rest under my belly button, over the band of my jeans. It felt like his hand was on fire. Immediately, my skin warmed in those areas.

'Good,' he murmured. 'I promised you that I'd keep you warm.'

He was definitely keeping me warm. 'You did.'

Under my breasts, his thumb began to move, tracing small, idle circles. Then, a few seconds later, the hand below started to move up and down, a slow continuous movement that caused my breath to start coming faster.

Each time his fingers moved over the flap covering the zipper, it tugged gently on my jeans, causing the seam of my pants to push against me. I had no idea if he knew that was happening. Knowing Cam, I'd have to go with a yes. In a matter of minutes, I was throbbing down there.

I let my head fall back against his chest, and my eyes drifted shut. The acute sensation he was creating was mind-blowing.

'Avery?'

'Hmm?'

There was a pause. 'Are you paying attention?'

'Uh-huh.' I shifted restlessly.

Cam chuckled, and I knew without a doubt that he was fully aware of what he was up to. 'Good. I wouldn't want you to miss any of this.'

I wasn't missing a single second of this.

Another fitful night of sleep beckoned me. I tossed and turned for hours after we got back from the drive-in, my body going through the same thing it had the night after our date. It was close to two in the morning when I gave in, slipping my hand under the band of my bottoms. It kind of felt dirty to be doing this in someone else's home, in their bed, with Cam just a door away. It didn't take long for me to find release, and I wasn't sure what that said about me.

I slept for a couple of hours before waking around six. There was no way I was going back to sleep, so I showered and changed before I worked up the nerve to leave my bedroom. I stood in front of Cam's door, like a total creeper. I wondered what he'd do if I woke him? Climbed into his bed—

I stopped myself before I finished that train wreck of a thought. If I tried to actually do that, I'd probably end up hurting myself in the process of trying to be seductive or flirty.

Pushing away from his door, I headed downstairs, hoping I didn't wake anyone. It seemed like every step creaked obnoxiously. As soon as I reached the foyer, I caught the scent of coffee and knew someone had to be up.

I hovered at the bottom of the stairs, hands twisting together as I debated between going back upstairs or making my presence known. I thought about all those times I'd woken in the middle of the night, usually from a nightmare, and would go downstairs, catching my mom sneaking drinks.

She had so not been a happy camper when that occurred.

I honestly shouldn't be roaming around someone's house. Seemed like that was breaking some guest rule. I had started

205

to turn to go back upstairs when Mrs. Hamilton stuck her head out of the kitchen.

Oh shit.

A warm smile appeared on her face. 'I didn't wake you, did I? I'm an early riser, even more so on Thanksgiving.' She waved a dishtowel. 'Making stuffing.'

'You didn't wake me.' I inched closer, sort of fascinated by the fact she was up this early making stuffing. 'Do you need help?'

'I could always use a hand in the kitchen,' she replied, motioning me forward. 'And I have fresh coffee.'

The allure of coffee was too much to resist. I followed her into the kitchen, my eyes widening at all the food spread across the kitchen island. A turkey sat on a platter, waiting to get stuff shoved up its cavity.

'Sugar and cream, right?' she asked.

I smiled a little. 'You remembered.'

'I think the key to the start of any good relationship is to remember how the other person likes their coffee.'

'Cam doesn't really like coffee.' The moment those words left my mouth, I flushed.

His mom pretended not to notice my red face. 'No, he's not big on coffee. Milk, on the other hand …'

'He drinks milk while eating Chinese.' I shuddered. 'It's so gross.'

She laughed as she handed me the coffee. 'He gets that from his father. Teresa is the same way. Speaking of which, you'll be meeting her within the next couple of hours.'

Knots formed in my stomach. Meeting his sister made me anxious.

'Have you made stuffing before?' she asked, moving over to the island.

'No.' I joined her on the other side, eyeing the loaves of bread, onions, milk, and eggs.

'My daughter usually helps me in the morning,' she said, placing the dishtowel on the counter. 'It's not difficult at all, so you're more than welcome to help or keep me company.'

'I can help. What can I do?'

Mrs. Hamilton's smile was wide. 'If you could start with the bread, that would be perfect. All you need to do is break the loaves up in this bowl.' She pointed to a large blue one. 'When you've finished that, we'll move on to the next step.'

'Okay.' I pulled my hair up into a ponytail and rolled up my sleeves, then washed my hands quickly.

'That's a pretty bracelet,' she commented as she started chopping the onion into small chunks.

'Thank you.' I tore apart the bread, probably a little harder than necessary. 'Cam told me that his sister was at a dance recital?'

'In Pittsburgh,' she said, pride pouring into her voice. 'It was an invitation-only recital. Richard and I would've gone, but we wanted to be home for Cameron. Teresa understands though. We rarely miss any of her dances.'

I finished the first loaf. 'What's next?'

'Onions, butter, milk, and seasoning. You get to mush it all with your hands.'

I waited for her to dump in the ingredients. As she did so, she told me how much she thought should go in and then I sank my hands into the gooey mess. Grinning, I laughed. 'Okay, this feels kind of weird.'

'It does. At least you're not eating it.'

'Raw?'

'Yep, Cameron and Teresa both would try to eat it raw.'

I made a face as I smushed everything together so that the milk and butter would get evenly distributed through the bread. After wiping my hands clean, I moved on to the second loaf of bread. 'I used to dance,' I admitted.

'Cameron mentioned that.'

My hands stilled around the bread. He'd told his parents that? I wasn't sure what to make of that.

'I would've known even if he hadn't said anything,' she commented as she dropped some of the onions in my bowl. 'You still move like a dancer.' She smiled. 'I danced, and after watching Teresa over the years, I've come to be able to recognize that in others.'

'It's nice to hear that. I mean, I don't feel like I still do.'

'You do.'

I was back to the mushing part again and I decided that was my favorite. I was weird.

'You never made stuffing with your mom?' Cam's mother asked.

It was an innocent question, but it caused a deep ache to slice across my chest. My mom and I hadn't been the closest two people in the world before the incident, but afterward, our relationship was nonexistent. 'I don't think my mom knows how to cook,' I said finally.

'You don't think?'

I shook my head. 'My parents aren't into cooking dinners.'

There was a pause. 'Cameron said they travel a lot during the holidays?'

'Yeah, and they kind of like doing their own thing, you know, daughter free.' I forced out a laugh, shrugging it off. 'I mean, I'm okay with that. I can't ski to save my life and being stuck on a ship in the middle of an ocean isn't something I'm into.'

Mrs. Hamilton was silent as we added the last of the ingredients and I dug my fingers into it, liking the way it slid through them. 'So what do you normally do when you're home?' she asked.

I shrugged. 'I wouldn't be by myself the whole time. They have a maid that usually cooks dinner for me before she goes home. It's really nice of her because she's not required to work during the holidays.'

'What about Christmas?'

'The same,' I admitted, surprising myself. I glanced up and found her watching me. 'It's not really a big deal. My family isn't very close, and so it's probably better this way.' After saying that, I figured it probably wasn't the best thing to say. 'Anyway, I'm done. What's the next step?'

'It goes in the turkey.' She smiled, but it seemed a little off. 'Want to do the honors?'

'Sure.' I waited for her to turn the bird around and then I completed the somewhat gross task of getting all in the turkey's personal space.

When I was done, I headed over to the double sink while she wrapped the turkey in foil and placed it in a roaster.

'Thank you for helping me, Avery.'

'No problem,' I said. 'I'm happy to have helped.' And I really was. 'It was fun.'

Mrs. Hamilton smiled at me, though her eyes were sad. 'Well, honey, you're always welcome here for the holidays. There are never enough hands when it comes to making food.'

I murmured a thank-you and finished washing my hands. As I turned, I caught sight of Cam standing just outside the kitchen. I had no idea how long he'd been there or how much of the conversation he'd overheard, but the soft look on his sleepy face told me he'd heard enough.

Chapter 19

Anyone with two eyes could tell that Teresa and Cam were close and they really did care about each other. The two of them were insane together, constantly picking on each other and causing general trouble wherever they went.

Teresa was a female version of Cam—tall, strikingly beautiful with raven-colored hair and bright blue eyes. She had the body of a well-disciplined dancer and was practically bubbling over with energy.

Much to my relief, Teresa was a sweetheart. I'd been afraid that she wouldn't like me for some reason or another, but she hugged me within the first couple of seconds of meeting me.

The Hamilton family were a bunch of hugging folks.

I hung out with Richard, Teresa, and Cam in the basement until Teresa and I went upstairs to help her mom get the sides ready for dinner, which seemed like the perfect moment to get away, because Cam and his father started talking about hunting and my skin was beginning to crawl.

Seeing mother and daughter working together and laughing had a strange effect on me. They were almost like strange creatures to me, the kind of family you saw on evening sitcoms.

I was envious of that relationship, but at the same time I sort of accepted that this would never be my mom and me.

While we got the dinner ready, Teresa was glued to her cell phone, constantly texting someone, which carried over to the dinner table.

'Who do you keep texting?' Cam demanded as he slopped a second heaping of yams on his plate.

Teresa smirked. 'That's none of your business.'

'I'm your brother, it's my business.'

Uh-oh. I glanced at them and saw Cam's eyes narrowed at his younger sister as she texted someone.

'Mom, you should tell *your* daughter it's rude to text at the table.'

Mrs. Hamilton arched a brow. 'It's not hurting anyone.'

Cam nudged me with his knee under the table, something he'd been doing every five minutes since we sat down. 'It's hurting my soul.'

I rolled my eyes as I knocked him back.

'That's sad,' his sister commented, dropping her cell in her lap. 'So, Avery, how did you end up in West Virginia?'

'I wanted to go someplace different,' I said, digging into the mashed potatoes. 'My family is originally from Ohio, so West Virginia seemed like a good place to go.'

'I have to be honest, I would've picked New York or Florida or Virginia or Maryland or—' Her phone chirped, drawing her attention like a shiny object to someone with ADD. She grabbed her cell and an immediate smile spread across her lips.

Cam knocked my knee as his eyes narrowed even further. He reached for more turkey, but suddenly veered off, snatching the cell from his sister's fingers.

'Hey!' she shouted. 'Give it back!'

Cam stretched into me, avoiding his sister's flailing arms. He scowled as he looked at her phone. 'Who's Murphy?'

212

Mr. Hamilton shook his head.

'It's none of your business! God,' Teresa snapped. 'Give me back my phone.'

'I'll give it back when you tell me who Murphy is. A boyfriend?'

Her cheeks flushed, and I figured Cam was a bit of the overprotective type. He held the phone away from her until she sat back, crossing her arms. 'Mom.'

'Cam, give her back the phone.' When Cam still held it, his mother smiled. 'We've met Murphy. He's a really good boy.'

Cam didn't look convinced, and I suddenly wondered if there was more to this. I looked over at Teresa, and her eyes were starting to shine. I turned my attention back to my plate quickly.

'He's really nice and I like him,' she said in a quiet voice.

Cam snorted. 'That's not a ringing—'

'He's not Jeremy,' Mr. Hamilton said, suddenly very serious and somber. 'Give her back the phone.'

Cam looked like he was going to hold on to that phone for the rest of his life, and where there hadn't been any tension in the house since I arrived, it was now very much in this room. I reached under the table and grabbed his upper thigh, startling him enough that he loosened his grip on her phone. I swiped it away from him.

'Hey!' His eyes narrowed. 'That was so not fair.'

I grinned as I stretched behind him, handing the phone to his sister. 'Sorry.'

'Thank you,' Teresa said, and I was sure I'd made a friend for life with that move.

Cam's look said there'd be payback later before he turned to his sister. 'I want to meet this Murphy.'

Teresa let out a loud sigh. 'Okay. Let me know when.'

Shock flickered through me. I would not have expected her to relent that easily to his demand. My gaze shifted between them, and while Cam seemed to relax, there was a tension in his jaw that hadn't been there before. Conversation picked back up, but there seemed to be something simmering behind it.

Or it could just be my paranoia.

After the feast, Cam and I were alone in the dining room, stacking the dishes. 'Is everything okay with your sister?' I asked.

Cam laughed, but it didn't reach his eyes. 'Everything is kosher. Let's play,' he said, catching my hands and pulling me toward the stairs leading to the basement. 'I bet you can beat me at pool.'

'I don't know about that.' But I let him lead me away.

'Oh, I suck ass at pool.'

I laughed. 'What about the dishes and—'

Cam stopped without any warning, causing me to crash into his chest. His hands fell to my hips as he lowered his forehead to mine. 'Forget the dishes. Come play with me, sweetheart.'

Crap. He had me at sweetheart.

I'd just changed into my pajamas and slid my legs under the covers when there was a soft knock on the bedroom door. I rose onto my elbows. My heart jumped as Cam opened the door halfway.

'Hey,' he said, a slight grin on his face.

'Hi.' The one word came out a half whisper, half croak.

That lopsided grin spread an inch. 'I wanted to say good night.'

A flutter took up residence deep inside my chest and my lower stomach. My hand clenched the edge of the down comforter. 'You already told me good night.'

'I did.' He stepped into the room, and my gaze slipped down the length of him. Cam made a gray shirt and flannel pajama bottoms look good. 'But I didn't. Not in the way I want to say good night.'

Oh dear sweet mercy me …

Cam quietly shut the door behind him. The click of the latch catching caused my heart to pound, with him being here while I was in bed wearing nothing more than a thin, long-sleeve shirt and cotton shorts. That was all.

I held my breath as I watched him make his way to the bed. He sat beside me, his hip resting against my leg. In the dim light of the room, his eyes shone like dark jewels as they moved over my face and down to my chest. Under his intense gaze, my nipples immediately puckered against my shirt.

His gaze flicked up to my face, and I sucked in a soft breath. The nest of butterflies were back in my stomach, trying to make their way out. 'I'm glad you decided to come here,' he said, voice gruff.

I shivered. 'I am, too.'

'Really?' Cam planted a hand on the other side of my hip. 'Did you just admit that?'

'Yeah, I sort of did.'

He leaned in so that his upper body hovered over mine. 'I wish I had my phone to record this moment.'

My gaze dipped to his mouth. A witty retort slipped out of my grasp. I wetted my lower lip and his lips parted. My chest rose sharply as I forced my eyes up to meet his. 'I've … had a wonderful time.'

'So have I.' The look in his eyes softened just a bit, but there was still a heated edge to his stare. 'So what do you think you're going to do for winter break?'

Knowing that he'd overheard the conversation I'd had with his mom, I didn't lie. 'I don't know. I thought about taking off for DC one of the days. I want to see the Smithsonian and the National Mall. I've never been.'

'Hmm, that could be fun. I could be your tour guide.'

A small grin pulled at my lips. 'That … that would be fun.'

'It would be,' he said, his voice warm on my cheek. 'Pick a date.'

'Now?'

'Now.'

'January second,' I said immediately, and then flushed. 'Will you be available then?'

'I'll be available whenever you want me to be.'

That delighted me to no end and my grin spread.

'Guess what, Avery?'

'What?' I wondered if he could see how fast my heart was beating beneath my shirt.

'Remember how you just said you were having a good time?' Cam lowered his head so that our mouths were scant inches apart. 'It's about to get better.'

'Is it?'

He shifted his head and his nose grazed mine. 'Oh, yeah.'

'Are you going to not kiss me again?'

His lips tipped up. 'That's exactly what I'm going to do.'

Warmth slid through my veins as my body tensed in a welcome, delicious way. My eyes fluttered shut as his lips brushed mine once and then twice, as if he was getting reacquainted with the feel of them. The slight, barely there touch was nerve-racking.

Cam shifted his weight onto his left arm and with his other hand, he spread his fingers along my cheek. He placed a kiss at the corner of my lips and the other side before sliding his hand back around the nape of my neck. His lips moved along my jaw, trailing a fiery path to my ear. A shiver danced along my skin, eliciting a deep, husky chuckle from

216

him. His lips pressed against the sensitive spot under my ear, and a moan crawled up my throat.

'Good night, Avery.'

And then he kissed me—kissed me like he had right before he'd left the night of our date. Kissed me like he was a man starving for oxygen and I was the only air he needed to breathe. The hand around my neck held me there, raised up on my elbows as his mouth devoured mine. And that was the only word I could use to accurately explain how he kissed me.

Cam devoured me.

My lips opened, needing almost no coaxing, and his tongue slipped in, teasing mine as his hand tightened behind my neck. He tasted like toothpaste and it had my senses spinning. A sound rumbled from deep inside his chest as he pushed back, sliding his hand out from under me.

The moment my head hit the pillow, a tiny burst of panic kicked the air out of my lungs. Where was this heading? I thought about his sister being down the hall and his parents sleeping on the floor above, but then he kissed me again, a sweet tender kiss as he cupped my cheek. The panic eased off; the thoughts slipped away.

Cam hovered above me and I wanted to feel him *on* me, our bodies pressed together. Once that need took root, warring emotions rose inside me. Was this too much? Not enough? He caught my lower lip between his teeth, and a moan escaped me.

I was going to go with not enough.

In an act of supreme bravery fueled by desire, I reached down and slid my hands under the hem of his shirt. Cam jerked as my fingers grazed his bare, taut skin. He stilled for a moment and then he pulled away. I almost demanded to know why—I'd come this far to actually touch him, and he was leaving me? What in the holy hell was up with that?

Cam reached down and pulled his shirt off, over his head. Oh.

Oh.

My breath hitched as I soaked him in. Cam's body was gorgeous. All smooth, tight skin stretched over rock-hard muscle. I wanted to ask about the tattoo and if it symbolized something to him, but I couldn't force the words from my mouth.

He yanked the comforter down, and my heart jumped. Immediately, I thought about what I had done in the bed. Our gazes locked, and I couldn't move or breathe. He climbed over me, his arms caging me in, surrounding me in a way that made me feel small ... and safe. My hands went to his stomach, flattening against his skin. The muscles of his abs spasmed.

Cam dropped his forehead to mine. 'You have no idea what you do to me.'

I didn't, but as he lowered himself onto me, I started to get a good idea. I could feel him against my stomach, through our clothes, hard and thick. I thought that would pull me out of the heady haze of desire, but it didn't. Heat flared between my thighs, and my pulse pounded throughout my body. I shifted under him, bringing him closer to where I ached for him.

'Fuck,' he growled, his large body shaking.

He captured my lips in a searing kiss as he settled between my legs, muffling the pleasant groan that had worked its way up my throat. His hips rolled into mine, and my nerve endings were suddenly on fire. The thin material of my pajamas was nothing between the hard, hot skin of his chest and mine. His hips made another slow thrust that had my toes curling as I gripped his sides. His kiss turned deeper, more urgent as he slid his hand from my cheek, down my neck. His hand brushed the swell of my breast, so close to the sensitive bud before following the curve of my stomach to the flare of my hips. He curved his hand around my thigh, lifting my leg around his hip. He settled deeper, pressing against my sex in a way that thrilled me at the same time that it stirred a conflicting emotion. When his hips rocked again, I whimpered against his lips.

'I like that sound,' he said, moving his hips. I made it again, flushing. 'Correction. I love that fucking sound.'

Sensations raced across my skin, building into an ache in my core. It was like the night in my bed but much stronger, more intense and so very real. His hand was on the move again, trailing up my side, jumping to my hand. His fingers tangled with mine for a second and then drifted up, under my sleeves as his tongue danced with mine.

Suddenly, he stilled above me and lifted his head. I forced my eyes open as I dragged in a deep breath. The look on his face; I didn't understand it.

'Cam?'

Without saying a word, he lifted my arm and turned it over. My heart dropped. No. No. It was like slow motion. His fingers moved, thumb sliding over the length of the deep scar that cut across my vein.

He looked.

I followed his gaze.

Disbelief exploded, suffocating all the wonderful feelings that had been building in me. His thumb moved again, as if he was trying to wipe the scar away, and then when it remained, he shifted his gaze to mine. There was no mistaking it. He knew—he knew what the scar was.

'Avery …?' he whispered, brows furrowed and face taut. 'Oh, Avery, what is this?'

Horror swept the disbelief away, like a rolling tide. The pained expression etched on his striking face reached down into me, sinking deep with razor-sharp claws, and tore me apart. The look on his face, it … it destroyed me in a way nothing else could since that night on Halloween.

The scar—I never wanted anyone to see it, to witness just how weak I'd been once upon a time. It went beyond humiliation.

Tearing my arm free, I scrambled out from underneath him. My body flashed between hot and cold as I yanked the sleeve down over my bare wrist.

'Avery …' He reached for me.

'Please,' I said, pushing myself to the edge of the bed. 'Please leave.'

Cam pulled his hand back. 'Avery, talk to me.'

I shook my head, lip trembling.

A muscle worked in his jaw. 'Avery—'

'Leave!' I jumped from the bed, stumbling back a step. 'Just leave.'

Cam froze for a second, as if he was about to say something else, but then he pushed off the bed. He backed toward the door as a deep shudder started working its way through my body. With his hand on the doorknob, he stopped.

'Avery, we can talk—'

'Leave.' My voice broke. 'Please.'

His shoulders stiffened, and then he did as I asked. Cam left, closing the door quietly behind him.

Chapter 20

I didn't go to astronomy class on Monday or Tuesday. I just couldn't bring myself to face Cam. Not after I'd seen the look on his face when he realized what the scar on my wrist was from. Not after having to pretend everything was okay in front of his mom and dad before we left. Even though I'd only known them for a short period, I thought they were wonderful and hated the fact that I was leaving knowing the likelihood of ever seeing them again was low. Not after the tense, never-ending ride home Friday morning or when Cam had followed me up to my apartment and tried to talk to me.

And definitely not after he tried to come over Sunday morning with eggs and I didn't answer the door.

I spent most of the weekend in bed, my eyes aching so badly from the nonstop sob fest that I didn't think was truly over. I'd avoided my phone. Brit texted. Jacob texted.

Cam had texted.

Cam had also tried to stop by Sunday night, Monday night, and Tuesday night. Every time he did it was like a punch to the stomach.

I just couldn't face him, because that look on his face had been as bad as the one on my mother's.

It had been about five months after the Halloween party when I had decided I couldn't take it anymore. The onslaught of e-mails, texts, phone calls, and Facebook messages had been bad, but at school, in real life? In the hallways, the bathrooms, the cafeteria, and the classrooms, people didn't just whisper about what they heard happened when Blaine and I went into his bedroom. They openly talked about it in front of me. Called me every combination of lying whore you could come up with. The teachers didn't stop it; neither did the staff.

So me and that picture frame that used to hold the photo of me and my best friend—the same girl who'd called me a slut that very day in the crowded hall at school—had gotten friendly.

My parents could barely look at me before I cut my wrist. But after? In the hospital room, Mom had lost it. For the first time in, like, forever, she had lost it.

She had stormed into the private room, Dad trailing behind her. Her sharp gaze shot from my face to my bandaged wrist.

Stricken panic had crossed her too-perfect features, and I thought that finally, she was going to pull me into her arms and tell me that everything was going to be okay, that we'd get through this together.

That look of pain had given way to disappointment, to pity, and to anger.

'How dare you shame yourself and your family like this, Avery. What am I supposed to tell people when they find out about this?' Mom had said, and her voice had shaken as she struggled to keep quiet in the hospital room, but she lost control. The next words were shrieked. 'After everything else, you go and do this? Haven't you put us through enough? What is wrong with you, Avery? What in God's name is wrong with you?'

The nurses had dragged Mom out of the room.

Strangely, what I remembered from that night had been that brief look of panic on her face and how I had mistakenly believed it had been there out of concern for me.

That stricken look had been on Cam's face, and I wanted to be somebody else, because I knew that stricken look would eventually turn into something else, into disappointment, into pity, and into anger.

And I couldn't bear to see that happen with Cam.

I would do anything to avoid that, even if it meant taking drastic steps. Somewhere between Tuesday night and Wednesday morning, I'd made up my mind about the current state of my life.

This ... this stuff with Cam had been doomed for failure from the beginning. Could a guy and a girl who were attracted to each other really be friends? I didn't think so. Things would get too complicated. They'd either act on those feelings or stay away from each other. We had tried to act on those feelings for a hot second. We kissed a couple of times. That was all. And in reality, it wouldn't have gone further.

I wasn't sure that I could've gone further. Well, especially now I didn't think so. Cam would eventually move on, and I would have an absolutely obliterated heart. Not broken, but completely destroyed, because Cam ... he was falling-in-love-with material. And I couldn't let that happen.

Maybe you already did, whispered an evil, terrible, bitchy voice.

So on Wednesday morning I went to my adviser and made up some excuse about there being too much schoolwork and me getting behind. The last day for complete withdrawal from a class had been at the end of October, so to get out of astronomy I would have to take an incomplete.

An incomplete would totally bitch-slap my GPA, but the truth was I was doing well enough in the rest of my classes that it wouldn't kill my overall.

There was a decision to make.

Face Cam and deal with the inevitable broken heart or take the incomplete.

I took the incomplete.

And as I left my adviser's office, I knew what I'd done wasn't so much making a decision. I was running. After all, wasn't that what I was good at? Running?

Brit and Jacob attempted to stage an intervention the following weekend. Both showed up at my apartment and if I hadn't let them in, I was confident they'd have beaten down my door or, worse, involved Cam.

I sat in my moon chair, staring up at them. 'Guys, really … ?'

Brit folded her arms, chin raised stubbornly. 'We are your friends and obviously you're facing a crisis of some sort, so we are here, and you can't get rid of us that easily.'

'I'm not having or facing a crisis.' God, had Cam told them what he'd seen? My stomach dropped, but I told myself he wouldn't have done that. At least I didn't think so.

'Really?' Jacob said, returning from the kitchen. 'Since you've come back from Thanksgiving break, you've been walking around like a zombie, and not the cool, fast, brain-eating kind. You look like you've been crying your eyes out, you've been avoiding Cam and all talk of him, and there is nothing good to eat in your kitchen.'

I raised my brow at the last statement. 'I haven't been avoiding Cam.'

'Bullshit,' Brit replied. 'I talked to Cam yesterday. He said you won't talk to him or answer his phone calls or your door when it's him, and you haven't been to astronomy.'

A sharp pain sliced across my chest. I almost asked if she had approached him, but figured it didn't matter. The less I thought about him, the better. Not saying his name helped.

Having my two friends give me the third degree about him wasn't helping.

'Did you guys get into a fight?' Jacob plopped down on the couch.

Had we? Not really. I shook my head. 'It's nothing, guys. We didn't get in a fight. I just haven't been in the mood to talk to him.'

Brit shot me a bland look. 'Avery, that's bullshit, too.'

I raised my hands helplessly.

'Why haven't you been going to astronomy?' she asked.

'I dropped the class.'

She gaped. 'You've dropped the class? Avery, the last day to drop was—oh, my God, you're taking an incomplete?'

'It's not a big deal.'

Brit stared at me, so did Jacob. 'Have you lost your fucking mind, Avery?'

I winced. 'No.'

Taking a deep breath, Brit glanced between Jacob and me. 'Jacob, can you get back to the dorm by yourself?'

His brows knitted. 'Uh, yeah, it's not that far of a walk, but—'

'Good,' she chirped. Leaning forward, she kissed him on the cheek. 'See you later.'

Jacob sat there for a moment and then shook his head. He gave me a quick hug before he left. 'Why did you kick him out?' I asked.

'Because we need to talk girl to girl,' she replied.

Oh dear.

She leaned forward, clenching her knees. 'What happened between you two?'

I struggled to come up with a good excuse for why I was avoiding Cam. 'It's just that I don't think pursuing a relationship with him is the right thing.'

'Okay. You're entitled to decide that, but no friendship? To the point you can't be in the same class as him?'

'We can't be friends,' I said after a few moments, already weary with this conversation. 'That's just it, okay? I really don't want to talk about this. I'm not trying to be rude, but there's nothing to say. I don't want to see him. End of story.'

I don't want to see him. The thing about that was that it was only partially true. I was too embarrassed and ashamed to see him, but I missed him. It had only been a week, but I missed his smart-ass comments, his wit and charm, and—I stopped myself with a shake of my head.

Brit pushed her hair off her forehead. 'All right, but I want to ask one question and I want a fucking honest answer, okay?'

My eyes widened. 'Okay.'

'Did he try something?'

'What?' I shrieked.

She met my stare. 'Did he hurt you or something?'

'Oh, my God, no.' I stood, running my hands down my hips. 'Cam didn't do anything. I promise you. He didn't do anything wrong. It's me. Okay. Please don't think that about him.'

Brit nodded slowly. 'I didn't think he would've, but I had to ask. I had to know.'

She stayed for a little while longer, switching the conversation to her latest hookup with Jimmie, and for a while I forgot about Cam and the whole mess.

When she left, she stopped at the door and turned back to me. 'Just in case you're wondering, when I talked to Cam, he was really worried about you. He was upset. Whatever went down between you two, I hope you guys can work it out, because ...'

'Because what?'

226

She pressed her lips together, exhaling through her nose. 'Because I think the guy really does care about you, Avery. And I think you really care about him. It would be a fucking shame if you guys couldn't fix this or work this out over some bullshit.'

With the semester winding down, I threw myself into finals. With the incomplete in astronomy, I needed to ace all my exams just to make myself feel somewhat better after making such a crazy decision. More than once over the last week or so, I had wanted to punt-kick myself in the face for taking an incomplete. In those very rare logical moments, I cursed myself every which way from Sunday. It was a stupid, stupid decision, especially over a boy, but there was nothing I could do now. I'd missed the last two weeks of class, and there was no way I could make up for that.

As I finished up my last final of the semester—music—I headed to the train station where my car was parked. Facing the brutal wind that seemed to blow straight in my eyes, I pulled out my cell. There were a couple of unread texts from Cam over the last week and one from the UNKNOWN CALLER, who apparently had gotten tired of calling me a whore over voice mail and moved on to texting it. Just like I avoided my cousin's e-mails, I did the same with Cam's texts.

I didn't delete them, though. I'm not sure why. I just couldn't do it.

There was a missed call from Brit. She wanted to get together before she headed home for winter break. Neither she nor Jacob brought up the stuff with Cam again, but it hung between us every time we were together. After leaving campus, I headed to the grocery store for a long overdue trip. I milled through the aisles, not really finding anything appetizing, just throwing stuff in my cart.

On the way out, I spotted Ollie heading into the pizza joint at the end of the strip mall. We were less than a mile from the apartments, so it wasn't a surprise to see him there, but I stopped in the middle of the parking lot, my heart pounding. He didn't look over my way, probably didn't even see me, but I saw him and I thought of that stupid tortoise.

A lump appeared in my throat, and I inhaled sharply. Tears burned the back of my eyes as I forced myself to walk to my car. Back at the apartment building, I unloaded the groceries, focusing on the mundane task until I felt the messy ball of emotion slide back down.

The inevitable happened as I lugged up the last of my groceries.

I heard Cam's door open and I knew it couldn't be Ollie. My heart stuttered and I tried to get the door open and get the groceries in before he saw me, except that wasn't possible. Dismissing the idiotic idea of leaving the groceries in the hall, I bent over, grabbing as many bags as possible.

'Avery.'

Squeezing my eyes shut, I froze, three bags of groceries dangling precariously from my aching fingers. My throat closed up as I *felt* him come closer. It was as if my body was aware of him on some kind of subconscious level.

'Let me help you.'

His deep voice wove its way through my chest, working a shiver from me. I opened my eyes, but kept my gaze glued to what I could see of my apartment. 'I got it.'

'Doesn't look that way,' he replied. 'Your fingers are turning purple.'

They were. 'It's fine.' I started into my apartment, but Cam moved quickly. He slid around me, and all I saw was his midsection. Thank God he was wearing a sweater. His hand came into view and he extracted the bags from my fingers, brushing over mine in the process. I jerked back, causing one of the bags to hit the floor. 'Shit.'

I stooped down, grabbing my hair conditioner before it rolled down the steps. Cam knelt, picking up the rest of my spilled items. In his hands were my shampoo, toothpaste, and tampons. Nice. Cursing under my breath, I forced my gaze up.

Cam's jaw was clamped shut, and I had to look away quickly, because seeing him wasn't good.

'If you laugh, I will punch you in the stomach,' I said, grabbing the rest of the groceries.

'I wouldn't dare think of laughing.' A hint of amusement filled his tone.

He followed me into my apartment, moving past me and putting the bags on the counter. I did the same, my heart pumping with him in my kitchen. 'You didn't have to help, but thank you,' I said, hands shaking as I pulled the milk out of one of the bags. He was still in the kitchen, standing in front of the door. 'I really need to—'

'Do you really think you're going to get rid of me that easily now that I'm in here?' he asked.

I shoved the milk into the fridge and went to the frozen stuff. 'I could only hope.'

'Ha. Funny. We need to talk.'

Stacking the frozen dinners into a pile, I carried them to the freezer. 'We don't need to talk.'

'Yes, we do.'

'No, we don't. And I'm busy. As you can see, I have groceries to put away and I—'

'Okay, I can help.' Cam strolled forward, heading to the counter. 'And we can talk while I help you.'

'I don't need your help.'

'Yeah, I think you kind of do.'

I whipped around, leaving the freezer door open. Cold air blew across the back of my neck, but I barely felt it over the panic and anger of having to face him. 'What is that supposed to mean?'

'It doesn't mean what you think it does, Avery. Jesus.' He thrust a hand through his messy hair. 'All I want to do is talk to you. That's all I've been trying to do.'

'Obviously I don't want to talk to you.' I stormed over to the counter, swiping the pack of hamburger meat off the counter. Tossing it into the freezer, I slammed the door shut. Several items rattled inside and on top of the fridge. 'And you're still here.'

Cam took a deep breath as the muscle along his jaw started thrumming. 'Look, I get that you're not happy with me, but you have to fill me in on what I did to piss you off so badly that you won't talk to me or even—'

'You didn't do anything, Cam! I just don't want to talk to you.' Pivoting on my heel, I left the kitchen and headed for the front door. 'Okay?'

'No, it's not okay.' He followed me into the living room, but stopped behind the couch. 'This is not how people act, Avery. They don't just up and drop a person or hide from them. If there's—'

'You want to know how people don't act?' Stung by the truth in his words, I lashed out. 'People also don't constantly call and harass people who obviously don't want to see them! How about that?'

'Harass you? Is that what I've been doing?' Cam let out a laugh, but it came out harsh. 'Are you fucking kidding me? Me being concerned about you is harassing?'

I opened my mouth, but that messy ball had returned, almost strangling me. 'I shouldn't have said that. You're not harassing me. I just …' I trailed off, running both my hands through my hair. 'I don't know.'

Cam's lips thinned as he stared at me. He shook his head. 'This is about what I saw, isn't it?' He gestured at my arm, and I tensed. 'Avery, you can—'

'No,' I said, holding my wrist. 'It's not about that. It's

230

not about anything. I just don't want to do this.'

'Do what?'

'This!' I closed my eyes briefly, dragging in a deep breath. 'I don't want to do *this*.'

'Good God, woman, all I'm trying to do is talk to you!'

His words tugged at my heart, but I shook my head as I met his gaze. 'There's nothing to talk about, Cam.'

'Avery, come on …' Cam sucked in his bottom lip, drawing my attention like he'd dangled a cheeseburger in the face of a starving frat boy. 'Okay, you know what? I'm not going to rake myself over fucking hot coals for this. Fuck it.'

I flinched as I took a step to the side. Totally deserved that, but it hurt—it sliced deep.

He brushed past me, reaching the door. 'Look, I'm heading home for winter break. I'll be back and forth, so if you need anything …' He laughed again, the sound humorless as he thrust his fingers through his hair. 'Yeah, you don't need anything.'

An ache poured into my chest as I watched him pull open the door. Cam made it out into the hallway, and then he turned around. 'You're staying here, all break by yourself, aren't you? Even Christmas?'

Silent, I folded my arms across my chest.

He looked away, jaw clenching. 'Whatever. Have a good Christmas, Avery.'

Cam stalked toward his apartment and I expected to hear the door slam but didn't, and somehow that was much worse. I closed my door, my eyes already blurry. *This was the right thing to happen,* I kept telling myself as I backed up from the door. Brit had been wrong. There wasn't anything to work out or fix. It was better this way. It had to be.

Except it didn't feel that way at all.

Chapter 21

Two things happened on Christmas Day. My father texted me to wish me a 'Merry Xmas.' *Xmas*. Couldn't even type out Christmas. So personal. Love you too, Dad.

And it snowed that evening.

I hadn't ever seen it snow on Christmas.

Caving in to the tiny trill of excitement, I pulled on my jacket and a pair of thick boots and then slipped out of my apartment. Even though I knew no one was home in Cam's apartment, not even Ollie, I glanced at their door as I reached the stairs. I wondered who was taking care of Raphael.

A heavy feeling settled in my chest as I forced myself down the steps and out from under the awning of the apartment building. Strings of multicolored lights hung from the windows of some of the apartments. Christmas tree lights shone from others. I hadn't put up any decorations. Didn't seem like it made sense to go through all that, but I had ordered myself a Christmas present.

A new messenger bag—distressed leather. A new bag for a new semester.

I don't know where I was heading, but I found myself in the little patch of field on the other side of the last building.

Fluffy white flakes already dusted the ground and were falling thickly.

Shoving my hands into the pockets of my jacket, I tipped my head back and closed my eyes. Tiny flakes dropped onto my cheeks and lips. Each little sliver was cold and wet. I stood there long enough that if anyone looked out the window, they'd think I'd lost my damn mind, but I didn't care.

Cam hadn't contacted me since the day with the groceries.

Not that I had expected him to, but there was a knot in my chest whenever I checked my phone and there was nothing from him. How twisted was that? I told him that I didn't want to talk to him, so he stopped. That was what I wanted, wasn't it?

A different kind of dampness covered my cheeks, mingling with the misty snow, and I sighed. Opening my eyes, I watched the snow fall for a few more seconds, and then I headed back inside.

As I stood outside my door, I looked over at Cam's and whispered, 'Merry Christmas.'

The day after New Year's, I'd had enough of my solitary confinement and did what I wanted to do. On the cold and blustery day, I pulled up Google Maps and drove into the nation's capital and visited the museums.

I was proud of myself by the time I found a place to park. I didn't take out a family of four driving in the city. But growing up near Houston sort of prepared me for the insanity of these kinds of roads.

The museums were packed, mostly with families, and I wasn't sure if that was normal for a day after a holiday. I spent most of my time in the Eternal Life in Ancient Egypt portion of the Smithsonian. Truly amazing to see the artifacts from thousands of years ago.

And the mummy was pretty damn awesome too.

The history nerd in me was all kinds of excited as I roamed the wide corridors, even though I was alone and every so many minutes, no matter how many times I told myself to stop, I thought about how Cam had seemed like he had wanted to do this with me. Granted, that had been right before he'd kissed me, so he might have been down for just about anything at that point.

I couldn't even fool myself into thinking he was still visiting home, because when I left this morning, I spotted his silver truck parked at the back of the parking lot. Cam was back at school.

I stopped in front of a display of pottery. Thinking about him kissing me so did not help. It made all of this worse. I turned, spying a teenage couple more interested in the feel of each other's mouths than all the wonder of history laid out before them.

A pang hit my chest.

Okay, maybe coming here wasn't the smartest of all ideas, but I couldn't stay home today.

Not when it was my birthday.

The big 2-0.

I hadn't heard from my parents yet. I'd figured they'd text or something, but by the time I left the capital, a little before four in the afternoon, I still hadn't heard anything from them.

Yeah, that carried a jellyfish type of sting.

I stopped at the Dairy Queen near my apartment and picked up one of those ice cream cakes. I wasn't a huge fan of ice cream, but whatever made up that crunchy stuff in the middle was absolutely divine.

With my little slice of cake, I curled up on the couch and made it through half the first season of *Supernatural* before passing out at an embarrassingly early hour.

I woke up sometime between four and five in the morning, feeling like fog had invaded my brain. Pushing myself into a sitting position, I winced at the vicious throbbing in my temples. Thinking it was from sleeping on the couch in an awkward position, I stood.

'Whoa.' I pressed my palm to my forehead as the room did a tilt-a-whirl. My skin felt hot. Was I sweating?

I started toward my bedroom to change, but only made it halfway before I veered off to the bathroom.

'Oh God,' I gasped out.

Cramps seized my stomach and I dropped to my knees, lifting the lid on the toilet. The ice cream cake and everything else I ate that day came up quick. It was impressive, and it didn't stop for hours. As soon as it seemed like the nausea had eased, I leaned back against the tub, resting my cheek on the cool surface. That felt good, but the calm feeling didn't last long. My tummy clenched and I barely reached the toilet in time.

It was official.

God had done the whole 'I smite thee' by striking me down with a nasty case of the influenza virus. How had I caught it? Did that matter? Hell no. Nothing mattered as I lay on the cool tile floor, my cheek smushed and most likely now carrying the pattern of the floor. I had no concept of how much time had passed. I knew I needed medicine, something from the store. Yes, the store would be a good idea. Chicken soup. Theraflu. Pepto ...

Stumbling to my feet, I shuffled back into the living room. The walls seemed funny to me, fuzzy and a little warped, like they were waving to me. After a minor adventure, I found my purse and keys and made it to the front door. Just as I unlocked it, I felt the ominous stirring in my stomach.

I dropped my purse and keys and spun. The walls danced. Not good. I made it a couple of steps and my legs did the strangest thing. They just stopped working. Done. Nothing. I dropped to the floor, but really didn't feel it. Crawling toward the kitchen, because I had enough sense left to not want to do this on the carpet, I made it to the sink. I hauled myself up and leaned over the sink, my stomach heaving until tears leaked down my cheeks.

Oh man, this sucked.

Finally, when the storm seemed to have passed, I slid down, leaning back against the cabinets under the sink. Okay. The store was out of the question. So was bed. I'm not sure if I stretched out or sort of fell over, but I was back against the cool floor again. At least the kitchen floor had more space.

A deep ache settled into my muscles and bones. My head throbbed so badly it hurt to open my eyes or to concentrate on anything other than the fact that it hurt. It felt like someone had shoved a wool brush down my throat. My brain felt like it was trying to run through muddy waters. Nothing really made sense to me. I heard the phone chirping from somewhere, and then sometime later, it rang and rang … and it rang. I wondered if it was my parents. Maybe they'd remembered that yesterday was my birthday.

I think I might've fallen asleep, because there was a banging that sounded far, far away. And I thought I heard my living room door open. I was at the point where I didn't care if it was a mass murderer. I'd welcome anyone willing to put me out of my misery.

'Avery?' There was a pause and then an 'Oh my God.'

The murderer knew my name and was the praying type? Lovely.

Cool hands touched my forehead. 'Avery, oh my God, are you okay?'

The murderer sort of sounded like Brit, so it was obviously not a murderer. I forced my eyes open into thin slits. Her

237

face blurred together for a second. Worry etched into her features and then her face wavered.

'Flu,' I mumbled. 'I have the flu ...'

'So that's why it smells like there was a vomit party in here.'

I winced. 'Ugh.'

'Yes, ugh, all of this is ugh.'

I heard something drop on the floor and then the cool hands were gone. My fridge door opened and wonderful, beautiful, cold air washed over the floor and me. I was in heaven, freaking heaven.

The door shut and Brit returned, water in hand. 'You need to drink water. Come on, help me help you sit up.'

Mumbling under my breath, I got my hands on the floor but my arms felt too weak. She got an arm around me and had me leaning against the cabinet. A water bottle appeared by my dry lips.

'No.' I tried to knock her away, but I couldn't lift my arms. 'You ... get ... flu ...'

'I got the flu shot, so no. Drink this water, Avery. Drink it.' She put it to my mouth again, and the water leaked in, scorching my throat. 'It probably hurts, huh? If you drink this water, I'll go to the store and get you some stuff, okay? I think you have a fever.' Her hand pressed against my forehead. 'Yep, you have a fever.'

I think I drank the water and then I think I face-planted on the floor afterward. Everything blurred. Brit was talking to me and I think I responded. No idea what was coming out of my mouth. She left me on the floor at some point and then I heard her again, out in the living room, speaking in a low voice. The pain in my head was too much to open my eyes.

Arms slipped under me, and for a second I was floating. Then I shifted, resting against something warm and hard.

I moaned, turning my head toward it. There was a familiar, soothing scent that tugged at me, lulled me under until I was lying on something much more comfortable and there was something cool and damp pressed to my forehead.

I slept on and off, waking every so often to realize I wasn't alone. Someone sat beside me on the bed, holding a cloth to my cheeks. I murmured something before falling back asleep. I'm not sure how long this lasted, but finally my eyes opened, and it was like coming out of a coma. The light filtering through the window was too harsh, and the throbbing was still in my head but duller than before.

I opened my mouth, but immediately started hacking.

Footsteps pounded from the hall and suddenly Brit was in my bedroom doorway, a glass of water in one hand and a mug in the other. 'You're alive! Thank God, I was beginning to think I accidentally killed you by forcing meds down your throat.'

I looked at her dumbly. 'I took medicine?'

'Yep.' She bounced over to me and sat on the bed. 'You've taken medicine twice and you're about to take it again. You need to drink all of this water. And then you need to drink this—more medicine. My mom, who's a nurse by the way, said that since it seems like your fever broke last night, you should be fine. Well, you should be better.'

'Last night?' Covering my mouth with my hand, I started hacking again as I took the water from her. We had to wait for *that* to pass. 'What … time is it?'

Brit sat on the edge of the bed, holding a steaming mug. I could already smell the lemon. 'Time? Honey, day would probably be the better question. It's Saturday.'

I almost choked on my water. 'I've been … out of it for … a full day?'

'A full day and a half,' she said, sympathetic. 'When I texted and called you and you didn't answer, I got worried. That's why I came over. You were pretty bad. Mom said it was probably from dehydration.'

Mulling that over while I finished off the water, I placed the glass on the nightstand and took the mug from her. Another coughing fit hit me, and only by some miracle did I not spill it on myself. 'Did you … stay here the whole time?'

'Not the entire time. I had help.'

'Thank you,' I said. 'Really, thank you. I'd still be lying on … the floor if it weren't … for you and Jacob.'

She shook her head.

Suddenly, something very important occurred to me. I glanced down at myself. I was wearing a long-sleeve sleep shirt. My bra was still on and I was in pajama bottoms—oh my God—my bracelet was off. My head jerked up way too fast, causing the ache to spread across my face. The bracelet sat on the nightstand. 'Did you …?'

'Yes and no,' she said, messing with the short ponytail at the top of her head. 'I helped you get into the bottoms.'

'Then who …?' A sinking feeling had me thinking I was going to have to run for the bathroom again. 'Oh my God …'

Brit winced. 'Don't hate me, Avery, but I didn't know what else to do. I couldn't get you off the floor. For someone who is so little, you weigh a ton, and I have more muscles than Jacob. Cam was right across the hall, and it seemed like the quickest solution.'

Oh my God, I couldn't even wrap my sick brain around this little piece of news. If Brit hadn't stripped me from my sweat-soaked sweater, it had to have been Cam, which meant he was the one who placed the bracelet on the nightstand.

I closed my eyes.

'Are you feeling like you're going to hurl again?'

'No,' I said hoarsely. 'So … so Cam was here?'

'He carried you to the bed and stayed with you while I ran to the store,' she said, crossing her legs. 'When I came back, he'd changed your shirt and he swore he didn't peek at your goodies. Though I was staring at his goodies. He was shirtless the entire time. Even though I had every window in this house open to air out all your funk.'

All my funk. Cam was all up in my funk.

'He was like the perfect nurse. Had a damp cloth to your face, keeping you cool.' Brit sighed a dreamy sound. 'He even stayed with you while I cleaned up your mess.'

'Thank you,' I said again, finishing off the mug. 'I mean it, thank you so much. I owe you.'

'You do.' She flashed a quick grin. 'You also owe Cam.'

I collapsed back against the bed, closing my eyes. 'I bet you had to beg him to come over.'

'No,' she replied, poking my leg until I looked at her. 'I didn't have to ask him twice. He dropped what he was doing and came right over to help you.'

Chapter 22

The sickness had lingered and turned into a disgusting, hacking cold that I treated obsessively with every over-the-counter medicine known to man. By the first day of spring semester, I was still coughing, but I felt well enough to go to class.

On the way downstairs, I grew some lady balls and went over to Cam's apartment. I needed to thank him, face-to-face and not over text. With my heart pounding like I'd run up and down the stairs, I knocked on his door.

Heavy footsteps sounded on the other side of the door seconds before it flung open, revealing Ollie in all his messy glory. A sleepy smile crossed his lips. 'Hey there, glad to see you up and walking around.'

'Thanks.' I felt my cheeks warm. 'Is Cam up?'

'Yeah, let me check. Hold on a sec.' He left the door open a crack as he disappeared back in the apartment. A few moments—moments that felt like forever—he returned, a little less rumpled. 'Actually, he, um, left already for class.'

'Oh.' I smiled to hide my disappointment. 'Well, I'll … see you around.'

'Yeah.' Ollie nodded as he ran a hand through his shoulder-length hair. 'Hey, Avery, I hope you're feeling better.'

'I am. Thanks.'

Giving him a little wave, I readjusted the strap of my new bag and then pulled out my gloves as I headed down the stairs and out into the bright, freezing morning. I stopped a few spaces behind my car, my heart tumbling.

There it was—Cam's truck.

He hadn't left for class. He'd been in the apartment. The truth was as cold as the weather. Ollie had gone back to ask him, and Cam hadn't wanted to see me.

I saw Cam around campus a lot over the next few weeks. It seemed we had a schedule that placed us near each other, and every time I saw him, he was with Jase or with Steph.

Whenever I saw him with her, there was a nasty little feeling that settled in my stomach. I had no right to that feeling. I knew that, but it didn't stop me from wanting to take off and karate-chop Steph into next week.

But that wasn't the worse part of spotting him. Most times he would see me, and if our gazes collided, he *always* looked away. It was like we hadn't been friends for almost five months or shared any intimate moments. It was like we didn't even know each other.

It reminded me of how things had become with my friends in high school after the Halloween party. As if our time together had been erased.

On Friday, a small opening occurred. Cam was alone, crossing the main street, heading toward Knutti, his head down and hands shoved into the pockets of his hoodie.

'Cam!' I yelled his name so suddenly that it caused a rather pathetic-sounding coughing fit that was left over from my cold.

He stopped, lifting his chin. Wisps of dark hair curled out from under the knit cap he wore.

I struggled up the rest of the hill, chest and legs aching. Out of breath, I stopped in front of him. 'Sorry,' I croaked out, taking several deep breaths. 'Need a second.'

His brows knitted. 'You sound terrible.'

'Yeah, it's the Black Death and it never goes away.' I cleared my throat, forcing my eyes to meet his. For a moment, as I stared into those crystalline eyes, I forgot why I had forced him to stop.

Something crossed his face and then he averted his gaze, a muscle thumping in his jaw. 'I've got to get to class, so …?'

Cam in a hurry to get to class? The apocalypse was about to occur. I fought the urge to just walk away at that point, because it was painfully obvious he had no interest in this conversation, but I stood my ground. I owed it to him.

'I just wanted to say thank you for helping Brit out when I was sick.'

His lips pursed as he focused on something beyond me. 'It's not a big deal.'

'It was to me,' I said quietly, wishing he'd look at me. 'So thank you.'

Cam nodded curtly and then took a deep breath. His gaze flickered back to me and then away. His shoulders tensed. 'You're welcome.'

'Well …' I ran out of something to say because everything that came to mind shouldn't be spoken. Like *I'm sorry for being such a bitch*. And *I wish you hadn't seen the scar*.

'I've got to go,' he said finally, backing toward the side entrance of the building, where several students smoked. 'I'll see you around.'

'I'm sorry,' I blurted out, my heart stuttering.

Cam turned around, eyes narrowed, and it was like he was waiting for something, but then he shook his head. 'Me too.'

I didn't stop him again.

Tears burned the back of my throat, and somehow I made it to English 102, which was in the same building as him. The morning was a numb blur and when I met with Jacob and Brit in the Den for lunch, I barely followed their conversation as I picked at my sandwich. I think they were used to it though, because neither of them pointed it out.

As Brit and I walked to Whitehall for economics, I told her about my run-in with Cam. 'He didn't want anything to do with me.'

'I don't think that's the case, Avery.'

'Oh, it is. He was in a hurry to get the hell away from me. Actually said he couldn't be late for class, and come on, Cam never cares about that.'

Brit tugged her cap down over her ears as we stopped near the pavilion in front of the social sciences building. 'Can I be real with you?'

'Yes.'

She clasped her glove-covered hands together. 'You know I love you, right? So I'm just going to put this out there. You have avoided Cam since Thanksgiving, and to me, him, and baby Jesus, it seems like that was what you wanted. For him to just go away.'

I opened my mouth, but what could I say? That was what I wanted.

'And so he has gone away. You can't blame him for that. The guy is only going to put up with so much, you know?' She pursed her lips. 'And after ignoring him for that long, he's probably not going to be thrilled talking to you.'

'I know,' I admitted. 'It's just …'

'You've finally pulled your head out of your ass and you're worried it's too late?'

Was that it? I wasn't sure, but I hoped not, because at least with my head in my ass, what happened between us was a little less depressing.

'Give it some time,' she said, dropping her arm around my shoulders. 'If he doesn't come around, then fuck him.'

'Fuck him,' I repeated, but I really didn't feel it.

Brit squeezed me anyway. 'That's my girl.'

Friday night, I stared at my econ homework, convinced it was a totally different language designed to confuse the hell out of people. Concentrating was proving difficult for several reasons. Several times I found myself staring at the TV screen, not really seeing what was on the television, my mind going in different directions, most of them leading back to Cam.

I was getting sick of myself.

My phone suddenly went off, ringing from deep inside my bag. Digging it out, I groaned when I saw the caller's name. My cousin. I was a bit surprised that he was actually calling me after the dozens of e-mails I'd ignored.

But the fact that he was calling me was what made me bite the bullet and answer.

'Hello,' I said, my voice monotone.

There was a silent moment and then, 'You answered the phone?'

'Why wouldn't I?' Yeah, that sounded ridiculous even to me. 'What's up, David?'

'Have you read any of my e-mails?' The uppityness that was normally in his tone was absent. Shocking.

'Ah, I read one or two, but I've been busy, with college and all.' I stood and nudged my bag under the coffee table. 'So …'

David's sigh was quite audible. 'You don't know anything? Have your parents tried to contact you?'

I snorted. 'Um, no. They forgot my *birthday*.'

'Sorry about that,' he replied, and I could practically see his cringe. 'I thought that they might have tried to tell you about what's been going on here. It sort of has to do with you.'

Walking into the kitchen, I frowned as I grabbed a soda out of the fridge. 'How does anything back there have anything to do with me?'

There was a pause, and the bomb of all bombs was dropped. 'It's about Blaine Fitzgerald. He's been arrested.'

The can of soda slipped from my fingers and clanged off the floor. It rolled under the table. I stood there, staring at the fridge. 'What?'

'He's been arrested, Avery. That's why I've been trying to get ahold of you. I thought … I don't know, I thought you would like to know.'

My legs felt weak, so I turned and clutched the counter with one hand. The room tilted as if I was sick again.

'Avery, are you there?'

'Yes,' I said, swallowing. 'What happened?'

'It was at the start of summer, but it was kept quiet until about the middle of August, when he was arrested. There was a party being thrown. Some younger kids were there, from what I heard,' he explained, and I closed my eyes. 'It was a girl you went to school with. I think she was a year younger than you—Molly Simmons.'

I remembered seeing her name in one of his e-mails and assuming something totally different. 'What … did he do?'

David didn't answer immediately. 'He was charged with sexual assault and several other offenses. He goes to trial in June, but has been out on bail. It's not looking good for him. There's a lot of evidence. The only reason I know any of this is because his father came to mine to represent his case. My father turned the case down. I want you to know that.'

I didn't know what to say to that. Thank you for not representing the asshole? I didn't know what to say at all. I was stunned. I'd always wondered if Blaine had done what he'd done to me to someone else and if my silence would enable him to do it again. I had hoped not—I'd prayed that wouldn't be the case.

'The girl he … raped contacted your family.'

I didn't know what I was more shocked about: the fact that this girl contacted my family or that David had actually said *rape*. 'What? Why? I haven't said anything. I've kept my—'

'I know, Avery. I know you didn't say anything, but she went to the same high school as you. She heard the rumors about you and Blaine, and, well, she put two and two together. She went to your parents first and I'm sure you know how well that went.'

I needed to sit down before I fell down.

'When they refused to even speak to her, she came to me.' David paused. 'I didn't tell her anything, Avery. That's not my place, but I think she's been trying to get ahold of you. I don't know how she got your information.'

'I don't think she has.' I plopped down on the couch. Then again, I deleted almost every e-mail I didn't recognize. 'The girl? Is she … okay? I mean, did she seem like she was okay?'

David cleared his throat. 'Honestly? No.'

Rubbing my brow, I let out a low breath. 'Of course she's not. That was a stupid question.'

'You might want to, uh, check your e-mail or something. She really seemed like she needed to talk to you and that was back in August.'

'I can't say anything to her. If I do and it gets out, his family will sue me and my family for *millions*.' Bile rose in my throat. 'It's a part of my nondisclosure.'

'I know,' David said. 'But like I said, I thought you'd like to know what's happening.'

My head was full of so much I could barely pick one question to ask. 'And the charges? You think they're going to stick? That he's going to go to jail?'

'From what Father has seen, the charges are going to stick. He's going to go to prison, Avery, at least for several years.'

My eyes fluttered open. Relief swamped me, so potent, so powerful that it was like having a ton of bricks removed from my chest. Never in my wildest hopes had I expected this. Blaine wasn't going to jail because of what he had done to me, but justice was being served. Finally. I just hated that this had to happen to another girl—a girl who probably faced a terrible amount of censure for coming forward but had stuck to it. A bit of the relief turned into guilt and shame. What if I had told my parents no? What if I had held my ground? This might not have happened to Molly. And only God knows how many other girls this could've happened to that we'd never know about. My stomach roiled at the thought.

'Anywaaay …' David drew the word out. 'I just wanted to let you know.'

'Thank you,' I said, meaning it. 'I'm sorry about not responding. I thought … well, it doesn't matter what I thought.'

'I know what you thought. I haven't really given you a reason to think anything other than that.' He paused, and my eyes widened. 'Look, I want to tell you that I'm sorry.'

'What?'

'All these years, well, I never knew what really happened, but I should've done something,' he said. 'I'm sorry. I'm sorry you had to go through what you did.'

Emotion crawled up my throat. Nothing short of amazing happened. Not only was David removed from my fantasy 'shit list;' those two words, such simple words, were like a bright beacon in the middle of the night. My fingers trembled around the phone. I squeezed my eyes shut, but a tear snuck out.

'Thank you,' I whispered hoarsely. 'Thank you.'

Chapter 23

I was still in a state of shock most of Saturday, so much so that after I met with Jacob and Brit for our study date with coffee, I couldn't even remember what the hell I had done with them, and then after eating a quick dinner of mac 'n' cheese, I realized that I had left my bag in my car, along with my phone.

Too distracted and a little bit lazy, I didn't even put shoes on as I yanked open my door and stepped out into the hallway, drawing up short when I spotted Ollie coming up the stairs with a case of beer in his hands.

'Hey!' He smiled. 'What are you doing out here … in your socks?'

'Uh, I was running to my car to get my bag.' I shifted my weight. 'Thirsty?'

Ollie laughed. 'While I'm always thirsty, this is not for me. There's a fight tonight and we've got a few people over.'

'Sounds like fun.'

'Yeah …' He glanced at his door, switching the case to his other arm. 'Why don't you come over?'

My heart jumped. 'Oh, I don't know about that. Maybe another—'

'Come on, the main fight hasn't even started yet, so you haven't missed anything.'

I hesitated. 'I don't know …'

Ollie stuck out his lower lip, and it was so ridiculous that I laughed. 'Cam will be happy to see you.'

'Yeah, I don't think—'

'Sounds like a plan right there,' he interrupted. 'Don't think about it. Come over. Just for a little while, okay? Maybe we can take Raphael for a walk.'

I laughed again, thinking of Ollie and the poor tortoise as I glanced back at their apartment. Why shouldn't I stop by? It would be a normal thing to do, and Ollie lived there. He could invite me. And if I was honest with myself, I wanted to see Cam.

I … I missed him.

Taking a deep breath, I nodded. 'Okay. Just for a little while.'

'Great!' Ollie looped his free arm through mine, and before I could change my mind, he led me down the hall.

'Wait! I don't have shoes on.'

'Who cares?' He gave me a goofy grin as we crossed the short distance. 'Shoes are overrated.'

My heart rate kicked up as Ollie nudged the door open. Immediately the sound of laughter and fighting amplified, and for a moment, I was a little overwhelmed. Everyone was focused on the TV. Ollie let go of my arm and set the case in the fridge. He picked up two shot glasses off the counter in the kitchen. What in the hell was I doing here?

'Jose welcomes you.' He offered me one of the tiny glasses.

My hand shook a little as I took it. The voice in my head told me no, but goddamnit, I was tired of that voice. It was the same voice that had told me to tell Cam to go away. The same voice that had told me to listen to my parents. The same voice that had told me to let Blaine take me into that room.

254

That voice had done nothing but fuck me over. I downed the shot, and immediately my eyes watered as the liquid scorched my throat.

'Holy smokes,' I muttered, blinking rapidly.

Ollie laughed as he replaced the shot with a bottle of beer, and then he grabbed my arm, pulling me back into the living room. 'Look who I found!' he shouted.

Several heads turned, and my fingers tightened around the neck of the beer. I didn't see anyone except Cam, and the moment I laid eyes on him, I knew this was a bad, bad idea.

It seemed like months since I'd last seen him.

Cam sat on the couch, baseball cap on backward. He was leaning forward, yelling at the two guys on the TV who were beating the crap out of each other. The burgundy hoodie was unzipped, revealing a white shirt underneath. Beside him on the couch was Steph.

I took a healthy drink of the beer.

She looked perfect, as usual: hair a glossy brunette, tight black turtleneck stretched over her breasts. She must've said something, because Cam finally looked over, and it was like being punched in the chest.

Surprise flickered across his striking face, and then his gaze dropped to what was in my hand. His brows shot up and then our eyes locked. My heart seemed to skip a beat. To me, it seemed like everyone stopped talking and started staring, but in reality, only seconds passed and no one probably even noticed anything.

One side of his lips curved up. 'Hey.'

'Hey,' I replied lamely.

He continued watching me for a few more moments and then turned back to the screen, shoulders straight and tense. He didn't want me here. It was written all over him, and, besides, Steph was beside him.

I started for the door, but somehow Ollie ended up behind me and the next thing I knew, he had me sitting in an empty recliner, facing the TV. Two shirtless guys in spandex shorts were punching each other in the face.

Hmm.

Tensed, I drank the beer faster than I probably should've. Steph's husky chuckle crawled into my stomach and started clawing at my insides. Over the course of minutes, she was practically in Cam's lap, one hand wrapped around his biceps. She leaned in and whispered in his ear. Cam shook his head, and the most perfect pout filled out her lips. What had she said?

Someone—Ollie, maybe?—handed me another shot of Jose that warmed my stomach and washed away Steph's claws.

'Like the socks.'

Glancing up, I saw one of Cam's friends. I didn't know his name or really recognize his face, but he had a nice smile. I stretched my legs out, wiggling my toes in my rainbow-colored socks. 'Thanks.'

He ran a hand over his close-cut brown hair and clasped the back of his neck. 'So you normally watch UFC fights?'

I looked at the screen. A guy was kicked back into the cage. 'This is the first time I've watched one of these.'

'You don't sound like you'll be watching one of these again.'

Opening my mouth, I was surprised to hear a giggle come out. 'Yeah, I don't know if this will be something I watch regularly.'

'Well, that's a damn shame,' the guy said with a slight grin. 'Cam orders this every month and you coming would be something else to look forward to.'

I didn't say anything to that and turned back to the TV, running my hand over my knee. The shots and beer were making my muscles warm and my thoughts fuzzy. The guy asked if I wanted another drink and I realized my bottle was empty.

'Sure.' The smile that crossed my face felt overly wide and bright.

Returning with a cold one, he sat on the arm of my chair, and beyond him, I saw Cam look up and narrow his eyes. 'Here you go.'

'Thanks.' I took a drink, now at the point where I could easily ignore the nasty aftertaste that filled my mouth. My gaze collided with Cam's for a second, and I forced myself to look away. I ended up staring up at the guy beside me. 'I'm sorry. I didn't catch your name.'

The guy nudged my shoulder. 'I don't think we've met before. I'm Henry.'

'Avery,' I said.

He repeated my name with a smile. 'Like it. It's different.'

'Like my socks?'

Henry laughed as he glanced at the screen. 'Yeah, like your socks. So you going to college, Avery?'

I nodded. 'You don't?'

'Nope. Graduated a couple of years ago. I know Cam from … well, from this thing we do.' He took a swig from his beer as I tried to figure out what that meant. He looked down at me, brows furrowed. 'Are you old enough to be drinking?'

I giggled. 'Nope.'

'Didn't think so. You look pretty young.'

'I'm not that young. I just turned twenty.'

'Thank God you're legal,' he said, shaking his head as his brows rose. 'I just won't tell anyone about the beer in your hand.'

Cocking my head to the side, I tried to figure out his age. 'How old are you?'

257

He glanced down at me. 'Old enough to know better.'

Before I could get him to elaborate on that, Cam yelled out. 'Hey, Henry, come here a second.'

Henry pushed off the arm of the recliner and made his way around a couple of the other guys. Steph sat back and crossed her arms as Cam motioned Henry to lean down. I had no hope of hearing what Cam was saying to him, but then Henry backed away and headed over to where Jase was leaning against the bare stretch of wall.

More than curious about what was going on over there, I felt the strong urge to do some investigation. I opened my mouth, because why the hell not, but Steph had a hold on Cam's arm, and I was distracted. He was whispering to her. She jerked her hand back and shot me what could only be described as a 'bitch' look. Frankly, it was a fucking work of art and I was sort of jealous of that level of mastery.

I glanced over at Henry, and he looked up. He winked, and I smiled in return, feeling sort of giddy. My skin prickled along my neck and I turned to where Cam sat. He was staring at me, and I started to smile at him, too, but then he glanced toward Henry.

Cam muttered something, and Steph shot to her feet, stalking back toward the hall bathroom, yanking the door open. Then Cam was up, coming toward me, and my giddiness was all consuming. A big, stupid smile broke out across my face. It had been so long since we'd talked, and I missed him, I really did.

Cam was … he was special … to me, and I wanted to go back in time, to Thanksgiving, and not have overreacted. I wanted to take back dropping astronomy and I wished I hadn't avoided him. I wanted to not be that girl who did stupid, stupid things like that. I wanted Cam to smile at me like he used to.

He wasn't smiling now, that's for sure. 'Come with me for a sec?'

I'd go anywhere with him.

Jumping up, I swayed as the room seemed to tilt to the side. 'Whoa.'

His jaw clenched as he caught my arm. 'You okay to walk?'

'Yes. Of course.' I took a step and bumped into Cam. I giggled at the doubtful look that crossed his face. 'I'm okay.'

Cam shot Ollie a dark glare as he led me into the brightly lit kitchen, backing me up against the counter. He stood between me and the doorway, arms folded over his chest. 'What are you doing, Avery?' he asked in a low voice.

I held up my bottle. 'Drinking. What are you doing?'

His icy blue eyes narrowed. 'That's not what I'm getting at and you know that. What are you doing?'

Damn. Hello, attitude. I tried to give Cam the bitch look Steph had mastered, screwing my face up until I'm sure I looked like I was having a seizure. I sighed and gave up. 'I'm not doing anything, Cam.'

'You're not?' He raised his brows. 'You're drunk.'

'Am not!'

He gave me a bland look. 'A drunk's famous last words before he falls flat on his face.'

'That has not happened … yet.'

Cam shook his head and then he grabbed my arm, pulling me back into the living room. I thought he was going to make me sit beside him or something, like I was in a time-out, but he opened the front door and led me out into the chilly hallway.

'Um …' Not what I was expecting.

'You need to go home, Avery.' He let go of my arm and pointed at my apartment door like I had no idea where I lived.

My mouth dropped open as I clenched the bottle to my chest. 'Are you serious?'

'Yes. I'm fucking serious. You're drunk, and that shit is not going down in front of me.'

'What shit?' I took a step back, bewildered. 'I'm sorry. Ollie invited me—'

'Yeah, and I'm going to kick his ass later.' Jaw set in a hard line, he ran his hand through his hair. 'Just go home, Avery. I'll talk to you later.'

The back of my throat burned. A thousand thoughts raced through my head as I stared at him. 'You're mad at me—'

'I'm not mad at you, Avery.'

Sure as hell didn't seem that way. I shuffled side to side. 'I don't want to go home. There's no one there and I ...' I trailed off as the burn in my throat grew.

Cam drew in a deep breath, closing his eyes. 'I'll come over later and we'll talk, okay? But go home. Please just go home.'

Chapter 24

I opened my mouth, but there was nothing I could say. Cam had actually kicked me out of his apartment. He was begging me to go home. The burn encompassed my lungs now, and red-hot tears pricked the backs of my eyes.

'Okay,' I mumbled.

'Avery …'

'It's totally okay.' Turning away, I stumbled back up the hall and to my door. I heard his open and close before I could even open mine. Pressing my forehead against my door, I squeezed my eyes shut, but a tear snuck out, running down my flushed cheek.

Cam had kicked me out, and my apartment was empty. I was empty. Everything was empty. It would be just me and my stupid beer bottle.

Okay. Maybe I was slightly drunk.

I moved away from my door, not sure where I was going, but I couldn't go inside my apartment. By an act of God, I made it down the five flights of steps and out onto the sidewalk without breaking my neck.

The cold pavement seeped through my thick socks, numbing my feet as I stumbled along, taking another drink.

I found a vacant parking spot and plopped my ass down on the curb. Tilting my head back, I stared up at the sky riddled with stars. Hey, there was the Corona Borealis.

Still didn't look like a fucking crown.

Or maybe it wasn't the Corona Borealis. How the fuck would I know?

The stars … they were pretty, though, and so far away and really blurry. Tears built in my eyes and coated the back of my throat. My arms fell between my legs, bottle dangling from my fingers.

It was official. I really was Señorita Fucktard. And I'd fucked everything up with Cam—the 'what was' and the 'what could've been.' Because there could've been something there, and I was just so fucking stupid. Worst of all, I'd slaughtered our friendship and he had been such a good friend. In the short time I had known him, he'd become the best friend I'd ever had. Seriously.

Wiping my cheek on my shoulder, I took another drink. A cool wind whipped around me, tossing my hair across my face as I lowered my head. I wasn't cold, though, which probably meant I was pretty drunk.

I was such a lightweight.

And why was I sitting on the curb? I honestly didn't know, but it was better than being inside my apartment, all alone. And, yeah, I was alone out here, but it didn't feel that way. I was pretty sure there was a squirrel over by the tree, so that counted for something, right?

I laughed and the wind seemed to pick up the sound, tossing it up in the bare branches, where they rattled like dry bones.

Lifting the bottle to take another drink, I realized it was empty. 'Well, shit on me …' Still, I sat there, staring out across the parking lot, not really seeing anything. I don't know how long it was, but when I glanced up, I couldn't see any of the stars behind the thick, dark clouds and my face felt numb. I wondered what Molly was doing right now. Did she feel any different than me because she had done the right thing? Any better or worse?

'Avery!'

I jumped at the sound of my name and dropped my empty beer bottle. It clanked off the asphalt and rolled under someone's car. Whoops.

Cam stalked across the sidewalk toward me, the wind tossing strands of wavy hair across his forehead. What happened to the cap? I liked the cap. The look on his face twisted up my insides. 'What in the fuck are you doing out here?'

'I … I'm looking at the stars.'

'What?' He stopped beside me and knelt down. 'Avery, it's like thirty degrees outside. You're going to get sick again.'

I shrugged and looked away. 'What are you doing out here?'

'I was looking for you, you little dumbass.'

My head swung in his direction, and my eyes narrowed. It may have been only thirty degrees outside, but the liquor was warm in my tummy and it fueled my temper. 'Excuse me? You're out here, so you're a dumbass, too, you dumbass.'

His lips twitched as if he was trying not to smile. 'I told you I was coming over to talk to you. I checked your apartment first. I knocked and you didn't answer. The door was unlocked and I went inside.'

'You went inside my apartment? That's kind of rude.'

He looked unbothered by that. 'Yeah, I saw you sitting up here from your window.'

It was taking my head a little longer than normal to process everything. 'Is the fight over?'

He sat down beside me, shoulder to shoulder. 'No. The main fight just began.'

'You're missing it.'

Cam didn't respond immediately. He thrust his hand through his hair, causing the ends to stand up between his fingers. 'God, Avery …'

I squirmed, and the liquor sloshed in my stomach.

A muscle in his jaw worked as he focused on the cars I had been staring at earlier. 'Seeing you tonight? I was fucking surprised.'

'Because of Steph?' I blurted out, and blamed the alcohol for that.

'What?' He shot me a look. 'No. Jase invited her.'

'Looked like she was there for you.'

He shrugged one shoulder. 'Maybe she was, but I don't give a fuck.' Then he turned to me, head tilted to the side, hands now on his knees. 'Avery, I haven't messed around with Steph since I met you. I haven't messed around with *anyone* since I met you.'

My heart thumped in my chest. 'Okay.'

'Okay?' He gave a little shake of his head. 'See, you don't get it. You never fucking got it. You've avoided me since Thanksgiving break. Dropped the goddamn class and I know that was because of me, and every time I tried to talk to you, you fucking ran from me.'

'You didn't want to talk to me the day I thanked you for helping me out,' I pointed out.

'Gee, I don't know why? Maybe because you made it painfully clear you didn't want anything to do with me. And then you just show up tonight? Out of the fucking blue and get *drunk*? You don't get it.'

I wet my cold, dry lips. Everything he said was true. 'I'm sorry. I am drunk, a little, and I am sorry, because you're right and … I'm rambling.'

He stared at me a moment and then barked out a short laugh. 'All right, it's not the time for that conversation, obviously. Look, I didn't mean to be such a dick inside there, making you leave, but—'

'It's okay. I'm used to people not wanting me at their parties.' I pushed to my feet. The stars seemed to twirl a bit with the movement. 'No big deal.'

Cam stood, watching me carefully. 'It's not that I didn't want you there, Avery.'

'Um … really?' I laughed, and it sounded hoarse. 'You asked me to leave.'

'I—'

'Correction.' I held up my hand and my fingers blurred a bit. 'You *told* me to leave.'

'I did. It was a dickhead move, but it's the first time you're at my place, you come in there, start drinking and then …' He took a deep breath, letting it out slowly. 'Henry was all over you and you're giggling—'

'I'm not interested in him!'

'It didn't look that way, Avery. You're drunk and I didn't want you doing something you'd regret,' he said. 'I don't know what the hell goes on in your head half the time, and I had no idea what you were doing here tonight, but I've *never* seen you drink like that and I didn't know what you were going to do. I didn't want someone taking advantage of you.'

'Been there, done that,' I tossed out recklessly, and then clamped my mouth shut. Oh my God, I was never drinking again. Ever.

He raised his hands and then stopped halfway. He just stared at me, a terrible understanding crossing his face. 'What?'

I'd made a big mistake—a big, big mistake. Flight-or-fight response kicked in, and of course, I did the flight thing. I started around him.

'Oh, hell no.' Cam was right in front of me, hands on my shoulders. 'What did you just say?'

Damage-control mode took over. 'I don't know what I said. Okay? I'm drunk, Cam. Duh. Who the fuck knows what's coming out of my mouth? I don't. I really don't know what I'm even doing out here.'

'Shit.' His eyes were a dark, midnight blue as he stared into mine. 'Avery …' A pained look crossed his face, and his fingers tightened on my shoulders. 'What are you not telling me? What *haven't* you told me?'

My throat constricted. 'Nothing! I swear. I promise you. I'm just running my mouth, okay? So stop looking at me like there's something wrong with me.'

'I'm not staring at you like that, sweetheart.' His brows slammed down as he searched my face.

I wanted to know what he was thinking, because I knew he had to be lying. That one little slip of the tongue had me desperately trying to come up with a way to erase it. I could lie and tell him I just got really drunk once and embarrassed myself. Sounded believable, but I had absolutely no control of my mouth apparently.

Then Cam did the one thing that sent my thoughts spinning.

He pulled me against him, wrapping his arms around me. I froze for only a second or two and then I placed my hands on his sides. I closed my eyes and pressed my cheek against his chest.

I inhaled his scent, surrounding myself in it. 'I've missed you.'

His hand moved up my back, burying deep in my wind-blown hair. 'I've missed you, too, sweetheart.' He leaned back and lifted me a good couple of inches off my feet and then sat me back down. Sliding his hands to my cheeks, he laughed. 'You feel like a little ice cube.'

'I feel hot.' And that was true. My skin was numb, but I felt his hug and I felt his hands sliding over me. I raised my

266

lashes and our eyes met. 'Your eyes are really beautiful, you know that?'

'I think that's the shots of tequila talking,' he replied, grinning. 'Come on, let's get you inside before you freeze.'

Cam stepped back and let go of my shoulders. I was a little tipsy on my feet, and when he reached down and threaded his fingers through mine, the biggest, stupidest grin lit up my face. It was like he hadn't asked me to leave his apartment and I hadn't been sitting outside for God knows how long like a loser.

Might have been the tequila and beer, but I wanted to run around like a lunatic.

Luckily I didn't attempt that, because the stairs proved to be a tricky beast. I think the depth between each step kept changing on me. Back in my too-toasty apartment, Cam shut the door behind us. He still held my hand tightly in his as he turned to me. He didn't say anything, and a nervous anticipation swelled inside me.

'You're missing the fight,' I said again.

'So I am.' He tugged me around the couch and then down, so I was sitting beside him. Only then did he let go of my hand. 'How are you feeling?'

'Okay.' I smoothed my damp palms along my jeans. 'Your friends are probably wondering where you are.'

Cam leaned back against the cushion, throwing his arm along the back of the couch. 'I don't care.'

'You don't?'

'Nope.'

I sat forward and looked over my shoulder at him. He appeared to be waiting for something. Unable to stay seated, I jumped up and nearly face-planted on the coffee table. Would have if Cam hadn't caught my arm.

'Maybe you should sit down, Avery.'

'I'm okay.' Wiggling free, I moved around the table

carefully, just in case it decided to move on me. The nervous energy buzzed along with the alcohol. I tugged my sweater off my skin, feeling hot. 'So … what did you want to do? I can, um, turn on the TV or put a movie in, but I don't have any movies. I guess I can order one from—'

'Avery, just sit down for a little while.'

Instead of doing that, I picked up a fallen pillow and placed it on the couch. Straightening was a little difficult, but I flitted over to the moon chair. 'You don't think it's hot in here?'

Amusement filled his blue eyes. 'How much did you drink?'

'Um …' I had to really think about that. 'Not much— maybe like two or three shots of tequila aaand two beers? I think.'

'Oh wow.' Cam leaned forward, his lips tipping into a grin. 'When's the last time you really drank?'

'Halloween night,' I blurted.

He looked confused. 'I didn't see you really drink Halloween night.'

'Not this past Halloween night.' I stood, tugging on my sleeves, and my fingers brushed the bracelet. 'It was … five years ago.'

'Whoa. That's a long time.' He scooted forward and then stood. 'You got water in here? Bottled?'

'In the kitchen,' I said, wetting my lips.

He disappeared and reappeared pretty quickly, handing a bottle over. 'You should drink this.'

I took it, but I wasn't thirsty.

'So that made you, what? Fourteen? Fifteen?' He sat back down on the edge of the couch.

'Fourteen,' I whispered, my gaze dropping to where his hands hung between his knees.

'That's really young to be drinking.'

Sweat dotted my forehead. Setting the bottle down, I picked up a hair tie from the coffee table and pulled my hair up into a messy bun. 'Yeah, you didn't drink when you were fourteen?'

A little grin appeared. 'I snuck a beer or two at fourteen, but I thought your parents were strict?'

I snorted as I dropped into the moon chair. 'I don't want to talk about them or drinking or Halloween.'

'Okay.'

Feeling sweaty, I tugged my sweater up. It got stuck around my head for a second, and then finally, I got the itchy material off. Knocking the loose strands of hair out of my face, I glanced over at Cam. You'd think I didn't have a tank top on underneath by the way he was staring at me, but it was more than that.

I stood once more, wanting to be far away from that conversation, because Cam was looking at me again like he was seeing more than I was showing. I thought about how he'd looked when he saw the scar on my wrist and outside minutes before.

It was the same look.

Like he was piecing together a puzzle and the pieces were starting to fit. For some reason, through my disorganized thoughts, I thought about Teresa and how he was when he'd realized she was talking to a guy. He'd taken protective older brother to a whole new level. Had she ...?

I shook my head and pushed those thoughts away, because it made me think of how there hadn't been anyone looking out for me.

But I didn't want him looking at me like that. I didn't need him to watch out for me, to worry about what I was doing or what would happen. I needed him to ...

Look at me the way he had the first night he'd kissed me and then again in the bed at his parents' house. I wanted him to see me like that.

'What are you doing?'

I stopped in between the kitchen and hallway. My fingers were curled around the edges of my tank top, and there was a different kind of interest in his stare, a keen wariness. My heart was racing, and my thoughts were crashing into one another. I liked Cam—a lot. Even if it was crazy and doomed for heartbreak. My heart already hurt. And I'd missed him and he'd missed me and he was here now when he could be with his friends, with Steph.

Part of me stopped thinking completely. The other part told me to do what was expected, what someone like Cam would want and need, because wasn't that why he was here? Because we weren't talking, and I wanted to be that girl from before.

I took off my tank top before my brain caught up with everything. Oddly, that part wasn't hard. Cool air washed over my flushed skin, spreading tiny bumps. The hard part was looking up when I heard Cam inhale.

'Avery.'

My heart was thumping so fast and my pulse pounded. Blood rushed to my face, but I looked up.

He was staring at me, the wariness in the tense line of his jaw overshadowed by the way his chest rose like he was breathing just as fast as I was.

Slightly dizzy, I leaned against the wall, letting my arms fall to my sides. Cam stood a few feet away, and I hadn't seen him move around the couch. He wasn't just staring at me. Oh no, it was much, much more than that. I felt devoured by his stare, like I had felt when he'd kissed me, as if he was committing every detail to his memory. Warmth traveled down my throat, across my chest, and to the lacy edges of my black bra. His lips parted, and I bit down on mine. When he dragged his gaze back up, an intense feeling built low in my stomach. Heat poured into his crystalline eyes, deepening the brilliant hue.

There was a twinge of uncertainty blossoming in my chest, under the delicious tensing, and my throat dried. I didn't want to feel that. I wanted just the warmth and the breathless feeling.

'Cam?'

He shook his head, hands closing into fists at his sides. 'Don't.'

'Don't what?' I asked.

His eyes squeezed shut. 'This—don't do this, sweetheart.'

'Isn't this what you want?' I swallowed.

Cam's eyes flew open. 'I don't expect that, Avery.'

My confidence wavered like a thin tree in a storm and then completely collapsed. I sucked in a breath, and it got stuck in my throat. 'You don't want me.'

Cam was in front of me within a second, so fast I hadn't even seen him move. His hands were planted on either side of my head and he leaned down, his face inches from mine. Tension rolled off his body in waves. Air fled my lungs as my body went rigid.

'Fuck, Avery. You think I don't want you?' His voice came out low, almost a growl. 'There's not a single part of you that I *don't* want, you understand? I want to be on you and *inside* of you. I want you against the wall, on the couch, in your bed, in *my* bed, and every fucking place I can possibly think of, and trust me, I have a vast imagination when it comes to these kinds of things. Don't ever doubt that I want you. That is not what this is about.'

My eyes widened as confusion swirled through me, muddling my thoughts further, which at this point seemed impossible.

He leaned in, resting his forehead against mine. The contact sent my pulse pounding. 'But not like this—never like this. You're drunk, Avery, and when we get

271

together—because we *will* get together, you're going to be fully aware of everything that I do to you.'

It took a few moments, but what he said finally sank in through the liquor haze and confusion and made sense. Closing my eyes, I turned my head to the side, feeling the way his skin slid alongside mine. 'You're a good guy, Cam.'

'No, I'm not.' He exhaled deeply, and his breath was warm against my cheek. 'I'm only good with you.'

Chapter 25

What Cam had been waiting for happened shortly after I took my shirt off and showed him my bra. He'd gotten me to sit down and wrapped a quilt around my shoulders, covering me up. We were watching a horrifically bad science fiction movie when all that liquor decided it didn't want to be in my belly anymore.

Tearing off the quilt, I scrambled over Cam's legs and lap. 'Oh God …'

'What? You're sick.' Cam was on his feet.

I rushed toward the bathroom and slammed the door behind me. Dropping to my knees, I lifted the lid and started heaving. Every muscle in my body went through the motion. Tears streamed down my face as my body shuddered. It seemed wrong to be going through this after having the flu.

Over all the retching noises I was making, I hadn't heard Cam come in, but he was there, kneeling beside me. His hand smoothed the length of my spine, a continuous, endless soothing stroke as he scooped the hair that had escaped my bun out of my face. He stayed, murmuring unintelligible words to me that did wonders, even through the violent dry heaving stage.

When it was all done, he helped me lean against the bathtub while he grabbed a small towel and ran it under the water. He knelt down, wiping the soft material across my face like he had the night of the Halloween party and when I'd been sick. 'Feel better?' he asked.

'Kinda,' I murmured, closing my eyes against the brightness. 'Oh God, this is so embarrassing.'

He chuckled. 'It's nothing, sweetheart.'

'This is why you stayed, right?' I moaned, feeling like a giant idiot. 'You knew I was going to be sick and here I was, taking off my clothes.'

'Shh,' he said, tucking the loose strands of my hair back. 'As charming as it was to watch you vomit up your guts, that's not why I stayed and you know it.'

I closed my eyes again, feeling a bit floaty. 'Because you want me, but not when I'm drunk and puking all over the place?'

Cam burst into laughter. 'Yeah, you know, that sounds about right.'

'Just making sure we're on the same page,' I murmured. It kind of struck me then that I was still just in my jeans and bra, but I honestly didn't care. Tomorrow would most definitely be a different story.

'We're not.'

I pried one eye open. 'Ha.'

'Thought you'd like that.' He swiped the cool, damp cloth along my chin.

'You're very … good at this.'

'Had a lot of practice.' Cam tossed the towel aside, grabbed a new one, and repeated the steps. 'Been where you are quite a few times.' He ran it down my neck, over my bra straps, and then along the length of my arms. 'Want to get ready for bed?'

My other eye flew open.

He shook his head, and the dimple appeared in his left cheek. 'Get your mind out of the gutter.'

'Oh.'

'Yeah, oh,' he said, standing. With his back to me, he rummaged around the sink. A faucet turned on. He was back in front of me again, holding a loaded toothbrush. 'Thought you'd want to get the taste out of your mouth.'

My fingers made grabby motions. 'You are wonderful.'

'I know.' He handed it over and then replaced the toothbrush with one of those paper cups I never used. When I was all done, he knelt again and rocked back on his heels. He unzipped his hoodie and shrugged it off. 'I've been trying to get you to say I'm wonderful from the first time you plowed into me. If I'd known that all it would take was handing you a toothbrush, I would have done that a long time ago. My loss.'

'No. It was my ...' I pushed myself up a little, watching as he reached down and pulled the shirt off his head. 'My loss—what are you doing?'

'I don't know where your clothes are.'

'Uh-huh.' My gaze dropped, and I think I needed the damp towel again.

'And I figured you'd want to get out of your clothes.'

In the bright light, I saw the detail on the sun tattoo like I never had before. There had to be a thousand little marks inside the sun, giving it such a realistic, fiery detail. 'Yeah ...'

'So the easiest thing would be to let you borrow my shirt.'

My eyes went even lower, over the dusky nipple and then down, tracing each ripple of his stomach muscles. 'Okay.'

'Then you'd be more comfortable.'

There was a fine dusting of dark hair that appeared under his navel and traveled south, below the band on his jeans. It looked like someone had placed their fingers on either

275

side of his hips, indenting the skin there. 'Sure,' I murmured. How did someone get muscles there? Like what kind of stomach exercises did you have to subject yourself to?

'You haven't been listening to a single thing I've said.'

I dragged my gaze up. 'Nuh-uh.'

There was that dimple again as he clasped my hips and helped me up so I was sitting on the edge of the tub. 'Don't lift your arms yet, okay?'

Sitting still, I gripped the edges of the tub as he pulled the opening of his shirt over my head.

'Keep your arms down.' He let go of the shirt and slipped his arms around me. A second later, his agile fingers unclasped my bra.

'What are you doing?' My stomach dropped, and boy, after what had just gone on in there, that was not a good feeling.

He laughed as the straps slid down my arms, making me shiver. 'Like I said before, get your mind out of the gutter. Your virtue is safe with me.'

'My virtue?' I wasn't sure if I wanted it to be safe with him.

He peeked up. 'For now.'

'For now?' I whispered.

Cam nodded. 'Put your arms through.'

I did as I was told and then he made a show of rolling up the sleeves before sliding his hand down my left arm, stopping above my bracelet.

'Don't—' Panic shot through me as he unhooked the bracelet. I tried to yank my arm back, but Cam looked up, tightening his grip.

'I've already seen it, Avery.'

Pressure clamped down on my chest. 'Please, don't. It's embarrassing and I can't take back that you saw this. I wish I could, but I can't.'

He wrapped both his hands around the bracelet and wrist as he met my gaze with his steady one. 'It's because of this, isn't it? Why you freaked out on me? Wouldn't talk to me? Dropped the class?'

A lump rose so quickly in my throat that I couldn't speak.

'Oh, sweetheart.' Softness crept into his voice and his stare. 'We've all done stuff we aren't proud of. If you knew ...' He shook his head. 'The point is, I don't know why you did this. I just hope that whatever the reason was, it's something that you've come to terms with. I don't think any less of you because of it. I never did.'

'But you looked so ...' My voice was too hoarse.

The bracelet slipped off, but his one hand still covered my wrist as he put the bracelet on the edge of the sink. 'I was just surprised and I was concerned. I didn't know when you got this and I'm not going to ask. Not right now, okay? Just know that you don't have to hide it around me. All right?'

All I could do was nod, because I was always trying to hide it.

Cam lowered his head as he lifted my wrist, turning my arm over so my palm was facing up. He pressed his lips to the scar, and the breath caught in my throat. I looked away, squeezing my eyes shut. Something cracked inside me, a proverbial wall I'd built around me.

'I'd just turned fifteen,' I said, my voice hoarse as I blurted out the words before I lost my nerve. 'That's when I did it. I don't know if I really meant to do it or if I just wanted someone to ...' I shook my head. 'It's something I regret every day.'

'Fifteen?' His tone was devoid of judgment.

I nodded. 'I would never do anything like that again. I swear. I'm not the same person I was then.'

'I know.' Several moments passed, and then he placed my arm on my leg. 'Now it's time to take your pants off.'

The abrupt change in subject caused me to laugh. 'Nice.'

When he helped me stand, the shirt almost reached my knees, and my bra lay on the floor between us like a sad, lonely thing. When he reached for the buttons on my jeans, I smacked his hand away. 'I think I can do that.'

'Are you sure?' A brow arched up. 'Because I'm here at your service, and taking your jeans off is something I feel I'd be exceptionally wonderful at.'

'I'm sure you would be. Put your hoodie back on.'

He took a step back and leaned against the sink. All that male flesh completely on display. 'I like when you look.'

'I remember,' I grumbled, turning away. I felt naked without my bracelet. With a little shimmy, I stepped out of my jeans. When I faced Cam, he was still all kinds of half naked.

Cam swiped his hoodie off the floor and then took my hand. 'You think you'll be good out of the bathroom?'

'I hope so.'

We headed back into the living room, and I thought he was going to leave then, as it was well after two A.M., but he found me some aspirin, made me drink a bottle of water, and then sat on my couch. He gave my arm a little tug. 'Sit with me.'

I started to move around his legs, but he stopped me.

'No. Sit with me.'

Having no idea where he was going with this, I shook my head. Cam leaned back and then tugged on my arm a little harder. I went with it, letting him pull me into his lap. My side against his front, legs stretched out on the cushions beside us. He yanked the quilt up over my legs, and once he had me situated the way he wanted, he wrapped his arms around my waist.

'You should try to go to sleep,' he said, his voice barely audible over the hum of the TV. 'It'll help in the morning.'

I relaxed against him, faster than I thought possible. Snuggling closer, I rested my head against his chest. 'You're not leaving?'

'Nope.'

'At all?' I closed my eyes.

His chin grazed the top of my head and then his lips brushed across my forehead. A sigh leaked out from between my lips. 'I'm not going anywhere,' he said. 'I'll be right here when you wake up, sweetheart. I promise.'

It took a couple of moments to realize the blinding light was from the sun shining through my living room window and that I was still in Cam's lap. My head was against his shoulder, and his chin was resting atop mine. His arms were secured around me like he thought I'd wake up and run off.

In my chest, my heart got a little workout.

Memories from last night were a little disjointed at first, but when they started to make sense, I alternated between being thrilled, embarrassed, shocked, and then thrilled again.

Cam was still here and last night he'd said that he wanted me, that we would be together, even after he knew what I had done to myself and after I'd been a total bitch to him.

I almost couldn't believe it. Maybe I was dreaming, because I didn't feel like I deserved this.

Placing my hand on his chest, I felt his heart beat steady and strong under my palm. His skin was bare, warm, and real. I needed to see his face to fully believe that this was happening. I shifted in his lap.

Cam groaned, a deep, rich sound.

Eyes going wide, I stilled. Holy moly, I could feel his arousal against my hip. His arms tightened around my waist, and I felt his heart kick around the same time mine did.

'Sorry,' he said, his voice thick and gruff. 'It's morning and you're sitting on me. That's a combination meant to bring any man down.'

Warmth swamped my cheeks, but heat raced through my veins and I was reminded of how he had felt when he had rocked against me before. Not the best thought to be having right now. His grip on my waist loosened and his hand dropped to my hip. Through the thin shirt—*his* shirt—my skin tingled.

Okay. Maybe it was the perfect thought to be having right now.

'Do you want me to get off you?' I asked.

'Hell no.' His other hand traveled up my back, his fingers tangling in the ends of my hair. 'Absolutely fucking not.'

My lips cracked a grin. 'Okay.'

'Finally, I think we're actually agreeing on something.'

I leaned back a little, so I could see him. Disheveled from sleep and with the faint trace of stubble on his jaw, he looked absolutely stunning. 'Did last night really happen?'

One side of his lips curved up, and my chest swelled. I'd missed that smile. 'Depends on what you think happened.'

'I took my shirt off for you?'

The hue of his eyes deepened. 'Yes. Lovely moment.'

'And you turned me down?'

The hand on my hip slid lower. 'Only because our first time together isn't going to be when you're drunk.'

'Our first time together?'

'Uh-huh.'

Muscles in my stomach tightened. 'You're really confident about there being a first time between us.'

'I am.' He leaned back against the cushion.

I needed to focus. 'We talked, right?' My gaze fell to my bare left wrist. 'I told you when I did this?'

'Yes.'

I peeked at him. 'And you don't think I'm a raving bitch?'

'Well ...'

Cocking my head to the side, I pinned him with a look. Cam's grin spread as his hand slid farther up my back, reaching the nape of my neck. 'You want to know what I think?'

'Depends.'

He guided my head down so that our mouths were inches apart. 'I think we need to talk.'

'We do.' I agreed even though it made me nervous, of course, but resolve replaced my apprehension.

Cam suddenly gripped my hips and lifted me off him, placing me on the couch beside him. I missed his warmth immediately. Confusion rose as he stood. 'I thought we needed to talk,' I said.

'We do. I'll be right back.'

I had no clue what he was up to.

'Just stay there, okay?' he said, backing toward the door. 'Don't move from that spot. Don't think about anything. Just sit there and I'll be right back.'

I watched him curiously. 'Okay.'

A lopsided grin appeared. 'I mean it, don't think about anything. Not the last couple of minutes or last night. Not the last month. Or what's coming next. Just sit there.'

'All right,' I whispered. 'I promise.'

His eyes met mine for a second longer, and then he left, and of course I thought about everything in those five minutes he was gone. By the time he returned, I'd almost convinced myself that he wasn't coming back.

Except he did.

I twisted around, peering over the back of the couch, and once I saw what he had in his hands, I smiled widely. 'Eggs—you brought eggs.'

'And my skillet.' He nudged the door shut with his hip. 'And I brushed my teeth.'

'You didn't put a shirt on.'

He cast me a look as he headed into my kitchen. 'I know it would break your heart not to be able to see me shirtless.'

As he disappeared through the door, I dropped my head to the back of the couch and let out a girly sound that I hoped was muffled.

'Avery, what in the hell are you doing?'

I lifted my head. 'Nothing.'

'Then get your ass in here.'

Grinning, I scampered off the couch and started toward my bedroom.

'And don't you dare change.'

I stopped, making a face.

'Because I really like seeing you in my clothes,' he added.

'Well, when you put it like that …' I turned around and made my way back to the kitchen. Lingering in the doorway, I watched him do something I had seen him do at least a dozen times.

He looked over his shoulder at me. 'What? You missed my eggs that badly?'

I blinked my misty eyes clear. 'I didn't think I'd have you in my kitchen making eggs again.'

The thick bands of muscle across his shoulders flexed, and I couldn't help but admire the sensual valley. They curved deep into his skin as he leaned forward, adjusting the controls on the stove. 'You missed *me* that much?'

For once I didn't hesitate. 'Yes.'

Cam faced me. 'I've missed you too.'

I took a deep breath. 'I want to say I'm sorry for how I acted when you … well, when you saw my scar. I've never let anyone see it.' I sucked my lower lip in and took a step

282

forward. 'I know that's not an excuse, because I was a terrible bitch, but …'

'I'll accept your apology on one condition.' He folded his arms across his chest.

'Anything.'

'You trust me.'

I cocked my head to the side. 'I trust you, Cam.'

'No, you don't.' He walked over to my small table and pulled out a chair. 'Have a seat.'

Sitting down, I tugged the hem of his shirt down as he headed back to the stove, putting the tiny skillet over the burner.

'If you trusted me, you wouldn't have reacted the way you did,' he said simply, cracking an egg. 'And that's not me judging you or any of that kind of shit. You've got to trust that I'm not going to be an ass or freak out over that kind of stuff. You have to trust that I care enough about you.'

My breath stalled.

He turned, his eyes as clear as glass. 'There's a lot I don't know about you and I hope we fix that. I'm not going to push you, but you can't shut me out. Okay? You have to trust me.'

There were a lot of things he didn't know, but I didn't want those things to interfere. Not now. Not ever. 'I trust you. I will trust you.'

Cam met my gaze. 'I accept your apology.'

Then he turned back to the stove, scrambling my eggs. Next came the OJ. We really didn't say anything more until he sat down with his four boiled eggs. 'So where do we go from here?' he asked. 'Tell me what you want.'

I stopped, my fork full of egg. My gaze flicked up and he was holding one of the eggs. 'What I want?'

'From me.' He bit into the egg, chewing slowly. 'What do you want from me?'

Placing my fork down, I sat back and stared at him. It suddenly occurred to me that he was going to make me say it and … and I needed to say it. I thought about Molly and what she had to say a hundred times. This was easy compared to that. 'You.'

'Me?'

'I want you.' My cheeks were burning, but I pressed forward. 'Obviously, I've never been in a relationship and I don't even know if that's what you want. Maybe it's not—'

'It is.' He finished off the egg.

My chest tightened. 'It is?'

He chuckled. 'You sound so surprised, like you can't believe it.' He picked up another egg. 'It's really kind of adorable. Please continue.'

'Please continue …?' I shook my head, flustered. 'I want to be with you.'

Cam finished off the second egg. 'That's the second thing we're in agreement on this morning.'

'You want to be with me?'

'I've wanted to be with you since the first time you turned me down. I've just been waiting for you to come around.' His lips curved up. 'So, if we're going to do this, there are some ground rules.'

He'd been waiting for me? 'Rules?'

He nodded as he peeled the third egg. 'There's not that many. No shutting me out. It's just you and me and no one else.' He paused, and my heart was jumping. 'And finally, you keep looking damn sexy in my shirts.'

A laugh burst from me. 'I think all of them are doable.'

'Good.'

I watched him finish off his eggs and as happy as I was, the nerves got the best of me. 'I've never done of any of this before, Cam. And I'm not easy to get along with all the time. I know that. I can't promise this will be easy for you.'

'Nothing fun in life is easy.' He emptied his glass of milk and then stood, coming to my side. He took my hand and pulled me to my feet. His arms went around my waist as he tilted his head down, and when he spoke, his lips brushed my cheek. 'I'm serious about you, Avery. If you want me for real, you have me.'

Closing my eyes, I placed my hands on his chest. 'I want you for real.'

'Good to know,' he murmured, tilting his head to the side and his lips grazed mine. Anticipation swelled like a bubble. 'Because if not, this would get a whole lot awkward.'

I started to laugh, but then his mouth was on mine, quieting me. The kiss was soft at first, a tender exploration of my lips. But it had been too long since he'd kissed me last. And it had been too long since I had felt like this. I wanted more.

Sliding my hands up his chest and then the sides of his slightly rough cheeks, I thrust my fingers deep into his messy, soft hair. That was all the encouragement Cam needed. He deepened the kiss, parting my lips as his tongue slipped in. His hands slid to my hips and then up to my waist. He tugged me against him and the kiss went from innocent and sweet to downright sexy in a matter of seconds.

Cam lifted me, wringing a startled gasp from me that was quickly lost in him. Instinct took over and I wrapped my legs around his waist. In one powerful lunge, he moved forward and my back was against the wall and his chest was flush against mine. My body softened, dampened between my thighs as I felt him there, evidence of how badly he wanted me. Every inch of my body tightened as heat poured into me.

For the first time, there wasn't a smidgen of panic. Nothing but wonderful sensations that made me feel alive, and for once, I was completely in control. There was a freedom in that I had never experienced before, and I threw myself into that kiss. He made that terribly sexy sound that rumbled through his chest and then mine.

It seemed like forever before he lifted his mouth. 'I need to go.'

I let out a shaky breath. 'You're leaving now?'

'I'm not a saint, sweetheart,' he all but growled. 'So if I don't leave now, I won't be leaving for some time.'

A pulse went from the tips of my breasts to my core. 'What if I don't want you to leave?'

'Fuck,' he said, sliding his hands down to my thighs. 'You're making it very hard to be the good guy you said I was last night.'

'I'm not drunk.'

He pressed his forehead to mine, chuckling softly. 'Yeah, I can see that, and while the idea of taking you right now, against the wall, is enough to make me lose control, I want you to know that I'm serious. You're not a hookup. You're not a friend with benefits. You're more than that to me.'

I closed my eyes, breathing heavily. 'Well, that was … really sort of perfect.'

'I'm really sort of perfect,' he replied, gently untangling my legs. He sat me on the floor and I would've fallen right over if he hadn't held on. 'Everyone else knows that. You're just a little slow on the uptake.'

I laughed. 'What are you going to do?'

'Take a cold shower.'

'Seriously?'

'Yep.'

I laughed again. 'You coming back over?'

'Always,' he said, kissing me quickly.

'Okay.' I opened my eyes, smiling. 'I'll wait for you.'

Chapter 26

My life changed in very little ways in such a short period of time that it all added up to this monumental deal, at least to me. Cam had spent all day Sunday with me, and I'd woken up this morning to a good morning text from him.

Before I even had a chance to break the news to Brit and Jacob about the status change between Cam and I, they saw it firsthand while we waited outside for Brit to finish her cigarette before heading into Whitehall on Monday.

Cam came out of nowhere, slipping up behind me and wrapping his arms around my waist. I stiffened for a fraction of a second before forcing myself to relax. He pressed his lips to my cheek, and the shiver had nothing to do with the cold air. 'Hey there.'

The cigarette fell out of Brit's mouth.

Jacob blinked once, then twice, and then again. 'What the …?'

I gripped Cam's forearms as he trailed his lips to my ear, blazing a path across my skin. 'I think Brittany's going to set her shoe on fire.'

My gaze dropped and I broke free from his hold. 'Oh, my God, Brit, your shoe!'

She glanced down and gave a little shriek. Kicking the lit cigarette off her shoe, she jumped back. 'I almost burned to death. And it would've been your fault!'

'My fault?'

'Yes. Because you didn't tell me about this.' She gestured wildly at a grinning Cam. 'That!'

'Are you two, you know?' Jacob pointed at us. '*Together? Together?*'

I didn't get a chance to answer. Cam spun me around and kissed me, right there between the two buildings. It was no friendly peck on the lips. When our tongues touched, my bag slipped off my arm and hit the frosted ground.

'Holy crap,' Jacob muttered. 'I think they're going to make babies.'

Cheeks flaming, I pulled back. Cam looked absolutely shameless as he pressed a kiss to my forehead. Over his shoulder, I saw Steph and her friend gaping at us. Guess she didn't get the memo either.

'I've got to catch up with the professor before class begins, so I've got to run,' he said, backing up. 'See you after class?'

'Yes.' My lips tingled, along with various other parts of my body. 'See you then.'

When I turned back to my friends, both of them stared at me like I had just flashed them my goods. Bending down, I picked up my bag. 'Okay, before both of you start yelling at me, it just happened, like yesterday, and I hadn't had the time to say anything.'

Brit folded her arms. 'You haven't had a second to call, or I don't know, send a text message?'

'We sort of hung out all day yesterday, went to dinner and then—'

'Did you guys have sex?' Jacob grasped my shoulders, giving me a little shake. 'Oh my God, girl, details—I need details. What is the size of his—?'

'We didn't have sex.' I smacked his hands away. 'Geez, we just got together yesterday. Give me some time for that.'

'I would've been screwing him since August,' Jacob advised.

I shot him a bland look.

They grilled me on what had happened as we headed into Whitehall and through the beginning of class. By the time I left them to wait for Cam outside, I was sure I'd smoothed over my friend fail.

I stood just outside the awning, leaning against one of the pillars. I probably looked weird, because of the beaming smile plastered across my face, but I hadn't really stopped smiling since yesterday morning.

My smile slipped an inch when I saw Cam coming out of the doors, Steph attached to his side. The only thing that kept me from acting like a tiger and pouncing on her was the fact that Cam didn't look too thrilled.

Steph tossed her glossy mane of hair over one shoulder as they approached me. 'Hi,' she said with what I thought was a whole buttload of false cheer.

'Hey,' I replied, holding her gaze.

Cam slipped up to my side, threading his fingers through mine. 'Your class let out early?'

I nodded. 'Just a few minutes ago.'

Steph was glaring daggers through our joined hands. 'Are you going to be at Jase's party next Saturday, Cam?'

There was a party? As stupid as it was, I so did not like the idea of Cam going to a party where Steph would be. Wrong. Wrong. But an ugly feeling snaked through me whenever I thought of those two hooking up in the past.

'I don't know yet.' Cam squeezed my hand. 'Depends on if Avery wants to go.'

Her perfect mouth dropped open, and I think I loved Cam. 'If Avery wants to …? Whatever.' She stalked off, joining the girl I'd seen her with at the Halloween party.

I looked up at Cam. 'Well, she didn't seem too happy about that.'

He shrugged.

We started up the hill, toward Knutti. 'So you guys weren't more than just friends with benefits?'

Cam sent me a sidelong glance. 'We hooked up every once in a while, but like I told you this weekend, I haven't been with anyone since I met you.'

'I know. It just seems like she wanted more.'

'Wouldn't you?'

'Geez, we really need to work on your confidence.'

Cam chuckled as he pulled me to his side. We huddled against the wind whipping down the hill. 'I can think of a few other things we can work on.'

'Perv,' I mumbled even though my mind was right there with him.

He pressed his lips to my temple. 'Guilty as charged, sweetheart.'

Cam didn't go to the party at Jase's Saturday night. He hadn't even brought it up, and I wasn't sure if I should have. I felt a little guilty about him not going, because I didn't want to interfere with his friends, but he didn't seem bothered by the fact that he was missing out on an epic game of beer pong.

We went out to dinner in a nearby town and then came back to my place. If I had any doubts about the seriousness of our relationship, they were vanquished that evening.

Cam brought Raphael over to my apartment.

Nothing got more serious than allowing a tortoise to crawl across your kitchen floor.

'He needs to get his exercise,' Cam said, sitting in front of my fridge, legs spread. 'If not, he just gets fat and lazy, sitting in his shell.'

'Poor Raphael.' I picked him up and turned him back around so he was heading toward Cam. 'It has to be boring in the aquarium.'

'It's a terrarium,' Cam corrected. 'And he has a rocking terrarium. Got him a new one for his birthday.'

'You know when his birthday is?'

'Yep. July twenty-sixth.' He paused, eyeing me. 'When is your birthday?'

I crossed my ankles. 'Uh, you have a while until you have to worry about that. When's yours?'

'June fifteenth. When is yours, Avery?'

This was about to get awkward. 'It was January second.'

Cam leaned forward, his brow raising. Several seconds passed as he stared at me. 'I missed your birthday.'

'It's not a big deal,' I said, waving it off. 'I went to the Smithsonian and then I got sick, so it's probably a good thing you weren't around.'

His expression tensed. 'Aw, man, that's why you said you wanted to go there on the second. You were alone? Shit. I so feel—'

'Don't.' I held up my hand. 'You don't need to feel terrible. You didn't do anything wrong.'

Cam watched me for a few more moments, expression sheltered. Finally, he said, 'Well, there's always next year.'

I smiled at that. Next year. Wow. Thinking that far in advance was a little scary and exciting.

After a little while, Cam scooped the turtle up and stood. 'Be right back.'

While Cam took his pet back to his apartment, I rushed into the bathroom and quickly brushed my teeth. I was done seconds before he came back. He pulled his wool sweater off, draping it over the back of the couch. The gray shirt he had on underneath stretched over his broad chest, and when he stretched before he sat down, the shirt rose, exposing a span of taut skin.

My heart rate kicked up as I watched him from the hallway. Cam and I kissed—a lot—and he liked to cuddle, so in a week, I'd grown used to him having his arms around me and his lips on mine, but we hadn't done anything like we had Thanksgiving night, even though I imagined that he wanted to. So there were many nights I went to bed thinking about him, and while I could get some relief from what was turning into a constant low simmering ache, it wasn't enough.

He wanted me.

I wanted him.

We were together.

And I trusted him.

Biting down on my lip, I toyed with the edge of the sweater dress I wore. I'd taken off my boots and tights when we'd gotten back and now tiny bumps spread across my bare legs.

Was he waiting for me to make the first move? He seemed so … careful with me, as if he was worried that I'd run away from him. I wanted to run *to* him. Cam glanced over at me, brow raised. The room was dark with the exception of the glow from the TV. 'You going to come over here or stare at me the rest of the evening?'

My cheeks flushed as I pushed away from the door. I could do this. I didn't need to wait on him to make a move.

Gathering my courage, I walked over to him. He stared up at me with those extraordinary eyes as he lifted a hand. I placed mine in his, but instead of sitting beside him, I climbed into his lap, straddling him.

Cam immediately straightened, his hands flying to my hips. 'Hey there, sweetheart.'

'Hey,' I replied, heart pounding so fast there was a good chance I was going to have a heart attack.

His gaze dipped, thick lashes shielding his eyes. 'Did you miss me this much? I was only gone a few minutes?'

'Maybe.' I placed my hands on his shoulders as I lowered myself down. My grip tightened as I felt his arousal pressing against the softest part of me.

His hands traveled up my sides slowly, so slowly that I thought I would die by the time he cupped my cheeks. 'What are you doing?'

I wetted my lips and his lashes lifted, revealing a deeper shade of blue. 'What does it look like?'

'I can think of a few things.' His thumbs moved over my cheeks. 'All of them have me extremely interested.'

'Interested?' My breaths were coming out fast and short. 'That's good.'

Then, because it seemed like he was letting me take the lead on this, I brought my head down to his. Our lips brushed once, twice, and then I pressed mine to his more firmly. He followed me, our kisses becoming deeper, slower, and infinitely more as his tongue tortured mine in a way that had me shaking and wanting so very much more.

His hands slid back down at a slow, languid pace, causing my back to arch into the movement. Even though the only experience I had with this was what we'd done Thanksgiving night, it seemed like my body knew what to do. I rocked my hips and his hands tightened on my waist. A shudder worked its way down his large body, and it was both a bit frightening and a lot exhilarating.

One of his hands balled in the material of my dress, inching it up my thighs. The other drifted back up, over my front and then across my breast. He cupped me, his thumb smoothing over the tip, teasing the hardening peak through the clothing. A moan rushed me and it came out, a sound that seemed to thrill Cam.

'You liked that?' he asked, his lips brushing mine.

Did he really need confirmation? 'Yes.'

His thumb moved in a slow, torturous circle over my tip. I tried to catch my breath as his lips left mine. He nipped at my chin and then down my neck. My back arched more, pushing my breast farther into his hand as my hips rolled again. The sexiest sound rumbled from his chest as he leaned back and looked at me.

'Tell me what you want, sweetheart.' His hand moved to my other breast. 'Anything. And I'll do it.'

There was one thing I needed from him. 'Touch me.'

Cam shuddered again, and the action made me hot. 'May I?'

I nodded, having no idea what I was agreeing to, but I trusted him. Both of his hands were on my shoulders, sliding under the wide neckline of my dress. I stilled as he slipped the material down my shoulders, exposing my bra. He kept lowering the dress, until I could pull my arms free and the material bunched around my waist.

'Beautiful,' he murmured, trailing his fingers along the lacy edges of my bra. 'Look at that blush. So fucking beautiful.'

My response was lost as he lowered his head, closing his mouth over the tip of my breast. Through the thin satin of my bra, his mouth worked me as he gripped my hips, pulling me against him harder. My senses were overwhelmed from each hot pull of his mouth and the feel of him there, pressing against my core. My hands fluttered to his head as mine kicked back. He moved to my other nipple and a teasing bite had me crying out.

I was lost in him, surrendering to the feelings he was

stirring inside me. I already felt close to toppling over the edge and when his hands dropped to my thighs, running up under the hem of my skirt, I tensed in the most wonderful way.

His lips scorched a path up my neck, teasing my lower lip. 'Tell me something, sweetheart.' His hand moved to the inside of my thigh, making tiny circles that came close to my core. 'Have you come before?'

My entire body flushed, and when I didn't answer, his hand moved farther down my thigh, away from where I wanted him. Damn him. 'Yes,' I whispered. 'I have.'

'By yourself?' he asked, moving his hand back up my thigh.

I wiggled closer, and he groaned. Dropping my forehead to his, I closed my eyes. 'Yes.'

As a reward for answering his question, one long finger skimmed over the center of my panties and my entire body jerked in response. The knot in my belly tightened and his finger trailed back and forth in a feather-light touch that drove me crazy.

Desire clouded my thoughts, and I knew I wanted to make him feel what I did. I wasn't completely oblivious on the how to. I slid my hand down his chest, over his flat stomach. I hesitated at the band of his jeans.

Cam stilled and then nipped at my lip. 'What do you want, Avery?'

'I want to … I want to touch you,' I admitted, surprising myself. 'But I don't know what you like.'

He made that sound again that had me trembling as he placed his other hand over mine. 'Sweetheart, anything you do is something I'm going to like.'

'Really?'

'Hell yeah,' he said, shifting back so that there was space between us. 'Whatever you want to do to me, I'm going to love it. You don't have to worry about that.'

Emboldened by that statement, I flicked the button of his jeans open and then pulled down his zipper. Holy crap. I gasped at the sight of hard, pink flesh. No boxers. Nothing. Cam went commando.

Cam chuckled at my discovery. 'Easy access.' And then he reached down, easing himself out.

I couldn't help but stare and I felt like a goober for doing so, but there was something entirely hot about seeing him like this, knowing that he wanted me and I welcomed him. I hesitated, though, and while he'd said I could do anything and he would enjoy it, I doubted that and I wanted to please him. I wanted to make him feel good.

I watched his hand wrap around the base and stroke up. 'I've thought about you,' I whispered.

His hand stilled. 'How?'

'When I … touched myself, I thought of you.'

'Holy fuck,' Cam growled. 'That is the hottest thing I've ever heard.'

Cam kissed me then, harder and rougher than before. It didn't scare me. If anything, it excited me more. He guided my hand to him and I wrapped my fingers around his thickness. He jumped against my palm and his chest rose sharply.

He said something against my mouth that I couldn't make out and then he moved my hand up the length of him and then back down, establishing a rhythm that I kept up after he let go of my wrist. With one hand free now, he clasped the back of my neck as his other returned to the center of my thighs. Both of us were breathing fast when he cupped me through my panties. His palm pressed against the bundle of nerves as his fingers pushed into my heat, and I was lost. As he kissed me deeply and as I stroked him, I rode his hand. He thrust into mine, the movements small but forceful. His body shook as I felt the familiar tightening in my core. The knot unraveled, spiraling out through me. I came hard, his name a harsh whisper. His hand stayed there, rubbing me slowly through my panties as tremors rocked my body. And then he followed, his body thrusting up and spasming.

Forever seemed to pass before Cam gently pulled my hand away. I was limp and sated as he tucked me against his chest, holding me close, his heart pounding as fast as mine. He dropped a kiss on the lids of my eyes and then on my parted lips. We didn't speak in the aftermath, and I learned that sometimes words weren't necessary.

But in the back of my head, I knew there were words I needed to say. Truths that should be spoken before we went any further. Things I needed to deal with.

'Hey,' Cam said, his voice soft. I'd tensed without realizing it. 'You okay? I didn't—'

'It was perfect.' I kissed his jaw, wishing I had a switch on my brain. 'This is perfect.'

I just hoped it lasted.

Chapter 27

Economics became infinitely more interesting when I used the time in class to replay everything that Cam and I had done after his friends had left and Ollie had gone to bed the night before.

He'd taken me back to his bedroom, quietly closing the door behind him. Nervous energy had built in my stomach as he'd stalked toward me and cupped my cheeks. Since the night on my couch, we'd kissed and touched a lot, but it seemed different in his bedroom, more intimate, with more possibilities.

I tried not to think about actual sex, because I wasn't sure I could go through the act. If it would feel good for me or if it would remind me of what happened. I knew it would hurt, because I was still very much a virgin, but would the pain become something deeper?

He hadn't wanted more that night and I wondered if, in some way, he knew.

Cam had taken my sweater off, but he'd left my bra and jeans on. His shirt had joined my discarded clothes, and when he'd kissed me, his hands had tangled in my hair. We'd fallen onto his bed and he'd slid his leg between mine.

As his kisses had trailed down my throat and centered over my lace-covered breasts, he'd dropped his hands to my hips, urging me to move against him. He'd drawn my hardened nipple into his mouth as I rocked against him, my head kicked back and mouth clamped shut to keep quiet. He'd brought me to an orgasm like that, no hands on me, through my jeans and panties. And when I slid my hands into his loose sweats, palming the hard, heavy length, he thrust against my hand, very much like I imagined he would inside me.

I had stayed for a while, cuddled up against him. We'd talked about everything and nothing, long into the night. I'd left when he'd started to doze off, and he'd been awake enough to try to coax me back into his bed. He'd gotten up, though, and had walked me to my apartment door. Cam had given me the sweetest kiss good night.

There was a good chance that I'd fallen in love.

Okay. I probably already had months ago, but now it seemed more real; it was attainable, and—oh, God—I actually knew what love felt like—bubbly warmth. When I was around him or thought about him, I felt like I imagined the bubbles in champagne did, constantly floating to the top. *Did I just think that?*

A big goofy smile appeared on my lips.

Brit caught my eye and made a face.

Flushing, I decided I should pay attention for the last ten minutes of class. The professor was talking about gas pump lines in the early 1980s. Something to do with supply and demand. I was so going to have to read that chapter.

'God, you have it so bad,' Brit said to me after class, as we walked out of Whitehall. 'It's all over your face.'

I grinned. 'I do.'

Brit looped her arm through mine as we stepped outside. Flurries floated to the ground and the clouds were thick.

'I'm glad you guys worked it out. You two are so damn cute together it's almost disgusting.'

'He's …' I shook my head. 'I'm lucky.'

'He's lucky,' she corrected, nudging me as we trudged up the hill. 'So what are you getting him for Valentine's Day?'

'Valentine's Day?' I stopped suddenly. Several people behind us grumbled as they walked around Brit and me. 'Oh shit, that's next week.' I turned to her, eyes wide. 'I have no idea.'

Brit giggled as she tugged on my arm. I started walking again. 'You should see your face,' she said. 'It's like you just realized that the world is ending next week instead of there being a stupid, man-made holiday.'

I ignored that. 'I have no idea what to get him.'

'What have you gotten previous boyfriends?'

'Nothing,' I replied, too panicked to care about what I was admitting. 'I've never had a boyfriend before.'

Now it was Brit's turn to stop and back up traffic. 'What? Like, never? Holy crap, I knew you were a little, um, sheltered, but come on. I think Amish kids have more experience than you.'

I shot her a dirty look. 'You're not helping, and I'm seriously freaking out here.'

'Okay. Okay. Make fun of you later. Got it.' She wrinkled up her nose. 'We'll go shopping after class.'

Later that afternoon, the snow was still coming down, but the roads were clear for the drive into Martinsburg. At the mall, I was still seriously at a loss, staring at the little red hearts dangling from the ceiling at the department store.

Brit picked up a pair of black satin boxers with red hearts on them. 'Uh …'

'No,' I said. Besides the fact that was the corniest shit I'd ever seen, Cam didn't always wear underwear.

She pursed her lips. 'Well, there's always the standard gifts. You can get him some cologne, a wallet, a tie, or a shirt.'

'That's really lame.'

'I didn't say they were good ideas.'

I pouted as we headed into another store. The trip was a total bust with the exception of Brit trying out every body lotion. By the time we left, she smelled like she worked in a Bath & Body Works sweatshop.

Back at my apartment, I scoured the Internet for a good gift. I wanted it to be special, because with Cam, I felt like I was waking up. I saw things differently, more clearly. I wasn't sure if it was him or how I was with him or if I was finally *changing*. Either way, Cam played a role in this, and I wanted to get him a gift that mattered.

After about an hour, I decided that shopping for a guy *sucked*.

I racked my brain. If I could get him a lifetime supply of eggs, he'd be down for that.

Groaning in frustration, I got up and peeked out the window. Snow was coming down thick and fast, blanketing the ground and the cars. The news had said there'd be accumulation, but I doubted the campus would close.

Pulling my hair up in a messy ponytail, I headed toward the kitchen when it suddenly struck me. Something that Cam had mentioned a few times.

He'd talked about wanting to catch a DC United game.

Squealing, I raced back to my laptop and checked out their website. Clicking on their schedule, I ordered two tickets for an early April game, thinking that the weather would be a lot more stable then.

I closed my laptop, feeling good about my purchase. He could take me or, if he wanted to, one of his friends. I was okay with that as long as he was happy with what I got.

Less than an hour later, Cam showed up, damp from the snow. 'Pizza night?'

'Sounds good to me.' I kissed his cheek as I took the box from him. 'How are the roads?'

'They suck.' He grabbed two cans of sodas out of the fridge. 'Which brings me to this brilliant idea I've had.'

I grinned. 'Your ideas can be a bit scary.'

'My ideas are never scary or bad.'

'Well …'

'Name one,' he challenged.

I didn't have to think hard. 'How about when you tied a string around Raphael's shell and called it a leash?'

'That was an innovative idea!'

'The poor thing just stood there and put its head in its shell.'

Cam scoffed. 'That's really no different from any other day.'

I laughed. 'True.'

'This idea is great.' Slapping slices of pizza on two paper plates, he winked at me. 'They're saying that it's supposed to snow through tomorrow morning.'

I was caught between glee and annoyance. Snow was great. Walking on campus with snow or ice on the ground was not.

'And I seriously doubt that any of the classes will be canceled tomorrow,' he continued as we walked into my living room. 'But a lot of people will be out and the teachers will expect that.'

'Okay.' I sat on the couch, scooting over for him.

'So I was thinking we should skip tomorrow, stay right here, and watch shitty movies all day.'

My first response was to say I couldn't skip a whole day's worth of classes, but as I met Cam's mischievous gaze, I said screw it. 'That is a brilliant idea.'

'I know, right?' He tapped his head. 'I'm full of great shit.'

'Yeah, you're definitely full of it …'

'Ha.'

I giggled as I bit into the cheesy goodness. Cam ate half the pizza and when Ollie stopped by, he finished it off. It amazed me how the two guys could eat so much and be in such drool-worthy shape. I ate two slices and gained an extra ass.

Sitting between the two boys, I dozed off while they watched a minimarathon of a reality show about moonshining. When I woke up, Ollie was gone, and although I was lying against Cam, his body was unnaturally tense.

I sat up, yawning as I pushed my hair out of my face. 'Sorry. I didn't mean to fall asleep on you.'

He looked at me, expression unreadable. Unease stirred like a pit of vipers in my stomach. His jaw was so tight that I wondered if he was going to crack his molars.

'Is everything okay?' I asked.

Cam exhaled softly as he glanced at the coffee table. 'You got a message while you were sleeping.'

My gaze followed his, landing on my cell phone. At first I didn't see what the big deal was, but then anxiety rose like a fast-moving storm. Wide awake, I shot forward and grabbed the cell phone. Tapping the screen, my heart jumped.

You're a lying whore. How can you live with yourself?

I dragged in a breath, but it got stuck. I stared at the message, wishing it would simply vanish from existence.

'It flashed across your screen when it came through,' he said.

Hands shaking, I deleted the message and sat the phone down. Hurt and a wave of irrational anger rolled through me. Those two emotions felt better than the threatening panic. 'You looked at the text?'

'It's not like I did it on purpose.' He leaned forward, hands splayed over his knees. 'It was right there, sitting on your screen.'

'But you didn't have to look!' I accused, backing off the couch.

Cam's eyes narrowed. 'Avery, I wasn't sneaking through your stuff. The damn text came through. I looked before I could stop myself. Maybe that was wrong.'

'It was wrong!'

'Okay. It was wrong. I'm sorry.' He drew in a deep breath. 'But that doesn't change the fact that I saw that text.'

I was frozen, standing in the middle of my living room. This was pretty damn close to my worst fear coming true. Him finding out what happened held the first spot, but this was a close second and just as horrifying.

'Avery,' he said in a low, careful voice. In that moment, I realized he wasn't mad at me. Not in the slightest, and not even after I yelled at him for looking at the wretched text. Somehow that was worse than him being angry with me. 'Why would you get a text like that?'

My heart threw itself against my ribs painfully. 'I don't know.'

A dubious look crossed his face.

'I don't know,' I said again, latching on to the lie with everything I had in me. 'Every so often I get a text like this, but I don't know why. I think it's a wrong number kind of thing.'

Cam stared at me. 'You don't know who that's from?'

'No.' And that was the truth. 'It says unknown caller. You saw that.'

His shoulders tensed at that, and then he clenched his knees. Several seconds passed while my pulse pounded.

'I'm sorry for freaking out on you,' I added in a rush. 'It just surprised me. I was asleep and I wake up and I could tell something was wrong. Then I thought … I don't know what I thought, but I'm sorry.'

'Stop apologizing, Avery.' He scooted to the edge of the couch. 'I don't need to hear that you're sorry. I want you to be honest with me, sweetheart. That's all I want. If you're getting messages like that, I need to know about that.'

'Why?'

His dark brows knitted. 'Because I'm your boyfriend and I care if someone is calling you a whore!'

I flinched.

Cam looked away, chest rising. 'Honestly? It pisses me off, even if it's an accidental text. No one should be sending you shit like that.' His gaze settled on me again. An eternity stretched out between us. 'You know you can tell me anything, right? I'm not going to judge you or get mad.'

'I know.' My voice sounded small to my own ears and I hated that. I said louder, 'I know.'

His eyes met mine. 'And you trust me, right?'

'Yes. Of course I do.' I didn't waver.

Again, there was a pregnant pause that had me assuming the worst. 'Shit,' he all but growled, and my heart sank. Did he know? What was he thinking? The truth—everything— rose to the tip of my tongue, and then he closed his eyes. 'I haven't been entirely honest with you.'

'What?' That was the last thing I expected him to say.

He rubbed his palm along his jaw. 'I tell you that you should trust me and that you can tell me anything, but I'm not doing the same thing. And eventually you're going to find out.'

Whoa. Forget the text message. Forget saying anything. What the hell was going on? Almost numb, I hurried around the coffee table and sat a few feet away from him on the couch. 'What are you talking about, Cam?'

Lifting his head, he pierced me with such a tortured stare that it made my chest ache. 'You know how I told you we all have done shit in our past we aren't proud of?'

'Yes.'

'I can say that from firsthand experience. Only a few people know about this,' he said, and I suddenly thought of the day he'd gotten upset with Ollie and then at the party when he'd gone after that guy. There seemed to be something that Jase had been telling him without really saying it. 'And it's the last thing I want to tell you.'

'You can tell me,' I assured him, and yeah, I felt like a twat considering all that I wasn't telling him. I pushed those thoughts away, focusing on Cam. 'Seriously, you can talk to me. Please.'

He hesitated. 'I should be graduating this year, along with Ollie, but I'm not.'

'I remember you telling me you had to take some time off.'

Cam nodded. 'It was sophomore year. I hadn't been home a lot during the summer because I was helping coach a soccer camp in Maryland, but whenever I did go home, my sister … she was acting different. I couldn't put my finger on it, but she was super jumpy and when she was home, she spent all her time in her bedroom. And apparently she was rarely home, according to my parents.'

My stomach sank as I crossed my legs. I hoped I was wrong, and I didn't know where this was heading.

'My sister, she's always been this bleeding heart, you know. Picking up stray animals and people, especially stray guys. Even when she was a tiny thing, she always buddied up with the most unpopular kid in the class.' His lips quirked up at the corners. 'She met this guy. He was a year or two older than her and I guess their relationship was serious—as serious as they can be when you're sixteen.

307

Met the kid once. Didn't like him. And it had nothing to do with the fact he was trying to get with my little sister. There was just something about him that rubbed me the wrong way.'

Cam slid his hands down his cheeks and then dropped them between his knees. 'I was home over Thanksgiving break and I was in the kitchen. Teresa was in there and we were messing around. She pushed me and I pushed her back, on her arm. Not even hard, but she cried out like I'd seriously hurt her. At first I thought she was just being dumb, but there were tears in her eyes. She down-played it, and I forgot about it for that night, but on Thanksgiving morning, Mom walked in on her in a towel and she saw it.'

I held my breath.

'My sister ... she was covered in bruises. Up and down her arms, on her legs.' His hands closed into fists. 'She said it was from dancing, but we all knew you couldn't get bruises like that from dancing. It took almost all morning to get the truth out of her.'

'It was her boyfriend?' I remembered the conversation at the table, and Cam's sudden interest in who she was talking to made sense.

A muscle popped in his jaw as he nodded. 'The little fuck had been hitting her. He was smart about it, doing it in places that weren't so easily noticeable. She stayed with him. I didn't know why at first. Come to find out that she was too scared of him to break up.'

Cam stood suddenly, and my gaze followed him. He went to the window, parting the curtains. 'Who knows how long it would've continued if Mom hadn't walked in when she did. Would Teresa have finally told someone? Or would that bastard have just kept hitting her one night and killed her?'

Emotion crawled up my throat as I sucked my lower lip between my teeth.

'God, I was so pissed, Avery. I wanted to kill the fuck. He was beating up my sister and my dad wanted to call the police, but what were they really going to do? Both of them were minors. He'd get his hands slapped and get counseling, whatever. And that's bullshit. I wasn't okay with that. I left Thanksgiving night and I found him. Didn't take much, fucking small town and all. I knocked on his door and he came right out. I told him he couldn't come around my sister anymore and you know what that little punk did?'

'What?' I whispered.

'He got all up in my face, puffing his fucking chest at me. Told me he would do whatever the fuck he wanted.' Cam barked out a quick, harsh laugh. 'I lost it. Angry isn't even the word to use. I was *enraged*. I hit him and I didn't stop.' He turned around, but he wasn't really seeing me. 'I didn't stop hitting him. Not when his parents came out or when his mom starting screaming. It took two police officers to get me off him.'

Oh my God, I didn't know what to say. As I watched him sit in the moon chair, I couldn't imagine him hitting someone and not stopping. Not even after seeing how angry he'd been at the guy at Jase's party.

Cam rubbed his cheeks again. 'I ended up in jail and he ended up in a coma.'

My mouth dropped open before I could stop my reaction.

He looked away, lowering his chin. 'I'd been in fights before—normal shit. But nothing like that. My knuckles were busted wide open and I didn't even feel it.' He shook his head. 'My dad ... he worked his magic. I should've gone away for a long time for that, but I didn't. Guess it helped that the kid woke up a few days later.'

309

With every passing second, my muscles locked up, one after another.

'I got off easy—not even a night in jail.' Cam smiled, but there was no warmth to it. 'But I couldn't leave home for several months while it got worked out. I ended up with a year's worth of community service at the local boys' club and then another year's worth of anger management. That's what I do every Friday. My last session is in the fall. My family had to pay restitution and you don't even want to know how much that cost. I had to stop playing soccer because of the community service gig, but ... like I said, I got off easy.'

He had gotten off easy.

Just like Blaine had gotten off easy.

No. I stopped myself right there. These were two different situations—Blaine was a rapist and Cam had beaten the guy who'd beat his sister. What Cam had done was wrong; violence should never be the answer to violence, but the guy had hurt his sister.

'I understand,' I said, and I realized that even though their situations were similar in a way, they were vastly different. And I was shocked myself. The old me—all she would've been able to think about was how both had gotten off because of who they were, who their parents were, and money. But I wasn't her anymore. And sometimes good people did bad things.

His head swung to me. 'What?'

'I understand why you did it.'

Cam stood. 'Avery—'

'I don't know what it says about me, but you were defending your sister; beating the crap out of someone isn't the answer, but she's your sister and ...' And if I had a brother and he'd reacted that way after what happened to me? Well, he would have been my hero, as terrible as that was. 'There are some people who deserve an ass kicking.'

He stared at me.

I unfolded my legs. 'And there are probably some people who don't even deserve to breathe. It's a sick and sad thing to say, but it's true. The guy could've killed your sister. Hell, he could have beaten some other girl to death.'

Cam continued to stare at me like I'd sprouted a second nose. 'I deserve to be in jail, Avery. I almost killed him.'

'But you didn't.'

He didn't say anything.

'Let me ask you a question. Would you do it again?'

Several seconds passed and then he said, 'I still would've driven to his house and I would've hit him. Maybe not as badly, but honestly, I don't think it would've changed anything. The bastard beat my sister.'

I took a deep breath. 'I don't blame you.'

'You're …'

I shrugged. 'Twisted?'

'No.' A real smile broke the tension in his face. 'You're remarkable.'

'I wouldn't go that far.'

'Seriously,' he said, coming to the couch. He sat beside me. 'I thought you would be disgusted or angry if you knew.'

I shook my head.

Cam dropped his forehead to mine, and he clasped my cheeks gently. His eyes searched mine. 'It feels good getting that off my chest. I don't want there to be secrets between us.'

I smiled as he leaned forward, kissing the corner of my lips, but I barely felt the touch. Cam settled back, pulling me against his chest. I snuggled closer, but coldness still seeped deep into my bones. He'd shared this major secret

311

with me, even though he'd feared I would judge him somehow, and I had remained quiet, keeping my secrets close to my heart. That wasn't fair, and I couldn't shake this terrible premonition that it would somehow come back around.

How can you live with yourself?

Cam kissed the top of my head, and my breath caught.

I wasn't sure how I did.

Chapter 28

I hadn't really noticed it till then, but there had been a stress that Cam carried with him; the weight of keeping a secret he thought would destroy something he cared about. How I hadn't recognized it before was beyond me.

But it was good now ... mostly.

Part of me suspected that one of the reasons why he'd finally told me was because he didn't believe what I said about the text. That maybe he hoped by opening up with me that I'd do the same.

I wished that was the case, but my secret would destroy what I cherished most.

Us.

But since it was Valentine's Day, I refused to think about it. I was having the most perfect day and I wasn't going to ruin it.

Cam had shown up at my door in the morning with a single red rose and with one after every single one of my classes. By the afternoon, I had half a dozen, which turned into two dozen when he arrived at my apartment that evening. I hadn't been sure of our plans, so I was relieved to see him in jeans and a sweater and nothing fancy. It was late, after nine, since Valentine's fell on a Friday, and I wasn't sure if we were even going out.

Thanking him for the roses, I took them into the kitchen and added them to the vase. He remained by the door. 'What are you doing?' I asked.

His grin was mischievous. 'Stay right where you are and close your eyes.'

'I have to close my eyes?'

'Yep.'

I arched a brow as I tried to hide my burgeoning excitement. 'So it's a surprise?'

'Of course it is. So close your eyes.'

My lips twitched. 'Your surprises are just as scary as your ideas.'

'My ideas *and* my surprises are brilliant.'

'Remember when you thought it would be a good idea to—'

'Close your eyes, Avery.'

Grinning, I dutifully closed my eyes. I heard him walk away and then a couple of moments later he reentered my apartment. 'Don't peek.'

Telling me not to peek was like putting a slice of cake in front of me along with a fork and telling me not to eat it. I shifted my weight. 'Cam ...'

'A couple more seconds,' he said, and I heard something heavy roll inside.

What the ... ? More than curious, I struggled to not open my eyes. I honestly had no idea what he was up to, and with Cam, anything was possible.

His hand wrapped around mine. 'Keep your eyes closed, okay?'

'They're closed.' I let him lead me out of the kitchen and into my living room.

Cam let go of my hand and slid his arm around me from

314

behind, pressing his cheek against me. Months ago I hated when anyone stood behind me, but I loved it when he did. The feel of his arms, the strength of his embrace, the intimacy behind it.

'You can open your eyes now.' His lips brushed my cheek, sending shivers across my skin. 'Or you can stand there with your eyes closed. I like that, too.'

I laughed as I placed my hands above where his rested on my stomach and opened my eyes. My jaw hit the floor. 'Oh my God, Cam …'

Before me, sitting on a stand, was a fifty-gallon *terrarium* completely decked out with sand and rock bedding, leafy foliage, and a hidey-hole, and inside was a tortoise almost the size of my hand.

He chuckled. 'You like?'

'Like?' Stunned, I nodded as I pulled free, placing my hands on the glass. The little guy inside pulled his head back. 'I … I love it.'

'Good.' He stood beside me. 'I thought Raphael could use a play date.'

I laughed again, blinking back tears. 'You shouldn't have done all this, Cam. This is … too much.'

'It's not that much, and everyone needs a pet tortoise.' He bent his head, kissing my cheek. 'Happy Valentine's Day.'

Spinning around, I wrapped my arms around him and kissed him like there was no tomorrow. When I pulled back, his eyes were pools of blue fire. 'Thank you.'

He kissed me again, soft and achingly tender. 'You're welcome.'

Sliding my arms to his waist, I leaned against his chest. 'Is it a boy or a girl?'

'You know, I really don't know. Supposedly you can tell by the shape of the shell, but hell if I know.'

I grinned. 'Well, boy or girl, I'm going to name it Michelangelo.'

Cam threw his head back and laughed. 'Perfect.'

'We just need two more.'

'So true.'

Wiggling free, I smiled up at him. 'Be right back.' I rushed into my bedroom and grabbed the card I'd stuck the tickets in. When I got back to the living room, Cam was adjusting the heat lamp on the terrarium. He turned, smiling softly. 'Happy Valentine's Day,' I said, all but shoving the card in his hands. My cheeks flushed. 'It's not as cool as your gift, but I hope you like it.'

'I'm sure I will.' Lips curved up on one side, he carefully opened the envelope and pulled the card out. I hadn't written much in it, because I had no idea what to write. I'd settled on a quick message and my name.

I held my breath as he opened the card. The half grin spread into a full smile as he slid the two tickets between his fingers. He peered up through his lashes. 'This is an absolutely amazing gift, sweetheart.'

'Really?' I clasped my hands together, pleased. 'I hoped you'd like it. I mean, I know not playing soccer sucks and I hope this doesn't make you sad going to the game and you don't have to take me—'

Cam claimed my mouth like a man half starved. There was nothing slow about the kiss; it was a whole different level of seduction. 'Of course I'm taking you. The gift is perfect,' he said, nipping at my lower lip in a way that caused heat to sweep over me, leaving me needy. 'You're perfect.'

An insidious voice crept in. *If he only knew how far from perfect I really am.* I pushed that thought away, letting myself fall into his kiss. That wasn't hard. Not when he drank from me as if he'd been deprived of the act for far too long.

His hands dropped to my hips and he pulled me to him. Against my belly, I felt his arousal. Cam was a … sexual man, so it came as no surprise he was that hard that quickly, but it always amazed me how badly he did want me but never pushed for what I knew he'd be oh-so down for.

When his grip on my hips tightened, I looped my arms around his neck. We seemed to be in some unconscious agreement, because he lifted me as I wrapped my legs around his waist. I moaned as he pressed against me and his tongue swept across mine.

He started walking, and my blood thundered in my veins. I knew where he was heading, and excitement and nervousness warred inside me. He laid me on the bed and I leaned back, down the center. Pausing long enough to tug his sweater off over his head, he then placed his hands on either side of my head. The power and strength in his arms and body was overwhelming but not frightening.

Reaching up, I traced my finger over the flames surrounding the sun on the left side of his chest. 'I love this tattoo,' I admitted. 'Why did you get it?'

A half grin appeared. 'You really want to know?'

'Yes.'

'It's pretty lame.'

I followed the sun around his pec. 'I'll be the judge of that.'

'I got it after the fight.' Cam shifted so his knees were against my outer thighs and slid his hands under my shirt. I lifted up, helping him take it off. I have no clue where it ended up. He sort of just tossed it behind him. 'I was kind of messed up for a while. Couldn't go back to school, was stuck in my home, and I'd done that to myself. I was worried that there had been something wrong with me to lose it like I did.'

My hands fell to my sides as he placed one of his on my bare stomach. The tips of his fingers reached the underwire of my bra and the front closure.

'I was depressed,' he admitted. His hair tumbled forward, falling over his forehead as he placed his other hand beside my head. 'I was pissed off at myself and the world and all that bullshit.' Pausing, he ran his hand down my belly and then back up, causing me to wiggle. That slight smile was back. 'I think I drank just about every liquor my dad had in his bar over the course of a couple of weeks. I knew my parents were worried, but ...'

Cam trailed off as he lowered his head, kissing the space between my breasts. I sucked in a sharp breath and he did it again. 'Jase came to visit me often. So did Ollie. I probably would've lost my fucking mind without them. May I?' He looked up, eyes filled with intent, his fingers on the clasp of my bra.

My heart jumped. This was a first for us. Mouth dry, I nodded.

'Thank you,' he said, and I thought that was a strange thing to be thankful for. His gaze lowered again, and my breath caught. He unhooked the delicate clasp, but didn't part the cups. 'It was something Jase had said to me while I was drunk off my ass. Don't know why, but it stuck with me.'

I drew in a ragged breath as he trailed a finger down the center of my chest. 'What did ... what did he say?'

Cam glanced up through thick lashes. 'He said something like things can't be that bad if the sun is out and shining. Like I said, that stuck with me. Maybe because it's the truth. As long as the sun's shining, shit can't be that bad. So that's why I got a tattoo of the sun. Sort of a reminder.'

'That's not lame,' I said.

'Hmm ...' He plucked up the edge of my bra and gently pushed it to the side and then repeated the same motion on the other cup. Cool air teased the tips of my already hard breasts. I was completely bare for him from the waist up. 'God, you're beautiful, Avery.'

I think I said thank you, but I wasn't sure if the words were coherent or not. He ran his hands over my breasts and my back arched off the bed at the contact of his flesh against mine. He said something too low for me to understand as he smoothed his thumb over my nipple. Beside my head, his arm flexed.

Cam looked up, meeting my gaze as he lowered his hand to the button on my jeans. There was a question in his eyes, and I nodded, wanting to know what he was going to do more than I was afraid.

He tugged my jeans off, then my socks. He commented on the skull and bones design, but the pounding in my body made it hard to pay attention. He then slid the bra off completely and when he had me just in my panties, his slow perusal of my body was like stepping out in the flaming August sun of Texas.

Our lips touched as he eased his weight onto his side. The kisses were slow and deep as his hand traveled over my chest. His touch was teasing and practiced as his kisses trailed over my chin, down my throat. I tensed in that second before his hot mouth closed over the tip of my breast. He'd done this before through my bra, but nothing could compare to the feeling of there being nothing between us. My blood turned to molten lava and my hips moved restlessly in tiny circles. As he sucked deep, his other hand traveled down, skimming my skin and then sliding under my panties.

My toes curled as his finger brushed the nub. New, stronger sensations pulsed throughout me. My head fell back as he slowly worked his head down, his fingers following the length of me.

He raised his head, his eyes boring into mine as he slipped the tip of his finger inside me. I gasped, my fingers digging into his arms.

'Is this okay?' he asked, voice deep and smooth.

Drawing in a breath, I nodded again. 'Yes.'

A small, intimate smile tugged at his lips as he pushed a little harder. My body was aflame as he started a pace, his eyes locked with mine. My entire body was shaking. The knot that formed whenever he touched me was much deeper and intense.

'You're so tight,' he murmured, and then his kiss consumed me.

My hips were moving faster and he twisted his palm, pressing down on the sensitive nub. The feel of his bare chest rubbing against mine, his hand in my panties, his finger inside me—all of it was too much. I clenched around his hand, my thighs squeezing, and broke the kiss, crying out his name as release thundered through my body.

Cam made a deep sound as he nipped at my throat. 'I love how you say my name.'

I could barely breathe, let alone speak, as he continued to move inside me, working out every last spasm. When the tremors finally subsided, he eased his hand away and I was flushed all over and heady. I wanted to give him more than what I'd been doing. Nervous and excited, I pressed my hands to his chest lightly and he rolled onto his back. Taking a deep breath, I straddled him and before I lost my nerve, I slid down him and unbuttoned his jeans, tugging them down his legs.

Cam caught on the moment I wrapped my fingers around him and my warm breath blew across his tip. His hands immediately fisted in my comforter.

'Oh shit,' he growled.

I smiled at the tortured sound of his voice and then I

closed my mouth over him. His entire body jerked and his back bowed. I really didn't have a clue when it came to doing this, but I figured it didn't take much.

And it didn't.

Cam enclosed one hand around mine as I took him and his other hand rested on the back of my neck with the slightest pressure, guiding my less than skilled movements. I wasn't embarrassed or worried about doing it wrong. If his body and deep groans were any indication, I was doing enough right for him to be enjoying this.

He pulled me away before his release shuddered through him, sitting up halfway and capturing my mouth as he came. I loved the way his body shook, but most of all, I loved that I felt safe and secure enough to do this. Tired, I broke away, easing onto my back as he did the same, his chest rising and falling sharply. 'This was the best fucking Valentine's Day ever.'

A deep, throaty laugh escaped me. 'I have to agree.'

His hand found mine between our bodies and squeezed. 'You hungry?'

'No.' I smothered a yawn. 'Are you?'

'Not yet,' he replied.

I had no idea what time it was, but I felt boneless, and it would take an act of God to get me out of this bed. Or chocolate. One thing I did know was that I didn't want him to leave. I worked up the nerve to ask for what I wanted. 'Stay with me? The night?'

Cam's hand trailed over my bare shoulder. 'You don't have to ask twice.' He kissed the edge of the shoulder. 'Be right back.'

I rolled onto my side as he left, pulling the covers up over me. I heard water running in the bathroom and then he was back, sliding in behind me. With his arms around my waist and the length of his body pressed against mine, I smiled sleepily and thought about the sun.

Everything was perfect.

Chapter 29

The sun was shining all February and through March. I spent half of spring break hanging out with Cam and Ollie at school and then the later part back at Cam's parents' house, and we even got to hang out with Brit while she was home.

I found it strange that Brit didn't seem to know what had happened between Cam and his sister's ex-boyfriend, but I didn't bring it up. What Cam had told me had been personal, and no matter how strong my curiosity over whether or not she knew, I wasn't going to violate that trust between us.

Especially when there'd been so many opportunities for me to open up to him. No matter how many times I told myself I would do it, I simply couldn't get the words past my tongue. The idea of confiding in Cam terrified me. It wouldn't be easy, and I really didn't even know where to begin.

Instead I went out of my way to make sure my phone was never unsupervised around Cam. I was still receiving the texts and phone calls, at least two times a week, and I shied away from my e-mail. Several times over the last two months, I *almost* responded to the text. Or I *almost* pulled up my e-mail and responded to one of the messages.

Just like with Cam, I pretended it wasn't happening rather than deal with it. I hated that part of me, loathed it really, because I was still running instead of facing anything.

As winter loosened its hold on the tiny speck of the state and the ground began to thaw, Cam was deciding whether he should pay a visit home over the mid-April weekend or hang out here and be lazy while Jacob spent lunch trying to convince Brit to accompany him to some kind of volunteer garden planting adventure.

Brit swirled her fry in a glob of mayo. Ollie watched her, his handsome face twisted in awed disgust. She was completely oblivious. 'I'm not going to spend my last four-day weekend of the semester planting daisies.'

'It's not daisies.' Jacob sighed. 'It's a botanical garden of wonder and love.'

Cam was sitting at the table next to me. He dropped his head on my shoulder, hiding his snicker. I went with the old hand-over-the-mouth method.

'That just sounds stupid.' Brit popped the mayo-covered fry in her mouth, and Ollie groaned. 'I'm going to spend the four days being a veg.'

'Would you rather spend your time being a cucumber or making your soul feel happy?'

Cam's shoulders started to shake.

'I think I will go with being a piece of broccoli,' Brit replied.

Across from us Ollie finally dragged his gaze away from Brit's place and looked at Jacob. 'Are you serious?'

'Yes!' He smacked his hands down. 'Why not paint the world in beautiful flowers of all different colors?'

I stared at him. 'Are you high?'

Jacob looked affronted ... for maybe two seconds. 'Maybe a little.'

Laughing, I glanced at Brit. 'You should help him build his happy garden.'

She snorted. 'You can help him.'

'Oh, no.' Cam lifted his head as he slipped his hand over my leg, just above my knee. 'She's all mine this weekend. No garden of love.'

'Unless she's planting in *your* garden of love?' Jacob queried.

I rolled my eyes. 'Cute.'

'Sounded like she was doing some planting last night.' Ollie moved the tiny paper cup of mayo farther away from Brit. 'At least from the noises coming from your bedroom.'

My mouth dropped open. 'Whatever!'

'Did you have your ear plastered to my bedroom door?' Cam's hand inched up, and my cheeks were suddenly burning for a whole different reason.

Ollie shrugged. 'What else am I supposed to do?'

'Freak,' Cam tossed back.

The three of them launched into a discussion about vegetables, leaving Cam and me on the outside of the bizarro conversation, which was okay with me. I wasn't a fan of vegetables.

'I have another great idea.' Cam propped his chin on my shoulder, voice low.

I turned my head just the slightest bit toward him. 'Oh dear …'

'You're going to love it.'

Warmth bubbled up my chest, and I wanted to say I love you, but sitting in the Den, while our friends were discussing the pros and cons of asparagus, didn't seem like the best moment to blurt that out. So I settled with a 'What's your idea?'

'Take the rest of the day off and chill with me.'

That sounded like an excellent idea. 'I have class.'

'You have art. That doesn't really count as a class.'

'How so?'

He lifted his head, pressing his lips to the space beside my ear. 'You told me you almost fell asleep on Monday.'

'Almost,' I reiterated.

Cam now kissed the spot under my ear, and I shivered. 'Trust me. What I want to do is so much better than art.'

My mind went straight to one thing. Sex. Like, real sex with real penetration.

Oh my God, I couldn't believe I just thought that. Was there a fake penetration I was unaware of? Actually, sort of. We'd done everything except sex. We've touched, groped, he'd gone down on me and I on him, but sex? There had been none of the actual act, but the last time, what Ollie was claiming he heard, it had seemed like we were heading there. There had been a certain intent.

I'd panicked and basically went down on Cam. Not that he was complaining, but I couldn't keep doing that. We had to take our relationship to the next level. Besides, I was probably the only twenty-year-old virgin on campus, and how long would Cam wait for me to be ready? We'd been together for four months and guy time was like dog years so that was like two years.

Anticipation tingled throughout me, but under the excitement, unease formed like a ball of ice in my chest.

Cam circled his arms around my waist, pulling me out of my chair and into his lap. The people at our table basically ignored us, but the ones at the tables around us were starting to stare.

He was totally unfazed by the attention as he tossed his head back, grinning widely. 'So what do you say?'

'You two are so sickly sweet it's actually cute,' Jacob said, interrupting us. We looked at him. 'If you don't skip art and run off with him, I'm going to kick your ass.'

'Well then, how can I say no?'

I just hoped that when it came down to it, I could say yes.

Cam really was extraordinary.

And I don't know how he managed to continuously surprise me with his thoughtfulness or how it was even possible for him to be so wonderful. Or why it took me so long to pull my head out of my ass and see that.

When we'd left the campus, he met me by my car and ushered me over to his truck.

'What are we doing?'

'You'll see.'

The secretive half smile had me on edge. It wasn't until we hit I-70 and I saw the sign that I knew where we were going. I twisted toward him and in my excitement, I almost choked myself with the seat belt.

Cam laughed.

'We're going to DC? Aren't we?' I exclaimed, practically bouncing in my seat.

He slid me a sly side look. 'Maybe.'

'And we're going to the Smithsonian, right?'

'Quite possibly.'

I flipped forward, clasping my hands together. 'Why?' I blurted out. 'I mean, I know history bores you, so why?'

'Why?' He laughed again as he messed with his baseball cap. 'I told you that I'd go to the Smithsonian with you and I didn't get to do it with you on your birthday, so I thought why not today?'

Why not today? That was one of the things I loved most about Cam. His ability to do things on the spur of the moment, no thought or plan behind them. He literally lived in the moment and nothing held him back, not even the trouble he'd gotten into, because he had moved past that.

I knew that was mainly because he'd accepted what he'd done and the consequences of his actions. It may have taken him a few weeks after it happened, but he'd come to terms with it.

I admired that in him.

Once we got to DC, we spent the rest of the afternoon and most of the evening going from exhibit to exhibit. Cam seemed more interested in touching me and stealing kisses than what we were looking at, and I was okay with that. I thought of the couples I'd watched last time and realized I had become one of them. It was so normal, so perfect. There was no difference between us and them, and I reveled in that.

It was late when we got home, and since there were no classes on Thursday, we had the whole night. Buzzing from our impromptu trip, I dropped some of the stinky tortoise bites onto a little bowl and slipped it into Michelangelo's home.

As I closed the lid on the terrarium, Cam came up behind me, placing his hands on my hips. He turned me around, and I stretched up, placing a kiss on his lips.

'Thank you for today,' I said, looping my arms around his neck. 'I had a lot of fun.'

'I told you that my idea was great.'

'They usually are.'

'Holy shit.' His eyes widened in exaggerated surprise. 'Did you just admit that?'

I grinned. 'Maybe I did.'

'Uh-huh, you've always known my ideas hit a ten.'

'On a scale of one to a hundred, yes.'

'Ha. Ha.' He slid his hands up until they rested on my rib cage. 'Guess what? Got another idea.'

'Does it involve eggs?'

A deep laugh burst from Cam and then he tugged my hips against his. 'It doesn't involve eggs.'

I had a good idea of what it involved. My stomach dipped. 'It doesn't?'

He shook his head. 'But it does involve something equally tasty.'

My cheeks heated as I turned my head to the side.

His lips followed the movement, tracing my cheekbone. 'And it involves you, me, a bed, and very little, if any, clothing.'

Tingles shot down my spine. 'Does it now?'

'Yes.' Cam slid his hand down under the band of my jeans so that his fingers rested over the swell of my rear. He brushed his lips over my brow. 'What do you think?'

I wasn't thinking. I tilted my head back, and Cam obliged my silent invitation. His lips were on mine, and then his hands were under my shirt. He broke away long enough to tug my shirt off and then his. Lips melded together, we started walking, our hips bumping into the couch, and he lost his balance. He fell backward, half on the couch and half off. Giggles broke free between our kisses and our laughter died as our hands got more involved. With a skill beyond me, Cam managed to get my jeans off while I sprawled on top of him, and then he displayed a whole different kind of talent.

His hands traveled northward, cresting over my breasts, finding the nipples covered by satin. I arched against his hands, biting back a moan as Cam made that sexy sound as his hips pushed up against mine. A rush of heat flooded my core as one hand left my breast and slipped down the curve of my stomach. His hand slid under my panties. He palmed me, rubbing his thumb in just the right place to make me cry out. The desire—the need to lose myself in nothing but sensation, even for just a few moments, took over. My skin was on fire as I put my weight on my knees and reached down, unzipping his fly.

'Avery,' Cam groaned, thrusting into my palm.

Upon hearing my name on his lips, tension built deep inside me. Our bodies rocked together, but still apart. Then the tension was spiraling, breaking apart and shattering. I threw my head back, biting down on my lip. Bliss washed over me.

Cam shifted under me and the next thing I knew, he was standing and I was wrapped around him like a little monkey. My body was still trembling when I hit the bed. In a heated daze, I watched him strip. Completely.

My God, he was beautiful.

He hooked his fingers under my panties and I lifted my hips so he could pull them down. It wasn't the first time that he'd stripped me bare, but it was the first time that we both were so naked. There were different stages of nakedness, I'd learned over the past four months. This was the final stage. My stomach fluttered.

Cam hovered over me, his lips trailing a path across my body. My fingers were in his soft hair as he came back up, claiming my mouth. He shifted above me and I felt him on my thigh.

My heart stuttered and then sped up.

A tremor coursed over his body, or maybe it was mine causing his to do that, because I think I was shaking. I didn't know if it was from excitement or something else. My hands found his chest and they flattened there.

'Do you want this?' he asked, his voice strained as he held himself back.

'Yes,' I said, and I told myself that I did. And I did want this. I wanted to cross that final line with Cam.

His eyes met mine for a moment and then he bent his head, kissing me as he lowered his body upon mine. I felt him there, the tip of him slipping through my wetness, and I don't know what happened. Maybe it was the weight of him on top of me or the feel of him between my thighs. For a frightening second, I wasn't in my bedroom or under Cam. I was back on the couch, my cheek pressed roughly into the coarse fabric. Cold air rushed over my exposed lower body, followed by a rough, demanding hand. I tried to push the memory out of my head and focus on what was really happening, but once it crept in, I couldn't get it out of my head.

Every muscle in my body locked up and the knot of unease from earlier in the day returned with a vengeance. It was like being hit with an arctic blast. I went cold on the outside and inside. Panic dug in with razor-sharp claws.

I twisted my head to the side, breaking the kiss as I pushed against his chest. 'No. Stop. Please stop.'

Cam froze above me, his chest rising and falling deeply. 'Avery? What the—?'

'Get off.' My skin was crawling as pressure clamped down on my chest. 'Get off. *Please*. Get off me.'

He rolled off me in an instant, and I scrambled across the bed, grabbing the comforter and tugging it up over me. I shot to my feet, backing up until I hit the dresser. Bottles of lotion rattled. The soft thud of them hitting the floor snapped me out of it. My heart was racing so fast I thought I'd be sick.

'Oh God,' I whispered hoarsely. There was a good chance I was going to hurl the baked pretzel we'd shared earlier.

Light from the hallway cast strange shadows over half of Cam's pale face. His eyes were as big as the moon. He stared at me, brows pinched with concern. 'Did I hurt you? I didn't—'

'No. No!' I squeezed my eyes shut. 'You didn't hurt me. You didn't even … I don't know. I'm sorry …' I trailed off, having no idea what to say.

331

Cam took several deep breaths, planting his hands on the bed. 'Talk to me, Avery. What just happened?'

'Nothing.' My voice cracked. 'Nothing happened. I just thought—'

'You thought what?'

I shook my head. 'I don't know. It's not a big deal—'

'Not a big deal?' His brows flew up. 'Avery, you just scared the shit out of me. You started panicking like I was hurting you or—or like I was forcing you to do this.'

Horrified, I felt my stomach drop. 'You weren't forcing me, Cam. I liked what you were doing.'

Several seconds passed and then he said, 'You know I would never hurt you, right?'

'Yes.' Tears clogged my throat.

'And I would never force you to do anything you didn't want to do.' He spoke slowly, each word precise. 'You understand that, right? If you're not ready, I'm okay with that, but you have to talk to me. You have to let me know before it gets to that point.'

Clenching the blanket, I nodded.

There was another gap of silence, and his stare pierced mine. A certain level of comprehension flashed across his features, and I bit down on my lip. I wanted to know what he was thinking and then again, I didn't.

'What are you not telling me?' he asked, like he'd done the night out in the parking lot.

I couldn't say anything.

His jaw clenched. 'What happened to you?'

'Nothing!' The word burst from me like a cannon. 'There's nothing to talk about, dammit. Just fucking drop it.'

'You're lying.'

There. He said it. He called me on it.

Cam took a deep, long breath. 'You're lying to me. Something happened, because that?' He gestured at where we'd been twined together moments before. 'That wasn't about not being ready. That was about something else, because you know—*you know*—I would wait for you, Avery. I swear. But you have to tell me what's going on in your head.'

My chest ached at his words, but I couldn't say anything.

'I'm begging you, Avery. You've got to be up front and honest with me. You said that you trusted me. You've got to prove it, because I know there is more to this. I'm not stupid and I'm not blind. I remember how you acted when we first met, and I sure as hell remember what you said that night you were drunk.'

Oh God. The floor shifted under my feet.

He was on a roll. 'And that text message you got? Are you telling me that has nothing to do with this? If you trust me, you will finally tell me what the hell is going on.'

'I do trust you.' The tears reached my eyes, blurring him.

Cam watched me for a second and then stood, grabbing his jeans off the floor. He tugged them on, zipping them up but not buttoning them. He faced me, expression tense. 'I don't know what else to do with you, Avery. I've told you shit that I'm not proud of. Stuff that hardly anyone in this world knows and yet you keep shit from me. You keep *everything* from me. You don't trust me.'

'No—I do.' I started forward but stopped when I saw the look on his face. 'I trust you with my life.'

'But not with the truth? That's such bullshit, Avery. You don't trust me.' He stalked past me, heading out to the living room.

I followed him, my hands shaking. 'Cam—'

'Stop it.' He grabbed his sweater off the floor and faced me. 'I don't know what else to do and I know I don't know everything in the world, but I do know that relationships don't work this way.'

Fear punched me in the chest. 'What are you saying?'

'What do you think I'm saying, Avery? There are some obvious issues with you and, no, don't fucking look at me like I kicked your puppy. Do you think I'd break up with you because of whatever the hell went on with you? Just like you thought I'd think differently of you when I saw the scar on your wrist? I know you think that and that's bullshit.' Sorrow and raw anger flooded his voice. 'How can there be any future for us if you can't be honest with me? If you can't really trust that how I feel about you is strong enough, then we have nothing. This is the shit that ends relationships. Not the past, Avery, but the *present*.'

My breath caught. 'Cam, please—'

'No more, Avery. I told you before. All I asked from you was to trust me and not shut me out.' He turned to the door. 'And you don't trust me and you shut me out again.'

And then he was gone, the door slamming shut behind him. I made it to the couch before my legs gave out. Sitting down, I pressed my knees to my chest. There was a cracking in my chest, my heart, and the pain was so very real.

My mouth opened, but I didn't make a sound.

I never made a sound.

Chapter 30

I stayed in bed and slept most of Thursday and Friday. A thick and suffocating feeling lay over me like a too-heavy blanket. I'd screwed up. Royally. That was the self-pitying mantra that I repeated over and over. It was the truth, and it was all I could think about.

Not how I planned on kicking off my spring recess.

Burying my head in the pillow, I stayed away from my phone, because if I checked it and Cam hadn't called, then I'd feel worse. Pointless thing was I knew he wouldn't call.

And there was no doubt in my mind that I was *in love* with him. There was a difference between loving someone and being in love and I had let it slip through my fingers.

Cam had had enough.

He'd trusted me, and in a way, I'd thrown that trust back in his face. If he'd known everything, things could've gone down differently between us Wednesday night. But I had remained silent, like I had all these years.

At some point during Saturday, the deep cutting sorrow gave way to something else. I threw off the blanket and stood in the middle of the room, breathing in raggedly. Spinning around, I picked up a bottle of lotion and threw it across the room. The bottle hit the closet door and then thudded off the floor.

Not satisfied, I grabbed another bottle and threw it harder. That one hit the wall, cracking the plaster. There went my security deposit.

I didn't care.

Anger rose around me like a hot steam. I whirled, pulling the comforter and sheets off the bed.

Then I attacked my closet.

I hated the boring sweaters, the turtlenecks, the cardigans, and the ill-fitting shirts. I hated everything, but most of all, I hated myself for doing *this*. Crying out, I yanked them down. Hangers rocked and fell to the floor. Tears blurred my eyes as I turned, seeking something else to destroy, but there really wasn't anything. No pictures to throw. No paintings to rip from the walls. There was nothing. I was so pissed— pissed at myself.

Moving to the hallway, I leaned against the wall, squeezing my eyes shut. Breathing heavily, I kicked my head back and bit back a scream.

The silence was *killing* me.

And that's all there ever was. Silence. It was all I knew. Keep quiet. Pretend nothing had happened, that nothing was wrong. And look how well that was turning out.

I slid down the wall and opened my eyes. They were as dry as I felt on the inside, brittle.

Who did I have to blame for that? Blaine? His parents? Mine? Did it matter? Never once did I stand up to my parents and tell them what I thought. I just shut up and took it— took it until I could run away.

Problem was, running away wasn't working anymore. It never worked in the first place and how long did it take me to figure that out? Five years, almost six? And how many miles? Thousands?

And then, like fucking clockwork, I heard my phone ring from the living room.

Shoving to my feet, I stalked out there, the back of my skull tingling as I saw UNKNOWN CALLER flash across the screen. I grabbed the phone and pressed the answer button.

'What?' I said, my voice shaking.

Nothing. More fucking silence.

'What the fuck do you want from me?' I demanded. 'What? You have nothing to say? You've only been calling and texting for nine months. I'd think you'd have a shit ton to say.'

There was another pregnant pause and then, 'I can't believe you answered.'

My eyes widened. Holy shit, the voice belonged to a girl. The person who was calling me and most likely e-mailing me was a girl.

A girl.

Who knows what I expected, but I sure as hell didn't expect a *girl*.

I could only say one word. 'Why?'

'Why?' The girl coughed out a dry laugh. 'You have no idea who you're talking to, do you? You didn't even read a single e-mail I sent you? Not one?'

She was questioning me? 'Well, when I saw the content in a couple of them, I decided to not torture myself.'

'I've been e-mailing you since *June*, trying to talk to you. There was nothing wrong with the first couple of e-mails I sent you. If you just read one of them, you would've seen that. Then again, why should I even believe that you didn't read them, since you have such an infamous background of telling the truth?'

Plopping down, I frowned. 'Who *are* you?'

'God, this is fucking unbelievable. My name is Molly Simmons.'

My eyes widened. 'Molly?'

'You sound like you recognize my name. I guess you did read the e-mails.'

'No—my cousin told me about you.' I was on my feet again, pacing. 'I didn't read your e-mails. I'm not lying about that.'

'Well, that would be the first time you told the truth if that's the case,' she said, and I heard a door slam.

I didn't know what to say. Shell-shocked—I was absolutely dumbfounded. 'I don't know … God, I'm so sorry for what you—'

'Don't you dare apologize,' she cut in, her voice razor sharp. 'I'm sorry means absolutely fucking nothing to me.'

My mouth hung open as I shook my head, which was stupid, because it wasn't like she could see any of that.

'You're a fucking lying whore. Because of you—'

'Hey! Seriously. You're calling me a whore? You have to see how messed up that is.' My hand tightened around the phone. 'Honestly, every single disgusting message you have sent me is messed up. And I don't even understand why you'd do this.'

'Why?' Her voice turned shrill. 'Are you fucking serious?'

'Yes!'

There was an audible breath. 'Tell me one thing. What was true? What you told the police or what Blaine told everyone?'

I sucked in a breath.

'Which is it, Avery? Because if it was true, why did you drop the charges knowing what he was capable of? Because you had to know that there was something wrong with him and that he'd do it again.'

My shoulders caved in and I whispered, 'You don't understand.'

338

'Oh, I understand completely. Either way, you're a liar.' Molly's breath crackled over the phone. 'Do you know why I wanted to get in contact with you? Because I needed to talk to someone who'd been through what I had been through and I thought—' Her voice cracked. 'It doesn't matter what I thought or why I wrote. You didn't even take the time to read a single fucking e-mail. The least you could do is to tell me the truth.'

I closed my eyes, resting my forehead on my palm. My head was still spinning from what happened with Cam, and this blew my mind. There had been so many e-mails from accounts I didn't recognize. Many with my name as the subject. And I hadn't opened them because I hadn't wanted to deal with it, but I never thought it was her.

Then again, would that really have changed anything? Would I have opened them and reached out to her? Legal aspects of the nondisclosure aside, would I?

I'd be lying if I said I thought I would.

'Are you there?' Molly demanded.

'Yes.' I cleared my throat, lifting my head. The ball in my chest unraveled a little. 'I didn't lie.'

'So it was true?' Her voice sounded closer to the phone. 'And you dropped the charges.'

My body tensed like a coiled rope. 'Yes, but you—'

'Why would you do that?' Her voice was raw. 'How could you? How could you stay silent this long?'

'I—'

'You're a coward. You cling to your silence because you're a coward! You're still the same scared, fourteen-year-old girl pretending to be over it years later!' she shouted, and my ear popped. 'This happened to me because you didn't tell the truth. You can tell yourself whatever you want, but that's the truth. And we both know it.'

Molly hung up on me.

I sat there, staring at my phone. Anger still boiled inside me, but some of what she said had sunk through the red haze and it made sense.

'You cling to your silence because you're a coward! You're still the same scared, fourteen-year-old girl pretending to be over it years later!'

She was right.

God, she was so right. All these years and I had never uttered the words since that night. I was too scared to tell anyone, to even tell Cam. And that was why he'd walked out of here, because he had also been right. I hadn't let go of the past, and there was no future unless I did so. All I'd been doing this entire time was pretending—pretending to be okay, to be completely happy, to be a survivor.

And I wasn't a survivor. For too many years, I'd been nothing more than a victim on the run.

Molly didn't know the whole story. Probably wouldn't change anything if she did, but *surviving* and being a *survivor* were two different things. That's what I'd been doing this whole time. Just surviving, waiting for the day when what Blaine had done to me would not tarnish everything that was good in my life.

I dropped my head into my hands. Tears welled up in my eyes.

There were things I could've done differently. I couldn't change what had happened to me, but I could've changed the way I reacted, especially now when I was so far away from those who had hindered any attempts to overcome it. But to be honest, it was more than that. It had always been more than Blaine. It had been my parents—it had been me.

The only way I could truly move on was to confront what had happened, to do something I had been punished for doing in the first place.

It wasn't the past that was coming between us.

It was the present.

Cam had been right.

Suddenly, I shot to my feet. I was moving before I knew what I was doing. It was when I stood in front of Cam's apartment door that my heart leaped in my throat. It was probably too late for us, but if I told him—if I could explain myself—then that was a start. Either way, I owed it to Cam.

I owed it to myself.

I knocked and heard footsteps a few seconds later. The door swung open, revealing Cam. His eyes immediately closed and his mouth opened, and I knew he was going to tell me to leave.

'Can we talk?' I asked, voice cracking halfway through. 'Please, Cam. I won't take up much of your time. I just—'

Cam's eyes flew open and then narrowed as he looked at me. 'Are you okay, Avery?'

'Yes. No. I don't know.' Part of me wanted to turn and go back to my apartment, but I refused to allow myself to run. Not anymore. 'I just need to talk to you.'

Taking a deep breath, he stepped aside. 'Ollie's not here.'

Relieved that he hadn't shut the door in my face, I followed him into the living room. Cam picked up the remote, muting the TV as he sat on the couch. 'What's going on, Avery?' he asked, and his tone suggested that he didn't expect me to answer truthfully, and that hurt.

It hurt because he had no reason to expect me to be up front about anything.

I sat on the edge of the recliner, unsure of where to start. 'Everything.' And that was all I could say at first. 'Everything.'

Cam scooted forward, twisting the cap he wore backward. An adorable habit that said he was paying attention. 'Avery, what's going on?'

'I haven't been honest with you, and I'm sorry.' My lower lip started to tremble and I knew I was seconds from losing it. 'I'm so sorry, and you probably don't have time for—'

'I have time for you, Avery.' He met my gaze with a steady one. 'You want to talk to me, I'm here. I've been here. And I'm listening.'

As he held my gaze, fight or flight kicked in. Instinct. Run. Don't deal with it. But Cam kept holding my gaze and something unlocked inside me. It wasn't easy, but the words were bubbling up. I wouldn't run.

Calmness settled over me and when I took a breath, it came out slowly. 'When I was fourteen, I went to this party on Halloween,' I heard myself saying, sounding as if I were in a tunnel. 'I was there with my friends. We were all dressed up and there was this guy there. It was his house and … and he was three years older than me and friends with my cousin.'

I took another deep breath, my gaze dropping to my hands. 'He was really popular. So was I.' A dry, humorless laugh came out. 'That might not seem important, but it was. I never thought someone like him could do—could be like he was. And maybe that was stupid of me, like a fatal flaw or something. I don't know.' I gave a little shake of my head as I looked up. 'I was talking to him and I was drinking, but I wasn't drunk. I swear to you, I wasn't drunk.'

'I believe you, Avery.' Cam closed his eyes briefly as he steepled his fingers under his chin. 'What happened?'

'We were flirting and it was fun. You know, I didn't think anything of it. He was a good guy and he was a good-looking guy. At one point, he pulled me into his lap and someone took our picture. We were having fun.' I laughed again, another harsh sound. 'When he got up and pulled me into one of the empty guest rooms on the ground floor, I didn't

342

think anything of it. We sat on the couch and talked for a little while. Then he put his arms around me.' I rubbed my hands together continuously, hoping to ease the knots forming in my stomach. 'At first I didn't mind, but he started doing things I didn't want him to. I told him to stop and he laughed it off. I started crying and I tried to get away from him, but he was stronger than me, and once he got me on my stomach, I couldn't do anything really, except tell him to stop.'

Cam had gone very still. The only way I could tell he was breathing was by the steady thrumming of the muscle along his jaw. 'Did he stop?'

'He didn't,' I said quietly. 'He never stopped, no matter what I did.'

A moment passed and Cam straightened. He looked like he wanted to stand but changed his mind. 'He raped you?'

Closing my eyes, I nodded. Talking about it, it was almost like I could feel Blaine's hands. 'I am still a virgin.' I forced my eyes open. 'He didn't touch me there. That's not how he … raped me.'

Cam stared at me, and I saw the moment he understood. Comprehension flared in his eyes. His hands closed into fists in his lap. The muscle in his jaw sped up. 'Son of a bitch,' he said, lips thin. 'You were *fourteen* and he did *that* to you?'

'Yeah.' The knots in my stomach grew.

Another moment passed, and Cam thrust his hand through his hair. 'Shit. Avery. I suspected something. I thought that something like that might have happened to you.'

I wrapped my arms around my waist. 'You did?'

He nodded. 'It was the way you acted sometimes, how jumpy you could be. But I'd just hoped it didn't go that far. And when you told me you were still a virgin, I thought that was the case.'

That was an understandable assumption.

343

'Avery, I'm so, so sorry. You should have never had to go through something like that, especially at that age ...' His jaw clenched down and he looked like he was going to stand again but stopped. 'Please tell me that motherfucker is in jail for this.'

'He is now.' I focused on the muted TV. 'It's a long story.'

'I have time.' When I didn't say anything, he spoke again and his voice sounded strained. 'What else, Avery? Please talk to me, because I'm seconds away from booking a flight to Texas and killing a motherfucker.'

I rocked back, pulling my knees to my chest. Knowing that I owed him everything, I took another deep breath. 'After he stopped, I really don't think he had a clue that he'd done anything wrong. He just left me there on this couch and when I could get up, I knew I needed to tell someone. I knew I needed to go to the hospital. I was in so much ...' I squeezed my eyes shut as a shudder rocked through me. The following minutes after Blaine had left me had been as horrifying as the attack. 'I couldn't find my friends, but I found my purse, and I ended up walking out of the house and I kept walking until I remembered I had my phone with me. I called 911.'

Unable to sit any longer, I dropped my feet to the floor and stood. 'I ended up at the hospital and they did an exam. The police showed up and I told them what happened and it was the truth.'

'Of course it was the truth,' he said, his gaze following me.

'By the time the police left the hospital, the party was over, but Blaine was at his house. They arrested him and took him in. I went home and I stayed out of school for the next two days, but everyone found out that he'd been arrested for what he'd done.' I stopped in front of the TV. 'And then his parents showed up.'

344

'What do you mean?'

I started pacing again. 'His parents and mine were—*are*—country club buddies. All they ever cared about was image. My mom and dad have more money than they could ever want, but ...' A thickness coated my throat and my vision blurred. 'The Fitzgeralds offered my parents a deal. That if I dropped the charges and remained quiet about what happened, they would pay me and them an ungodly sum of money.'

Cam's nostrils flared. 'And your parents told them to go fuck themselves, right?'

I laughed, but it came out more of a sob. 'They showed my parents the picture that was taken of Blaine and me at the party and they said that if this went to court, no one would believe the girl in the "slutty costume sitting in his lap." And my parents, they didn't want to deal with the scandal. They wanted it all to go away, so they agreed.'

'Holy shit,' Cam whispered hoarsely.

'It happened so fast. I couldn't believe what my parents were telling me to do. They hadn't really talked to me about it before, but they ... they had been so worried about what everyone would think if the whole thing went public—the pictures and the fact that I *had* been drinking. I was just so scared and confused, and you know, I'm not even sure they believed me.' I tugged my hair back, hating what I was about to admit. 'So I signed the papers.'

Cam said nothing.

'I agreed to take the money, half of which went into my account so that when I turned eighteen, I had access to it, and I agreed to pull the charges and to not speak about it again.' I dropped my hands to my sides. 'That makes me a terrible person, doesn't it?'

'What?' Cam's brows flew up. 'You're not a terrible person, Avery. Jesus Christ, you were fourteen and your parents

345

should've told them to fuck off. If anyone is to blame, beside the fucker who did that to you, it's them. You don't have any fault in this.'

I nodded slowly as I sat on the recliner. 'Within days, everyone at school turned on me. Apparently, there was nothing in the agreement about Blaine keeping his mouth shut. He told people that I had lied. That I had done all those things with him willingly and then falsely accused him. Everyone believed him. Why wouldn't they? I'd dropped the charges. I wouldn't talk about it. School was … it was terrible after that. I lost all my friends.'

Cam ran a hand over his jaw. 'This is why you stopped dancing?'

'Yes,' I whispered. 'I couldn't stand people looking at me and whispering about what they'd heard or talking openly about it in front of my face. And I did this …' I raised my left arm. 'My mom was so pissed.'

He stared at me, as if he couldn't comprehend the last thing I had said. 'She was mad because you …' Trailing off, he shook his head. 'No wonder you don't go home to see them.'

'It's why I picked here, you know. It was far enough to just get away from all of it. I thought that was all I needed to do—to distance myself.'

'That message I saw? It was someone who knew about what happened?'

I nodded again. 'Whoever came up with the saying you can't escape your past really knew what they were talking about.'

The muscle popped faster in Cam's jaw. 'What else has been going on, Avery? You said this *Blaine*'—he spat the name out—'was in jail? But who's been messaging you?'

Leaning forward, I pressed my forehead into my open hands. My hair slid forward, shielding my face. 'I've been

346

getting these messages since August. I just thought it was some asshole and ignored it. And my cousin had been trying to reach me, but I ignored him too because … well, for obvious reasons. I finally talked to my cousin over winter break, the night before I came over to your apartment.'

'The night of the fight?'

'Yeah,' I said. 'He was trying to get in touch with me to tell me that Blaine had been arrested for doing the same thing to another girl at the start of summer. My cousin actually apologized. That meant a lot to me, but … I didn't know that this girl has been the one who's been contacting me this entire time.' Taking a deep breath, I told him how it all came about with Molly.

When I was done, Cam was shaking his head. 'What happened to her is fucking terrible and I'm glad that bastard's ass is going to jail. Better yet, he should be fucking castrated, but what happened to her isn't your fault, sweetheart. You didn't make him do that to you or her.'

'But me not telling anyone allowed him to do it again.'

'No.' Cam stood, his eyes full of fire. 'Don't fucking tell yourself that. No one knows what would've happened if you didn't drop the charges. You were fourteen, Avery. You did the best you could in the situation. You *survived*.'

I lifted my head then. 'But that's it, you know? All I've been doing is surviving. I haven't been living. Look at what I've done to us. And yes, I've done this! I pushed you away *again*.'

His expression softened. 'But you're telling me now.'

'I've let what happened to me five years ago still affect me! When we almost had sex? I wasn't afraid of you, or that there'd be pain. It wasn't that. I was afraid that once we started, that what Blaine had done would ruin it for me or that I would ruin it for myself. I am a coward—I *was* a coward.' Coming to my feet, I folded my arms across my

347

waist. 'But it's too late, isn't it? I should've been honest with you months ago so you knew what you were getting into and I'm so sorry that I wasn't.'

'Avery ...'

The back of my throat burned as tears flooded my eyes. 'I'm so sorry, Cam. I know telling you now doesn't change anything, but I needed to tell you that you didn't do anything wrong. You were perfect—*perfect* for me—and I love you.' My voice broke again. 'And I know you can't look at me the same now. I understand.'

Cam's arms had fallen to his sides. He looked shell-shocked. 'Avery,' he broke in, voice soft, and he was suddenly in front of me, cupping my cheeks. 'What did you say?'

'That you can't look at me the same?'

'Not that. Before that.'

I sniffed. 'I love you?'

'You love me?' His eyes searched mine intensely.

'Yes, but—'

'Stop.' He shook his head. 'Do you think I look at you differently? I told you I always suspected that something happened—'

'But you had hope that it wasn't that!' I tried to pull away, but Cam's hands dropped to my upper arms, not allowing me to run. 'You looked at me before with *hope* and you don't have that anymore.'

'Is that what you really think? Has that been what has been stopping you this whole time from telling me?'

'Everyone looks at me differently once they know.'

'I'm not everyone, Avery! Not to you, not with you.' Our gazes locked. 'Do you think I still don't have hope? Hope that you will eventually get past this? That it won't haunt you five more years from now?'

I didn't know what to say, but my heart was racing as he slid his hands down to mine. He placed them on his chest,

348

right above his heart. 'I have hope,' he said, his gaze never leaving mine. 'I have hope because I love you—I've been *in* love with you, Avery. Probably before I even realized that I was.'

'You loved me?'

Cam dropped his forehead to mine and his chest rose sharply under my hands. 'I love you.'

My heart stuttered. 'You *love* me?'

'Yes, sweetheart.'

There was a strength in those words, and there was a power in the truth. Something broke wide open inside me, like the foundation of a great, thick wall finally giving under the weight. A hailstorm of emotion whirled inside me, seeking a way out. I couldn't stop it. I didn't even try. Tears streamed down my face, so fast that I couldn't see Cam's face through them.

A sound from the back of his throat came and he pulled me to his chest, circling his arms around me tightly. He held me, whispering soothing, nonsensical words. At some point, he lifted me into his arms and carried me back to his bedroom. He laid me down on his bed and climbed in beside me, cradling me to his chest. Once the tears came, they didn't stop. They were the big, ugly kind of sobs you couldn't speak or breathe around. There was also something renewing in those tears, as if each tear that fell somehow symbolized that I was finally letting go.

I cried for Molly and all that she had to go through. I cried for Cam and everything I had put him through. I cried because, in the end, he still loved me. Most of all, I cried for everything that I had lost and for everything I knew I could now gain.

Chapter 31

Lying beside me on my bed, Cam reached over and picked up a strand of my hair. He twirled the reddish-brown lock around his fingers and then smacked it across my nose. 'So what does it feel like to finally be a sophomore in college?'

I caught his hand and untangled my hair, grinning. 'I'm not officially a sophomore. Not until school starts again in the fall.'

'I deem you a sophomore now.' He plucked up my hair again, this time trailing it across my cheek. 'What I say goes.'

'Then how does it feel finally being a senior? Next year *is* your last.'

'Amazing,' he replied, tracing my lower lip with the ends of my hair. 'It feels amazing.'

Wiggling closer to him, I wrapped my fingers in the collar of his shirt. 'It feels pretty damn good to be a sophomore.'

'Would be better if you didn't sign up for summer classes.'

'True.' I was taking bio over the summer to get it out of the way. And it would work out. Cam was helping out with a summer soccer camp for kids, so he'd be here most of the

351

time. I was going to miss Brit and Jacob though. They'd already headed home.

Smiling softly, I managed to get closer. Cam spread his arms and I placed my head on his shoulder, throwing an arm and a leg over him.

'Close enough?' he asked.

'No.'

He chuckled as his fingers trailed up and down my spine. My body relaxed under the soft ministrations. His lips brushed my forehead and I smiled.

Things were different between us since I'd told him the truth. It had been rough and awkward immediately afterward. Whether Cam admitted it, he hadn't been sure how to proceed forward with our relationship, what he should say or do; and it wasn't like a miraculous change occurred overnight. Three weeks had passed before anything sexual happened between us. It wasn't that he hadn't wanted to, but I knew he hadn't wanted to push me. It took me taking control and basically attacking him for him to get the message. Of course, we hadn't had sex, yet, but the first time we were intimate after I opened up to him had regained any ground we'd lost in that aspect.

In a small way he did look at me differently, but it wasn't as I feared. He knew the whole story now and that did change us.

For the better.

I was more of myself, the way I was *before*. I'd even gone to a party thrown at Jase's the previous weekend. There'd been moments of unease, but Cam had been there to help me through it instead of me having to deal with it on my own. I had danced with Cam.

He'd really enjoyed that.

There weren't any secrets between us, and we had the whole summer ahead of us to explore, but there were things on my mind. Resolving the issues with Cam had been important and a much-needed step, but there were still things I needed to face, needed to take care of—and they were big things.

Rolling on top of Cam, I straddled his hips. 'Hey.'

His eyes got that heavy, sensual look to them as he placed his hands on my waist. 'Hey there.'

'So I've been doing some thinking.'

'Oh God.'

'Shut up.' I laughed and then lowered my head, kissing his lips. 'Actually, I've been doing a lot of thinking. There's something I want to do.'

'What?' His hands slid down over my shorts and rested on my thighs.

I bit my lip. 'I want to go home.'

Cam's brows shot up. 'Like back to Texas?'

'Yes.'

'For how long?'

Placing my hands on his stomach, I sat back. A flicker of tension ricocheted across his face as I pressed down on him. Part of it was on purpose. 'You're not getting rid of me that easy. For just a day or two.'

His grip tightened. 'Damn. There goes my master plan of spending the summer like a sex-crazed bachelor.'

I rolled my eyes.

'What do you want to do if you go back there?' he asked, smoothing his hands over my thighs.

'I want to see my parents,' I admitted. 'I need to talk to them.'

'About what happened?'

'I've never talked to them about it, not since that night.' I tapped my fingers along his chest. 'I need to. I know this sounds like it being a bitch fest, but I need to tell them that what they did was wrong.'

Cam let go of my thighs and placed his hands over mine. 'It doesn't sound like a bitch fest, but do you think it's wise? I mean, do you think it's going to help you and not ...'

'Hurt me?' I smiled softly. 'There's really nothing more my parents can do that will hurt me, but I feel like I need to confront them. Does that make me a bad person?'

'No.'

'I need to do this.' I took a deep breath. 'I also need to talk to Molly.'

'What?'

'I need to talk to her and try to explain why I did what I did. I know it's risky, and if it comes back and bites me in the ass with the nondisclosure, then it does, but if I can get her to understand just a little bit, then maybe it will help her and she'll stop contacting me.' And that would be a hell of a nice change. Since we had talked she still sent me messages. Sporadic ones, so I guess that was an improvement, but I wanted them to end.

I wanted to move on completely.

Cam's eyes met mine. 'I don't know about that. The girl seems like she's not the most stable person out there.'

'She's not crazy. She's just mad, and she has a reason to be.'

'And you're not the reason why it happened to her. You know that, right? You're not responsible.'

I didn't say anything, because I wasn't sure if that was the truth. If I hadn't dropped the charges, Blaine wouldn't have gotten away with what he'd done and that may have been enough to stop him from doing it again. Or not. That would be a great unknown.

'I need to do this for myself and for Molly,' I said finally. It wasn't going to be pretty. 'I don't want to run anymore, Cam. And I know I can never really put this behind me.

What happened … well, it will always be a part of me, but it won't be me. Not anymore.'

Cam was silent for a moment. 'You know what I think?'

'I'm awesome?'

'Besides that.'

'What?'

'I think you've already made it that far, Avery. I think you have accepted it will be part of you, but it's not you. You just haven't realized that.' His hands moved to my hips. 'But if you want to do this, then you'll do this, and I'll be there with you.'

'You want to go with—' I squealed as Cam rolled suddenly and I was on my back and he was above me.

'You're not doing this by yourself. Hell to the mother-fucking no,' he said, resting his weight on his arm. 'I'm going with you. And you're not talking me out of it. When do you want to do this?'

'Got any plans this weekend?'

A silent laugh shook his shoulders. 'Jesus.'

'I need to do this.'

He dropped a kiss on the tip of my nose. 'I don't think you do, sweetheart, but if you think you do, then that's what matters.'

I loved his belief in me. It was beautiful. 'You really want to come with me?'

'That's a stupid question, Avery. And, yes, there is such a thing as a stupid question. That was one of them. Of course I'm going to be there with you.'

My lips spread in a smile. 'I love you.'

'I know.'

'Cocky.'

'Confident,' he replied, lowering his head to mine. He kissed me softly, but my body stirred to life. 'I love you, sweetheart.'

355

I started to wrap my arms around him, but he rocked off me and grabbed my hand. 'Hey! Get back here.'

'Nope. We got stuff to do.' He hauled me off the bed. 'And if you start feeling me up, we aren't going to get anything done.'

'What are we doing?'

Dipping down suddenly, he picked me up, put me over one shoulder, and spun toward the door. 'We've got some tickets to book.'

It seemed absolutely insane that we were in Texas two days later, but here we were, checking into a hotel not too far from my parents' house. Not wanting to delay what I needed to do today, as soon as we dropped off our luggage, we hit the road. I didn't tell my parents I was coming to Texas, so I had no idea if they'd actually be home.

Cam let out a low whistle as he followed the winding road around the bend and my parents' estate came into view. 'Good Lord, that's a home.'

'It's really not,' I said as my gaze crawled over the manicured, bare lawn and then the massive brick structure. 'Your parents have a *home*. This is just a really big shell.'

He parked the rental in the center of the circular driveway, near the marble fountain that bubbled with water. Eyeing it, he smiled slightly. 'I don't think I've actually seen a house with a fountain in front of it in real life.'

I took a deep breath, nervous but determined. 'I can do this.'

'You can.' He squeezed my knee gently. 'You sure you don't want me to come inside?'

'Yes.' I looked at him, smiling. Of course I wanted him in there with me. 'I need to do this by myself.'

He settled back in the seat. 'If you change your mind, text me and I'll be right there.'

I leaned over, kissing him softly. 'You're amazing.'

His lips curved against mine. 'So are you.'

Kissing him once more, I then opened the door and climbed out. If I stayed a moment longer, I would change my mind. As I shut the door, Cam stopped me.

'Just remember that whatever they say doesn't change the fact that you're a beautifully strong woman and nothing that happened was your fault.'

Tears filled my eyes, and a steely resolve fortified my spine. 'Thank you.'

Cam winked. 'Now go do good things.'

Giving him a watery smile, I turned and headed up the wide stairs and across the porch. A fan in the ceiling stirred hot air and lifted a few strands of my hair. I raised my hand to knock and then shook my head. I reached into my pocket and pulled out the key. I didn't need to knock.

The lock gave and with one more glance back at where Cam waited, I stepped inside my parents' house.

Nothing had changed. That was my first impression as I quietly shut the door behind me. Everything was clean and shiny. There was no smell or sounds. Nothing welcoming about the cold foyer.

I walked under the golden chandelier and entered the formal sitting room. 'Dad? Mom?'

Silence.

I sighed as I passed white furniture my mom would have a shit fit over if anyone dared to sit in. I checked the dining room and then the living room. Finally, after checking out the study and then the kitchen, I headed upstairs.

The steps made no sound.

On the second floor, I headed toward the end of the hall, to the last door, and pushed it open.

It was my bedroom—key word being *was*.

'Holy shit,' I whispered, slowly walking into the room.

All my stuff was gone—my books, my desk, the posters, and the other little odds and ends I'd left behind. Not that it really mattered, but jeez, nothing about this room would make anyone think I used to live in it.

'We packed your stuff up.'

I jumped and spun around. She stood in the doorway to what used to be my bedroom, dressed in beige linen slacks and a tucked-in white blouse. Her strawberry-blond hair was coifed, her face void of any line or physical imperfection.

'Mom.'

A delicate eyebrow arched. 'Your stuff is in the attic if that is what you're here for. We had the help move it up there after I spoke with you in the fall.'

'You forgot my birthday,' I blurted out.

She tilted her head to the side in a smooth, elegant movement. 'We did?'

I stared at her a moment and all I could think was, *What a bitch*. Anger rose, but I pushed it down. Anger got you nowhere with Mrs. Morgansten. You had to beat her at her own game—stay calm, stay collected. 'I'm not here for my stuff.'

'Are you here to move back in?' she asked, and she didn't sound hopeful. She sounded like nothing. I wondered if she'd gotten plastic surgery for her voice. It was as expressive as her face.

'No.' I almost snorted. 'I'm here to talk to you and Dad. Is he home?'

She didn't answer immediately. 'He's out on the veranda.'

Most folks would call that a covered porch, but not Mom. 'Well, let's go.'

Not waiting for an answer, I brushed past her and headed downstairs. She trailed slightly behind and I could feel her eyes boring into the back of me. I started counting. I made it to five and the bottom step before she opened her mouth.

'Have you gotten a haircut recently?'

'No.'

There was a slight huff. 'I can tell.'

I sighed. 'Then why did you ask?'

Mom didn't respond until we reached the den that led out to the porch. 'What are you wearing, by the way?'

'Thrift store shit,' I replied, even though that wasn't true.

She tsked softly. 'Very nice, Avery.'

I rolled my eyes as I pushed open the back door, half tempted to race back through the house and start rolling around on all the white furniture. Dad was sitting on one of the chaise longues, reading a newspaper. Before I could open my mouth, Mom did.

'Look who decided to pay us a visit.'

Dad lowered the newspaper as he looked up. Surprise flickered across his face. 'Avery.'

'Hey, Dad.'

Sitting up, he folded the newspaper and placed it aside. 'We weren't expecting you.'

No 'how have you been' or 'happy to see you.' I sat in one of the wicker chairs. 'I know. I'm not going to be here for long.'

'She wants to talk to us.' Mom remained standing. 'I cannot fathom what it could be about, but there is a rental in the driveway and there's a boy in the car.'

I ignored that comment. 'This has nothing to do with the rental or who is in the car.'

'I'd surely hope you didn't come all this way to talk about that,' she replied.

I took a long, deep breath. 'I spoke to David.' My father stiffened, and Mom was surprisingly quiet. Good signs. 'He told me about Molly Simmons and Blaine Fitzgerald and what happened last summer—what will happen this summer.'

'Avery …'

'No,' I said, cutting Mom off before she could say anything else that would surely piss me off. 'I haven't broken the agreement. I've kept my mouth shut all these years. I've done exactly what you two told me I should do.'

Mom drew herself up. 'David had no right to call you—'

'Why not?' I demanded. 'Is it against the law to let me know that Blaine raped another girl, just like he raped me?'

Dad sucked in a shrill breath, but Mom, she got whiter, if that was possible. 'There is no reason to put that out there so crudely,' she said, crossing her arms. 'We know what you said—'

'What I told you that night at the hospital is the same thing I told the police. Blaine raped me. It was you two who decided I should drop the charges, which made everyone think that I had lied.'

'Avery,' my father began.

I didn't let him get any further. 'The reason why I even came here is because I need to let go of what happened to me, and the only way I can do that is by telling you two what I should've said then.' I took a breath, one I didn't need. 'You two were wrong. You were so unbelievably wrong in what you decided.'

Mom stepped forward. 'Excuse me?'

'You heard me.' I stood, my hands balling into fists. 'You should've told his parents to go fuck themselves. You should've told them to get the hell out of your house. You should've gone to the police and told them what his parents were trying to do, which was to bribe *your daughter* into silence. And for what? So you wouldn't have to go to court? So that no one would ask questions? And you all could still go to the *club* and things wouldn't be awkward? Meanwhile, I was labeled a lying whore by everyone? And Blaine was free to do it again to another person? How culpable are we? You should've stood beside me and believed me! You

360

should've gotten me help. I'm your daughter. You should've been thinking about me.'

Dad looked away, and I could understand why. Maybe he'd always suspected the truth. I would be ashamed, too.

'Things haven't turned out that bad for you, Avery.' Mom let out a noisy breath. 'After all, look at what you've been able to do with that money. Go to college. Furnish your own apartment.' Her lip curled. 'You make it sound like we did nothing for you.'

'Nancy,' my father said, lifting his head.

'What?' She raised her chin. 'Never once did she think this was hard on us.'

I stared at my mom, but I wasn't surprised. Part of me wished I were. I wasn't that hurt by her words. 'You know, that's the problem, Mom. You've only ever been concerned about how everything is so difficult for you.' I shook my head as I glanced at my dad. 'I'm doing better. In case you guys actually care. I'm doing well at school. I have friends and I've met a wonderful man who knows what happened to me. So those are the things that haven't turned out bad. I hope one day I can say the same thing about us.'

My father pressed his lips to the back of his fingers, still staring out into the garden. I took one more look at him and turned to my mom. She met my stare with a steady one, but fine lines had started to show at the corners of her lips. No matter how unaffected she looked, I knew I had nettled her.

'I didn't come here to make you two feel bad,' I said, swallowing. 'That isn't what this is about. I needed to say something, finally. And I need you guys to know that I forgive you, but don't ever expect that you can tell me what to do with my life ever again.'

My mom held my gaze a moment longer and then looked away, her jawline tight. I gave them both a few seconds to say something, but silence crept between us. So be it.

I walked toward the door, my back straight and my head high. It wasn't forced. It was real. Another weight lifted off my chest, leaving only one thing left to do. But that was tomorrow, and today—today was a good day.

Smiling slightly, I walked through the formal sitting room. On my way out, I grabbed a throw pillow that probably cost a month of rent and tossed it onto the floor. Childish? Yes. Did it make me feel good? Oh yeah.

As I stepped out onto the porch, I saw that Cam was outside of the car, his baseball cap pulled low as he inspected the water fountain. My smile widened as I saw him run his hand through the water.

He turned, and when he spotted me, he jogged around the car and met me halfway. 'How'd it go?'

'Ah …' I stretched up, tilting my head to the side so that I could move in under his cap. I kissed him. 'It went as expected.'

His hands immediately landed on my hips, a sure sign that the quick kiss had affected him, even standing in front of my parents' house. 'Want to tell me about it?'

'Over dinner?' I stepped back, and he caught my hand. 'I'm going to take you to Chuy's—'

'Avery?'

Cam stiffened, his grip on my hand tightening as I turned toward the sound of my dad's voice. He was halfway across the porch, coming straight for us.

'If he says something ignorant, I cannot promise I will not lay him out right here, right now,' Cam warned in a low voice.

I squeezed his hand. 'Hopefully that won't become an issue.'

362

'Just saying,' he muttered.

We waited for my dad to reach us. He took in Cam and where our hands were joined.

'This is Cameron Hamilton,' I introduced, because it seemed rude not to. 'Cam, this is my father.'

Cam extended his free hand, but his jaw was tight and his eyes were an icy blue. 'Hi.'

My father shook his hand. 'Nice to meet you.'

Cam said nothing.

'What's up, Dad?' I asked.

His eyes met mine for a second and then flickered away. Up close like this, in the harsh light of the Texas sun, I saw how much my father had aged. In that moment, I realized that what had happened had taken its toll on him. He, unlike my mom, hadn't covered it up through numerous procedures and makeup.

My dad took a deep breath and then said, 'You know what I've missed most of all? I miss watching you dance.'

Chapter 32

Over dinner, I filled Cam in on the conversation I had with my parents. I thought he might launch his steak knife into a wall when I told him about my mom's attitude.

'Really,' I said, 'I'm not surprised. She's always been … cold, and it's just gotten worse over the years.'

Cam's jaw flexed. 'You're nicer than I am.'

I shrugged. He wouldn't think that if he was party to my internal dialogue. 'I'm glad I talked to them. And Dad? The whole dance thing was his way of showing some level of regret. At least he got what I was saying, you know?'

He nodded. 'So how do you feel about it?'

Good question. I sat back. 'I don't really feel anything. I mean, like I said, I'm glad I did it, but I don't know. It's like having to go to the dentist. You don't want to, but you know you have to, and afterward, you're just glad you did it.'

Reaching over the table, he spread his hand over mine. 'You still want to see Molly tomorrow?'

'Yes.' I'd gone through my e-mail after we'd booked our tickets and found one from her. Wasn't hard. There had been many. I sent her a quick note explaining that I'd be in town and I wanted to see her. I'd been partly surprised when she responded within the hour saying yes. 'I still want to see her.'

Cam looked away, jaw tight. He wasn't big on the idea, but he was supporting me nonetheless. This was one of the moments that I realized how lucky I was to have run into him in the hallway outside of astronomy. I needed to realize that more often.

And I needed him, like, *needed* him.

I didn't want to talk about my parents or my impending visit with Molly any longer. I wanted to show Cam how much I did love him. Not because it was what I thought was expected of me, but because it was what I wanted.

'Ready to head back?' I asked, my heart rate picking up speed.

We paid the check and traveled the short distance back to the hotel. It was still early and being so close to Houston, there was a lot to show Cam, but I was feeling stingy with my time with him. I didn't want to share.

Cam sat on the edge of the bed, his baseball cap tilted backward as he thumbed through the buttons on the remote. Curtains were drawn on the large window across the room, and only a bit of fading sunlight slipped in.

'I'm going to take a quick shower.' I gathered up my toiletries and started backing toward the bathroom.

He slid me a long look, opened his mouth, and then nodded. A certain light had filled his eyes, making me shiver with awareness. I smiled and then darted into the bathroom. Closing the door behind me, I dumped my bag on the sink counter. I hadn't brought any clothes in with me and I wondered if Cam had noticed that.

And if he had, what was he thinking?

Was it the same thing I was?

I took a quick shower, getting the inevitable airplane funk off me. I took the time to clear my thoughts of the conversation with my parents. It didn't take much. My pulse was already thrumming, and my entire being was focused on him.

Stepping out of the shower, I wrapped a thick towel around my chest and combed the tangles out of my hair. My stomach kept dipping like I was on a roller coaster. I brushed my teeth and then there was nothing left for me to procrastinate with.

Opening the door, I found Cam where I left him, except he was lying on his back, his legs dangling over the edge of the bed. The cap rested beside him, and the remote lay on his flat stomach.

I stopped at the door.

Cam turned his head and immediately sat up. Locks of dark hair tumbled over his forehead, brushing his brows. Beneath the thick lashes, his eyes were a vibrant shade of blue.

Skin tingling with a thousand tiny pinpricks, I walked over to where he sat. He angled his head back, his throat working as I stopped in front of him, my fingers curled around where the towel was knotted.

His lashes swept down and his lips parted. 'Avery.'

Placing one hand on his shoulder, I climbed up onto the bed, my knees on either side of his thighs. His hands landed on my towel-covered hips. 'Cam?'

His lips slanted up on the side, and the dimple began to appear in his left cheek. 'What are you up to?'

'Nothing,' I said, recognizing the breathlessness in my voice. 'Everything.'

'Those are two opposite things.'

'I know.' I lowered myself down onto his lap, shuddering when I felt his arousal through his jeans, pressing against my heat. 'Kiss me?'

I didn't wait for his answer. I bent my head down and brushed my lips over his once, twice, and then again, slipping the tip of my tongue over his lower lip and then inside. His grip on my hips tightened, but I was totally in control as I coaxed his mouth open, deepening the kiss. His lips moved against mine, following my lead. I was sure I would melt into him, into the bed.

'Touch me.' My lips brushed his. 'Please.'

Cam obliged.

He slipped his hands under the hem of the towel. Both were on my thighs, sliding up and down slowly. Each pass brought his fingers closer to where I wanted him desperately. One stopped along the back of my thigh while the other came tantalizing close to my core.

'Now,' I said, lifting my head.

Cam chuckled as his fingers inched back up. His knuckles brushed my dampness and then retreated. A groan of frustration escaped me. 'What do you want?' he asked, those lashes hiding his eyes.

'I want you to touch me.'

Another close call as his knuckles brushed me once more and then his hand slid back down my leg. 'I am touching you, sweetheart.'

'You know what I mean.'

'I don't.'

'Please.' I dropped my head to his. 'Please touch me, Cam.'

Cam tipped his head back again. Our noses brushed and then our lips. 'Well, when you say it like that, I think I get what you mean.'

'Finally,' I groaned.

He laughed again and then nipped at my chin as his hand drifted up the inside of my thigh. I jerked as he cupped me fully. 'Like this?'

'Yes.'

His lips pressed down on the center of my throat as his finger slipped inside. 'And this?'

My eyes closed as my back arched. 'Uh-huh.'

Cam shifted his hand and his thumb pressed down on the nub of nerves. I gasped as he worked another finger inside me and his body tensed beneath mine. 'What about this?'

I angled my hips forward, moaning as my body heated. 'Oh, yeah. Definitely that.'

'Definitely that,' he murmured, his fingers pumping.

Another moan escaped me, but I wanted more. I wanted to feel him inside me, needed him to be. A wild desire born from lust and something far, far stronger. Opening my eyes, I locked mine with his. Slowly, I untied the knot on my towel and let it slip down my back, falling onto the floor.

Cam's hand stilled and his breathing quickened. He reached up with his free hand, cupping my breast. 'Fuck, Avery …'

I placed my hand over his, my heart pounding. 'Don't stop.'

His thumb moved over my hardened nipple and he growled, 'I wasn't planning on it.'

'Not what I meant,' I whispered. Reaching down with my other hand, I found the zipper on his jeans. 'I want you, Cam.'

'You have me,' he groaned. 'You so fucking have me.'

A delighted smile appeared as I wrapped my fingers around his wrist. With a level of control I didn't realize I had, I pulled his hand out from between my thighs. 'I really want you.' I flicked open the button on his jeans and pulled his zipper down. My fingers skimmed his hardness and he shuddered. 'Don't you want me?'

'More than you know,' he said, lashes lowering as I palmed the length of him. He groaned. 'Avery …'

I let go of him, long enough to tug his shirt off and toss it aside. He was all golden skin and sleek muscles. 'I want this, Cam.'

He grabbed my hips, his chest rising sharply. 'Are you sure, Avery? Because if you're not, we don't have—'

Silencing him with a kiss, I slid my hands over his chest. 'I'm sure.'

His hands flexed on my hips and then in one powerful movement, he had me on my back and he was above me, his eyes bright and intense. He swooped down, claiming my lips in a feverish kiss with so much power and passion. Then he stood, pinning me with a molten stare as he shucked off his jeans. My gaze traveled over his chest, the tattoo, the magnificent abs, and then lower. Cam was huge and an awfully naive part of me wondered how this was going to work.

Cam's heated gaze drifted down my bare skin. My heart fluttered unsteadily; my stomach was full of anticipation. 'I could stare at you for a lifetime. It would never grow old.'

'Even when I'm old?'

'Even then.'

Then he lowered himself, trailing his lips over my legs and stomach. He reached my breasts, suckling and nipping until they felt heavy and swollen. Cam took his time, slowly moving over me, licking every inch of my skin like he sought to memorize my body or claim it. I didn't care. He could do it for eternity. Intense heat built in my stomach and spread lower, turning into a glorious ache. For the first time, I wasn't afraid or unsure of the awakening desire. I wanted to explore it. I wanted Cam to explore it.

My body arched against his, aching and tense as he drew out every breath, every moan and whimper. Desire, rife and powerful, spread through me. I had never felt this way before.

Cam brought his lips back to mine, supporting himself with his arm, continuing to delve into my mouth while he gently worked one finger into me and then two. Soon he

370

had me bucking under him. Then he lifted his head and there was something intoxicating in his gaze—wild. It mirrored what I felt inside me. He worked me to the edge and then slowly withdrew his fingers.

I whimpered, 'Cam.'

He chuckled as he slid down my body and then his mouth was on me, his tongue moving until my head thrashed and my hips rolled with abandonment. I felt all over the place, half crazed with need, and when he rolled his fingers over the bundle of nerves, I came, crying out his name.

Cam rose swiftly, his gaze fixed on mine as my body trembled. He nudged my thighs apart and there was a twinge of unease, of coldness and darkness, but I pushed it away. I was *ready*. His erection rested against me and then he slipped in, maybe an inch.

'I love you,' Cam said softly, one hand flat against my cheek. 'I love you so very much.'

I wrapped an arm around his. 'I love you.'

He kissed me deeply as he dropped a hand to my hip and then his hips thrust into mine. Sharp, stinging pain shot through me. Tears of surprise pricked my eyes, and I froze at the incredible pressure of fullness.

'Are you okay?' he breathed, stilling.

I nodded and then said, 'Yes.'

Cam's eyes searched mine as his arm shook around mine. He remained still, buried deep inside me as he lowered his mouth to mine. He kissed me slowly, tenderly, and so deeply that I felt a different kind of tears rise to my eyes. My chest swelled with love and then, finally, the dull ache faded and the pressure inside me started to feel good. I tentatively raised my hips.

He groaned. 'Av ...'

I did it again, rocking against him. He cradled my hips, thrusting forward, wringing a cry of pleasure from me. I gripped his shoulders as I wrapped my legs around his waist, bringing him deeper. He moved over me, in me, the intensity increasing until it became a feverish pace. My head spun with the bliss building inside me. He moved faster and his touch was everywhere, his mouth on my breasts, piercing me. Hips grinding, Cam slipped a hand between us and it was too much. I threw my head back, shuddering around him. The moment was incredible. The spasms rocked my body in tight, sensual waves.

'Avery,' he grunted my name, burying his head in my shoulder. Two quick thrusts and he came as the last of the tremors rippled through me.

Our hearts pounded together, our skin slick with moisture. Minutes went by, maybe hours. I don't know. When he pulled out slowly, carefully, he kissed me in a way I don't think he ever had before.

'That was … there are no words.' He shook his head, eyes brilliant. 'You okay?'

'Perfect,' I told him, spreading my hands over the sides of his face. 'You were perfect.'

Cam dipped his mouth to mine. 'Only because I was with you.'

Chapter 33

Stepping into the shower the following morning, I felt the hot water pelt deliciously sore muscles. I turned into the spray, letting it wash over my upturned face. Last night … all night … A big smile pulled at my lips. It had been amazing. Not just the sex—and the sex had been awesomely wonderful—but everything that had come afterward. We were closer than we were before, and it hadn't been the act of sex bringing us together.

It had been the act of complete trust in each other.

Hearing the soft slide of the shower door, I opened my eyes and turned as Cam stepped in behind me. Completely naked. My gaze dipped. And hard.

My cheeks flushed as I folded shy arms across my breasts. Yeah, we were closer, but that didn't mean standing in the bright light of the bathroom buck-ass naked wasn't intimidating.

'You're beautiful.' Cam smirked a little as he eased my arms away. 'And you want to hide yourself?'

'Not all of us are blessed with your confidence.'

'Uh-huh.' He ran his thumb over my pebbled nipple and then he kissed the corner of my lip as his hands slid up my arms. Water coursed down my back. 'I got lonely out there. Thought I'd join you.'

'You were lonely?' I stepped closer to him.

'Yes.' Cam let his arms fall to my waist. He closed the rest of the distance between us. Our slick skin pressed together and parts of my body got all happy about that. 'I ordered breakfast. We have about twenty minutes.'

'Twenty minutes to get fresh and clean?'

'We only need a couple of minutes for that.'

'And what about the rest of those minutes?'

Cam didn't tell me how he wanted to spend those moments. He showed me … in great detail. Kissing me once before latching his mouth on to my breast. A ball of lava formed in my belly as he turned me sideways, the water spraying down on us. Dazed, I fluttered my hand to the strands of his wet hair. They sifted through my fingers like silk. He slipped his hand between my thighs as he dragged his mouth to mine. He knew exactly how to touch me, how to bring me to the brink of losing control.

'Hold on,' he ordered.

I wrapped my arms around his neck, letting out a short breath as he lifted me up, pressing my back against the wet tile as he settled between my legs. He brought us together with a slow, torturous thrust. My moans filled the bathroom as his hips pumped. My heart was thundering, a flutter deep in my chest and stomach.

Somehow we ended up out of the shower, my back against the cool floor and Cam over me, his body rocking with mine, my thighs squeezing him as the shower still ran. One hand was on my breast, the other buried deep in my soaked hair. His mouth was hot and demanding, consuming.

'Cam!' I cried out, my back arching as my release powered through me, explosive and crashing. His arms went around me as he lifted me up, seating me in his lap. My knees

374

skidded over the now wet floor. Lightning zinged through my veins. His body shook as he held me to him tightly, thrusting once more, grinding my hips against his as he came.

For a while, the only sound was our ragged breathing. We were limp in each other's arms, my head on his shoulders, my hand resting above where his heart was pounding.

'You—'

'I'm okay,' I cut him off, giggling. 'I'm not going to break.'

'I don't know.' He brushed my hair back from my face. 'You—' A knock on our hotel door cut him off. 'Shit. The food's here.'

I wiggled off his lap and he climbed to his feet, slipping in the puddles we'd left on the floor and almost wiping out. He made it to the door in one piece. 'Cam!'

'What?' He looked over his shoulder.

Throwing him a towel, I giggled. 'You're about to answer the door with your junk hanging out.'

'Good call.' He wrapped the towel around his hips as he cast me a wicked grin. 'Although the masses would love to see my junk.'

I laughed as I dipped back under the lukewarm spray. His junk was rather impressive.

Molly's house was in a decent part of town. Middle income, neat and clean. We stopped in front of a one-story ranch and I scanned the numbers on my phone to make sure we had the right house.

'This is it.'

Cam parked the car along the curb, a slight frown on his face. 'Are you sure you need to do this?'

'Yes. I owe it to her.'

He turned the car off. 'You don't owe her anything.'

I looked at him. 'I do. It's not that I blame myself for what happened to her, but if I don't talk to her, she's never going to understand why I didn't say anything. And I need her to.' Because I really would like to go one week without getting a nasty message from her.

Drawing in a shallow breath, he pulled his hands off the steering wheel. 'And of course you want me to stay out here?'

I nodded.

He sighed. 'I don't like this.'

Leaning over, I kissed his cheek. 'But you like me.'

'I love you.' He turned his head toward me. Sliding his hand around the back of my neck, he brought his mouth to mine. 'Doesn't mean I'm happy about sitting out here while you go into some random, possibly psycho chick's house.'

'She's not psycho.'

'Says you.'

'Says me.'

His lips curved up on one side. 'If you're not out in five minutes, I'm coming in, guns blazing.'

'You don't have a gun.'

'She doesn't know that.'

I laughed softly. 'I'll need more than five minutes.'

'Six.'

'More,' I replied.

'You don't need this, sweetheart.' When I said nothing, he groaned. 'Seven.'

'You're being ridiculous. I'll be okay.'

Cam sighed again. 'Okay. Please be careful.'

'I will.'

Before I could slide out from his grasp, he tightened his grip and captured my mouth. The kiss started off softly, turning deeper and hotter as his tongue slipped inside,

376

moving in ways that reminded me of what he'd done last night and this morning. I moaned into the kiss, and when he pulled away, I was panting.

A wicked glint filled his blue eyes. 'The faster you are out of there, the faster you get more of that.'

'That is so wrong.' I slipped away, but I was grinning.

'I love you.'

I would never get tired of hearing that. 'I love you too.'

Pulling myself from that car was almost impossible, but I did it. My sandals smacked off the cracked pavement as I hurried to the front door. I'd been out in the late-morning sun for only a few seconds and sweat already dotted my brow.

I raised my hand to knock, but the interior door flew open, revealing a short, skinny girl with black hair and large gray eyes—wary eyes. They shifted to me and then over my shoulder. She was a pretty girl, one who looked bone-tired and weary.

'Who's that?' she demanded.

I recognized her voice immediately. 'That's Cam. My boyfriend.'

Her face puckered as if she tasted something sour. 'He can't come in here.'

'I know.' I was quick to reassure her. 'That's why he's staying in the car.'

Molly's expression slipped into a scowl, but she stepped aside. Opening the screen door, I followed her inside the dark living room.

'Is this your parents' house?' My eyes scanned the many pictures lining the walls and the well-worn furniture.

'Yes.' She stalked into the living room and picked up a remote. Turning the TV off, she tossed the remote onto the couch beside her. 'They're at work.'

'It's nice.'

She smirked. 'Says the girl who's from Red Hill.'

The jab at the stretch of road my parents lived on wasn't missed. I sat in a chair, crossing my ankles. 'Okay. I'm glad you wanted to see me.'

Molly didn't sit, but she stood only a few feet from me. 'Are you really?'

'Yes.'

She laughed harshly. 'I somehow doubt that considering our last conversation and the fact you've spent a good nine months or so ignoring me.'

Okay. This was not going to be easy. 'I'm not a big fan of reading e-mails from people I don't know after being in high school and getting bombarded with hate mail. And there's the *fact* that you sent me a ton of not-too-pleasant messages.'

Crossing her arms, she lifted her chin. 'You know why I sent you those messages.'

'Because I didn't respond in the beginning and because you blame me.' When she didn't say anything, I leaned forward. 'I wasn't lying when I said I knew nothing about you until I spoke to my cousin in January of this year. I didn't check the first e-mails. That's the truth.'

She pressed her lips together. 'So you're still sticking with the "not a lying whore" story?'

I exhaled through my nose as I stared up at her. Anger pricked at my skin, but like with my mother the day before, I kept my cool. 'Like I told you on the phone, I hadn't lied to the police.'

'Then why did you drop the charges?' she demanded.

'It's a long story.'

She spread her arms out. 'Obviously I have time. Tell me.'

Her demanding tone was making it a struggle not to be bitchy back. Keeping my voice level, I told Molly everything about that Halloween night and the days afterward. For the most part, her expression remained unyielding and

378

as unforgiving as a seasoned cop's. The only crack in the exterior was when I told her what Blaine had done. I didn't have to ask her to know that it was the same. When I was finished, she turned away, shoulders bowed but spine straight.

'I'm not allowed to tell anyone this, but I needed to tell you.'

'Did you tell your boyfriend?'

'Yes.'

She kept her back to me, silent.

'I wish my parents wouldn't have agreed, and I wish I hadn't either. I wish I was as strong as you are and that I—'

'You don't know anything about me.' She spun around, eyes a flinty gray.

I held up my hands. 'But I do know you are strong—stronger than me. You did the right thing, and I know it couldn't have been easy.'

'It wasn't easy.'

'I know.' I think this chick just wanted to be argumentative.

Her sharp chin jutted out. 'Nothing about this was easy. Talking to the police—the detectives and then the lawyers. Having to keep going over every fucking thing he did to me? In detail? Wasn't easy. And I wouldn't have had to go through any of that if you had stuck with the truth!'

'I'm sorry—'

She moved so fast and I was so unprepared for it that I just sat there.

Molly smacked me, snapping my head to the side. Tears of pain and surprise pricked my eyes.

She had smacked me right across the face.

I almost couldn't believe it. The entire side of my face burned red-hot, stinging. Damn. For someone so skinny she could deliver one hell of a good bitch slap.

Fury stamped down the shock, and my hands itched to repay the favor. But I got Molly's anger. Her pain was still so fresh, and it was cutting too deep. I'd been in her shoes, was still there every so often. The anger never really left. Maybe it never would. So I got why she was so furious.

That was one of the reasons why I wasn't currently introducing my fist to her face.

'You deserved that,' she said, voice shaking.

My cheek stung as I stood. 'Maybe I did. But I didn't deserve what Blaine did to me, and I don't deserve all the shit you're giving me for something I decided when I was fourteen and had very little choice in.'

'Your parents didn't put a gun to your head and make you sign those papers, did they?'

I shook my head. 'What would you have done if you were fourteen and your parents demanded that you do that?'

Her mouth opened.

'Don't even answer that, because it doesn't matter. I am sorry—but if you hit me again, I will hit back. I'm sorry that this happened to you. And I'm sorry that you have to go through a trial and all of that. And *trust me,* the biggest thing that I'm sorry about is signing those fucking papers and agreeing. But I can't change that. All I can do is let it go.'

'Well, you have fun letting it go then.'

Standing here, staring at the girl with whom I shared a terrible commonality, I felt … empty. There were no harking angels or golden light of revelation. I felt the same way I did walking out of my parents' house. Nothing. In a sudden insight, I knew Cam was right. I didn't need to do this to move on. I hadn't really even needed to confront my parents. Although that had felt terrific.

I had begun to move on the moment I had told Cam the truth.

It just hadn't happened overnight. Letting go had been a slow process that took a bitch slap in the face to figure out.

I didn't need to be here.

I needed to be out there, with Cam, and back home, in West Virginia, with my friends. I needed to continue letting it all go.

I started for the door.

'Where are you going?' Her bony fingers dug into my arm, stopping me. 'Avery?'

Removing her hand from my arm, I kept my voice even. 'I'm leaving, Molly. I'm going back out there to a man who loves me no matter what happened in my past or what stupid decisions I've made. I'm going home, which isn't the house on Red Hill, and I'm going to go see my friends. That's where I'm going.'

Molly's throat worked, but she said nothing as I walked to the door. I stopped and turned back to her. 'Look, if you want to call me to just talk or something, you obviously have my number. Call anytime you want, but I've learned from my mistakes. If you send me any more messages that piss me off even the tiniest bit, I will call the police and I will press charges against you.'

She clamped her mouth shut and took a step back.

'I wish you the best. I seriously do. Good-bye, Molly.'

She didn't stop me as I left and didn't come outside like my father had. I slid into the cool interior of the car and let out a ragged breath.

'How'd that—why is your face so red?' Cam caught my chin and gently turned me toward him. 'Did she hit you?'

'Yeah.' I winced at his explosive curse. 'But I think it made her feel better after she got it all out of her system.'

His eyes narrowed. 'That does not make it fucking okay.'

'I know.' I wrapped my hand around his and pressed it to my sore cheek. 'But it's over. I've said what I need to, and I don't think I'll be hearing from her again.'

Cam opened his hand, gently palming my cheek. 'Avery …'

'You were right. I didn't really need to do this, but I'm glad I did. I'm okay with it.' Closing my eyes, I turned my head, pressing a kiss to his palm. 'Take me home, Cam. That's where I need to be.'

Chapter 34

The only problem with summer once you grew up was that it was over before it felt like it got started. Or that could have something to do with taking summer classes, which seemed to suck the life right out of summer.

Prying one eye open, I groaned. First I saw my bracelet— not the silver one. Cam had replaced it with several loops of rope that carried an infinity charm. Then I saw the time. Why had I set the clock for this early? I didn't have class until nine.

The bed shifted beside me.

And Cam didn't have class until ten. It was going to be a light semester for him as he was winding down on his college career.

A sleepy smile pulled at my lips as I rolled onto my stomach, stretching my legs out and pointing my toes. The sheets slipped over my bare skin and ended up somewhere at the foot of my bed. Either there was a perverted ghost in my bedroom or Cam was wide awake.

Lips pressed down between my shoulder blades as a hand flattened on the base of my spine. Fingers trailed up, causing a wave of little bumps to race across my skin.

'Good morning, sweetheart.' Cam's voice was thick with sleep.

Ah, this was why I set the alarm for so early, which was so different from a year ago. Then I had been worried about being late, annoyingly anal about it, in fact. Now I set the clock an hour early for a little bit of one-on-one time.

'Morning,' I mumbled, closing my eyes as he ran his hand up and down, stopping at the cleft of my cheeks and going straight to the nape of my neck.

He kissed the center of my back and then his lips were on the flare of my hip. Warm breath danced over my lower back and then he kissed my right cheek.

I giggled, wiggling.

'You know what they say about a guy who kisses a girl's ass? Literally?'

'He knows his place?'

'Ha. Ha.' He swept my hair off my neck and kissed me there. 'He's absolutely in love with the girl.'

'Is that so?'

'So,' he murmured, grasping my hip with one hand.

'Where did you learn that?'

'On the Internet.'

'Classy.'

'You know what else I've learned?' He lifted me up and slipped his arm under me. 'That women's breasts are at their perkiest in the morning.'

'What?' I laughed.

'Yep,' he replied, cupping my right breast. 'I have to check out that theory.' He squeezed gently, and my nipple tightened. He moved on to my other breast and did the same thing. 'I think what I've read is right. Your breasts are exceptionally perky this morning.'

Breaking into a fit of laughter, I smacked his hands away, but my laughter quickly died off when his hand returned with a lot more purpose. His fingers worked their magic on the tips, and it wasn't long before my hips were moving in restless circles against the sheet.

'I love how your mind works,' Cam said, shifting behind me.

I looked over my shoulder. 'Huh?'

He nodded at the clock. 'Setting it early. You, my dear, are brilliant.'

'I know.' I smiled, and then rested my cheek on my pillow. My heart was already racing, my body ready. I was ready. 'So you going to do something with the extra time or wow me with your knowledge of the seedier side of the Internet.'

'Bossy.' His lips brushed my shoulder, and his hands went back to my hips. 'And I would send you screaming to campus with my knowledge of the seedier side of the Internet.'

'Good to know.'

Cam lifted me again. 'Can we?'

He always hesitated and asked before we did it like this. Something about that always warmed me; the thoughtfulness of it all and the fact he was aware that there were still moments when I was awkward as all hell when it came to intimacy or when I just didn't want to be touched. Those moments were few and far between, but still existed, and he watched for them and adapted.

We both had adapted.

During the summer, I had started meeting with one of the campus counselors once a week, and I would continue until it was no longer needed. And maybe one day, I could help someone with my story and experiences.

'Yes,' I said, and for extra emphasis, just in case he was confused, I pushed my rump against him. Cam growled deep in his throat. My smile spread.

He settled between my legs and I drew my arms up to my shoulders, putting my weight onto them. Lifting up slightly, I turned my head and his lips immediately found mine. I loved the way he kissed me, like he was drinking in my very essence. One kiss from him and I was melting in his hands. That's how good they were.

Cam broke the kiss as he shifted his hips forward, slipping into me from behind. The pace was slow and unhurried and yet still so absolutely shattering with each stroke. I dropped my forehead to the pillow, my breathing ragged as I rocked back against him. His hands landed on mine, threading through my fingers as his pace picked up.

'I love you.' His voice was a beautiful, hoarse whisper in my ear that sent me over the edge. Release took us both, seconds apart.

It was my whisper in his ear that took us both when we finally made it to the shower.

I ended up four minutes late for class, but I walked in anyway, shot the professor a sheepish grin, and took my seat.

The weather was pleasant and not sweltering hot, so our little group took our lunch outside, sitting under the shade of one of the thick oaks near the library.

Jacob tipped his bowler hat up, the one from last year's Halloween party, as he frowned at the dozen or so Styrofoam cups in front of him. He was building a pyramid. I didn't ask.

I popped my straw through my cup as I kicked off my flip-flops. Brit reached for my toes, and I shot her an evil look. 'You touch my feet, you die.'

'She's serious.' Cam nudged me. 'I touched her pinky toe once and almost lost a finger.'

'That's not the only thing you almost lost.'

'Oh, that sounds serious.' Brit glanced at her tub of mayo and then her fries. She sighed. 'I miss Ollie. I loved grossing him out with my fries.'

'Well, you have all of us to gross out.' Jacob's lip curled. 'Which you are doing right now.'

'It's not the same.' She pouted. 'Ollie was hot.'

'Excuse me?' Jacob almost knocked over his pyramid of awesome. 'I'm hot.'

Cam frowned. 'So am I.'

I elbowed him in the stomach.

'Well, since I must explain the obvious.' Brit plopped her fry in the mayo with flourish. 'Jacob, you don't like girls. Cam, you're hopelessly devoted to Avery, and that left Ollie.'

I grinned.

Jacob looked up, his lips slipping into a small grin. 'Well, there is one more.'

Twisting at the waist, I followed his gaze. Jase was across the road, heading for us.

Brit sighed. 'Yeah, I couldn't handle him.'

'Why not?' I asked, eyeing Cam's friend.

She made a noncommittal sound. 'He's not the relationship kind, or so I hear.'

'And do you want a relationship?' I asked her.

'No.' She laughed, dabbing her fry. 'But I have a feeling with someone like him, you get one taste and you will always want more.'

'Sort of like crack?' Jacob suggested.

'Or Cheetos,' Brit supplied.

Cam made a face as he swiped some of my fries. I sent him a death glare that I ruined when I kissed his cheek.

Jase dropped down beside us, stretching out his long legs. He looked a little off, his near-perfect features pale. 'Okay. Am I hallucinating or did I just see your sister walking into Knutti?'

'You're not hallucinating,' Cam replied. 'You saw her. She enrolled here late.'

'Oh.' Jase's eyes narrowed as he stared off into the distance. 'That's ... that's good.'

I caught Cam's eyes and he shrugged. With his gaze still focused on something no one else saw, Jase reached over Cam and hijacked a handful of my fries.

'What the hell?' I exclaimed.

Cam laughed. 'Your fries are not safe.'

'Obviously,' I muttered, eyeing them both.

Jase winked at me, and he was as ridiculously attractive as Cam doing it. 'You all coming to the luau this weekend?'

I nodded, and it struck me again how much difference a year made. This time last year, I wouldn't have even considered a party, especially one being thrown by a frat. I smiled to myself as I finished off the rest of my fries before the boys devoured them.

'Are you guys really having a pig?' Brit asked. 'Because last year, that wasn't a pig. It was a wild turkey and that was gross.'

Jase laughed. 'We'll have a pig this time.'

Beside me, the side pocket of my messenger bag vibrated. Curious as to who it could be, because everyone who contacted me was sitting here, I flipped open the pocket and pulled out my phone.

It was a text—a text from a normal telephone number. A Texas area code.

It's Molly. Can we talk when u have the time? Please.

A little tremor went down my arm as I stared at the message. Molly hadn't contacted me since I left Texas. Nothing from her, and the texts before that were never this friendly, even though this didn't scream best friends forevah.

I immediately texted back. *Yes. Call you this evening.*

Several minutes passed as I stared at the phone. Molly had texted back with an okay, and I was still stunned.

'Everything okay?' Cam asked, placing his hand on my lower back. Concern pinched his brows.

'Yes.' I dropped my cell back into my bag. Everything was okay. Maybe not perfect, but life wasn't meant to be perfect. It was messy and sometimes it was a disaster, but there was beauty in the messiness and there could be peace in the disaster.

I don't know where I'd be or what I'd be like if I hadn't decided to uproot my life and break free from my past. I knew it wouldn't be like this. And I also knew if I hadn't met Cam, I wouldn't be sitting here right now. Maybe I would've come around eventually on my own, but I was woman enough to admit that I had help.

And I was woman enough that whenever I looked up at the night skies and saw the Corona Borealis—or something that vaguely resembled it—I thanked it.

Leaning back against Cam's chest, I tipped my head back as I reached up, cupping his cheek. I drew his mouth to mine and kissed him softly. 'Thank you.'

His lips curved up on one side. 'For what?'

'For waiting for me.'

READY FOR MORE?

Turn the page for a sneak peek at the next fabulous story
from J Lynn

BE WITH ME

Coming February 2014

And don't miss TRUST IN ME - an ebook-only novella
in Cam's own words...

Out October 2013

Chapter 1

Sweet tea was apparently going to be the death of me. Not because it contained enough sugar that it could send you into a diabetic coma after one slurp. Or because my brother had nearly caused a triple-car-pileup by winging the truck around in a sharp U-turn after receiving a text message that contained only two words.

Sweet. Tea.

Nope. The request for sweet tea was bringing me face-to-face with Jase Winstead; the physical embodiment of every girly-girl fantasy and then some, outside of campus, and in front of my brother.

Oh sweet Mary mother of all the babies in the world, this was going to be awkward.

Why, oh why did my brother have to text Jase and mention that we were at this end of town and ask if he needed anything? He was supposed to be taking me around so I could get familiar with the scenery. Although the scenery I was about to witness was sure to be better than what I'd been seeing of the county.

If I saw another strip club, I was going to hurt someone.

Cam glanced over at me as he sped down the back

393

road. We'd left Route 9 years ago. His gaze dropped from my face to the tea I clutched in my hands. He raised a brow. 'You know, Teresa, you could put that in a cup holder.'

I shook my head. 'It's okay. I'll hold it.'

'Okay.' Cam drew the word out, focusing on the road.

I was acting like a spaz, but I needed to play it cool. The last thing anyone in this world needed was Cam finding out why I had a reason to act like a dweeb on crack. 'So, um, I thought Jase lived up by the college?'

That sounded casual, right? Oh God, I was pretty sure my voice had cracked at some point during that not-so innocent question.

'He does, but he spends most of his time at his father's farm. He's got a little brother.' Cam slowed his truck down and hung a sharp right. Tea almost went out the window, but I had a death grip on it. Tea was going nowhere. 'You remember?'

Of course I did. I obsessively remembered everything I'd ever learned about Jase in a way I imagined Justin Bieber fans did about him. Embarrassing as that sounded, it was true. Jase, unbeknownst to him and the entire world, had come to mean a lot of things to me in the last three years.

A friend.

My brother's saving grace.

A harmless crush on my end.

But then a year ago, right at the start of my senior year in high school, when Jase had tagged along with Cam and visited home, he'd become something very complicated. Something that a part of me wanted nothing more than to forget about—but the other part of me, that side refused to let go of the memories of his lips against mine or how his hands had felt skimming over my body or the way he

394

had groaned my name like it had caused him exquisite pain.

Oh goodness …

My cheeks heated behind my sunglasses at the vivid memory and I turned my face to the window, half tempted to roll the window down and stick my head out. I so needed to pull it together. If Cam ever discovered that Jase had kissed me, he would murder him and hide his body on a rural road like this one.

And that would be a damn shame.

Jase had a five-year-old brother named Jack. It was just his father and Jack at the farm. I didn't know what had happened to the mother, if she had died or up and left one day. Cam never mentioned it and out of the conversations I'd had with Jase, up until last year, when he stopped coming home with Cam, he never talked about his mom.

My brain emptied of anything to say and I so needed a distraction right now. The perspiration from the tea and my own trembling hands were making it hard to hold onto the cup. I could've asked Cam about Avery and that would've worked, because Cam *loved* talking about Avery. I could've asked about his classes or started talking about mine, but all I could do was think about the fact that I was finally going to see Jase in a situation where he couldn't run away from me.

The thick trees on either side of the road started to thin out and through them, green pastures became visible. Cam turned onto a narrow road. The truck bounced on the potholes, making my stomach queasy.

My brows lowered as we passed between two brown poles. A chain link lay on the ground and off to the left was a small wooden sign that read WINSTEAD: PRIVATE PROPERTY. A large cornfield greeted us, but the stalks were dry and yellow, looking as if they were days away from withering up and dying. Beyond them, several large horses grazed behind a wooden fence that was missing many of its middle panels. Cows roamed over most of the property to the left, fat and happy looking.

As we drew closer, an old barn came into view. A scary old barn, like the one in *The Texas Chain Saw Massacre*, complete with the creepy rooster compass thing swiveling on the roof, and several yards beyond the barn was a two-story home. The once-white walls were gray, and even from the truck I could tell there was more paint peeling off than there was on the house. Blue tarp covered several sections of the roof and a chimney looked like it was half crumbling. Red dusty bricks were stacked along the side of the house, as if someone had started to repair the chimney but grew bored and gave up. There was also a cemetery of broken-down cars behind the barn, a sea of rusted-out trucks and sedans.

Shock rippled through me as I sat up a bit straighter. This was Jase's farm? For some reason, I pictured something a little more … up-to-date?

Cam parked the truck a few feet back from the barn and killed the engine. He glanced over at me, following my stare to the house. Unlocking his seat belt, he sighed. 'His father's had a really hard time. Jase tries to help with the farm and stuff, but as you can see …'

The farm needed more help than Jase could provide.

I blinked. 'It's … charming.'

Cam laughed. 'It's nice of you to say that.'

My fingers tightened around the cup in defense. 'It is.'

'Uh-huh.' He flipped his baseball cap around, shielding his eyes. Tufts of brown hair poked out from the back rim. 'Fuck this farm.'

'What?'

He shook his head. 'If it wasn't for this farm, Jase could be anywhere he wanted, playing soccer or whatever. He's stuck here because of this damn farm.'

I hadn't known that. Jase had only talked about Jack, never his family or their finances, but before I could question Cam further, movement out of the corner of my eye caught my attention.

Racing out from the side of the barn, a little boy seated in a miniature John Deere tractor hooted and hollered, his chubby arms bone straight, his hands gripping the steering wheel, and a mop of curly brown hair shining under the bright August sun. Pushing the tractor from behind was Jase, and even though I could barely hear him, I was sure that he was making engine noises. They bounced along the uneven gravel and ground, Jase laughing as his little brother shouted, 'Faster! Go faster!'

Jase appeased his brother, pushing the tractor so it zigged and zagged to a stop in front of the truck as Jack squealed, still clenching the steering wheel. Plumes of dust flew into the air.

And then Jase straightened.

Oh man, my mouth dropped open. Nothing in this world could've made me look away from the splendor in front of me.

Jase was shirtless and his skin glistened with sweat. I wasn't sure what ethnicity he had in his family background. There had to be something Spanish or Mediterranean, because he had a naturally tan skin tone that remained that way all year round.

As he walked around the tractor, his muscles did fascinating things. His pecs were perfectly formed and his shoulders were broad. He had the kind of muscles one got from lifting bales of hale and tossing them places. Where? I had no freaking clue. It didn't matter. Boy was ripped. His

397

stomach muscles tensed with each step. He had a very distinctive six-pack. Totally touchable. His jeans hung indecently low—low enough that I wondered if he had on anything underneath the faded denim.

A flush spread across my cheeks and traveled down my throat as I dragged my gaze back up, mouth dry as the desert.

Sinewy muscles in his arms flexed as he pulled Jack out of the driver's seat, lifting him into the air above his head. He spun around in a circle, laughing deeply as Jack shrieked and flailed.

Ovaries go boom.

He sat Jack down on the ground as Cam opened the driver's-side door, yelling something at Jase, but I had no idea what he said. Jase straightened again, dropping his hands to his hips. He squinted as he stared into the truck.

Jase was absolutely gorgeous. You couldn't say that about a lot of people in real life. Maybe celebrities or rock stars, but it was rare to see someone as stunning as he was.

His hair was a mess of rich russet waves falling into his face. His cheekbones were broad and well defined. Lips were full and could be quite expressive. A hint of stubble shaded the strong curve of his jaw. He didn't have dimples like Cam or me, but when he did smile, he had one of the biggest, most beautiful smiles I'd ever seen on a guy.

He wasn't smiling right now.

Oh no, he was staring into the truck with a searing intensity.

Parched as I was, I took a sip of the sweet tea as I stared through the windshield, absolutely enthralled by all the baby-making potential on display before me. Not that I was in the way of making babies, but I could totally get behind some practice runs. At least in my fantasies.

Cam eyed me and made a face like I'd lost my damn mind. I might have. 'Dude, that's his drink.'

'Sorry.' I flushed, lowering the cup. Not that it mattered. Wasn't like Jase and I hadn't swapped spit before.

On the other side of the windshield, Jase mouthed the word *shit* and spun around. Was he going to run away? How dare he? I had his sweet tea!

In a hurry, I unhooked my seat belt and pushed open the door. In my haste, my foot slipped out of my flip-flop and because Cam just had to have a redneck truck, one that was feet off the ground, there was a huge difference between where I was and the ground.

I used to be graceful. Hell, I *was* a dancer—a trained, damn good dancer—and I had the kind of balance that would make gymnasts go green with envy. But that was before the torn ACL, before my hopes of dancing professionally ended when I came down from a jump wrong. Everything—my dreams, my goals, and everything I had worked for had been over in an instant.

And I was about to eat dirt in less than a second. There was no stopping it.

I reached out to catch the door, but came up short. The foot that was going to touch the ground first was connected to my bum leg and it wouldn't hold my weight. I was going to crash and burn in front of Jase and end up with tea all over my head.

Out of nowhere, two arms shot out and hands landed on my shoulders. One second I was horizontal, halfway fallen out of the truck, and the next I was vertical, both feet dangling in the air for a second. And then I was standing, the cup of tea clutched to my chest.

'Good God, you're going to break your neck,' a deep voice rumbled. 'Are you okay?'

I was up close and personal with the most perfect chest

I'd ever seen, and I watched a bead of sweat trickle down the center of it and then over the cut abs, disappearing among the fine hairs trailing up from the center of his stomach, forming a line that continued under the band of his jeans.

Cam hurried around the front of the trunk. 'Did you hurt your leg, Teresa?'

No. I was fine. More than fine. I hadn't been this close to Jase for a year and he smelled wonderful—like man and a faint trace of cologne. I lifted my gaze, realizing that my sunglasses had fallen off.

Thick lashes framed eyes that were a startling shade of gray. The first time I'd seen them, I had asked if they were real. Jase had laughed and offered to let me poke around in his eyes to find out.

He wasn't laughing right now.

I swallowed, willing my brain to start working. 'I have your sweet tea.'

Jase's brows rose.

'Did you hit your head?' Cam asked, stopping beside us.

Heat flooded my cheeks. 'No. Maybe. I don't know.' Holding out the tea, I forced a smile, hoping it didn't come across as creepy. 'Here.'

Jase let go of my arms and took the tea, and then I wished I hadn't been so eager to shove it in his face, because maybe then he'd still be holding me. 'Thanks. You sure you're okay?'

'Yes,' I muttered, glancing down. My sunglasses were by the tire. Sighing, I picked them up and cleaned them off before slipping them back on. 'Thanks for ... um, catching me.'

He stared at me a moment and then turned as Jack ran up to him, holding out a shirt. 'I got it!' the little boy said, waving the shirt like a flag.

'Thanks.' Jase took the shirt and handed over the tea. He ruffled the boy's hair and then, much to my disappointment, pulled the shirt on over his head, covering up that body of his. 'I didn't know Teresa was with you.'

A chill skated over my skin in spite of the heat.

'I was out showing her the town so she knows her way around,' Cam explained, grinning at the little tyke, who was slowly creeping toward me. 'She's never been down here before.'

Jase nodded and then took back the tea. There was a good chance that Jack had drunk half of it in that short amount of time. Jase started to walk toward the barn. I was dismissed. Just like that. The back of my throat started to burn, but I ignored it, wishing I had kept the tea.

'You and Avery are coming to the party tonight, right?' Jase asked Cam, taking a sip of the tea.

'It's the luau. We're not missing that.' Cam grinned, revealing the dimple in his left cheek. 'You guys need help setting it up?'

Jase shook his head. 'The newbies are in charge of that.' He glanced over at me, and I thought for a second that he'd ask if I was coming. 'I've got a few things to take care of here first and then I'm heading back home.'

A small hand tugged on the hem of my shorts, causing me to look down and into gray eyes that were both young and soulful.

'Hi,' Jack said.

I grinned. 'Hi to you.'

'You're pretty,' he said, blinking.

'Thank you. You're very cute.'

Jack beamed. 'I know.'

I laughed. This boy was definitely Jase's little brother.

'Alright, that's enough, Casanova.' Jase finished off the

tea and tossed the cup into a nearby garbage can. 'Stop hitting on the girl.'

He ignored Jase, sticking out his hand. 'I'm Jack.'

I took the little hand in mine. 'I'm Teresa. Cam's my brother.'

Jack motioned me down with his little finger and whispered, 'Cam doesn't know how to saddle a horse.'

I glanced over at the boys. They were talking about the party, but Jase was watching us. Our gazes collided, and like he'd been doing all week since I'd started at Shepherd University and run into him, he broke eye contact with distressing speed.

A pang of disappointment lit up my chest as I focused my attention back on Jack. 'Want to know a secret?'

'Yeah!' His smile grew big and broad.

'I don't know how to saddle a horse either. And I've never even ridden one before.'

His eyes grew as wide as the moon. 'Jase!' he bellowed, spinning toward his brother. 'She's never ridden a horse before!'

Well, there went my secret.

Jase glanced at me, and I shrugged. 'It's true. They scare the crap out of me.'

'They shouldn't. They're pretty chill animals. You'd probably like it.'

'You should show her!' Jack rushed up to Jase, practically latching himself to his brother's legs. 'You could teach her like you teached me!'

My heart lurched in my chest, partially at the proposition of Jase teaching me anything and partially due to my fear of those dinosaurs.

'It's "taught," not "teached," and I'm sure Tess has got better things to do than ride around on a horse.'

Tess. I sucked in a breath. It was his nickname—he was

402

the only person who ever called me that. I don't even know why he called me that, but I didn't mind it. Not at all. While Jack demanded to know why I had told him my name was Teresa and Jase explained that Tess was a nickname, I was sucked back into the memory of the last time he'd called me by it.

'You have no idea what you make me want,' he said, his lips brushing my cheek, sending shivers down my spine. 'You have no fucking clue, Tess.'

'Mine if I use the john before we get out of here? I gotta get back,' Cam said, drawing my attention. 'I promised Avery dinner before the party.'

'I'll show you,' announced Jack, grabbing Cam's hand.

Jase arched a dark brow. 'I'm sure he knows where the bathroom is.'

'It's okay.' Cam waved him off. 'Come on, little bud, lead the way.'

The two of them headed off toward the farmhouse, and we were officially alone. A hummingbird took flight in my stomach, bouncing around like it was going to peck its way out of me as a warm breeze picked up, stirring the hairs that had escaped my ponytail.

Jase watched Cam and Jack jogging over the patchy green grass like a man watching the last life preserver being picked up as the *Titanic* started to sink. Well, that was sort of offensive, as if being alone with me was equivalent to drowning while being nom-nommed by cookie-cutter sharks.

I folded my arms across my chest, pursing my lips. Irritation pricked at my skin, but his obvious discomfort stung like a bitch. It hadn't always been like this. And it definitely had been better between us, at least up until the night he kissed me.

'How's the leg?'

The fact that he'd spoken to me startled me and I stuttered. 'Uh, it's not too bad. Barely hurts anymore.'

'Cam told me about it when it happened. Sorry to hear that. When can you get back to dancing?'

I shifted my weight. 'I don't think I will.' The real answer was that I didn't know. Neither did the doctors or the physical therapist or my dance instructor, but I'd rather prepare myself for never than believe that I could dance once again. I didn't think I'd survive that heartbreak a second time. 'So, yeah, that's that.'

'God, that sucks. I'm really sorry, Tess. I know how much dancing means to you.'

'Meant,' I murmured, affected more than I should've been by the genuine sympathy in his voice.

His gray eyes finally made their way back to mine, and I sucked in a breath. His eyes … they never failed to stun me into stupidity or make me want to do crazy-insane things. Right now they were a deep gray, like thunderclouds.

Jase wasn't happy.

Thrusting a hand through his damp hair, he exhaled deeply and his brows pinched. A muscle in his jaw ticced. The irritation turned into something messy, causing the burn in the back of my throat to move up to my eyes. I had to keep telling myself that he didn't know—that there was no way he could've known, and that the way I was feeling, the hurt and the brutal wound of rejection, wasn't his fault. I was just Cam's little sister; the reason why Cam had gotten into so much trouble three years ago and why Jase had started making the trip to our home every weekend. I was just a stolen kiss. That was all.

I started to turn, to go wait in the truck for Cam before I did something stupid and embarrassed myself by crying. My emotions had been all over the place since I injured my leg, and seeing Jase wasn't helping.

'Tess. Wait,' Jase said, crossing the distance between us

with one step of his long legs. Stopping close enough that his worn sneakers almost brushed my toes; he reached out toward me, his hand lingering by my cheek. He didn't touch me, but the heat of his hand branded my skin. 'We need to talk.'

ACKNOWLEDGMENTS

Writing acknowledgments never gets easy, no matter how many of them I've written. I want to first thank Molly McAdams and Cora Carmack for their equally awesome blurbs and support. Sarah—your cover art is amazing and I fell in love with the cover from the moment I saw it. To my agent Kevan Lyon, a huge thank-you for being the most supportive agent in the business. Thank you to Marie Romero for working her copyediting magic on my typos, and to Valerie for always being willing to organize a book tour for me last minute and doing an amazing job. None of this would've been possible without you, the readers. I cannot thank you guys enough for reading my books. To this day it still amazes me that anyone does. Last but not least, a big thank-you to Stacey Morgan. She was the first person to hear about *Wait for You*—an idea I came up with while in the shower—and was with me from day one on this book. THANK YOU.

The W6 Book Café

Who's your favourite #bookboyfriend?

Who do you wish was taking you out tonight?
Tweet us at **@W6BookCafe** using hashtag
#bookboyfriend and join the conversation.

Follow us to be the first to know about
competitions and read exclusive extracts
before the books are even in the shops!

 Find us on Facebook
W6BookCafe

 Follow us on Twitter
@W6BookCafe